Demon's Curse

Book One in the
Imnada Brotherhood Series

ALEXA EGAN

Pocket Books
New York   London   Toronto   Sydney   New Delhi

Pocket Books
A Division of Simon & Schuster, Inc.
1230 Avenue of the Americas
New York, NY 10020

This book is a work of fiction. Names, characters, places, and incidents either are products of the author's imagination or are used fictitiously. Any resemblance to actual events or locales or persons, living or dead, is entirely coincidental.

First Pocket Books paperback edition January 2013

POCKET and colophon are registered trademarks of Simon & Schuster, Inc.

For information about special discounts for bulk purchases, please contact Simon & Schuster Special Sales at 1-866-506-1949 or business@simonandschuster.com.

The Simon & Schuster Speakers Bureau can bring authors to your live event. For more information or to book an event contact the Simon & Schuster Speakers Bureau at 1-866-248-3049 or visit our website at www.simonspeakers.com.

Manufactured in the United States of America

10 9 8 7 6 5 4 3 2 1

ISBN: 978-1-4516-7290-9
ISBN: 978-1-4516-7294-7 (ebook)

For the boys

Acknowledgments

It takes a village to raise a child and it takes a group of skilled, dedicated, and very helpful people to publish a book. It starts with my always amazing super critique duo, Do Leonard and Maggie Scheck, whose laughter, inspiration, hard work, and friendship I've come to rely on more than I can say. Kevan Lyon is always there with large doses of answers, suggestions, and reassurance. Emilia Pisani has championed this project from idea to finished product, and the fantastic crew at Pocket Books has been amazing in bringing my vision to life. And of course, I have to mention my wonderful family, who never fails to keep me on my toes and make life interesting. Thank you!

Prologue

They had not died gently. No imitation of sleep in their ripped and bloodied corpses. No quiet repose in their twisted limbs and staring eyes.

Mac had counted three already: two in the muddy farmyard, and another by the garden fence. As he stepped onto the house's porch, a figure threw himself out the door, knocking Mac aside in his rush to escape. He'd only time to glimpse a swarthy head of hair and shirtsleeves drenched in blood before the man hurtled into the wood at the far side of the lane.

Inside, Mac stepped over a woman's fallen body, her skirts sodden crimson, but for one edge that retained the original springtime yellow. Her hair was a wiry gray, her face, seamed with fine wrinkles like old parchment, now a ghastly white. Her eyes, wide and horrified in death.

By the hearth lay a heap of homespun skirts, one plump outstretched arm lit by a spill of light across the floor from a broken window. A maidservant, perhaps.

Bloody hell, what had happened here? Where was Adam?

Major de Coursy's shout from the back of the house signaled the discovery of another body. "Mother of All . . . shit . . . shit . . . shit!"

Gray's vocabulary had coarsened over the last five years. There remained barely a trace of the priggish lordling about him now. Some claimed war turned civilized men to savage beasts, and then there were those who were born that way.

Like Mac. Like them all. Gray, Adam, David.

Imnada—shapechangers and telepaths. A race of impossible origins and uncertain future.

From Lisbon, across Spain, over the rugged Pyrenees, and finally to this out-of-the-way farm on the Belgian border, the four of them had crept and sniffed, prowled and stalked, gathering what intelligence they could for king and country. Tracking the movements of Napoleon's army. Assessing intent. Relaying attack routes. That is, until Adam's urgent pathing brought them here. To this . . .

"I've found him!" Gray's voice came again. "Come quickly!"

Mac followed the shout down a short passage to a heavy wooden door partly blocked by another crumpled body.

Within, all was shadows. Heavy drapes had been pulled across the three long windows, letting only thin bars of slanting twilight into the room. The fire in the grate had burned down to a few smoldering embers, and even the candles were little more than melted stubs, only one still flickering in its pool of wax. Books lined the walls that weren't taken up with cabinets full of treasures and trinkets, including a macabre smiling skull. A globe sat within a mahogany stand. A map table stood spread with charts of the continents and the heavens above. On the desk, an enormous volume lay open as if someone had recently been reading.

Mac was vaguely aware of David crowding in behind him. But his attention was all for Adam crouched naked by the hearth, his shoulders heaving with rage and panic. One hand balled into a clawed fist, the other brandishing a sword, black with blood. He bore the rough form of a human, but his hunched stance and the elongated bones of his face held traces of the lynx that was his animal aspect.

"I had to do it. They knew."

That's when Mac noticed the man sprawled dead at the base of the desk, his coat gaping open to reveal a vicious wound.

"I couldn't let him live." His words echoed in Mac's head as a pathing.

Gray shed his scarlet coat and draped it across Adam's bare shoulders. His voice came low and urgent. "They knew what, Adam? What did these people do to deserve death? Was it about the French? Had they learned about the emperor's movements? About the coalition's defenses?"

But, struggling with the shift, Adam was unable to answer. He groaned, sinking to the floor, a shimmer of magic masking his return to human form.

Mac crossed to the desk, callously stepping over the crumpled body on the floor. He'd seen too many corpses to be overly concerned by one more. Pulling the open book around toward him, he leafed through the fluttering pages for clues. "Not the French, Gray." Mac met his major's shocked stare. "Us. The man was Other."

Gray's piercing blue eyes narrowed.

Mac's lips thinned as he continued reading. "The book's a compendium on the Imnada." He flipped pages, his heart sinking with every entry. "The man must have spent his entire life researching the clans."

"For what purpose?" Gray asked, twisting his ring round and round, the great diamond winking in the dim light.

David spat his disgust. "There can be only one purpose where Fey-bloods are concerned."

The men eyed one another, their shared thoughts equally dark. Equally fearful.

The Imnada's continued survival depended upon keeping their race's existence a secret. It had been thus for centuries upon centuries, ever since the Fealla Mhòr, the Great Betrayal, when the magical Fey-blood Other turned upon the Imnada with merciless ferocity, almost wiping the shapechangers from the earth. Only terrified retreat into the wild corners of the world had kept the Imnada alive. Only seclusion behind the great concealing power of the Palings guarded the few remaining pockets of their kind. All clan members knew the swift and brutal penalty befalling those careless enough to allow discovery by an out-clan.

Death if the culprit was lucky.

Exile if he or she was not.

"Shit," Gray muttered. "Just what we don't need this close to battle."

"Fey-blood," Adam murmured from his place on the floor. He was now fully human, but still incredibly weak. "Said he sensed the animal heart of me . . . forced the shift . . . no choice . . . had to kill . . . protect our secret . . . protect the clans . . ."

David knelt beside Adam, his gaze rage-filled. "The Fey-blood forced the shift against your will?"

Gray shrugged, but the tightness of his jaw hinted at his anger. "Must have. Look at him. He's so drained he can barely move. He'd not have shifted during the waning crescent of Berenth on his own."

Mac agreed. The Imnada's powers derived from the goddess moon, mother to all Imnada. As she grew from the slender young crescent of Piryeth to the fullness of Silmith, so did the strength and the ease in which the Imnada accomplished the shift from man to animal and back. As she aged to the waning sliver of Berenth, so did their abilities, leaving them weakened and vulnerable. On the nights of Morderoth when the goddess fled the skies completely, the Imnada's powers to shapechange disappeared as well, leaving them as defenseless as any human.

So had this Fey-blood Other really triggered Adam's shift through his magic? A terrifying thought.

Mac scanned the book, his mind churning with every new entry. "These pages are full of references to the Imnada. Somehow this Other must have discovered Adam was of the five clans. Adam did what he had to."

"But slaughtering the entire household?" Gray protested.

"You know the laws," Mac answered. "It was them or us. What would you have done?"

Gray scanned the room once more, his gaze coming to rest on the body of the Fey-blood. "There must be another way," he mumbled, his frustration clear.

"What now?" David asked. "We're due back to camp by dawn." His face pressed into harsh weary lines. Which one of them wasn't exhausted? Surviving on a knife edge? They'd been scouting for weeks, hoping to ascertain the disposition of French troops. It was only now, so close to Morderoth, that they'd completed their mission and begun the march toward Brussels, where Wellington's staff remained billeted.

Gray straightened, shoulders back, head up, as if sensing an answer on the evening breeze. But it was not the major who spoke.

The corpse on the carpet moved in a sudden gurgling breath. "You'll pay for your crimes."

Mac slammed the book closed. "He lives."

"Imnada . . . treacherous . . . demons . . ." the man gasped, his agonized gaze passing from soldier to soldier. "My family . . . Where . . ."

David's gaze flickered, his jaw clamped shut.

"Dead . . . you killed them . . . so shall you all be punished for the crime of one . . ."

"We murdered no one," David cried in defense, but Gray held up a hand. As the highest-ranking officer, Major de Coursy still held sway, and David fell silent, though Mac felt resentment in the younger man's thoughts.

"*Mest gelweth an'a noa pystrot a'gan'a mamsk hath an'a kollyesh esh a'na cronil,*" the Other whispered, his body shuddering in pain.

The gibberish meant nothing to the three of them. Not until Adam straightened, the coat sliding from his shoulders to the floor. "Stop him!" he shouted.

But the strange language came faster and stronger now, as if all the dying Other's remaining life were poured into the hellish words. "*Imnadesh Prytsk. Owgsk mollothegh. Dydhweytsk dea. D'wosk' an'a goedhvith. Dhiwortsk nana bya.*"

Adam fell, trembling. The rest of them remained transfixed as the Other spat his curse to the wind. The curtains billowed. The final candle was snuffed out, leaving the room in darkness. But a light burned blue and silver within the man's dying face as if his spirit hovered beneath his skin.

"Get out!" Mac shouted, a premonition of evil vising his chest. The air grew heavy. He couldn't breathe. Every hair stood at attention as if he were caught within the heart of a lightning storm. "Grab Adam! Now!"

Gray lunged for Adam. David scrambled for the door, Mac urging his friends onward, but the curse rode on swifter wings, and there was no escaping. Not the room. Not their fate.

Blue fire engulfed them. Unearthly wails, high and shrieking, beat against Mac's brain, breaking through every mental shield he threw up. The Other's curse sank into his blood, into the marrow of his bones. The taint moved through him like venom.

His limbs transformed, his body shifted, the change overtaking him even as he struggled against it. He could not control it. Could not stop it.

His companions fared no better. As the fireball burned without heat, without smoke, it crackled over fur and feather. It rippled in silver and aquamarine over beak and claw. And as the last red rim of the sun sank below the trees, it was wolf and panther, lynx and eagle, that emerged from the farmhouse to scatter like hunted beasts into the forest.

1

Bianca paid off the hackney with the last shilling she'd tucked in her reticule that morning. She could only hope the rain that had threatened all day would hold off a few hours more. She didn't relish a long, soggy trudge, especially since she'd stupidly worn her newest bonnet and a lovely pelisse in violet merino wool she could barely afford. She pinched her lips together. Actually, she hadn't been able to afford it at all, but Adam insisted the color became her perfectly. Like a graceful purple *Iris ensata,* he'd raved. Rain or no rain, it seemed fitting to wear the outfit to say good-bye to her dearest friend.

She regretted coming as soon as she descended onto the flagway. A mob thronged the area around St. James's. What did they imagine? That they might catch sight of Adam's naked, ravaged body? That he might rise from the grave to point an accusing finger? Expose his murderer to the world?

Whispers swirled around her.

". . . recognize her from Covent Garden . . . Viola

last spring . . . beautiful . . . no better than she should be . . . foreigner . . . actress . . . dead man's whore . . . murderess . . ."

A shiver raced up her spine, but as if she were preparing her entrance onstage, she firmed her shoulders, straightened her back, and lifted her chin, eyes sparking. Adam had been her friend. He hadn't deserved to die as he had, and she owed him a final farewell. Crowds and their ugly slander be damned!

Bianca passed through the churchyard to the grave site. Once beyond the ghoulish sightseers, she found herself almost alone in her grief. A minister presided over a trio of men standing awkwardly, their faces arranged in expressions of mourning, though she questioned their sincerity. After all, she'd never seen any of them before. Not once in all the time she'd known Adam.

Perhaps a clue rested in the uniformed crispness of one, his hat tucked beneath his arm, a sword hanging loosely from his hip. Bianca knew that Adam had served for years in the army, selling out after the emperor's final defeat at Waterloo the summer before last. Could these men be former brothers in arms?

They looked up as one when she swept forward to stand unapologetically beside them. She sensed a slow-burning appraisal from the golden-haired Adonis to her left, greatcoat hanging elegantly from his wide shoulders, cravat tied in careless perfection. A gentleman with the looks and—if she read him right—the knowledge of his own power to attract.

A regal gentleman at the foot of the grave eyed her down his straight aristocratic nose, lips pursing ever so slightly, hand tightening on the knob of his cane. It didn't take a mind reader to interpret his disapproval.

Only the officer spared her no more than a glance before returning his attention to the minister reading from his Bible.

Dismissing the three men with a jerk of her chin, she focused on the reason she was here. Adam Kinloch. A true friend and gentleman when so many others of her acquaintance wanted something from her. Her talent. Her favors. Her body.

Adam had never asked for more than her friendship. And in offering his in return, he'd reminded her of the life she'd lost when Papa died and Lawrence had swept her from the gardens and greenhouses outside Baltimore to the clogged and cluttered streets of London.

What sort of monster would have killed him in such a horrible, shocking way? Would leave him naked and gutted, abandoned like so much refuse to be scavenged by dogs and beggars?

Tears pricked the corners of her eyes, her stare burning to hold them back. No doubt these cold-eyed men assumed, like everyone else, that she and Adam had been lovers. She'd always let people believe what they wished. Better that than discovering the far more disturbing truth.

As if sensing her thoughts, the uniformed man met her watery gaze. His strange almond-shaped eyes were a pale green-gold, long-lashed and deeply set. His lips were full and sensuous. Smiling, he would have been devastating. But he didn't look as if he smiled often, if at all. In fact, he could have been carved from stone. From across Adam's grave, he watched her steadily as if he could see right into her heart. She knuckled her hands together, refusing to look away first. He wanted to stare? Fine. He could stare all he liked. She was used to eyes on her.

As the service concluded, the others drifted away, leaving her alone with the gravediggers clutching their spades.

She dropped the small nosegay she'd purchased from a flower seller into the grave. "I'll not forget you, my friend," she whispered. "And never fear, as you kept my secret, so shall I keep yours. You have my promise."

As the first scoop of earth thudded against the coffin's lid, the heavens opened, the autumn rain falling in a chilling drench that immediately drooped her ribbons and soaked through the expensive wool to her gown beneath.

Shielding her head as best she could with her reticule, she turned, almost knocking into the officer, who had lingered behind.

"Pardon," he said, his voice a gruff rumble, his gaze doubly intense at a distance of inches. He opened his mouth as if he might say more, but she dodged past him in her haste to leave this awful, forlorn, hopeless place.

The crowds had dispersed in the downpour. The sidewalk was empty but for a knife grinder hurrying for shelter and a man selling meat pies to a dripping-wet customer.

She lifted a hand to hail a hackney before remembering she had no fare. Instead she hastened east down Piccadilly on foot, all the while feeling a gaze leveled at her back, tickling her shoulder blades. She would not turn around, but her steps came faster until, cowardly as it made her feel, she was almost running.

*　　*　　*

"The woman knows, I'm sure of it." Captain Mac Flannery splashed brandy into his glass before downing it in one quick gulp, letting the heat travel soothingly through him. Without any explicit invitation, the group of old friends had ended up at Gray's town house after leaving the cemetery.

Mac poured another, trying to wash away the grave stench clinging to his nostrils, the roof of his mouth. The memory of earth striking the coffin lid as Adam was entombed. The Imnada did not hold with enclosing their dead in the ground but released their spirits with fire, the better to send them back through the Gateway to be reunited with their ancestors. Unfortunately, Adam's murder had garnered too much public attention to make that possible.

Instead, he'd died as he'd lived: in exile from his clan. His kind. Only Mac's intervention keeping him from a pauper's lye pit with the rest of the unclaimed dead.

"You think Adam betrayed us to an out-clan?" Gray demanded from his seat by the fire.

Mac hadn't seen de Coursy since the chaotic days following Waterloo. The estranged heir to the dukedom of Morieux lived a reclusive life in the north, rarely venturing to London, and even then shunning the usual Society entertainments. Some gossip blamed it on a horrible disfigurement acquired during the war. Others whispered he kept his mad wife locked in a tower. The most salacious hinted at black arts and satanic rituals carried out in the catacombs beneath his bleak Yorkshire estate.

If only the truth were that simple.

"Was that Bianca Parrino paying her last respects?" David St. Leger paused in shuffling a deck of cards to hold out his glass for Mac to refill.

"Who?" Mac asked, glancing at the faces of the men he'd once soldiered with. Men who at one time had been as close as brothers. The Fey-blood's curse had shattered that bond as it had destroyed so much in their lives.

Friendships forged by blood and steel had frayed like ragged cloth as if each of them had hoped to flee the curse by running away from each other. They should have known their fates and Fey-blood magic had tied them too closely for escape. They were bound by darker forces than the war.

"All work and no play, Captain Flannery." David gave a disgusted shake of his head. "Do they have you chained to your desk over there at the Horse Guards?"

Mac chose not to answer. This wasn't David's first refill.

"She's an actress at Covent Garden," he continued. "All the rage this year. Audiences love her."

Of course. That was why the woman at Adam's funeral had seemed so familiar. Mac had seen her penned likeness staring out at him from countless newspapers. They didn't do her justice.

Statuesque as any Nordic queen, she carried herself with a pride that bordered on the insolent. Hair blond as corn silk. Eyes a chilling blue. And just enough of an accent to give her an air of the exotic. But it was what she'd said more than how she'd said it that had truly rooted him to the spot. *As you kept my secret, so shall I keep yours.*

Had Adam been foolish enough to trust her with the Imnada's existence? And could this reckless confession have led to his murder?

"They say she's high in the instep as any duchess. Throws men into a quake with one glance from those alluring blue eyes," David said, refilling his own glass this time. "They also say she and Adam were lovers."

Gray rose to toss another log on the fire. "I find that hard to believe while the Imnada are forbidden marriage outside the clans."

"I never said he was marrying her. I said he was swiving her," David said with a leer.

Gray's face betrayed his disgust.

"Wrinkle your princely nose all you want, de Coursy, but you know as well as I do that as long as we lay under the curse, a quick shag is all you and I are ever going to get."

"That may be, but some of us still wish for more than a tumble with some faceless, nameless doxy."

David shrugged. "Wish all you want. It won't change the facts. Besides, what does it matter to the man they refer to as the 'Ghost Earl'? With that tall, dark, and mysterious act, you've got every woman in England panting for you, ring or no ring."

If David's smirk was any indication, Mac and Gray would do best to ignore him. St. Leger had always been a loose cannon. It was doubtful whether the curse had diminished his reckless ways.

Mac stepped into the breach. "Terminology aside, if Adam and Mrs. Parrino were lovers, she might know about the Imnada. About us."

"I still don't believe it," Gray declared. "Adam would never have betrayed us to an out-clan. It was his very determination to keep the Imnada's secret that led to the . . . to our . . ."

"Say it, de Coursy," David urged, his features rigid. "Or are you too frightened to speak of it out loud? Will the shade of our maker rise up from the grave and strike us down? Curse us again? What the hell could he do that's worse than what we already suffer? Forcing the shift . . . renunciation by the clans . . . Death would be preferable."

David's histrionics aside, Mac had to agree.

Tainted by Fey-blood magic, the four of them had been declared mortally damaged and a blight on the clans, their bloodlines forever corrupted. Worthless. Contemptible. Abominations.

And yet, they'd not been offered the swift mercy of a falling ax or a sharp snap of the neck. Instead, the Gather elders had pronounced a far harsher sentence of exile, severing the four of them from the protection and community of clan and holding, cutting them off from everyone they cared about, erasing them from the world they knew as if they'd never been born.

Mac's back twitched with the memory of the destruction the Ossine's enforcers wreaked upon his body as they stripped him of his clan mark. His bowels loosened as he recalled the violent shredding of his mental signum, as if a great claw had ripped through his brain. Both punishments had destroyed every bond with his past, leaving him adrift and alone. He'd only survived by hardening his mind and his heart against any pain and any loss, becoming as unfeeling and remote as a speck of dirt, focusing no further than the next day, the next cycle of the moon, the next season.

"Had your grandfather not caved to the Ossine's

commands, we'd have faced a quick end and you could have been the Ghost Earl in earnest then," David jibed.

"That's enough." Gray's terse command was unmistakable.

St. Leger lashed out, smashing his glass down on the tabletop, the shards spraying his hand, cutting his cheek. Blood slid down his face like a single crimson tear. "You're not my superior officer anymore. I don't take your orders."

"Did you ever?"

David froze for a moment, his expression unreadable. His body poised as if he might throw himself on Gray and beat him to a jelly. It wouldn't be the first time these two had come to blows. Like oil and water, they were, with Mac the inevitable peacemaker. He'd thought those days long past.

But as quickly as David's rage had ignited, it dissipated in a bout of laughter. "Damn, but I forgot what a right bastard you are." He passed the palm of his hand across his cheek, wiping away the blood.

"Feeling's mutual," Gray grumbled.

Mac swallowed back his aggravation. "That woman is aware of our existence. I'd bet on it. We're vulnerable—the Imnada are vulnerable—until we discover the extent of the danger."

Immediately his mind returned to Bianca Parrino. Her whispered words had set a queer pang jolting through him. Worry had taken root, and no amount of scoffing by these two chuckleheads would dissuade him.

"You think Adam was killed because he was Imnada? None know the clans survive. The enforcers have seen to that." David plunked himself down on a couch, dabbing at his cut with a handkerchief.

"Would you bet your life and the lives of every man, woman, and child within the clans on that assumption, David? Would you bet the lives of your family? Your friends?" Mac argued.

"Friends? Family? Where were they when the Gather pronounced our sentence? When our clan marks were obliterated and we were cast out half-dead into the world?"

"Not all of them wished us ill. There were those who spoke against our exile."

"For all the good it did us. No, Mac. We're *emnil*. Outlawed and living on sufferance. I say let the clans fend for themselves."

"Then forget the clans and remember Adam. He was our friend. We owe him justice, if nothing else," Mac challenged.

"Adam was no traitor," Gray reiterated. "He understood the allegiance owed the Imnada and the dangers in exposure to the outside world."

"People change," Mac shot back.

David's mouth twisted to a sneer. "Every night like clockwork, eh, Flannery?"

Mac sighed before tossing back another brandy.

They were a company again. The three of them. The accursed.

With his death, Adam had bound them together once more.

Wiping Froissart's seed from between her thighs, Renata stepped through the curtain into the inner chamber, dropping the heavy fabric into place behind her to muffle his snores and grunts. His foul breaking of wind. The creaks of the bed as he tossed and turned.

Pitching aside the rag, she toyed with the thought of killing him. How easy it would be. How quick. None would question it. They would mourn with her—the young, grieving widow. A thought quickly dismissed. The man was a pig, but he'd served his purpose. She had succeeded where all had called her mad to try. She had tracked those who slaughtered her father to this horrid gutter of a city. After a year and a half, vengeance would finally be hers. Only then would Froissart meet his final reward. Until that moment, she would prevent what attentions she could and endure what she could not.

"Is he asleep?"

A figure stepped from the shadows. She had known he was there, had felt his arrival as a tremor in the air, a touch upon her mind. She even knew when he parted the curtains to watch as Froissart spent himself inside her, his great bulk jerking and wheezing as he came. She'd felt his eyes upon her and smiled, her husband thinking the pleasure was for his sake.

"He is." Taking up her brush, she sat before an enormous mirror, one of four, each covering a wall of her dressing chamber.

Alonzo stepped behind her, pulling the brush gently from her hands. He slid it through her long black hair, tangle by tangle. He had always known how to soothe her. Milk-siblings, they'd shared a breast and then a nursery before he'd been packed off to the military and she to school with the priestesses of High Danu at Varennes. Until then, they'd been inseparable. As they were once again.

Tonight he smelled of tobacco and wine and leather and sex, and she felt an instant's jealousy for the whore who'd pleasured him. Then she looked up to catch his eager gaze upon her naked body, and her envy dissipated. She had nothing to worry about. He would always be hers.

"Froissart is a pig," he spat. "Why do you allow him to touch you?"

She laughed at the echo of her thought on his lips. They were so close, their minds flowed in tandem. Sometimes a mere flash of shared reflection. Other times, it was as a stream coming together with a river, thoughts rippling and diving and curling upon each other so there was no way to tell where one began and the other ended. So it had ever been since she'd discovered a mere skin-on-skin touch allowed her to travel into his mind—drift and spread into a corner to lie curled and watchful there. An invisible witness to all he saw and heard.

What began as a child's game had blossomed through study and practice into a rare and extraordinary talent: the ability to touch another's mind and, for brief flashes, to shape, influence, and even control. No longer was she constrained by actual touch: a lock of hair, fingernail parings, a drawn tooth, was all it took to open the door.

She kept these precious mementos in a case upon her dressing table, making use of them only when absolutely necessary. To indulge in such powerful magic spread her soul thin like high mares' tails stretching wispy across a wide sky. The body she left became an empty husk. Functioning but without a will. Quiescent. Vulnerable.

"I am strong, Alonzo, but even my powers have limits," she said. "It is easier to allow him his liberties and harbor my strength for more important business." She shot him a smoldering, pouty look. "But perhaps you don't ask for my sake but your own. Are you jealous, Alonzo? Do you wish to replace the toad Froissart in my bed? To possess my body as I possess your mind?" She ran the tip of her tongue across her lips. "To scream your release as you spill your seed within me?"

The answer was clear in his jealous gaze moving over her breasts, the creamy flat of her stomach, the jointure of her legs. A gaze reflected over and over within the four mirrors. Naked hunger stared out at her from every angle. His control held by a hair's width, his lust for her like an animal clawing at his innards.

"This pig-dog is worse than shit beneath your heel, Renata. He doesn't know you as I do. He sees you as nothing but a furrow to plow with his pig-dog babies. I would worship you as you deserve."

She shivered but did not yield to the tempting images heating her blood. She had come too far to give everything up for the feel of Alonzo moving inside her, the grip of his strong, broad hands upon her flesh. "That may be, but Froissart is useful to me. He is money and position. He is power."

"You have a hundred times more power than this bastard *abruti* in your little finger."

"Émile's power lies in respectability and connections. We need the cover of his embassy to shield us while we hunt. We found one, but my father's man claimed there were four soldiers at the house that day.

Four with swords and guns and death in their eyes."
She swung around, catching Alonzo by surprise. He
rocked back on his heels, clutching the brush like a
weapon. "Did you go to Kinloch's residence? Did you
find anything that might lead us to the others?"

"I searched his house but came away empty-
handed. Just books on plants and flowers. Pretty
drawings. Jars and bowls, coils of wire. The man was
naught but a gardener."

She turned away in disgust. So close they'd come.
So close to finding them all. And Alonzo had bungled
it. Allowing the man time to conceal. Time to run.
Though they'd caught him in the end. His time finally
ran out.

"I will have the men who slaughtered my father.
I will have them on their knees and at my mercy. A
mercy I shall not give."

"All's not lost. I went to the funeral. Watched to see
who attended."

Her eyes flashed up to meet Alonzo's hungry gaze
within the mirror. "And?"

"There were three men there, though no way to
know who or what they are."

She rose from her chair, catching up a silk robe to
cover her nakedness. "You risk coming to my rooms
to tell me this? That you may or may not have learned
something? That you may or may not have found the
treacherous Imnada vermin?"

"Are you so certain these men are Imnada? That
race is naught but dust and stories. The Other saw to
that centuries ago."

"We've had this argument before. My father's servant swears the chevalier trapped one of them. Forced

the monster to shift. All those years my father's theories were correct. Somehow the Imnada survived when we all thought them extinct. The beasts live among us still and remain as treacherous as ever."

"Then let us tell what we know. Go to the warriors of Scathach or the priestesses of High Danu; those with the power to root them out and destroy them once and for all."

"No!"

Rage bubbled up through her and, unthinking, she grabbed Alonzo's empty hand. Immediately the depthless black sea stretched out before her, ribbons of smoke twining about her, pulling her out of her own body and into his. For a moment she saw herself through his eyes. The long, rippling flow of black hair parted to hang on either side of shoulders pale as milk. Small, firm breasts, the dusky rose of her nipples visible beneath the diaphanous silk of her robe. The perfectly formed oval of a face; long, narrow cheekbones, lips parted, eyes shimmering gold with excitement.

"Renata," Alonzo groaned, making a small raspy sound deep in his throat. He shifted uncomfortably, and she was back. Hands at her sides. Alonzo's mind closed to her.

A whistling, grunty snore and a squeak of mattress ropes drew the two of them close in the dark.

"Trust me, Alonzo. I will reveal all in the end, but my own vengeance comes first. I have waited too long and sacrificed too much."

"As you will it." He nodded. "There was another at the churchyard. That actress everyone is talking about. Madame Parrino."

"Kinloch's slut? Interesting," she purred, tapping a

finger to her lips. "I wonder . . ." She closed her eyes, turning thoughts over to see what might lie beneath before once more facing Alonzo, brisk and commanding. "Follow her. Watch her house. See if any of those men come or go."

"Already done."

"I am relying on you. Do not fail me, old friend," she said, her voice pitched low, words slippery as the silk of her bed hangings.

He nodded once more before falling back into the shadows. Leaving her alone in the room with her thoughts—and her husband.

2

Mac scanned the newspaper. A mysterious killing in the St. Giles stews, a woman who claimed she'd spoken to the spirit of the late Duke of Hargreaves, a dangerous beast escaped from Exeter Exchange. He paced off the dimensions of the sitting room—again. He checked his watch for the third time. That couldn't be right. He couldn't possibly have waited for Mrs. Parrino for a full hour—he checked the door—and counting. What the hell was she doing up there, weaving the damn dress herself? He hadn't even seen the maid since she'd disappeared up the stairs to announce him.

He snapped the watch case closed, stuffing it back into his pocket. Counted the dots in the drapes for a second time—still four hundred and fifty-three. The flowers in the sofa upholstery—twenty-seven.

Why was he surprised? His sister, Siobhan, had spent hours in front of her mirror, while cathedrals had been built in less time than Lina took to ready herself for the day. He drew a short sharp breath as if in pain. Banished his ex-betrothed back to a cobwebby corner of his mind. He'd more important worries than the shallow, unfaithful heart of a beautiful woman.

At least that particular beautiful woman.

Whether Bianca Parrino fit into the same category remained to be seen.

Gray and David might think he chased shadows, but he couldn't shake the sense of impending doom. A trap slowly closing around them all. And while the Gather elders may have cast the four of them out, Mac couldn't sit idle when one of his race was attacked and their existence threatened. To turn his back on the clans was to give in to the despair that crouched waiting for any break in the stone he'd wrapped round his heart.

He fumbled with his *krythos,* turning over choices and consequences as he turned over the far-seeing disk. Dare he go against the terms of his sentence and use it to sound a warning? Or would doing so only bring down the Ossine's swift and deadly wrath? The shamans' authority had grown until their brutal enforcers were almost as feared among the clans as the Fey-bloods, and few dared challenge them. But surely this was important enough . . .

"Sir?" Mac wheeled around to face Mrs. Parrino's mouse of a maidservant. She flushed scarlet, her hands wrung in her apron. "My mistress says she's not at home to visitors."

As if taunting him, a man's voice carried down the stairs from the drawing room above. ". . . watched you for weeks . . . the man's dead . . . grieve forever . . ."

So Bianca Parrino wasn't turning *all* visitors away. Just him. Annoyance turned to stubbornness. He was a soldier. He'd lay siege to her bloody doorstep if he had to, but he wasn't leaving here without finding out what Adam had told her.

". . . don't struggle . . . have everything you could want . . ."

The sound of shattering glass brought Mac's head up. A high-pitched cry had him brushing past the maid to take the stairs in the space of a heartbeat.

He threw open the drawing room door to find a gentleman clutching a bloody handkerchief to his nose. Broken glass glittered across the carpet like diamonds, flowers scattered and floating in a spreading puddle beside an overturned side table.

The man dropped his handkerchief long enough to demand, "Who the devil are you?" before he clamped it back onto his swollen nose.

Mac stepped closer, his gaze moving slowly between Mrs. Parrino and her attacker. "Is there a problem here?"

"Not at all, Captain," Mrs. Parrino answered smoothly. "Lord Braemer just realized he was late for an appointment elsewhere, didn't you, my lord?"

The man's bluster subsided as he summed up his well-armed adversary. "Yes, so there's no need to take things amiss. Just a little misunderstanding between Mrs. Parrino and myself." He made a few more dabs at his nose before stuffing his handkerchief in a pocket. "I'd discounted certain nasty rumors circulating, but perhaps my faith was misplaced."

"And what rumors would those be?" she asked with barely a flicker of an eyelid.

"They say once the bloom was off, the gardener became the weed. Pulled viciously out of the ground and left upon the sidewalk to be swept up with the other trash." His smug gaze raked Mac up and down. "Now I see why. A new farmer is plowing the field."

Despite her chalky pallor, she faced the man down, blue eyes crackling. "You're mixing your metaphors, my lord. I believe it's best if you leave."

When the man looked as if he might argue, Mac settled a hand menacingly upon the hilt of his dress sword.

Lord Braemer plucked his hat and cane from a nearby chair. "Of course. We'll consider the matter closed and my offer retracted." Offering Mrs. Parrino a jerky bow, he hurried for the door beneath Mac's glower. "But a mere soldier? You sell yourself short, m'dear. If you planned on jumping into another's bed so soon, better by far to have chosen mine."

Tipping his hat as if he'd just concluded the most amicable of morning calls, Lord Braemer passed the apron-wringing maid on his way out. The door below shut with an audible click.

"Miss? Are you all right? His Lordship didn't hurt you, did he?" the maid asked.

Bianca Parrino turned a look of tongue-in-cheek amusement in Mac's direction. "No, Molly. This gentleman rescued me in the nick of time." Her gaze narrowed in dawning recognition. "You're the man from the cemetery."

"Captain Mac Flannery." He sketched her a terse bow.

"So brave, him charging up here," Molly gushed, her worshipping eyes fixed on Mac. "Just like a knight on a white horse."

Mrs. Parrino sagged onto a sofa, looking hopelessly at her torn gown. "Wasn't it? I don't know how I've survived so long without someone to protect me."

"Shall I lay out a change of clothes, mum?"

An almost imperceptible tremble shook the woman's fingers as she touched the torn fabric of her morning dress. "If you would, Molly. My muslin was no match for His Lordship's overwrought passions."

The maid dropped another adoring glance on Mac before scuttling out the door.

"She's gone," Mac said. "You can drop the pretense."

"Excuse me?"

He heard the annoyance glazing her voice, but he was too angry to care. She'd been manhandled by a damned lecher, and here she sat acting as if she'd not a care in the world. He might not be able to read thoughts outright—once common among the Imnada, that power surfaced rarely these days—but he definitely sensed the lie in her casual manner.

"Your flippant attitude as if being mauled was just another lark. Look at you: you're shaking."

Her blue eyes met his, their irises wide and dark as a stormy sea. "What would you have me do, Captain? Fall into hysterics? It's not the first time a man has assumed I'd welcome his attentions. It won't be the last. A hazard of my profession."

Damn, but she was lovely. All tumbled golden hair and creamy satin skin. No wonder that ass Braemer had made a fool of himself over her. What male with a pulse wouldn't? "Don't you have a companion living with you? A large, loud dragon of a woman to keep these louts at bay?"

"I prefer to live alone."

"Then at least employ a footman. Some big, hulking brute. That wee chit of a maid couldn't scare a pigeon."

"I'm perfectly capable of handling men who annoy me, Captain," she said pointedly.

Mac's gaze fell upon the bruise marring the pale flesh of her upper arm. "Oh, really? Is that mark what you call handling men?"

She threw herself to her feet. "No"—she stalked to the door—"it's what I call none of your business."

Alone in her bedchamber, Bianca clenched the torn fabric of her ruined gown as she grimaced at her reflection in the mirror. Hair a wild tangle down her back. A slight puffiness of her lips where Lord Braemer had slammed a sloppy wet kiss on them.

He'd offered her a fine house with a full complement of liveried servants. A carriage of her own. Jewels. Wealth. All a woman like her could want. His assumption about her character rankled. As if avarice and self-interest were unheard of among his vaunted class.

He'd been floored when she turned him down.

Had refused to take no for an answer.

How far would he have gone in persuading her?

How insistent would he have grown?

A wash of queasy panic splashed over clammy skin. Marriage had taught her the answer all too well. Men were bullies. They took what they wanted. Feasted on weakness. Gorged on fear.

Lord Braemer played the enamored lover as well as any actor, but she knew it for the role it was. After all, she'd seen it performed far more convincingly by Lawrence.

He, too, had been an attentive suitor until they were married. Then sweet-talking had become suspicion and consideration grew into controlling. She'd excused it as a new husband's adjustments to a wife. But time only increased his brutishness as it did his drinking and his whoring until she'd been glad of his long hours at the taverns and the low women he rogered, for it kept him away from home—away from her. Until the end, that is. Until he made no distinction between his wife and the cheap slags he frequented, and life became a held breath, his death her only means of escape.

She slammed a hand on the table, snapping herself free of the nauseating memories. Heaved a deep cleansing breath. Rolled her neck. Stretched her shoulders. And began the repair to her wardrobe.

Buttons. Ribbons. Combs. Pins. The correct drape of a fresh gown. The artfully arranged curl just so against her forehead. The deliberate process worked to restore her inner equilibrium. A woman's armor. A woman's mask. Amazing how much darkness you could hide behind a pretty face.

Finally, she slid open the top drawer of the cabinet beside her bed as if to reassure herself. Her pistol remained in its place, the dull gleam of its barrel winking at her as she touched the crosshatching of the handle, warm beneath her hand.

She'd be at no man's mercy again.

Shutting the drawer, she descended the stairs to the drawing room once more. Glancing down, she stumbled on the threshold and swallowed a muttered oath.

That dratted captain was still here.

Face set in an expression of regal tranquillity, she entered the drawing room as if she were meeting the enemy on a field of battle.

"I'm surprised you stayed. As my maid told you earlier, I'm not at home to visitors this afternoon."

"And yet, here I stand talking to you." There it was,

and just as devastating as she knew it would be—that beautiful mouth curving into a slow, delicious smile, softening the harsh lines and angles of his face, shining through his luminous green-gold eyes.

She returned his arrogant appraisal with one equally slow and studied. No decorative toy soldier, Captain Flannery bore a confident swagger with none of the posturing, and despite his spotless regimentals and the streamers of gold braid across his chest, he carried himself with a fighter's precision. This was a man who'd honed his muscled body and whip-fast reactions on the battlefields of Europe and not, like most of the men she met, in the training studios of upper-crust London. The afternoon light sheened his dark hair and picked out the hard lines around his mouth, the hollow beneath his jaw.

She glanced away, her gaze falling on the battered remains of what had been a bouquet of tall-stemmed white lilies interspersed with enormous purple asters. Lord Braemer's ham-handed love overtures had left them broken and strewn across the floor, but in Bianca's absence someone had gathered the blooms up and jammed them, lopsided and top-heavy, into an urn on her mantel.

"It was all I could find," he offered. "I'm afraid some of the wounds may be fatal." His voice came slow and deep, the slight breath of a brogue layered beneath his otherwise public school enunciation. "The big one there seems to have lost most of its petals."

She busied herself with rearrangement of the stems, hoping to hide the unwanted smile worming its way up through her system. It wouldn't do to offer him encouragement. No doubt most women melted like hot butter in his company. She refused to be one of those women. "I can purchase more at the market. If I'm lucky, they'll have dahlias and maybe some amaranth, though it's late in the season for those."

Her words fell into the silence like stones into a bottomless well. The captain studied her as if she were a particularly interesting specimen. Until then he'd concentrated on her face, those sparkling cat's eyes drilling a hole into her brain. But now his piercing gaze traveled over every inch, picking her apart in a fashion meant to intimidate and humiliate. "I'd not have taken you for a flower lover." His skeptical expression clearly revealed his inability to reconcile her diamonds and diaphanous silks with dirty nails and a gardener's secateurs.

"Appearances can be deceiving, Captain. Actresses know that better than most. My father was a botanist. I assisted him in his scientific work when I was a girl."

"And now?"

She dipped a shoulder in a shrug. "I attend lectures given by the Horticultural Society of London, visit Kew Gardens and the nurseries in Chelsea, and wander the market stalls at Covent Garden."

Another silence welled up between them, though this time she forced herself to accept it. She'd already revealed more than she'd intended. It was time to take the offensive. Crossing to the drinks cabinet, she poured her guest a brandy and herself a fortifying sherry. She needed it after the events of this afternoon. He accepted with a nod, his expression giving nothing away. "I'm curious," she said. "What kind of a name is Mac? It sounds made-up. Fictitious. Like a stage name."

"I could say the same of you. What kind of name is Bianca? You don't look or sound Italian."

"I'm American."

"That explains it."

"Explains what?"

"The accent. It's subtle. I couldn't place it."

"Much like yours."

"Oi can spake in a broad Oirish brogue if yer want me ter." His voice thickened, vowels and consonants rolling round his mouth like honey. She could be carried away on that delicious accent. He cleared his throat, once more clipped and public school proper. "Mac's short for Cormac. Cormac Cúchulainn."

She winced in sympathy.

A corner of his mouth twitched. "It could have been worse. I've been told my father considered Blathmach Ercc."

"The man sounds positively sadistic."

"How did you guess?" For a moment his eyes grew diamond-hard.

"Not holding a grudge over that atrocious name, are you?"

He gave a gruff snort that might have been laughter. "Goes a bit deeper."

"Did you seduce the neighbor's daughter? Gamble away your inheritance?"

"Those crimes might have been forgiven," he said, his expression thunderous.

Had the man simply come to glower at her? If that was the case, she'd had quite enough. "This conversation has been wonderfully scintillating, Captain, and I'm grateful for your assistance with His Lordship, but I've had an exhausting afternoon and really need to prepare for the theater."

She started to pass him on her way out the door.

"Wait." She gazed at his hand gripping her upper arm as if it had sprouted there. "I need to speak with you."

So here it was. She couldn't say she was completely surprised. The man dripped sensuality and self-confidence in bucketloads. "Let me guess." Her voice sharpened to a cutting edge. "You've come to tell me how much you adored me as Rosalind or as Cordelia in last spring's pageant. That I'm the most—insert 'fabulous,' 'talented,' or 'ravishing' here—actress you've ever seen. You can't sleep or eat due to the mad throes of this wild infatuation, and you'll do anything to make me yours."

Rather than cringing with embarrassment, the barest twitch of a smile lifted the corner of Captain Flannery's mouth. The tiniest hint of laughter lit his eyes. "Men say those things?"

"Some. Then there are those, like Lord Braemer, who believe expensive gifts are the way to a woman's heart. Fans, books, jewelry, flowers. You name it. I've had it sent round by some goggle-eyed fanatic with tented breeches and a pea brain. They think I can be bought for their thirty pieces of silver."

By now his eyes danced with laughter, and she was questioning how she'd managed to fall into a conversation with the man when she'd meant to freeze him with a haughty silence.

"I am not for sale, by the way," she added, trying to regain her footing and her upper hand. "So what's your lure, Captain?"

"Pardon?"

"How do you intend to try to sweep me off my feet? Are you here to read me a poem in honor of my eyes, or have you an expensive bauble that would perfectly grace my swan-like throat?"

The humor died as if someone had doused a light, and he was once more grim and implacable. "I came to speak to you about Lieutenant Kinloch."

All her righteous indignation drained away as if she'd been stuck with a pin. Grief blossomed like a physical pain under her ribs. "Adam's dead. What more do you need to know?"

"I need to know who killed him and why."

She sat upon a stone bench beneath a willow, its long, leafless skeins drifting like a curtain around her. She'd led him here after motioning meaningfully toward the drawing room door, where doubtless her maid crouched listening. He'd capitulated, following the slow sway of her hips, spine straight as a spear, as they made their way to her garden. This late in the season, few flowers bloomed in the tidy beds and the north wind carried hints of colder weather to come, but it was surprisingly tranquil even with the city's bustle a wall away.

Despite the ghostly pallor of her face and the tension tightening her mouth, she fairly glowed from the top of her perfectly coiffed head to the tips of her silver slippers. He almost waited for the trumpets and the celebratory cannonade. He'd never seen anyone as absolutely, iridescently radiant. So perfectly sleek and controlled. And yet, he'd witnessed for himself the bloodied Lord Braemer. This rose hid some vicious thorns.

"I still can't accept that he's gone."

Mac leaned against the garden wall, arms folded over his chest. Recalling David's smarmier insinuations, he asked, "Was Adam one of those who wrote odes to your eyes and brought you gifts?"

Her eyes spat blue fire.

"Gossip says the two of you were lovers."

"Then it must be true."

He winced but did not back down. "His home was broken into the night following his murder. The constable on duty was knocked over the head and came around to find the place completely ransacked, as if someone had been searching for something."

"The papers said it was footpads that killed him. A robbery gone wrong," she answered.

"I served with Adam for five years. Knew him for longer. It would take more than a thug with a knife to get the better of a seasoned soldier. He wasn't killed over a few coins for gin. The constable said his attacker was a big chap. Reddish hair."

A pensive line formed between her brows.

"Adam's house was searched. I want to know why, Mrs. Parrino."

"Do you think I can help you? Or are you hoping I'll confess?"

"Did you kill him?" he asked bluntly.

If she spat fire before, this time it was as if an entire fusillade had been leveled in his direction. "I won't even dignify that with an answer, Captain."

"The gossips claim you were the last person to see him alive."

"According to those same gossips, I've either made the Prince Regent weep with heartbreak or borne his secret love child. One of the reasons I pay little heed to what people say about me anymore."

"Then tell me about the last time you saw Adam,"

Mac said, ignoring her anger. "Convince me of your innocence."

"Why should I? You're not a magistrate, and like everyone else you'll believe what you want whether it's complete and utter hogwash or not. Besides, what's your opinion one way or the other?"

"Speculation has a way of growing. A dead man in St. James's Park nearly at the gates of Buckingham House is no small matter. People will be on the hunt for an answer."

"And you believe a man's whore is an easy scapegoat."

He shrugged. "A crime of passion is a momentary lapse, not likely to be repeated. Makes everybody feel better."

"Except me."

"So, tell me what I want to know and I'm an ally if things get sticky."

She snapped off a long willow tendril. It lay across her lap as she picked it apart. "Fine. You want to know what happened the last night I saw Adam? Absolutely nothing. He arrived at the theater just before I was due to go on and proceeded to pace around my dressing room like a caged bear while I finished applying my makeup."

He latched onto one word. Dragged it free, turning it round and round in his head. It couldn't be. She must be mistaken. "Night? Not earlier during the afternoon?"

"No, it was half past six or close to it. I remember because my dresser was complaining about Adam interrupting just as the bell rang announcing the half-hour warning. The performance was due to begin at seven. By the time I came back down to change between the first and second acts, he had left."

Mac's pulse thundered in his ears. "Did you see Adam often at night?"

Her gaze grew shuttered, no emotions marring the impenetrable mask of her face. "As our schedules allowed. He had his life. I had mine."

Mac barely heard her answer. His earlier fears of exposure to an out-clan drowned beneath the avalanche of a new discovery. One that could spell an end to the living death of an *emnil*. A return to the clans

His stomach tightened, nerves jumping beneath his skin, the same burn along his veins that accompanied his shift. The same wild exhilaration. "But that night? Are you certain it was after sunset?"

Now she was beginning to look on him as if he was mad. And maybe he was. But if she'd seen Adam after dark . . . If she was certain . . . If . . . if . . . if . . .

"As I've said more than once, yes, Captain Flannery, the sun was down when Adam arrived. It was dark when he left. The night usually is."

Mac fought the urge to shout his elation. To confess his excitement. To swing Bianca Parrino into his arms and kiss her as she ought to be kissed. But he couldn't fight the stupid grin he knew had plastered itself all over his face. Because if Bianca spoke the truth . . . if Adam had come to her that night . . . if Adam had been seen after sundown . . .

. . . then Adam had found a way to break the curse.

3

"'Dear Celia, I show more mirth than I am mistress of; and would . . . and would . . .'" Bianca shook her head. "'Dear Celia, I show more mirth than I am mistress of; and . . .'" Took a deep breath. "'Unless you could teach me to forget a banished father, you' . . . Drat!"

She should be able to recite Rosalind in her sleep. It was one of her favorite roles and one for which she was becoming known. She should not be stumbling over her opening line. She refocused with a rolling of her shoulders and a crack of her neck.

"'Dear Celia, I show more mirth than I am mistress of; and would . . .'"

Concentrate, Bianca. Captain Flannery with his impertinent questions and keen, searching gaze was long gone. And while Adam's murder and the whispers surrounding it proved all too sickeningly familiar, there was nothing they could do to her. She was innocent—this time.

"*'Dear Celia, I show more mirth than I am mistress—'*" She flung her script away.

Loss ached in her bones like cold weather. Did she believe the captain's theory that more lay behind the murder than a random attack on a dark garden path? That Adam might have known his killer? That she might be blamed for his death?

Her mind snapped back to the horrible, humiliating night she interrupted him entertaining that . . . that man.

Flannery had described an intruder with reddish hair. Tall. Dangerous. The pieces fit, but the picture they made only begat new questions.

Could she reveal what she knew without divulging Adam's secret? Would she allow her best friend's murder to go unpunished at the price of his reputation? Would she risk her own standing by keeping silent? Much as she hated to admit it, perhaps Captain Flannery had a valid point. Perhaps she did need to worry over the vicious rumors beginning to circulate if Adam's killer remained unfound.

"Toodles!" A voice interrupted her thoughts, followed by an explosion of rapping. "Bianca, sweeting. Are you there?"

Bianca swung around from the mirror. "Sarah! I didn't know you were in London. Weren't you supposed to be spending the autumn at Coldham with Sebastian's family?"

Brazen and beautiful in scarlet and gold, the new Countess of Deane flittered in like a frenetic butterfly. "He's decided to delay the trip until after the new year. He wants to wait for the worst of the scandal to die down before we beard the lioness in her den."

Bianca had known Sarah long enough to sense the disappointment behind her care-for-nothing attitude.

The shocking marriage of the powerful and wealthy Earl of Deane to a common actress had set the cat among the pigeons, and while outwardly Sarah disdained those who shunned her as an interloper, Bianca recognized her insecurities.

"Sebastian knows his mother better than anyone," Bianca soothed. "Besides, do you really want to spend the winter stuck in the country with the dowager and be cut to ribbons for your trouble?"

"Hmph. I've always wanted to play the lady bountiful role," Sarah challenged, the glimmer back in her eyes. "Visiting the poor, judging flower shows, sitting in the front pew at the village church. That sort of thing."

"And you'll be perfect when the time is right."

"But what if I let him down? What if he's disappointed in me?" Sarah prowled the cluttered dressing room, arms windmilling with dramatic flair. "Maybe he's already regretting the marriage. Maybe that's why he's delayed our trip."

"Stop it. Seb loves you. Anyone with eyes in their head can see that. He's head-over-heels smitten and no spiteful talk or nasty gossip will change his mind."

"I know you're right. I just never knew it would be so hard to live happily ever after."

"Is he here with you tonight?"

"I left him talking horses with Lord Grenville and Mr. Dunnett. It was that or slit my throat from sheer boredom." Sarah rolled her eyes. "He sends his good wishes. He wanted me to tell you how much he enjoyed that book you sent for his birthday. The man pored over it for two straight weeks with barely a break."

"It was Adam's idea," Bianca confessed. Grief robbed her of breath, and she fumbled with the edge of her shawl.

Sarah leapt from her seat to envelop Bianca in a flower-scented hug. "My darling, I'm so sorry. I read about it. Such a horror. It's gotten so one can't walk about the streets of London without an armed guard." She offered Bianca a handkerchief. "No tears, sweeting, you'll smear your makeup."

"Ever the practical one."

"Speaking of practicality, Mr. Hayworth's come again tonight."

Bianca's shoulders sagged, but what did she expect? She'd allowed Society to believe her one man's mistress. It was only natural others would try their luck now that Adam was gone.

"He's the heir to his uncle's viscountcy, you know," Sarah chided. "If you play your cards right, you can—"

"Win the heart of my lord as you did yours?" Bianca bought time in a refreshment of her hair, a check of her flounce in the mirror. "Neither Mr. Hayworth nor any of the flirtatious sprigs of fashion camped upon my doorstep are interested in matrimony. Besides, I've lived that charade already. I have no wish to repeat the performance."

Sarah offered her a schoolmarmish stare. "'The lady doth protest too much, methinks.'"

"And: 'Many a good hanging prevents a bad marriage,'" Bianca countered.

"Tish tush. We could trade quotes all night. You say they're all interested in bedsport only, but you don't know that for certain. You can't tar all men with one brush."

"If the brush fits . . ."

Sarah's expression took on a rarely seen solemnity, all the more forceful for being so unusual. "Banter aside, Bianca, you can't hide forever. What are you really afraid of?"

"Shall I list them alphabetically or in order of importance?" she quipped, but Sarah's gaze remained implacable.

Bianca met it without flinching, though her mind saw naught but dark memories. "You want to know what I fear?" she answered softly. "I fear love's end. I fear looking into my husband's eyes and seeing nothing but indifference where once I saw desire. I fear the heavy hand of jealousy and hate when all I crave is an affectionate caress." She scowled, banishing Lawrence's shade back to the recesses of her thoughts. "When one has been burned, it's only a fool who places his hand back into the fire."

"Or an optimist." Sarah's face broke into a smile. "Mark my words, Bianca. One of these days a man will make you forget that odious husband of yours."

Bianca responded with an unladylike snort. "Only if he whacks me over the head and I wake with amnesia."

The normal backstage bustle and chaos had quieted, most of the actors long since departed for engagements elsewhere. Only a few hardy souls remained— some prop and scene men organizing for tomorrow's performance, dressers tidying up costumes, maids dumping trash and sweeping passages, clerks counting tonight's till.

Bianca sat rubbing lotion into her hands, delaying the moment when she had to leave the serenity of her dressing room for another more difficult performance. That of carefree, glittering actress, bubbling with enthusiasm and sparkling with wit.

She grimaced at her reflection as she affixed her earrings. It might be hell sometimes, but it certainly beat the alternative—home to an empty house with only her thoughts for companionship. Better to exhaust herself dazzling the crowd than to lay awake for hours pondering the choices that had landed her here.

"Mrs. Parrino, are you in?"

A question hardly worth asking, since Mr. Harris, Covent Garden's manager and her boss, had not bothered knocking before barging through the door.

She rose to sweep the long draping silk of her scarf across her bare shoulders. "Just on my way out. Can it wait until tomorrow? I'm due to dine with the Astons and Lord Pollian."

"Actually, mum. It can't wait." Mr. Harris rolled back and forth on the balls of his feet, his red face redder than normal, his wig askew on his stubbled head. "You see, Mr. Kemble and I have been discussing the situation."

"What situation is that?"

"The . . . uh . . . the recent and unfortunate death of your . . . your particular friend, Mrs. Parrino. Now, I don't normally make it any of my business to poke my nose into the talent's lives. Long as you show up for work sober and you bring in an audience, you can do as you like on your own time."

"That's very liberal and decent of you."

"But there's a time when I have to make a stand and

that's when one of my company is being talked about in the same breath as a murder."

"Who would that be, Mr. Harris? And don't tell me it's Sally Randall. You know her. She threatens to kill off her no-good philandering husband every other day. We all know she's talk and no action."

"It is not Sally Randall. I'm afraid it's you. The stories are running like fire that you had that fellow murdered in the park last week."

Bianca's stomach tightened into a knot, her palms instantly clammy as she was reminded of the days and weeks following Lawrence's death when the fear of arrest hung over her like a pall. It had never happened, the coroner ruling her late husband's fall an accident, but the irony wasn't lost on her now. Cleared of a killing she'd caused only to be suspected of a killing she knew nothing about. Cosmic justice at its most absurd?

"Does anyone believe these stories?"

"Not much, no. But I can't have my Rosalind suspected of murder. It's not proper."

"Do you believe I killed Mr. Kinloch?"

"Of course not. I think I know you better than that. But it's not what I think that counts. It's what the public thinks. Mr. Kemble doesn't want any trouble, not with the place barely recovered from the last riots. Remember what happened in oh-nine? And that was over ticket prices! Imagine the tumult if our lead actress is carted off the stage mid-soliloquy by the Runners. We'd have the place in ashes around us."

"What do you propose I do, Mr. Harris? Pronounce my innocence like Anne Boleyn before the sword? If we gave credence to every rumor afloat in London, Princess Charlotte's paternity would be in doubt and

Lord Asbury would be selling his wife's services to Mr. Keeling for fifty pounds and use of his shooting lodge in Perthshire."

"Be that as it may, I'm going to have to ask you to step aside. Just until the gossip cools off and a new story catches fire."

"Mr. Harris—"

"Tomorrow night will be your last performance. That should give Sally time to prepare to take over. Think of it as a chance to rest. Take a little trip. Visit the seaside or the lakes. Go north for the shooting. Anything."

"Just don't turn up at your theater."

He nodded, smiling now that she had agreed without throwing a scene. "It's only until things get back to normal. Then you return, good as new."

"Is this a suggestion or an order?"

He grabbed her hand, pumping it as if he were drawing water from a well. "Thank you for being a jolly good sport, Mrs. Parrino. A week. A month. We'll be in touch."

She removed her sweaty hand from his grip with a thin-lipped smile. "That would be an order, then."

From his position across from the theater's stage door, Mac glanced up at the night sky. Clouds spread thick and reaching, a waxing orange moon slipping in and out between streamers of dank fog.

It was almost Silmith, the night of the full moon. In every clan holding from Ireland and Scotland to Wales and Cornwall, the Imnada would be paying tribute to the mother goddess. The Ossine would be offering tribute to her power. Younglings who'd reached maturity would be allowed on their first hunt beneath her watchful gaze. Promised mates would be joined in marriage, their first hours together blessed by her magic.

And under her harsh silver glare, swift and brutal punishments would be meted out to any transgressors of clan rule.

He shut that memory away, focusing instead on the ease with which he'd shifted to his panther aspect tonight, his body's transformation as smooth and fluid as the muscles beneath his glossy hide. He would enjoy the respite while he could, for as Silmith gave way to the waning quarter moon of Berenth, the debilitating violence of the curse intensified as ancient magics warred for control of his body. He hated the moonless nights of Morderoth, for then the shift became impossible, and he spent those long hours of darkness trapped in his human form, crushed between the goddess's powers and the Fey-blood's spell.

But could an end to the suffering be close at hand? A way to break the cycle of dawn and dusk that had come to rule his life? If Bianca Parrino spoke the truth, Adam had found the answer. But how? What had he discovered? And why hadn't he informed the rest of them? Elation and fury warred within Mac. Was Adam's silence a betrayal of their friendship? Or had he meant to tell them all and been killed before he found the chance?

Damn it to hell!

To be so close to freedom, then have the solution die with his friend, knotted Mac's gut. But there was still a chance, and Bianca Parrino was the key.

He had known it as soon as he laid eyes on her. As if the mother goddess herself had offered him a sign by searing Bianca's image on his mind, he'd been drawn from the sanctuary of his rooms despite the risks, her arctic-blue eyes acting like a lodestone.

He had to discover what she knew.

He had to see her again.

The performance had ended hours earlier. Crowds spilling from the theater like bees from a kicked hive. Loud, raucous laughter, shouts for passing hackneys, the jangle of harness as carriages jostled for the curb. Society men in elegant black with rainbow-hued women on their arms. The crude excitement of clerks and shopkeepers, lawyers and military men in glittering gold and silver braid. The fluttering fans and swaying hips of courtesans and demireps.

Then they were gone, the streets of Covent Garden empty as the theatergoers moved on to dinners and balls, clubs and concerts. The night would ring with the clink of china and the sparkle of witty conversation. Flirtations and scandal. Jealousies and petty vengeance. And finally, in the darkness, men and women would come together in passion. Hold each other close as the bliss subsided and sleep stole over them.

For Mac, night had become a purgatory to be survived. As long as he lay under the curse, there would be no woman to share more than a quick emotionless coupling. He was *emnil,* dead to the clans. Forbidden a marriage within his own race and burdened with the certainty that no human female would ever see him as more than a monster to be slaughtered as Adam had been.

For him there would be no home or family to replace the one stripped from him. No wife or lover to replace the beautiful Lina, who'd spurned him for the freak he had become.

Unless . . .

He stretched, loosening the pent-up swarm of excitement tightening his muscles.

. . . unless he broke the curse.

If Adam had been able to find a way to do it, so could Mac.

The moon had barely moved in the sky before the door opened. Even concealed beneath a heavy cloak, Mac recognized her. The velvety spice of her perfume, the slight musky scent of her creamy skin. The gleam of her shimmering hair.

Coming up on his haunches, Mac growled low in his throat.

Bianca spun around, eyes darting from shadow to shadow.

Pulling himself together, Mac sank back. Stupid mistake. He should know better. *Did* know better. He'd spent six years being professionally invisible for Wellington's army in the field. Now barely a year shuffling papers at the Horse Guards and he was losing his edge.

Bianca stood for a moment haloed by the light within until someone inside the theater called to her. Then she turned, illuminating the curve of one pale cheek and the sweep of dark lashes, the slender column of her throat and the dimple kissing her chin. If he weren't positive that she had no idea he was watching, he'd have sworn the pose was for his benefit. Sultry and yet uncontrived. A woman who knew her sexual power and took pleasure in it.

She remained thus for the barest of moments. Then a change in the light, a shift of her body, and her icy radiance became the chalky pallor of exhaustion. The deep wells of her eyes turned to shadows. The regal pose more closely resembled a woman bracing for a painful blow.

"I've changed my mind, Martha. I think I'll just go home to bed." Even her voice held a weary, forlorn air.

She headed toward Bow Street, Mac sliding from his alley hiding place to follow, one more shadow among the dark. Sometimes he wished his aspect had been sewer rat. Inconspicuous would have been a hell of a lot safer.

As she passed the front of theater, Mac caught movement out of the corner of his eye. A figure stood hidden behind one of the four portico columns, the pinprick light of his cheroot giving him away.

Mac paused as the stranger stepped out behind Bianca, his steps slow but certain.

Dread and frustration settled like a brick in Mac's gut. Did this stranger have anything to do with Adam's death, or was he merely a random footpad bent on an easy score?

The stranger's pace sped up. Mac closed in pursuit, the hair rising on his back as excitement warred with anticipation, his tail lashing in growing anger.

Bianca crossed over Russell Street, still unaware of the danger behind her.

The footpad stank of sweat, cheap gin, and cruelty. Mac lengthened his stride, muscles strung taut, body alive with a feral bloodlust.

Intent on his target, he never sensed the dogs until they launched themselves at him with furious growls and teeth like razors.

Behind you, Bianca! Run!

The blast of his pathing was all he had time for before the pack struck.

Bianca lay in bed, a damp, chilly breeze from her open window lifting the curtains. Raising gooseflesh on her arms. Rolling over, she burrowed deeper beneath the blankets. Turned back with a hefty sigh. Stared up at the ceiling. Examined her nails. Punched her pillow a few times.

Nothing. She was bone tired, her body screaming for much-needed sleep. And yet her brain whirred like a top.

Adam's murder . . . Captain Flannery's visit . . . Sarah's chiding . . . and the coup de grâce—her sacking by Harris. It all buzzed round in her head like gadflies.

Overwhelmed only by the last and strangest experience of the evening—a voice.

She'd heard it in her head. Loud. Insistent.

Too shocked to do anything but obey, she'd scampered the last few feet to the safety of the hackney stand and thrown herself into the closest carriage. Glancing back, she'd spotted a large man in greasy coat and battered hat. And then the hackney rounded the corner, and she could breathe again.

That's when she questioned herself—and her sanity. Was she hearing voices now? Not even in her worst days after Lawrence's death, when she'd been jumping at every shadow, had she heard any voice but her own, reassuring her she would be all right. He couldn't hurt her again.

Tonight's voice had not been hers.

Surrendering to the inevitable, she threw back the covers with a groan and, wrapping herself in a dressing gown, crossed to the window to look down on the rainy street below. A few lamps still flickered, but dawn lurked as a faint smudge in the east. Already the coal man was out with his sack, and there came the hollow rattle of a barrow as a dustman passed. Beyond that, the view was gray and misty. The houses across the way bleak and cheerless, their windows empty of life.

A movement caught her eye. A figure bundled in an oversized coat and wide-brimmed hat stepped out of the alleyway opposite and hurried, head down, toward Oxford Street.

Had he been watching her house? Spying on her?

Behind him, a second shape emerged, long and black and silent. Enormous as no alley cat she'd ever seen. Its intense gaze sought her out in her darkened window, eyes reflecting palest yellow-green in the light from a street lamp.

She yanked the drapes closed to a drumming heartbeat. Rubbed her eyes.

First hearing voices. Now seeing imaginary creatures. Perhaps Harris's suggestion had merit. Perhaps some time off was exactly what she needed. She'd been working too hard and sleeping too little. A few hours' reading should calm her nerves and weight her eyelids.

Her bag lay on the cabinet where she'd tossed it upon coming home. The great leather multi-pocketed satchel, which had belonged to her father, was one of the few things she possessed of his. A treasure despite its age and the sour, old-dog smell that clung to it. She could picture him even now, walking stick in hand as he tramped the high meadows behind their house, the bag slung over his shoulder. Calling out when he found a specimen that struck his interest. Fumbling with his field journal and a pencil, eyes bright as a starling's.

Smiling around the ache while rummaging in the depths for her brand-new copy of Sir Walter Scott's *Marmion,* she pulled out two small bouquets left for her with the watchman, now sadly wilted; a book of poems inscribed "To the goddess Artemis from her Actaeon" (yuck!); a beaded purse; a length of apple-green ribbon; a pair of leather gloves; and—wait a moment . . . now, that was odd . . . an old, weather-beaten leather-bound book with a guinea-sized divet in the center of the cover.

The things some people sent as symbols of their devotion made absolutely no sense to her.

In search of a note or an inscription, she cracked the book open, a shower of white petals falling into her lap from a dried stalk of ox-eye daisy, the leaves crackling to dust. Scott forgotten, she took a seat by her open window. Inhaling a shuddery, frightened breath of smoky, moist wind, she opened the book once again.

She turned to a random page near the front, a small curled fern pressed in the gutter. The handwriting was atrocious, tiny and close, the letters spilling one into another, words cramped tight into the pages. And very familiar.

Adam!

But how? When?

It must have been that last night at the theater. He'd

stayed for just a few agitated moments, but certainly long enough to stash this journal among her things. Was this what his killer had been searching for?

Studying the book more closely, she returned to the front cover. Inside, a heavy piece of parchment had been glued on three sides to form a pocket decorated with an odd crescent symbol. Running her fingers over the pocket, she felt a hard circular outline within. Barely one finger fit within the tight space between parchment and book, but enough for her to touch the edge of a smooth object hidden inside. Slowly, carefully, she eased the object loose a little at a time until it slid the rest of the way out.

A glass disk in a beautiful lapis blue, perhaps three inches in diameter, with four deep notches spaced evenly around the edge. She turned it this way and that. What on earth was it? She'd never seen the like.

She pushed the disk carefully back into the pocket. Whatever function it served, it had been important enough to hide. Perhaps answers would be found in the journal itself.

She flipped back through the pages. With much study, she made out:

Three miles northeast of San Millán. Few losses. Maucune's division escaped across the mountains. Flannery, St. Leger, and I share a barn. De Coursy arrived after durk. Good thing. I'd have hated to explain Gray's death to His Grace.

She pictured the severe, sharp-eyed captain hunched over a billet fire, sharing stolen poultry and cussing his superiors. Difficult to do. Far easier was imagining Captain Flannery hiking the hidden mountain tracks and lonely hillside forests of Spain in pursuit of the French army. He was a man bred for wars of old. Broad-shouldered. Iron-muscled. The past caught like amber in his long beryl-green gaze.

She gave herself a mental slap. Stupid woman. No dewy-eyed dream spinning for her, no sir. Both feet on the ground. Heart firmly locked away. Forget her resolve for a moment, and she had no one to blame but herself for the consequences.

She flipped ahead, discovering a long, flat-bladed leaf—perhaps an aster's. A small blue flower—gentian? larkspur? A sprig of some piney-scented herb—definitely, possibly wild thyme.

It had been too long since her days cataloguing beside her father. She'd forgotten too much since leaving America behind as Lawrence's bride.

Aire-sur-l'Adour. New moon of Morderoth. Shift impossible.

The fire flickered and burnt low as she read entries on the war years. Notes on scouting missions. Another mention of Captain Flannery. References to St. Leger and de Coursy.

By the time she skipped further along to a page bookmarked with a wilted primrose, petals brown, stem withered, she could barely make out the blur of shadowy pages, and the handwriting had gone from atrocious to nearly illegible.

She squinted to make out the plants listed by genus and species. Some common—willow, hemlock, vervain. Others less so, like marsh fern and burr medic.

Measurements had been penned beside each one as well as suggestions on which part of each plant should be used—root, leaf, or stalk. Farther down the page followed a procedure for preparation with normal details like cooking times and temperature veering into outlandish instructions, like "Should be completed during the new moon or bury for a day and a night tied with a scarlet ribbon."

What on earth? Bianca flipped through the next pages, but nothing else had been penned, the last few pages still waiting to be filled.

Rising to stir the fire, a paper fluttered free to drift across the carpet. She bent to retrieve it, catching back a gasp of astonishment at the face staring back at her—the same shaggy head of hair, the same wide-set, mocking eyes.

Adam's lover.

4

Mac tried focusing on the ordnance supply lists in front of him, to no avail. The amount of black powder in storage at the depot in Kinsale and the whereabouts of a lost shipment of carbines on the road between Portsmouth and Plymouth held little allure this morning. Instead, his head remained full of questions, mind leaping from thought to thought like a tennis ball.

The man at the theater. The man outside Bianca's house. Who was so interested in the actress that they stalked her? And why?

He rubbed a finger between his brows, his mind returning to that one instant when he'd looked back at Bianca's darkened town house and caught sight of her face in an upstairs window. Pale as the moon. Hair a loose ribbon of silver over a shoulder bare but for the thinnest of chemises. His own imagination had filled in the rest: delectable curves, creamy-soft skin, lips that could wring a hallelujah chorus from any man with a pulse.

He tried shaking himself free of the groin-tightening

images. Bianca Parrino had been Adam's mistress. She was off-limits.

And yet, their eyes had locked for a split second before he'd melted back into the alley, and he'd been struck by the infinite sadness in her gaze. He never should have pathed her that warning last night. It had been an instant's panic when common sense failed him. He'd seen the danger, understood the menace, and—damn it—he'd been unable to stop himself.

He only prayed he hadn't revealed too much with his heedless actions.

He tried easing his worry with the knowledge that when confronted with incidents out of the bounds of their understanding, most humans chose to ignore the truth and live on in ignorant bliss, never believing in the fantastical realms existing side by side with their own.

He prayed to the goddess it remained thus. He prayed—

"Captain Flannery, sir?" A pimply faced ensign hovered at the doorway, a sheaf of letters in his hand. "Captain Stockbridge just found these. They'd been mixed in among his mail."

Mac accepted the post from the young man, who started to say something else before Mac's forbidding expression had the fellow jerking a salute and making himself scarce. But his whispered comments back and forth with the sergeant on duty in the outer anteroom about worn-out old Flannery seemed to reverberate through the cramped office.

". . . queer duck. Not right in the head . . ."

". . . scout during the war . . . battle sick . . ."

". . . makes love to his requisition forms . . . useless . . ."

Mac had heard it all and worse over the last year

he'd been assigned to the army's headquarters. He felt his fellow officers' grudges and suspicions like a buzzing at the base of his skull, along with their disapproval and, in more than one instance, out-and-out dislike. They thought him a cold, emotionless bastard. A man who held himself aloof and above all others.

They blamed the war. Said it had changed him.

They didn't know how right they were.

Stuffing the letters unread and unremarked in his coat pocket, he turned back to his mountain of supply ledgers, the columns of inventory making his eyes cross and his head ache. How had it come to this? How had he become a cheese-paring, stoop-shouldered pen nibbler? On campaign, he'd always scoffed at Adam's constant scribbling in that damned book of his, the way he recorded every little tidbit as if how many times the four of them pissed between Tolosa and Vic-en-Bigorre mattered.

The ink from Mac's poised pen spread over the forgotten page, his idea bursting forth like a live shell. Of course! Why hadn't he thought of it before? Adam wrote everything down. He treated that battle-scarred book of his like a Bible. If the answers Mac sought were anywhere, they would be there.

Throwing himself to his feet, he ignored the tottering pile of requisition requests, consigned the damned pages of damned lists to the devil.

"Makes love to his requisition forms"? He'd feed them to the flames if he could. But what would be left to him then? Soldiering had become his life. Duty and honor had become wife and child to him. The only family he would ever know unless he changed fate and shattered the Fey-blood's life-destroying curse.

He pulled on his coat, grabbed his hat from the rack. Surprised the duty sergeant in the midst of picking his teeth. The man scrambled to his feet, casting Mac a faintly sneering side look. "Need somethin', Captain?"

"I'm going out."

"Where to, sir?"

He flashed the man a snarling whip slash of a smile. "This 'queer duck' has a mind to do some reading."

Stepping down from the hackney a few streets over from Spitalfields Market, Bianca scanned her surroundings with a wary eye. Downtrodden men hung about useless upon the corner. A hedge whore flirted with a sailor, her eyes devoid of emotion as she led her cull into a nearby alley. A gang of boys taunted a beggar. A man shoved a drunk from a dingy wineshop, where he fell face-first into the gutter. Scenes all too familiar from the final years of her marriage, when the money had run out and they'd taken two shabby rooms in Whitechapel, Lawrence spending his days drunk on cheap gin and sour wine.

Ignoring the angry shouting from an upper apartment and the scarlet-rouged bawds hawking their wares at the brothel down the street, she made her way to Adam's house.

She'd only visited here once. A few crushingly embarrassing moments she'd as soon forget. Flush with success in her first leading role and drunk on champagne and adoration, she'd come straight from a lavish midnight supper that had lasted till dawn. No one answered her knock, but upon spying the lit windows, and arrogantly confident of her welcome, she'd walked blithely in.

She'd discovered them in Adam's tiny parlor. The impression flashing through her brain like the flare of a lightning strike. Adam curled nude upon the floor. A shirtless man kneeling beside him, his shock of red hair alight with the fire's brilliant scarlet and silver glow, a tender hand resting upon Adam's shoulder. Words too low to hear between them.

She'd backed away, but the red-haired man caught sight of her. She still remembered the brutal glare of his eyes. The curl of his mocking smile.

She'd fled the house. Never returned. Never spoke of what she'd seen. Buried the memory away at the bottom of her mind. Adam's secret became her secret, an explanation for so much she'd never understood about his life.

Today the latch turned smoothly beneath her hand. Afternoon sun giving way to a dark and empty interior.

So much for locks and constables.

She stepped inside, shutting the door behind her. Took a moment to let her eyes adjust to the gloom. And drew in a breath of quick and painful fear.

Captain Flannery spoke the truth. The place was an absolute wreck.

Cupboard doors hung open. Drawers had been pulled out and overturned. Books and papers lay strewn across the floor in a blizzard of pages to mix with the smashed glass of cold frames, plants crushed and broken, their scent hanging like death in the air. As she passed through the cramped and tiny rooms, fear splashed clammy over her shoulders and squirmed in her stomach.

"I've seen close-range artillery fire do less damage," came a solemn voice just behind her.

Bianca spun around with a cry, colliding against a scarlet-clad chest sturdy as a tree.

The captain put out a hand to steady her. "Calm now, lass. It's just me. You look as if the devil were after you."

"How did you get in here?" she snapped, ashamed and embarrassed at her sudden, overwhelming urge to lean into his strength, let him wrap his arms around her and tell her it would be all right.

"The same way you did. The door" was his quiet comment as he righted a broken chair, stuffing spilled like entrails across the floor.

Alarm became anger, a more useful emotion. It allowed her to maintain a semblance of composure despite her thrashing heart and wobbly knees. "Are you following me? Is that why you're here?"

"I came in search of something."

"What kind of something?"

"Let's just say I'll know it when I see it." He took a deep breath and paced a few steps away, running his hand over a scarred tabletop. Bent to pluck a torn page from the floor by the hearth, his gaze narrowing. He shoved it into his pocket, but not before Bianca recognized the identical crescent symbol she'd noticed in Adam's journal drawn there.

"And why are *you* here?" he asked.

"Pardon?"

"What brings you to Adam's house alone and taut as a cocked pistol?"

"I suppose I hoped I'd find some clue or hint to the murderer's identity."

"And have you?"

"I found you. Does that count?"

"It would if I'd murdered him, but I'm as innocent as you of that crime."

"I'm glad at least one person thinks I'm innocent."

"Of murder, at any rate," he answered, a light hovering in his knife-blade stare. "The rest remains to be seen."

Fear and something else—something dark and forbidden—knotted her stomach and shivered like fingers up her spine. She lost her nerve and looked away, her eyes traveling over the wreckage of Adam's belongings. "Who could have done this? Thieves looking for trinkets to pawn?"

"Too much that could be sold remains. This was a search, plain and simple," he answered. The captain stepped closer, his body radiating heat like a blast furnace. "Did you ever see Adam with a book? Worn leather cover. Leaves and flowers pressed within it. A bookmark of ragged blue cloth torn from an old coat lining."

She clutched the strap of her satchel like a lifeline, unable to move. Unable to think.

"If you've seen it or might know where he kept it . . . I'd not ask if it weren't important."

She stared up at the flop of unruly, raven-black hair, the slash of dark brows. Noted a tiny white scar just beside his temple. The jump of his pulse at the hollow of his jaw. "What's so important about an old diary full of plants?" she asked, impressed at the steadiness of her voice.

"Only my life," he replied as he lifted a hand to her cheek, his fingers hovering bare inches above her skin. His eyes blazed a path over her face as if he might devour her, the space between them shimmering with expectation. "*Un fieuyn commdedig at neira,*" he whispered softly, his green-gold gaze vibrant as the sun upon the sea. "So beautiful. So cold."

His slow, seductive way of speaking moved like sugar through her veins. Desire jumped along her nerves. Wholly unexpected. Completely terrifying. Would he kiss her? Did she want him to?

Pulling free before she made a fool of herself, she cleared her throat. "I have to go."

He raised his arm as if he might catch her sleeve, but she jerked back.

"I'm late." She grabbed up her skirts, wheeling away. Away from his masculine strength and his grim, sorrow-filled gaze and a grief she'd felt welling from wounds she'd long cemented over. Grief echoed in his harsh, stony expression.

"Wait," he called.

She made it as far as the landing before staggering to a halt at the top of the stairs.

Three men climbed toward her, wide and solid as tree stumps. One with flabby hound-dog jowls and a smile gappy as a pitchfork. The second with a fire-scarred face, chapped lips pulled into a permanent grimace. The third, and most terrifying, with milky-white eyes, an expression empty as death. Two gripped long, ugly knives in their meaty fists; the third clutched a deadly-looking pistol.

"Here, now, what's yer hurry, pet?" Hound-Dog jeered as she retreated back into the parlor.

"Get behind me." Flannery pressed granite-hard against her back, breath warm upon the chilled flesh of her neck.

When she remained frozen, he put hands upon her shoulders, guiding her unresponsive body. "Now," he said firmly as the men bellied into the room.

Hound-Dog smirked, kicking aside a broken drawer. Stomping on the chipped edge of a bowl until it smashed as he herded the captain and Bianca ahead of him. "Bludge, Snips, and I want to know what a pretty bit like you is doing nosing about in a dead man's house with a fella like this one."

"Why not let the lady leave and we can settle this between ourselves." Flannery's steel gaze flicked between the three, a focused intensity in the coiled way he held himself. Violence rising off him like smoke. Here, then, was the battle-blooded soldier, the ancient warrior come to startling life. Just as breathtaking and twice as terrifying as she'd imagined.

In nervous agitation, the men closed ranks, gazes watchful as they eyed their adversary. Finally the man with the ruined face shoved to the front, brandishing his blade. "Nice try, lover boy, but mebbe we'll ask you the same thing. What's yer business here?"

Bianca jumped as Mac's lips brushed her cheek. "There's a carriage outside," he whispered. "When I say go, you run. Don't look back. Don't stop."

"Quit your muttering afore I cut out your tongue," Hound-Dog barked just before he sprang.

Mac reacted in a blur of movement that ended with Hound-Dog's knife in Mac's possession, the villain howling at a bloody slash running down one arm. Another movement too quick to follow, and he dropped like a rag doll beneath a fist to the jaw.

Bludge screamed and lunged, his blade whipping wildly.

Mac jumped aside, shoving Bianca clear before he stepped into the attack, knives meeting in a steely clash.

Now was her chance. Heart slamming into her throat, she inched along the wall toward the doorway leading to the stairs, cringing at each grunting curse, each smashing blow. Focusing on the cool, smooth wood of the chair rail beneath her fingers, she shimmied in tiny, agonizing increments, hoping all eyes were on the fight and off her escape.

The men dodged and struck back and forth across the ruin of Adam's tiny parlor, Mac always one step faster, his movements fluid as a dancer's. His face brilliant and stark and frightening in its cruelty. It was only when he avoided the obvious killing stroke for a deft and clever parry that she realized he was toying with them. The fight some sort of deadly game he played.

Another complicated maneuver straight out of Angelo's Fencing Academy, a sweeping lunge, and Mac's blade bit deep into the other man's thigh.

Clutching his leg, Bludge collapsed at Bianca's feet with a strangled scream, his face a sickly shade of green.

For a split second Mac's gaze found hers, his eyes ablaze with a lethal ferocity, a brutal smile lighting his dark features. Then a shot roared in the close space. The acrid smell of black powder and blood singed her nostrils and made her eyes water. Her ears rang with the echo of the explosion.

Mac reared back. "Run!" he yelled.

She blundered through the haze toward the door and down the stairs. There were shouts. A man's shrieking. She thought she heard her name called, and then she was through. Out in the street.

Before she caught her breath, arms wrapped around her midsection. Plucked her from the ground as if she were naught more than air. Tossed her into a carriage, the door slamming behind her.

"Holles Street," Mac ordered the driver, pressing his hand against a blossoming red stain on his side, bright against the darker crimson of his tunic.

"You've been shot." She gulped for air, praying she didn't faint. "Captain, you're hurt."

Eyes glazed with pain, he gave a slight shake of his head. "Looks worse than it is," he said, though his jaw remained tight, teeth clamped in a stubborn grimace.

She sat back against the musty seat, hoping the lurch and sway of the hackney would soothe her, but the looming, twisted grimace of Snips remained imprinted upon her mind before merging into another face: narrower, longer, eyes alight with the madness that always came over him with the drink. Slurred accusations of infidelity followed by vicious threats.

". . . devilish fog this autumn. Heard of a fellow got lost. Walked right into the Thames . . ." Mac's deep, lilting baritone broke into the endless spin of her thoughts. The crush of old fear. ". . . touch and go when the pickets were close. Never sure whether you'd be shot by your own sentries . . ." Sweat sheening his forehead, he sat stiff in the seat across from her. ". . . fields so green it makes your heart ache. A sky awash in clouds. There's a lake. Cold as the devil's heart, but it never stopped me from swimming . . ."

The yearning in his voice tugged at her own heart.

His usual arrogance stripped away for a revealing moment. "You should go home for a visit," she said gently.

Lines bit deep at either side of his mouth. "Impossible."

Mac leaned his head against the side of the carriage, and silence descended but for the rattle and squeak of the wheels.

No. His name was Flannery. Captain Flannery. She needed to stop thinking of him as Mac.

She sneaked a peek at the grave angle of his profile. Long, straight nose. Strong jaw. Stubborn mouth rimed in bitterness. A thin, bloody slash down his cheek. She dropped her gaze to his side and the spreading wound there.

"Are you certain you don't need a surgeon?" she tried again.

"I'm not one for doctors." He offered her a sheepish shrug before leaning back in his seat and closing his eyes. "They, uh . . . they frighten me."

"But—"

"Trust me, Bianca."

Before she could doubt her decision, she reached into her satchel, her fingers closing around Adam's journal. "You know, Mac Flannery? I'm beginning to think I can."

An entry about a scouting mission outside Orthez. Another relating an episode with a surgeon near Bayonne after a bloody skirmish. "Where did you get this?" Mac asked, still not quite believing he was holding Adam's fucking journal.

The last time Mac had seen it had been in Hainaut, when he and Adam shared a stew of cabbage and gristle, Adam scribbling away as usual until their fire burned to ash.

"Adam must have slipped it into my bag the night he went missing. I found it a few days ago."

Mac's skull heaved with desperate fear and desperate hope, his nerves scraped thin. "Have you read it?"

"There's more." She handed him a folded piece of paper. "I think this man killed Adam or knows who did."

Mac scanned the pencil sketch. It had been years, but there was no mistaking the slight upward slant to the eyes. The long patrician nose. The cynical twist of thin lips.

Jory Wallace.

An *emnil*. An Imnada outcast and rogue like Mac. Like the others.

His offense? Flouting tradition and Gather law by marrying an out-clan.

Mac had been a lad of ten when Jory's sentence was pronounced, but he recalled the incident as if it had happened yesterday: the long journey to Cornwall in company with his father. The great assembly in the hall at Deepings, seat of the Duke of Morieux, hereditary head of the ruling Gather, overlord of the five clans, and Gray de Coursy's grandfather. The ceremony and then the horror had impressed itself on Mac's young mind: the circle of angry faces, the calls for Wallace's immediate death, and the man's silent stoicism as they'd burned away his clan mark, his life forfeit if he ever dared attempt to pass through the Palings and return to the clans.

"You saw Adam with this man?" he asked, shaking off the bitter emptiness yawning before him. "When?"

"About six months ago. They were . . . together."
Dread and embarrassment rose from Bianca's body to
mix with the cinnamon-orange scent of her perfume.

"'Together'?"

"Adam was . . . that is, he preferred . . . he and this
man were . . ." Scarlet burned in her cheeks as she
straightened, a spark of defiance lighting her gaze.
"Adam and this man were lovers."

Mac nearly choked, the pain in his side flaring into
his brain. "Lovers? That's ridiculous!"

Sparks became flames. "I knew I shouldn't have
told you. I knew you would react in this way. But I
thought if it would help catch Adam's killer—if it
would bring him justice while quieting the rumors
making me out to be a murderous black widow—it
would be worth it."

"You of all people shouldn't believe such malicious
gossip."

"I wish that's all it was, but I was there. I saw
them together. Adam lay naked on the floor, and this
man . . . he was with him."

"So the rumors linking you and Adam . . ."

She shot him a scathing glare. "Were just that.
The distance between actress and whore is measured
in inches, Captain. People wanted to believe Adam
and I were lovers, and since the pretense kept him
safe, I never refuted it. But he's dead. No one can hurt
him now."

Mother of All! Of course! She'd witnessed Adam's
shift and taken it for an illicit assignation. Mac wasn't
certain whether to laugh or weep. Hell, had she arrived a few minutes earlier, there'd have been stranger
things than a naked man upon the floor for her to see.

"Don't judge him too harshly, Mac."

She'd said his name. She'd said his name, and Adam had not been her lover.

Unthinking, unbidden, and too stupid with unexpected relief to know better, he leaned forward and pressed his lips to hers. Her mouth beneath his was cool and soft and sherry-sweet. Once the kiss was over, the taste of her lingered. A wild buzz crackling beneath his skin. Arousal leaping like wildfire through his veins.

He waited for an eruption of temper that never came. Instead she offered him a strange look, eyes dark and inscrutable. Her hand rose as if she would bid him back to her.

The carriage lurched to a clattering stop, the driver shouting, "Holles Street, Cap'n!"

She sat up, a distant look in her eyes, and the moment between them passed as if it had never been.

A sticky hand clamped against his ribs, Mac opened the door for Bianca, the world reeling with more than recent discoveries. His side burned as if a torch had been held to his skin, and while the bleeding had slowed, it still seeped hot through his fingers at every movement. "You'll be safe now."

Bianca frowned, her lips pressed into a determined line, her hands clutching the strap of her bag. "I'll not leave this carriage unless you come with me. You're hurt and can barely see straight."

"Bianca—"

"Captain Flannery, it's that, or we order the driver to your lodgings and I'll tend you there. Either way, I'll not leave you until I know your wound is seen to."

He recognized that look of female pigheadedness.

If Bianca was anything like his sister, they'd sit here all night until she got her way. And he didn't have nearly that long. "You win."

She smirked over her success. "I usually do."

Renata paused in her letter writing to look out on the stream of people passing by her drawing room window. Was the gentleman standing on the corner a beast in man's clothing? Did the pair of women crossing the street change shape at the light of the moon? Was that fellow chatting with the peddler on the corner a dirty shifter?

It made her skin crawl to think these creatures walked unnoticed among humanity, able to work their treachery and do their murderous will, with the world none the wiser to their secret.

The Imnada are out there, Renata. I know it. And someday we'll prove it to the world.

Her father's words repeated so often throughout her childhood; an unrelenting refrain in spite of the criticisms and mockery heaped upon him by professors and scholars who scorned his research and dismissed his claims. They blamed Gilles d'Espe's mania on the tragic death of his wife, a woman Renata had never known but hated with every fiber of her being. It was this woman, long dead, who'd continued to hold her father's heart, allowing no other to take her place. No new love to grow.

Renata had tried. Desperate to prove her devotion, she'd assisted her father in gathering his Imnada lore, searching out rare texts and uncovering forgotten references. When he'd sought to launch expeditions to

Wales and Scotland in search of the elusive creatures, it had been Renata who organized sailing schedules and lodgings, provisions and guides. Any way to stay close to him. To carve a place within his life.

None of it had mattered.

A dead wife. A dead race. These were what he loved. He was blind to the living, breathing daughter in front of him.

She grew to hate this loathsome breed with the same fury she reserved for that bitch of a wife. Both had stolen her father's attention. And while one was naught but bones and beyond her retribution, the Imnada were not.

She dipped her pen into the inkwell, completed the last invitation in the stack. The recipients would gather for the skills of her cook and the perfection of her wine cellar. They would leave carrying the seeds of the shifters' destruction. The questions would grow. The word would spread. The Other would finally understand the threat they faced.

Father had been right.

The Imnada were out there. She had seen them.

They would pay for all they'd done to tear her family apart. She would prove her love once and for all. She would finally make Father proud.

5

The surgeon came and went, stitching the gash in the captain's side with much reproachful tut-tutting. "Is the gentleman staying here with you tonight?" he'd asked, his meaning clear.

"I certainly hope so or I'll have to postpone our orgy," Bianca snapped.

He sniffed his disdain even as he accepted her coins, but she'd already dismissed him and his small-minded contempt. Leaving his departure to Molly, she ascended the stairs to the guest chamber and tapped once before entering.

Molly had yet to clear away the remnants of the doctor's visit. A shallow basin of bloody water still sat on the floor by the bed, rags in a heap beside it. On the table, a half-empty brandy decanter and a glass stood amid a clutter of medicines.

She'd expected Captain Flannery to be asleep or, at least, in bed. Instead, he clutched the bedpost, wearing nothing but his bloodstained breeches and a sickly gray pallor. Spots of blood seeped through the layers of bandage wound tight across his ribs while sweat glistened on his powerful chest and shoulders and his eyes swam with pain.

A few inches in any direction. A few seconds slower in reaction time.

Bianca swallowed around the fear rising in her throat. "You claimed it was just a scratch. Look at you: barely able to stand."

"I can stand." He straightened. Immediately the color drained from his face, his mouth taut in a grimace. He slumped, letting out his held breath, hand resting against his side. "It's standing straight I have a problem with."

What was it about men and their stubborn need to appear invincible? They'd rather die than accept that they might be in pain or ill or, worse than worse, need a woman's assistance.

"How foolish can you be? That was no scratch to be fixed with sticking-plaster and basilicum powder. Ah, but I forgot: you're a soldier, impervious to pain."

"I wouldn't go so far as to say 'impervious.'" The ghastly pallor of sickness left his face, and he laughed. Or at least, that was what it sounded like. It came harsh and creaky. As if it had been a long time since he'd indulged. "Perhaps 'thick-skinned' would be more precise."

"'Thickheaded' would be more precise."

"Just when I think I have you figured out, Bianca Parrino, you surprise me." He reached out, his hand enfolding her own. His clean, wintry outdoor scent so different from the pomaded and perfumed men of her acquaintance. "I expect a tongue-lashing, and instead you're worrying over me."

"This *is* a tongue-lashing, and I am *not* worrying." She snatched her hand from his before he took her concern for more. "Merely stating the obvious, Captain. Denials aside, it's clear you're unwell."

"Say my name."

"Pardon?"

"Say my name, Bianca."

"Captain Flannery, I—"

Hunching his shoulders, he gave a snort of disgust.

"Cormac Cúchulainn Flannery," she said, enunciating each syllable with painful precision.

"Ouch. Low blow." His gaze seemed to shimmer like foxfire as a headache thumped behind her eyes.

"Mac," she said quietly.

A smile stole like a thief across his face. "Knew you had it in you."

She retreated from his unnerving warmth, looking for space to breathe and time to calm the uncomfortable buzz tingling her insides.

He dropped his hand to his side with something like regret in his eyes. "I have to go, Bianca."

"Go? You're in no condition to walk out of here. You have to rest."

Settling onto the edge of the bed, he fumbled with his boots, wincing as he bent to pull the first one on. "I can't stay. There are things I must do. People I must speak with."

"Then you'll come back and tell me who those men were, what's going on?"

He paused, second boot in hand, his stare seeming to pierce her to her core. "I don't want you mixed up in this. It's too dangerous."

"And your leaving is going to keep me safe? What

happened to the man who complained about my lack of protection? My mousy maid? This concerns me as much as anyone. While the stories linking me to Adam's death are running rampant, I'm without a job. I don't even want to think about what will happen if the stories grow to actual suspicions. Weren't you the one who offered to be an ally if things got sticky?"

"I was."

"Well, Captain, we're up to our necks in sticky, wouldn't you agree?"

He plowed a hand through his hair, exhaustion dogging his posture, sapping his words of their strength. "How is my spending the night here with you alone going to do anything but throw raw meat to the gossips?"

"I don't know. Maybe they'll be so distracted by my shameless behavior in taking a new bedmate, they'll stop dwelling on Adam's murder."

"More likely, they'll decide we're both guilty of conspiring to rid you of an unwanted lover. Lord Braemer thought as much, and with less cause than my sleeping in your bed."

"You'll be sleeping in my guest room."

"Semantics."

Mac had a definite point about the potential for disaster, but he spoiled it by rising from bed, stoop-shouldered and spine bowed as if it pained him to straighten. A stiff wind would blow the man over, and he wanted to charge back into the fray? He'd not stand a chance if those men returned. And she'd go from one very reluctant ally to no defender at all.

"Most red-blooded males in your shoes would be panting at the chance to spend a night with me." Explaining away her deception as necessary and for his own good, she furtively moved to shield the table with her body, unstoppering a bottle of laudanum to slosh an enormous dose into a glass of brandy.

"I'm not like most men."

Turning back with a smile, she held out the glass. "Oh, so you *don't* want to spend the night with me?" she teased, in a bid to distract him from her purpose.

"Is that a trick question?"

She offered him a practiced look of coy seduction. "Just a question."

He accepted the drink, tossing it back in one swallow. "Good-bye, Bianca."

She smiled in triumph. "Good night, Mac."

"If you outstay the time, upon mine honour, And in the greatness of my word, you die."

"O my poor Rosalind, whither wilt thou go? . . ."

"Alas, what danger will it be to us, Maids as we are, to travel forth so far! Beauty provoketh thieves sooner than gold . . . Now go we in content, To liberty, and not to banishment."

Tonight Shakespeare's words carried more of truth than Bianca would have liked. A woman fleeing for her life in the face of dangerous men. At least poor Rosalind had a sympathetic Celia as companion. Bianca's narrow escape had been in company with a grim-faced soldier whose roughened edges, beneath his pristine uniform, threw her into a tongue-tied frazzle. Something she wasn't used to—not in recent years.

She played the game, but it never touched her personally. She'd become an actress on and off the stage.

But not with Mac.

With every encounter, he managed to sneak beneath her props and costumes to the woman she was—or, rather, the woman she might have been had her life taken a different course.

And that was a complication she didn't need.

A jab to the ribs by the woman playing Celia refocused Bianca on the stage, the audience, the theater—a world that meant security and encouragement and admiration. A world where playing a role was all they ever asked of her, and the fantasy was everything. But all that might be lost now.

She took what might be her final bows to a drumming rain of applause and cheers, though scattered among the adoration were hints of darker emotions. A few hisses and catcalls from the lower benches. A spearing of hard-eyed disapproval from the upper boxes that chilled her bones like a cold wind. And just as the curtain closed, a half-eaten apple landed on the stage at her feet.

Was Mr. Harris right? Were her admirers so fickle that just the hint of a lurid story was enough to make them turn on her?

As she made her way backstage, fear and doubt and a lingering sour taste of panic left by this afternoon's attack pressed once more against a heart already weighted with grief. Not even her dresser's usual chatter was enough to soothe Bianca's nerves as she changed out of costume and wiped clean her face for the last time until who knew when. Even as she closed the lid on her cosmetics box, slid the last bit of costume jewelry away in a drawer, and tidied away the ribbons and combs and pins scattered across the top of her dressing table, the knowledge that this could be her last performance wasn't enough to erase the waxy gray of Mac's face. Instead, the memory of his fingers, sticky and red with blood, burned hot against the backs of her eyelids, and the vision of his ruthless, feral excitement as he fought still squirmed the pit of her stomach.

Normally she'd push aside the horrid events of the day with seven covers at table and non-stop champagne. Inoculate herself against the deafening quiet of the night with laughter and sparkle and conversation. Those ploys had always worked when memories of Lawrence's rage-filled violence surfaced and nightmares of the pain and humiliation suffered under his domination clustered close within the shadows.

But not tonight. Not when the rumors flew like barbs and she was uncertain of her welcome. Not when the only man who seemed to believe in her innocence lay recovering from a bullet wound in her house. Captain Mac Flannery had burst into her life like a rabbit from a conjurer's hat, but what role would he take on now that he'd arrived?

Ally? Maybe.

Enigma? Definitely.

Mac woke to darkness leavened only by the smoldering of a low-banked fire. For a moment, he had no idea where he was or what had happened. Then memories flooded back, and he clawed himself free of the entangling covers, paws skidding on the polished wood floor. Tail lashing the air like a flag.

He'd fucking shifted!

Mac's heart pounded. His skin going hot, then cold, then hot all over again. The blasted interfering woman must have slipped him a triple dose of laudanum when he wasn't looking. Clamping down on the terror igniting his blood, he listened for telltale screams or shouts or the pounding of boots up the stairs. Nothing. The house slept. The neighborhood remained silent. None had seen. None knew. Yet.

He stalked the room as he sought a way out of the trap closing around him. The mantel clock read three. If none in the household had looked in on him yet, it was doubtful whether they'd check on him now. Just a few more hours until dawn, and he'd be out of danger. One hundred and eighty minutes. Ten thousand eight hundred seconds.

He started counting. One . . . two . . . three . . . four . . .

A stirring of the air. A shush of a slipper against carpet. The orange spice of familiar perfume.

Bianca.

Events spun from bad to worse to infinitely horrible in the space of seconds. Drawing back into the darkest corner of the room, he curled into the shadows, his unblinking stare focused on the door, claws nervously extending and retracting, breath stilled in his chest.

The door opened, the light from her candle like a flickering spear across the floor, pointing to his hiding place. Her hair hung like a rippling silver wave on either side of her face, her robe loose to reveal the translucent linen of her nightgown.

She hovered within the doorway for what seemed an eternity. Mac's entire body crackled with unbearable tension. Every ache and pain was magnified to an agony. Then, as silently as she'd come, she pulled the door closed, leaving him once more alone in the dark with naught but bitter regrets and lonely hours for company.

Five . . . six . . . seven . . . eight . . .

Alonzo was there to hand Renata out of the carriage.

Stepping onto the flagway, she placed her gloved hand in his, pulling her shawl close around her shoulders against the pervasive dampness in the air. The flambeaux placed on either side of the entryway flickered low, and already a smear of gray across the sky signaled the coming dawn, but Renata's fatigue lifted as she shook off the hours spent flitting between Society entertainments on Froissart's arm.

"I have news," Alonzo said quietly.

A footman hovering over him with an umbrella, Froissart pulled his bulk free of the carriage, grumbling over the pains in his head, his heavy losses at cards, the poor state of the London streets, and the foul English weather.

"Come inside and have your man fix you a cup of milk with a dose of laudanum to help you sleep," Renata instructed over her shoulder to her husband before hissing under her breath, "Where have you been, Alonzo? It's been days without word."

Froissart spotted Alonzo, his face sharpening like a ferret's. "What's your cousin doing here? I don't like him skulking around."

Renata offered her husband a pouty frown, sliding close against him, reaching with just the lightest of mental touches to guide his mind where she wanted it.

"He's not my cousin, *ma puce*, but he is the only family I have left. The only connection to my lost home. You wouldn't send him away."

"Hmph," he snorted. "Let him stay if he amuses you. Surprised he's here in the first place. Did that opera dancer in Soho toss him out on his ear? An expensive piece, that one."

"I neither know nor care about his living arrangements or his . . . sexual appetites."

"No? Maybe that was Monsieur Gerrard who told me. I can't remember. Too much to drink, and my head hurts," he complained, Alonzo already dismissed from his thoughts.

Successful in turning Froissart's attentions aside, Renata eased free of his mind as they climbed the steps to the door, a servant waiting to swing it open before them. Another to take her wrap and muff. A third to hurry forward and assist Émile.

"Stop your badgering," Froissart shouted. "Renata! Tell these fools to stop gabbling about me like a pack of old women."

Froissart's valet hurried in from the kitchen with a glass upon a tray, handing it over with a small bow. Froissart, loosening his cravat, tossed back the spiked milk with a heavy sigh and a belch.

In the confusion, she drew near enough to Alonzo to whisper, "Come to me in one hour."

"I'm tired, and my head aches. Help me upstairs," Froissart whined. "No, not you"—he waved his valet away with a halfhearted swing of his meaty hand—"I want my wife to assist me. Renata!"

She pulled away from Alonzo, hatred barely concealed beneath a silky smile. "Coming, husband."

Excitement tremored along her limbs, her mind alive with possibilities and plans. The diversion helped as Froissart growled and bullied his way into her bedchamber, his manner coarse, his prick hard. Fortunately, the brief encounter left him spent and snoring even without the laudanum. By the time Alonzo knocked quietly at her dressing room door, she'd changed into a quilted robe and brushed out her hair while her husband slept off his aching head and sour stomach in the room beyond.

Alonzo answered her summons, pausing only briefly to adjust to the fragmented candlelight and his many-reflected shape within the mirrored walls. "The pig sleeps?"

"Like the dead." She placed her brush upon the table. "I hope you've more to show for the last few days than a case of the pox caught from that French opera dancer. If it's the one I'm thinking of, she's serviced every man in the embassy, including Émile. They call her the nun, she spends so much time on her knees."

His gaze grew shuttered, almost pained, and she smiled to herself. Women must use what weapons came to hand.

He drew farther into the room, taking up position in the shadows by the fire, light dancing over his devilish features. "One of the men from the cemetery has been seen in Madame Parrino's company and again at Mr. Kinloch's home. It's no coincidence. He's one of those who murdered the chevalier. I'm sure of it."

The words slid as painfully into her heart as they had the first time she'd heard the news. She'd vowed then and there: these creatures would suffer. She would make them bleed, listen to their pleas for mercy, watch their eyes slowly glaze over in death, and enjoy it. It was justice. "And where is he now?"

Alonzo clenched and unclenched the hand at his side. "He eluded me."

"You or those worthless gin-soaked thugs you paid to trail the Parrino woman? I told you not to trust in these English sons of dogs."

Alonzo dismissed her crudity and her complaints with a jerk of his head. "It does not matter. What's done is done, but come the new moon, he'll be yours. Unable to shift. Vulnerable, just like the last one. It will be easy to capture him then."

"No!" She spun around, her eyes darting toward the closed door behind which her husband snored in her bed, her bile rising with the memory of his hands upon her body, the swift, violent pounding as he took her. "I will not wait." She forced herself to relax, rising in a slow, graceful movement to caress Alonzo's cheek. "Once these Imnada demons are dead at my feet, I can lay my father to rest. I can move on. *We* can move on." Her gaze flicked once more to the door. "Together."

"What do you suggest?" he asked.

She returned to her seat, opening the collar of her robe to reveal an elaborate necklace of interlacing silver strands studded with rubies. A web of spun moonlight upon her pale skin, the stones like drops of blood. "Assist me with my necklace."

He stepped behind her, close enough that his breath tingled against her neck. His desire lighting the deep ocean blue of his gaze. Her own passion flared, and she leaned her head back for a moment against him, closing her eyes as his hand took up the silver necklace, his fingers on her skin sending shivers down her spine to pool wet and hot between her legs.

Their eyes met in the glass as he lowered the necklace into her open palm, understanding passing with a physical shock between them. With a smile cold as a blade, she closed her fingers around the silver links as if they might burn her, but only coolness met her fingers. "Silver. Who knew such a beautiful weapon could bring down such mighty beasts?"

6

"Is our guest awake yet, Molly?" Bianca asked, eyeing the laden tray the young woman juggled as she tapped the bedroom door behind her closed with her foot. "Don't tell me he's sulking. That laudanum was for his own good."

Molly shifted from foot to foot, her eyes flickering between her mistress and the wall behind her. "No, mum. It's not that."

Bianca tensed. "Is he feverish? Does he need his dressing changed?" She passed Molly to see for herself. "He didn't take his anger out on you, did he? Of all the ungrateful, self-centered—"

"He's left, mum."

Bianca spun round. "Gone?"

"Yes'm. The bed's made, his clothes are gone, and he's vanished."

"People don't just vanish."

"Must have been during the night or first thing this morn. I let Mrs. Skelton into the kitchens at half six to begin breakfast and didn't see nothing then."

"That can't be."

"I didn't want to bother him in case he was sleeping, so I never checked on him until just now. I'm sorry. I know I should have done it sooner, but Mrs. Skelton needed me—"

"It's all right, Molly. Not your fault our bird has flown his coop." Bianca entered the room as if expecting Molly's story to be just that. Bed neatly made, extra quilts folded at the foot. No clothes draped upon the chair. Adam's journal gone.

She pulled the door closed again. "I should have known. Good-bye it is," she whispered to no one.

By the time Mac returned to his lodging house, the throbbing in his side matched the throbbing in his head. All he wanted to do was sleep a few hours before he tackled Adam's journal. Instead he met David lounging outside the door to his rooms.

"Mother of All, Mac. What in blazes happened to you?"

"Bit of a run-in with Spitalfields' finest." Mac tried and failed at a reassuring smile as he ushered his guest into his apartment.

David gave the small, shabby rooms a cursory once-over. "What a dumpy flat."

"So it's not Brighton Pavilion," Mac answered.

"It's barely Brighton barracks," David shot back.

For the first time, Mac viewed the place through another's eyes. Scrupulously clean. Ruthlessly barren. No pictures on the wall. No knickknacks or childhood mementos. Nothing he couldn't fit into his campaign haversack and take with him at a moment's notice. Nothing he cared about losing.

"I don't need much. I'm only here when I have to be."

A silent understanding passed between them before David turned away to rummage among the liquor, pouring himself a tall whiskey. Another for Mac. "So, what happened? Footpads?"

"It was an ambush. At Adam's house."

David stiffened. "What were you doing there?"

"Mrs. Parrino and I—"

"Hold on. The actress Bianca Parrino? What the hell were . . . you're still on about his murder, aren't you? After Gray and I told you to leave it alone, you went ahead and poked your nose in anyway."

"Adam's murder wasn't a random killing. The attack on me yesterday proves it. Someone knows about the Imnada. Someone who wants us dead. The clans could be in danger."

"He's gone, Mac. Unmourned. Unshriven. And who from the clans showed at his service? None. To them, we're no different from the dirt filling Adam's grave. *Emnil.* Nothing."

Mac felt David's anguish like a frozen piece of his own heart, but he said nothing. Sympathy wouldn't assuage David's bitter resentment. The Gather had spoken. Their word was final, but mayhap if he knew . . .

"What would you say if I told you Adam had found a way to break the curse?"

Even as he spoke, Mac wished to take the words back. The wild flash of hope in David's eyes was almost heartbreaking. And then, just as quickly, it was gone. Replaced by his usual heavy-lidded cynicism.

"I'd say you received a knock to the head as well as that gash in your side."

"But if it's true, it could mean a lifting of our exile. We could go home, David. Think on it."

"I've better things to do than entertain crazy pipe dreams. Face it, Mac. We've exhausted every avenue. The Fey-blood's curse is forever. When will you finally surrender to the inevitable?"

"When I stop breathing. Here. Look at this." Mac handed David the journal. "Adam hid it with Bianca the night he disappeared. It's his diary, David. He never went anywhere without it. Remember? And there's more. Bianca saw Adam after sundown. She thought I was mad to press her about it, but she saw him. More than once."

"She couldn't have."

"Unless he broke the curse. Unless he found the answer. And if he did, maybe he wrote it down in here," he said, jabbing at the book.

"Well, did he or didn't he?"

"I haven't had a chance to go through it yet."

"All right, so let's just assume Adam did break the curse, and there's the ghost of a chance we may discover how he did it and reclaim our place within the clans. A big assumption, by the way, but I'll humor the man who looks as if he's been pummeled with bags of wet cement and say it's all plausible. What do you need from me?"

"I need you to keep an eye on Bianca."

"Look after Adam's beautiful ex-mistress? Now, there's a job I can get behind." He smirked. "And on top. And underneath. The possibilities are endless."

"If you value your manhood, you'll keep your possibilities to yourself."

"Are you marking your territory? Next you'll be

clubbing her over the head and dragging her back to your cave?"

"Leave her alone. I mean it."

David held up his hands in surrender. "All right. All right. No need to play defender of the realm. Why does Mrs. Parrino need guarding anyway? I thought you said the men targeted you, not her."

"Because something tells me she's important. I don't understand how, but I feel it. It's as if she's a key. And if we lose her, we lose our last chance to go home. Please, David. You're the only one I can trust."

David headed to the door. "Which says what about you, old man?"

"And be careful. Someone's hunting us. They killed Adam and now they're after me. It's not a coincidence. But is it because we're Imnada or because we served together?"

"Maybe it's both" was David's grim reply.

Feeling like a complete idiot, Bianca gnawed the end of her pen, the paper beneath her hand already smudged with cross-throughs and edits. The blotter beside her stained purple.

She neither wanted nor expected to see or hear from Mac ever again. He had Adam's journal. There was nothing more to draw him back to her. Whatever happened to him from here on out was none of her concern. And whatever happened to her, he'd made it clear he didn't care.

She should have known better than to trust in his avowals of support. She was on her own. Just as she'd always been. Just the way she preferred it. The way it had to be if she wanted to hold tight to her hard-won freedom.

Whatever tingly excitement she'd felt in his company would dull. Whatever scandalous dreams he inspired would fade. And she would most assuredly not wake with the image of his swoon-worthy body dancing across the surface of her mind or with impossible endearments whispered in a lilting Irish accent pushing against her heart.

No. Never. Not a chance in this or any other life.

She shook off her fancies with a firm shrug. She needed to control herself. Hadn't Lawrence caused the same flutterings and palpitations? Hadn't he been all that was kind and solicitous and tender—until he'd married her?

She clenched the pen tightly in her fingers, scribbling another hasty line.

"What are you writing over there, Bianca sweeting?" Sarah called from her place at the whist table. "Is it a love letter? Anyone we know?"

"What did she say? A love letter? I hope it's not that skinny Mr. Paisley who lives with his mother," Mrs. Commin commented. The earl's twice-widowed cousin living in East Grinstead had been overjoyed when an invitation to stay at Deane House had been extended. "A stiff wind would blow that man away."

"He's not skinny. He's wiry," Miss Hayes, Mrs. Commin's timid friend, said in Mr. Paisley's defense. "And his mother is very nice."

"Are we chatting or playing?" Lady Grigson complained. "I'm not getting any younger."

The elderly dowager viscountess had been one of the few Society women to buck prejudice and ac-

cept Sarah upon her shocking marriage to the earl.
A plainspoken woman with a gimlet glare and connections to every important family in England, she
spoke of Lord Deane's mother as "that upstart mill
owner's daughter" and assured Sarah that Sebastian
had enough money to buy entrée for his wife were she
a gypsy from Timbuktu.

. "Of course. It's your play." Sarah turned back to her
cards but not before Bianca threw her a threatening
we'll-talk-later glare.

She looked down upon the horrid scrawl with
a sigh. Perhaps she was jumping the gun by writing
to Mr. Jones at Dublin's Crow Street Theatre. But a
few months in Ireland might be just the change she
needed. A new city. A new job. A new start. She'd
not look too closely at why she'd chosen a theater in
Dublin above theater companies closer to home. It
certainly had nothing to do with a certain Irish army
captain.

". . . they call him the Ghost Earl. Isn't that delight-
fully thrilling?" Sarah gushed. "Such a mystery."

"The de Coursy family has always been a bit eccen-
tric," Mrs. Commin commented between tricks.

The women's chatter drew Bianca back from the
treacherous train of her thoughts. She listened, half-
heartedly dabbling at the page with her pen.

"You mean mad as a house of hatters," stated Lady
Grigson. "Obviously Gray de Coursy hasn't fallen far
from that tree."

Bianca sat up. Why did that name sound familiar?
Where had she heard it before?

"I heard the duke cast him off completely last year,"
Sarah said.

"Maybe so, but the Duke of Morieux can't stop the major from being heir now, can he?" Lady Grigson remarked, sounding like the voice of doom. "Besides, the duke should feel fortunate he still has an heir. Never wanted the boy to go for an officer. And from all I've heard, he was in the thick of things through most of the war."

The duke . . . Gray de Coursy . . . An officer . . . Of course. Adam's journal.

Gray's name had figured throughout the pages.

The gossip was interrupted by Sebastian's arrival, which turned the conversation away from de Coursy. Bianca concentrated once more on her sad muddle of a letter just as a shadow fell across the desk.

"Catching up on your correspondence?"

She looked up into the earl's quizzical face. One could be forgiven thinking Sebastian Commin past his prime when assessing his craggy features and gray-streaked dark hair. But then one noticed the broad-shouldered build of a pugilist beneath the elegant clothes and the shrewdness in his fiery gold gaze, and knew to tread very carefully.

"It began as a letter," she answered. "I'm afraid it's ended as fuel for the fire."

His eyes passed over her scribbling, his mild look of interest sharpening. "A strange little drawing there."

She followed his gaze to find she'd unconsciously sketched the crescent symbol over and over along the bottom of the paper. Shocked, she placed a hand over the page. "It's nothing. Just a mark I glimpsed recently."

"Did you?" His gaze grew solemn, his gold-flecked eyes burning brightly. "Step across to my study, Bianca. I'd like to show you something."

She rose and accepted his arm, the two of them passing through the corridor, past a pair of salons, to a dark-paneled door. Sebastian took a key from his pocket, fitting it into the lock, and pushed the door wide for her to enter ahead of him.

The book-lined room smelled of leather and parchment and ink and cheroot smoke. Knickknacks and curiosities lay scattered among the shelves and upon every cluttered cabinet and table surface. Little bits of carved stone. Small figurines in jade and quartz and one in ebony. A compass in a walnut case. A jeweled dagger beside a bowl of egg-shaped stones. A casket with a clasp wrought in diamonds.

Sarah had always made sport of her husband's fascination for the fantastic, his enormous collection of strange books and ancient artifacts. She called it his gentleman's hobby. But this room spoke of far more than a hobby. More like an obsession.

Bianca's mouth went dry and her prickling sense of unease returned and spread until it raised the hairs at the back of her neck.

He ascended a ladder next to the bookcase and pulled a book from the topmost shelf. Climbing down, he took a seat at his desk, clearing his throat with an awkward look of sorrow. "I was very sorry to hear of Lieutenant Kinloch's death. Sarah says my birthday gift was chosen on his advice."

"Adam found the volume at a queer little bookshop in Smock Alley. Said it would be perfect for you."

"Really?" Sebastian fiddled with his signet ring. "Interesting," he muttered again with an infuriating air of mystery as he handed her the book, open to a specific page. "That must be Theophilus Steen's shop.

I purchased this volume from old Steen last year. He's quite a character."

Bianca's eye fell immediately on the illustration. Not quite the same. The crescent was fatter and there was a small star design she didn't remember. But there was no mistaking it for anything but the symbol she'd doodled. The symbol scratched onto the bottom of the note to Adam.

She read the text beside it before meeting Sebastian's grave expression. "Who or what are the Imnada?"

Line Farm stood at the end of a quiet lane, set apart from the village by a belt of thorny, untended coppice and a crumbling ditch wide enough to corral a flock of grazing sheep. A churchyard ringed with yew stretched away to the west until it met a meadow thick with sweet clover. Jory Wallace had obviously wanted to keep nosy neighbors at bay.

Unlatching the gate, Mac entered the cobbled yard, trying on varying conversational gambits as he went. Discarding them just as quickly. His nerves jumped under his skin and his pulse thundered in his ears. His last sight of Wallace had been as he was dragged from the Gather's circle, face white as bone, with blazing eyes and a jaw set like granite. This meeting today could follow one of two paths: Jory might give Mac the moments necessary to explain his presence before he attacked.

Or he might not.

Nervous energy had Mac's mind leaping from David and his promise to watch over Bianca to the letter he'd posted to Gray before leaving London for Surrey. If the worst happened, at least his friends would know his fate.

Unfortunately, it would be too late to help. Mac would be six feet under.

The silence held a hushed expectancy. Prickles raced over his skin and up his spine, to settle cold at the back of his neck as he dismounted, and it took all his willpower not to reach for the weapon he carried in his saddlebag. Instead, he scanned the outbuildings for the unseen watchers he sensed, his gaze cutting through the long morning shadows.

"Bang! You're dead!"

Mac's heart shot straight into his throat at the sudden shout while his horse shied, throwing its head.

"Bang! Bang!" Another shout, this time from a barn to the right. "You've got to fall down now. I shot you fair and square!"

"Easy," Mac murmured to the big bay gelding, chagrined at his own skittish response. A year posted to a desk had wrought more changes than permanently ink-stained fingers and a brain packed with useless military trivia.

"Your gun misfired. And I dove under the bullet. You're the one who's dead."

So Mac was not the intended target. Merely caught between battle lines.

"That's not fair. I'm telling. Da!" The shout became a wail. "Daaaa! Henry says I'm dead." A young boy bolted from his firing position behind the chicken run, screaming all the way. "Daaaa! Tell him I'm not dead! Tell him he's a big, ugly liar!"

An older child stood up from his hiding place

at the edge of the trees, a long stick at his side. "You wanted to play. It's not my fault you're a poor shot."

Upon spying Mac, both boys rattled to a stop in mid-argument even as an enormous, rugged-shouldered man appeared from the barn, wiping his hands upon a rag, sweat darkening his red hair to a muddy brown. "Sam! Henry! I've told ye I need to be—" He spotted Mac, his gaze narrowing with suspicion, body braced as if expecting trouble. "What's your business here?" he asked, though his tone clearly implied he'd rather not.

"Jory Wallace?" Mac asked.

The two men eyed one another—the children looking silently from father to stranger with worried curiosity as the atmosphere grew storm-charged. It was the gelding that broke the standoff. It nickered, stretching its neck toward the smaller of the two boys with a twitch of its soft lips.

The boy smiled, patting its great dark head before glancing up at Wallace from under a shaggy crop of wheat-blond hair. "Look, Da. He likes me."

Wallace's lowered brows cleared as he tousled the boy's head. "Course he does, Sammy. Now take him to get some water. Henry, go with your brother."

The older boy looked as if he wanted to argue, but at a stern glance from his father he did as ordered, though he shot suspicious glances back over his shoulder as he went.

Wallace turned his attention to Mac, regarding him with as piercing an eye as a parade ground sergeant. "You're Sir Desmond Flannery's heir, aren't ye?"

"How do you . . ." Mac's words trailed off. "You remember me?"

Wallace gave a snort of disgust. "You've something of the look of your father and him I'll never forget. Big fellow. Shouted a lot. Wanted my head on a plate."

"That was him. Don't take it personally. He wanted mine as well."

A muscle tweaked in Wallace's jaw. "His own flesh and blood?"

"With Sir Desmond, family counts for nothing against the good of the clans."

Wallace shook his head before he motioned toward the house. "Come along inside, then, Captain. I've been expecting ye."

7

Bianca looked up from the book. "When I was a child, my father told me the legend of Robin Goodfellow." Her throat tightened at dusty, half-forgotten memories of nursery tales told before bed. Father sitting in a chair beside her, spectacles sliding down his nose as he read while Nurse tutted her displeasure. "He never mentioned anything about a race of animal faeries."

Leaning back in his chair, Sebastian steepled his fingers beneath his chin. Light from the window cast his long, solemn face half into shadow. "The Imnada weren't Fey. Nor were they completely human, but something different altogether. Though they possessed many preternatural gifts, their greatest was the ability to change shape at will."

"Sounds magical to me."

His gold-brown eyes shone warm with humor. "Normally, yes, but their enemies possessed much greater magic. And following the betrayal of their king, vengeful rage spurred them to wield those powers very effectively." Glancing at the longcase clock in the corner, he braced his arms upon the chair, half rising from his seat. "Ah, but we're keeping the women waiting. And your tea grows cold."

Bianca shot to attention, her fingers gripping the hand-tooled cover of the book, nerves buzzing. "Now, wait just a moment, you can't bring me to the edge of my seat, then just dismiss me back to tea and gossip. What happened? I want the whole story."

"Are you certain? There's no happy ending. Not for any of them."

"Show me a happy ending and I'll show you a fiction as great as any shapechanger prancing about the forest."

A guarded smile hovered over his mouth, fingers lightly drumming upon the desktop. "Very well. But how to begin?"

"All faerie stories begin with once upon a time."

"That works as well as any." Resting his chin upon his clasped hands, elbows planted on the desk, Lord Deane leaned forward, gaze alight with a troubadour's zeal. "Once upon a time, Other and Imnada existed side by side under the high king Arthur. It was a time when the barriers separating this world and the world of the Fey were fluid as a river's surface. Magic surrounded us. It lived in the turning of the planets and the turning of the seasons. From the smallest insect of the earth to the birds of the air, all interconnected like fine lace. All important to the eternal balance. And while those bearing the blood of the Fey and those bearing the blood of the beast maintained a wary distance at the best of times, still they lived united in peace under the king's banner."

His voice wrapped round her, pulling Bianca along with him into an ancient lost age until the room seemed to waver and fade. As if a curtain drew back to reveal a stage, before her stood enormous, dark, mist-tangled forests, rolling hills splashed with sun, the silver sparkle of twisted waterways all flowing toward the sea. A spring-scented breeze filled her head. Ruffled her skirts. Birds hopped and chirped in the undergrowth. A fox slunk low through the briars.

She blinked, rubbing her eyes. The forest vanished. There sat the desk. The window. Sebastian, his voice slow and measured as music.

Had she dozed? Had days and nights of too little sleep and too much worry finally caught up with her here in this quiet book-lined sanctuary?

"If you choose to see it as a dream, Bianca, then that is what it is and how it will reveal itself to you."

Sebastian had answered her unspoken question, his voice rippling and curling like the wind in the forest and the waves upon the river. His gold brown eyes the same autumn shade as the trees. The rustling of papers on his desk became the twitch and twitter of birds in a tangled thicket.

"The past speaks through me," he continued in that same hypnotic rise and fall. "But the words create the magic. You have but to listen to learn what has gone before."

His Lordship's encouragement freed Bianca from the continuing sense of dislocation. Of course. She'd napped. That was all. She'd fallen asleep to Seb's faerie story, and vivid imaginings had followed.

Vaguely, she knew she should be embarrassed. What sort of guest fell asleep in front of her host? A very rude one, came the answer. Yet, a fierce desire to return to that ancient wood overpowered her good manners. She would make her apologies afterward. Plead exhaustion or illness. Surely, Sebastian would understand.

Decision made, she relaxed back in her seat, letting the words and the dream carry her away.

". . . At that time the Imnada's leader was a man called Lucan. Despite the tensions between their races, he ranked high within Arthur's circle. They were friends as well as monarch and subject, and Lucan's warriors served faithfully within the king's armies . . ."

Once more Bianca found herself standing within the oak forest, sun streaming through the latticed branches to fall upon a carpet of scattered autumn leaves. A path snaked off to her left toward a crumbling riverbank. Two men walked there, heads bent in conversation. One dark. One guinea gold, encircled by a narrow crown.

". . . the king's half sister. A woman as beautiful as she was treacherous. Morgana bore the blood of both Imnada and Other. She was jealous of Arthur's power. She wanted it for her son Mordred. And through him, for herself. Morgana and Lucan became lovers and, bewitched by her beauty, Lucan conspired with her against the king . . ."

The vision changed like bits of shifting colored glass. The two companions became a man and a woman. The dark-featured soldier from before and a lithe seductress with hair red as a sunset and eyes of honey amber, yet empty of warmth.

They strolled the path, pausing at the stream to spread a blanket upon the ground. Clothing shed. Passions rising. Dream this may be, but it was too real for comfort. The man's gleaming herculean body. The woman's soft, shuddering moans. Bianca felt like a lecherous voyeur. The fox returned to sit at her feet. Barked once before slinking away into the brush. Bianca followed, the branches swinging back to hide the lovers from view.

". . . deciding the Imnada would be better served by a new king—one who bore their blood, Lucan persuaded his men to join with Mordred. On the morning of the final battle, the king positioned himself as he had always done, in the center of the line . . ."

The colors shifted once more, falling into new patterns. New landscapes. Bianca stood at the edge of the forest now. Ahead, the trees thinned to become a wide, sloping plain crowded with men. Banners snapped in a cruel, laughing wind. Horses pawed the ground, leaving gouges in the soft earth like gaping wounds.

". . . opposing armies fought for hours until finally Arthur gained the upper hand. But without warning, the Imnada changed sides, and what had been a victory turned to a rout as the shifters, ferocious and almost indestructible in their battle madness, swept down upon their former comrades . . ."

Like waves beating against the shore, armies raged and swirled in an unending stink of blood and death. Until at some invisible signal, there came a shifting in the lines and, like a storm unleashed, the plain went black with new shapes and new sounds. Screams of terror and defiance became howls and snarls of victory. Men swept forward with the strength and then the forms of beasts. Washing over the king's army like a cresting wave.

Alone upon a low hill, Arthur's banner billowed. The king fought against the onrushing horde. Golden head uncovered. Sword raised, blind to the man approaching from behind intent on murder.

Bianca screamed. Throwing herself toward the attack as if she might stop the events unwinding before her dreaming eyes. But as always in dreams, her feet sank into a quagmire. All her effort and she barely moved. There was no way she would reach the hill in time. Even as she left the sanctuary of the forest for the blood-slick chaos of the plain, it was finished. Arthur lay upon the turf, and Mordred stood triumphantly over the fallen king.

The world shook and shivered in a dazzle of broken light, the sun falling oddly upon the ground. Mist rolled out across the plain with a roar like thunder. Enveloping both the armies. Climbing the hill where the king drew his last painful breath.

". . . unraveling began. Arthur's golden age became an age of bloodshed and death as stories of the Imnada army's treachery spread among the Other. In the vengeance unleashed, first the Imnada warriors and then any shifter unlucky enough to be swept up in the purges was killed as ancient feuds reignited . . ."

Panic and helplessness pushed jumpy and skittering through Bianca's body. Caught up in the storm of vengeance loosed upon the shapechangers, a once tranquil countryside now burned with violence. Women and children cut down as they tried to flee. Men speared as they defended their homes. Whole villages torched. And at the edges of her sight, the twisting, writhing shapes of bird and beast struggling for their lives. Here a bear pierced by a quiver of arrows. There a pack of wolves, silver-gray fur sodden red as they plunged and ducked the swiping strokes of swords and clubs. Eagles riding the currents above, screaming useless defiance.

"There you two are. I began to wonder when you didn't come in for tea."

Sucking in a frightened breath, Bianca sat up. The dream vanished in foggy, eye-blinking confusion. Nothing remained but a headache, scratchy eyes, and a painful throb in her throat as if she'd been weeping.

Sarah stood in the doorway, candle shine gilding her hair. Sconces flickered, and a branch of candles burned upon a table. Another on Sebastian's desk. A cheerful fire danced within the grate against the night beyond the window.

Bianca glanced at the longcase clock. Heat stained her cheeks. She bit her lip. "I'm sorry. I can't believe I drifted off. That is . . . Seb was telling me a story and I . . . I must have been more tired than I knew."

Sarah threw a guarded gaze toward her husband before waving away Bianca's stammering excuses. "There's nothing to apologize for, sweeting. You're all done in. I've half a mind to bundle you upstairs and put you to bed for a proper rest."

Bianca forced a smile, trying not to reveal how deeply her dream affected her, how the weighty pain of loss clung like a shroud. She smoothed her hand over the book. For a flash, the plain of her dreams stood before her. The eerie, silver-lined mist hovering above the armies. The king shrouded within its pale folds as a mother draws a blanket round a child. The thunder becoming the echoing chime of bells.

She curved her arms around the book, loath to place it on the desk and lose her only source to the Imnada. "May I borrow this?"

Sarah lifted one slender brow in surprise. "Heavens. Why on earth would you want to wade through that dull muddle? I knew it. You're still upset over Kinloch's death. It's no wonder you've the pallor of a wheel of soft cheese and you're falling asleep where you stand. Now, come upstairs. I'll send a maid with a warming pan and we'll bring you a tray. Seb, tell her. She'll listen to you—"

He interrupted Sarah's monologue with a simple "Of course you may take it, although there's not much more in there than a few dry facts. Unfortunately, the man who collected the stories is dead. And few are left to care about a race all but forgotten to history."

Bianca glanced at the spine and the gold lettering stamped there—GILLES D'ESPE. "None of the Imnada survived?" Bianca asked, surprised to feel the sting of tears in her eyes.

"No, my dear. Nothing remains of the shifters but some dusty faerie stories and that mark you doodled," he answered.

The mysterious crescent. The mark of the Imnada. How and why had it found its way into Adam's journal and onto the torn piece of paper in his ransacked house? Coincidence? Or—her stomach sank into her slippers with a heavy thud—something far more disturbing?

Wallace placed two tumblers of whiskey on the table. "When Adam first sought me out, I feared he might have been sent by the Ossine's enforcers to finish what they began. I nearly took his head off with a pitchfork."

"That's when Adam explained what happened to us?"

Mac sat at a scrubbed pine-topped kitchen table. Obviously the heart of the house, it was a comfortable, lived-in room. The faded aromas of baking and stews and a woman's perfume hung in the golden dust-moted air.

If Mac closed his eyes, he could imagine himself in the kitchen at Concullum, Mother preparing luncheon to take to the men in the fields, her work interspersed with snatches of song. After her death, the singing had ended, and a weighty silence took its place. Father trapped in his grief, Siobhan too young to understand, and Mac struggling to hold the family together even as he yearned to venture beyond the fog-shrouded valley and the narrow world enclosed within the Paling.

Wallace pulled Mac from his memories as he slid into a seat opposite. "Aye, Adam told me the whole, though it only took a few hours before no explanation was needed. Saw it for myself, now, didn't I?"

"And you weren't . . . shocked or . . . appalled?"

A corner of Wallace's mouth twitched. "Can't say I wasn't shocked. A forced shift is a hard thing to watch when there's naught you can do to help. But I'm not one to hold a blood taint against a man. Not when my own name's been erased from the Ossine's scrolls. To the Imnada, Jory Wallace no longer exists." He leaned back in his chair, running a hand over his stomach. "Though, for a spirit, I'm a bit on the portly side. Marianne's cooking. The woman knows her way around a meal, that one does. Adam used to do all but lick his plate clean. Said he gained a full stone after every visit."

"Adam visited often?"

"Not at first, but by the end I teased him about paying rent. He didn't have to hide what he was when he was here or pretend to be what he wasn't. He could take to the fields and meadows with no greater worry than a poacher or two. Oh, and mayhap Squire Fruddy's dogs, but they're a worthless pack of hounds that wouldn't know a wildcat from a wildflower. Adam could run rings around the sorry curs."

Mac longed for that freedom with all his heart. To shift without fear, stretching every sense until he could feel the swift-moving mountain storms break in his chest and taste the winds whipping across the moors. To breathe the soft-scented air of meadow and woodland and run beneath a cloud-scudded sky until he burst with joy. To fully inhabit his body and draw on his Imnada powers when and how he chose—not at the whim of a Fey-blood's dark magic.

He'd spent his youth wanting to escape the restrictive confines of clan life. Now he'd pay any price to find a way back.

He clutched his mug to keep his hands from shaking. Focused on his reason for being here. Shoved aside pointless bitter regrets.

Wallace rubbed a finger against the tabletop. "I tried to help as I could—even went up to London once or twice, close to the new moon. Adam and I shared clan and holding once. I needed to honor that bond, even broken as it was. Adam didn't like me to see the curse working, but I couldn't leave the poor lad alone."

Mac understood Adam's dread of those nights of Morderoth. Trapped between man and animal, the curse flooded his body like shards of glass through his veins, his brain throbbing with a wracking, crushing pain and sight, naught but a river of blue and silver fire.

One of those visits to Adam must have been what

Bianca had witnessed and misinterpreted. Not two lovers, but a man ministering to a helpless friend.

He'd laugh if the whole horrible situation wasn't so goddamned bloody tragic.

"But Adam broke the curse," Mac said, pulling the conversation toward the point of his visit before he could fall into self-pity. "He found a way to combat the Fey-blood's magic."

"Aye, he did. He said it was his fault the four of you lived under the Other sorcerer's taint. Fell to him to repair the damage."

"It wasn't his fault. There was nothing else to be done. The Fey-blood knew too much. The threat had to be eliminated. Who could foresee what would come of it?"

"Mmm, yes. A useless, worn-out argument, by my way of thinking." Wallace's tone hardened, his hand tightening around his tumbler. "But a thousand years of indoctrination is hard to fight."

"I didn't mean your wife was a threat just because she's out-clan."

"Didn't you?" Wallace rose to poke once more at the kitchen fire, his arms thick around as tree limbs, his hands scarred and callused with work. He looked back over his shoulder. A keen-edged light in his eyes. "Well, since I'm the one happy with wife and children and you're the sorry bastard infected by the Other's twisted magic, I guess I can afford to be forgiving."

Mac winced at the truth of that bald statement of fact. The man pulled no punches. He was tough, but with reason.

"Adam was a good friend," Wallace continued. "I was away in Gloucester when I read about his murder in the papers. Rode straight for London. Don't know what I thought I'd do when I got there, but I knew Adam had recorded his discovery and that he'd have wanted you and yours to have it."

A redheaded man. Brawny. Tall. "It was you who gave the constable a clout on the head?"

"Aye, the idiot fool tried stopping me. Said I wasn't allowed in, but I knew once those blockheads laid hands on Adam's rooms, there'd be no hope at all. Not that it did me a bit of good. The place had already been turned upside down. Everything broken and busted and naught to be found among the rubbish but a few stray pages and a letter or two he'd never finished writing. I'm sorry, Flannery, but Adam's journal was gone, and with it any hope of breaking the curse."

Mac pulled the battered book from his coat pocket, laying it on the table between them. "Was this what you were looking for?"

"Jory Wallace? Damn, there's a name from the past. He's still alive? I figured he'd have turned up his toes long ago." David St. Leger tipped his chair back against the wall as he flipped a coin back and forth across his knuckles like some gaming-hell elbow shaker.

Tobacco smoke hung low in the crowded chophouse's greasy air as Mac poked at his fatty beefsteak. "Not only is Wallace alive, but he lives a mere thirty miles away."

"So, Adam and he knew one another. Not so hard to understand." Back and forth. Back and forth. The coin jumped and spun across David's knuckles. "Adam probably figured that, as a fellow *emnil*, they'd have lots to chat about."

Mac forced himself to ignore the annoying sleight of hand. This was David at his most infuriating. Aloof. Unpredictable. An enormous pain in the arse. "He did more than drink whiskey and swap stories. He helped Adam break the curse. I was right. Adam wrote it all down in his journal."

Catching the coin and pocketing it, David lowered his chair's front legs to the floor. "So we can just whip up another batch of whatever it was and it's over?"

"I don't know. Wallace thinks he can help. I've left the book with him. I plan on returning in a few days."

"Before you mire yourself in alchemical research, you might want to pay a visit to Mrs. Parrino."

"Is she safe? You kept an eye on her, didn't you?"

"Oh, ye of little faith. Of course I did, but that's what's interesting. She spent the day at Deane House."

"What's so interesting about that? Isn't his new wife an actress?"

"*Was* an actress. Yes, the marriage of Sarah Haye to the Earl of Deane is still the London gossip du jour, but it's not so much the man's wife I'm curious about. It's His Lordship."

Mac's fork paused on the way to his mouth, a lump settling in his throat. "What's curious about Lord Deane?"

"He's one of them, Mac. The Earl of Deane is a Feyblood."

Mac leaned upon the sill, staring out onto a smutty red sky, the dull pewter wash of nightfall creeping ever westward, and knew he had mere moments left.

He'd already disrobed, the October breeze cooling

the feral heat of his naked body. Drawing in a gritty, coal-smoky breath, he let it fill his lungs until they burned, then expelled it in a whoosh of frustration, disgust dropping like a weight into his chest. Pressing his forehead against the glass, he closed his eyes, wearier than he'd been in long years. Sighed—or maybe it was a groan.

What the hell was wrong with him? The soft silken touch of Bianca's lips, the heady, spicy notes of her perfume, the way her body fit perfectly against him as she looked on him all worried concern and nascent trust . . . And it had all been a lie.

He should have known better. After all, it wasn't the first time a woman had played him false. Lina had been the same: beautiful and smart. He'd considered himself the luckiest of men to have had the Ossine choose such a compatible mate for him.

The curse had destroyed that as it had everything else in his life.

Lina refused to follow him into exile. She'd laughed at his suggestion as if he'd made a great joke. After that, no matter how often he asked for her or how many letters he wrote, she never responded. Then the Gather elders confirmed his sentence.

His last sight of her had been at the great hall at Deepings just before he was handed to the Ossine for punishment. She stood between her father and mother, her disgusted gaze passing over him without recognition. In her eyes, he'd become a grotesque figure. Tainted. Spoiled.

A monster.

No doubt Bianca would feel the same if she ever discovered the truth.

He finished off his whiskey, hoping the reassuring burn would ease the tension across his shoulders, the tightness in his back, and the stiffness of his cock. It didn't.

He'd been right to mistrust Bianca. Right to believe that she was involved in Adam's death. David's surveillance proved she was in league with Fey-bloods. And Fey-bloods were the enemy. The slaughterers of his people. The monsters who stalked his childhood nightmares. And, in the end, the cause of his accursedness and exile.

With regret and not a little discomfort, he prepared himself to face the oncoming night as twilight became dusk, the sun sliding beneath the horizon.

He shuddered at the first cauterizing blast of heat that signaled the curse's awakening. Even on the night of Silmith, when the moon rode round and fat and shifting came easiest, the curse's possession was nothing like his voluntary transformation from man to animal. He still remained vulnerable while the magic enveloped him. Still knew the ecstasy of release as the chained parts of his being flooded free and he felt himself filled with a sleek, powerful strength. A predator with a predator's mighty grace.

But the curse blighted what should have been joy in realizing his aspect. Fire needled along his blood like venom. Muscles strained as bones warped; organs twisted as limbs stretched. His vision filled with a sheet of blue-white rippling flame. Even now, long after he should have inured himself to the futility of fighting the shift, he continued to try. Willing his body to obey. Struggling to break the immutability of a dead man's final words.

No use. It never was. The curse never yielded.

He spun from the window with a shout of pure rage, dragging his hand across a shelf, uncaring at the shattering of broken china, the splintering of wood, the smashing of porcelain.

Dropping to his knees, he squeezed his eyes closed, tears leaking beneath his lids as the curse consumed him. Above, the curtains billowed in a sudden wind, his shirt sliding off the bed to lie forgotten and unneeded on the floor beside him.

Sides heaving, he opened his eyes, his feline gaze cutting the darkness like a knife. His claws extended as he stretched his body loose of the last shreds of its humanity.

The night rolled out before him into a solitary eternity.

The dream of Bianca Parrino obliterated beneath a bitter, monstrous impossibility.

There were moments when he envied Adam the peace of death.

8

"Molly said you were out here grubbing in the dirt."

Bianca looked up from her mulch spreading to see Mac standing on her terrace, his gaze cold as the gray fall sky. Trowel in hand, she rolled back on her haunches, pushing her hair from her face. Dressed in a grubby coat and battered hat, she wasn't exactly prepared for company, but one look at his clenched jaw and the harsh planes of his face and she knew he'd not come for a comfortable afternoon call. "What brings you back? After all your fine words, I never thought I'd see you again," she said, working to remain civil but cool. Hard to do as her stomach tumbled and unwanted heat danced across her skin.

He stepped off the terrace and onto the lawn. "What can I say? You're becoming a bad habit."

Bianca rose, picked up her bucket of tools, and crossed the grass to meet him. "A habit you'll have to break. I'm leaving for Dublin in a few weeks."

His jaw jumped, face unusually grim, even for him.

"The queen of London theater is heading for an Irish stage?"

"Time away will be time for the gossips to forget. Perhaps I can as well."

"I hadn't taken you for a coward."

"Courage is tiring. Even the brave need a chance to rest between battles." Her gaze fell to his side." Do your ribs still bother you?"

"They'll mend."

She set down her bucket and peeled off her gloves. Why had he come back? He hadn't said. She should be wary of his continuing attentions and downright afraid of her unwelcome reactions to them. Too much about him remained a mystery. Too many questions had been left unanswered.

And yet, he had only to glance at her with that blade-sharp gaze and heat slid along her limbs to pool between her legs, her heart pounded in her chest, and pleasure prickled her skin. Just what she didn't want or need. She gave herself a mental slap, schooling her rebellious features into their usual expression of calm. "Why did you leave, Mac? I told you I didn't worry about what people thought. Those I care about know me better than that. The rest don't matter."

"Then why run away to Dublin? Is it the rumors about Adam?" His eyes hardened like flint. "Or something else?"

Caution slid sharp as a blade along her bones. "Excuse me?"

"Why did those men attack us, Bianca? Were they in the employ of Lord Deane? Is he behind Adam's murder?"

"What do you know about Sebastian?"

"I know you were at his house yesterday." Mac's eyes sparked, the very air around him crackling. "What did he tell you? What lies did he spin to convince you to betray Adam?"

Even as she tried to understand Mac's barrage of accusations, she lifted her chin, meeting him head-on, refusing to drown in those iridescent eyes. "I don't know what you're talking about. Sebastian hasn't told me anything. Or rather, he told me a story and he gave me a book to read because I asked him to. It's nothing to do with Adam."

"It's everything to do with him. It's the reason he died," Mac snarled. "He trusted you and you betrayed him. Am I next on your list?"

Faced with his irrational rage, she retreated to the cold, empty place where anger didn't touch her. Where harsh words and heated threats meant nothing. His questions pounded against her like stones hurled at a wall. She remained unmoved. Unfeeling. No matter how he tried, he couldn't dent her armor. No matter how she hurt, no hint of it touched her face. "Despite the insane ideas rolling around in that hard, hollow head of yours, I did not betray Adam, nor would I have ever betrayed him."

"Bianca, so help me—"

Instinct overcame pride and she flinched, taking a step back. One foot landed in the bucket. In one farcical moment, she lost her balance, floundering wildly, arms flailing, hat flying. Gloves went one way, tools another, and she dropped with a soft, squishy thud backside-first in the mud. "Damn and blast!"

His mouth thinned, his eyes widened, and a snort of laughter escaped him.

"You!" She struggled to her feet, coat spattered with dirt, hair tumbling out of its pins and scarf.

"Lost for words? I'm surprised, after hearing about your reputation for cutting a man to ribbons with your tongue," he sneered.

"I'll show you what I can do with my tongue," she snapped.

"Is that a threat or a promise?"

"Neither. That is . . . that didn't come out right."

But he'd already grabbed her, crushing the breath from her lungs as his body molded against hers, his mouth blazing a trail over her lips, the power of his kiss turning her bones to jelly. Now she was furious, confused, muddy, and completely and frustratingly aroused.

The heavens chose that moment to open, unleashing a deluge, soaking her to the skin. He lifted his head, rainwater sluicing over his cheekbones and saturating his coat.

It was all the time she needed to tear herself from his arms and run like hell.

Had he completely lost his mind? He'd come here to confront her and ended with his tongue down her throat. Not exactly the confrontation he'd envisioned. Yet, all it had taken was a flash of those blue eyes and a tilt of that stubborn chin for his original intentions to swerve dangerously out of control. He chased her down in a small back parlor, sweat splashing hot across his back despite the cold weather, as he fought down the urge to kiss her senseless.

"It's best if you leave, Captain," she said. "Leave and never come back."

"You haven't answered my questions."

"You mean your accusations? You're right. I haven't and I won't. Besides, it's obvious you wouldn't believe me even if I did."

"I don't know what to believe anymore."

"Good-bye, Mac. We won't be seeing one another again." By now her teeth chattered, her body hunched against the cold and the wet. She shouted for Molly as she pulled her coat off, dropping it to the floor.

Questions and indecision gnawed at him. Was David wrong? Had he misunderstood and Bianca had a perfectly reasonable explanation? Why would she ally herself with a Fey-blood? What would she gain? Was she lying now? Was Mac the biggest fool ever born?

Round and round he went, with no answers in sight, only anger at himself for giving in to the dazzle long enough to be hoaxed. For believing in her. Perhaps even for dreaming a little. It had been too long since he'd felt this strange swimming of his senses. Too long since he'd held a woman he hadn't paid for. Too long since he'd had someone in his life who mattered. Bianca shouldn't matter. But she did. More than he'd ever meant her to.

She started to leave, but he grabbed her wrist before she could escape. "Wait a moment."

"For what?" She flicked a glance at his hand gripping her arm, anger and disappointment in her gaze. "Adam was my friend, Mac. That's a bond I don't take lightly."

"Nor do I."

Her level stare seemed to drill straight through him. "I didn't kill him. Believe me or don't. It makes no difference anymore. I'll be gone in a few days and we never have to meet again."

A painful knot formed low in his gut at the idea, which he fought to explain away. He still had questions about the curse. Bianca was his only connection to Lord Deane. He needed her—and not like that, though with her wet gown clinging to her curvaceous body, certain parts of him were definitely experiencing more need than others. "What if I told you I believed you? Would you still go to Dublin?"

"Of course. There's nothing for me in London until Adam's murderer is found or the gossip dies."

"*I'm* here."

She shot him a dubious look. "That's supposed to convince me?"

"Let's say I had hopes." He released her, shrugging out of his coat to drape it over her shoulders before her lips turned blue. It was completely waterlogged, but better than nothing. "Where's that maid of yours? You're sopping wet."

She reached up to wipe the hair from his face. "You're just as wet and drippy as I am."

He sucked in a quick breath at her touch. Covered her hand with his own, noting the dirt beneath her half-moon nails. The smudge up one wrist. He wanted to lay his lips upon the pulse fluttering there. Hell, he wanted to lay his lips on every part of her sweet body.

She glanced at their linked fingers. "Your hand is so warm."

"'Warm hands, cold heart.' Isn't that the saying?"

"I've never heard that before."

If she thought his hands were warm, she'd be shocked by how hot the rest of his body grew with every shivering, trembling breath she took. Every brush of those long black lashes against her cheeks. Desire burned like a lit fuse along every nerve ending until his arousal grew embarrassingly evident, inner warnings shoved aside by flat-out lust.

"How about 'But kiss, one kiss! Rubies unparagon'd, How dearly they do't,'" he quoted.

"Cymbeline. The soldier knows his Shakespeare."

"Aye. I can read and write and everything."

Her lips curved, soft and full and pink as rosebuds. How would they taste? What would they feel like wrapped around . . .

Shit, he was a bloody goner.

Bracing for a stinging blow, he drew her against him, leaning in for a kiss, the taste of rain and earth and wind in the sweet velvet lushness of her mouth. But no virago's temper met his embrace. Instead she breathed soft gasps as she opened to him, his tongue sweeping in to taste her wet, sweet heat. Her scent rose from her damp skin to wrap round him with exotic hints of orange and spice. He cupped her head in his hand, delving deeply, the shivers running through his body having nothing to do with the weather but with a hunger growing every second that he plundered her mouth with kisses.

His hand skimmed her side, the rounded slope of her hip, the long plane of her torso to the swell of one perfect breast. He thumbed her pebble-hard nipple, eliciting a whimper from deep in her throat, her body swaying against him, one arm coming round his neck to tangle in his hair.

"The sweet lovers. How touching. I wonder if you'd think the same if you knew what he was, Madame Parrino," came a thickly accented voice from just behind them.

Mac and Bianca turned as one to face the startling newcomer: a tall man in a long black greatcoat. Over his shoulder, he carried a canvas bag.

"I hope you don't mind me inviting myself in. I sent your maidservant on an errand. A nice long one. So much easier than trying to dispose of a body."

Bianca stiffened in Mac's arms. "Who are you?"

The man's gaze flicked toward Mac, intent written in the brilliant, gold-flecked eyes as he swung the bag to his side and reached into it. "Your savior against a treacherous, blackhearted monster."

Mac went rigid, his panther strength boiling up from that secret well where it slept until called upon—or until the curse pulled it screaming forth. His muscles wound taut as a low snarl curled up into the back of his throat. "Fey-blood."

The man pulled his hand from the bag. "A gift from my mistress, Captain!" he shouted as he tossed a net fine as spiderwebs toward Mac, the binding silken mesh settling heavy and entangling over his shoulders.

Silver.

All Mac's doubts vanished as a low drone vibrated from the base of his skull down his spine and along his ribs. The Fey-bloods knew of the Imnada's existence. And, more frightening, knew how to destroy them.

"Leave him alone!" Bianca grabbed the man's thick arm and tried to pull him away. The stranger looked down at her, his golden eyes narrowed to violent slits, his mouth curling in a leering, fiendish smile. "Stupid *putain*, you may have your uses yet."

She stumbled as he shoved her off, her hem tangling under his boot heels. Losing her balance, she flailed as she fell, striking the edge of a chair before she sprawled lifeless on the floor.

"Bianca!" Mind aflame, Mac struggled to drag the strength-sapping weight of the silver net from his shoulders.

"Crull! Hoyse!" the man shouted. "*Vite!*"

Shadows fell over Mac. Someone knocked him to the floor. Hands grabbed him by the elbows, shoving him onto his stomach, dragging his arms painfully behind him. A boot struck him in the ribs. Another slammed against his head. He fought back, but only managed to tangle the net more firmly around him, snared by the buttons on his jacket.

"It is useless to struggle," the Fey-blood warned, his black coat billowing like raven's wings as he pulled a wicked knife from a sheath at his waist.

Useless or not, Mac wasn't about to surrender without a fight. Wrenching loose and rolling up onto his knees, he lunged for the man, his fist slamming into the Fey-blood's chest.

"*Fils de pute!*" he cursed, though he did not run.

Why should he? If he knew the lethal power of silver on the Imnada, he knew enough to be patient and let the net weaken Mac until there was no fight left in him. Already his muscles cramped with pain, his breathing labored as the element acted on his body like a poison.

Another attack met another retreat before the Fey-blood's cohorts stepped in. A fist to the jaw knocked Mac back on his knees. A blow to the gut left him doubled over and retching. He struggled, but the blows came too swiftly. There was no time to react. No time to strike back. The poison sucked him into a downward spiral in which every breath hurt and his heart crashed against his sore ribs.

He shot another glance toward Bianca, lying in a crumpled heap of silks and petticoats, her hair spilling free of its pins to lie in a ripple of gold around her head. A thin trickle of blood dripped onto her pale cheek from a cut on her scalp. He tried dragging himself toward her, hoping to discover whether she yet lived, but the Fey-blood stood in his way, towering over him, his face twisted with disgust and hate.

"The stories talk of the Imnada's incredible strength and cunning in battle, but they were wrong. You are weak. Weak and powerless."

Mac barely felt the vicious kick to his ribs as he retched, hands curled into fists against his chest, agony radiating through his body as if he were being cleaved in two. His lungs worked like a bellows, yet he couldn't breathe. Spots danced in front of his eyes, his vision narrowing to a pinprick.

"You'd love to kill me, wouldn't you, shifter? So close and yet so far, eh?"

Each taunt was accompanied by a flick of the Fey-blood's blade. Each wicked jeer matching a wicked punch to the ribs or a kick to his side from heavy boots. Mac tried curling away from the worst of it, but nowhere was he safe against the violent onslaught.

"We will kill you, your comrades, and then the rest of your filthy unclean race. It will be just as before, when the rivers ran with shifter blood and our swords feasted on your flesh."

"Are Fey-bloods always this melodramatic?" Mac shot back, spitting blood, the words clawing their way out of a painful throat.

His bravado earned him a clout to the side of the head that left his ears ringing.

"If she didn't want to kill you herself, I'd enjoy gutting you like the dirty hell-spawn you are."

She? For a moment, as Mac watched, something—or someone—else seemed to enter the man's lethal gaze. A woman. Mac sensed her presence. A musky-sweet scent in the air. A shadow's flicker caught out of the corner of his eye. If he focused, he could feel her tangled thoughts fuzzing his already fuzzy brain.

So the man's purpose was to capture Mac, not kill him outright. This left a chance. Slim, but he'd take it. It might be the only one left to him. Sucking in a last shallow breath, he twisted away from his captors' grasp, lunging for the man's knife. Forcing it from his grip. Celebrated his success for a mere heartbeat's time before the Fey-blood's battle magic struck. Enough to slow him. To knock him from his stride.

He ducked as another scorching ripple seared the air above him, striking the wall at his back. He never saw the toppling bookcase until it fell, slamming him to the ground. A boot swung toward his head. He threw up a hand as it connected. Lights pinwheeled across his vision.

He never saw the second blow.

Never felt the third.

Images came to Renata along ribbons of smoke, sparks dodging and darting within the spiraling columns erupting from an endless black sea. Alonzo was her eyes and ears. Through him, she observed, she planned. Able to travel where a woman of fortune and standing could never remain unnoticed or unmolested. Away from duty's confinement. Freed of her husband's clinging control.

Even as a tiny part of her mind remained aware of her surroundings—the rumpled bedcovers, the soft gray light pouring through the lace at her windows—she became one with the smoke, traveling out across the depthless void to crouch behind Alonzo's eyes as she clutched the locket containing a curl of his dark hair.

The smoke rolled thick and black-red, revealing the dimly lit interior of a house. A man, bent and stumbling, a hand pressed against his stomach. He possessed a face of chiseled lines and angles, a clean jaw, a thin nose, lips that if not pressed grimly together would curve deliciously upon a woman's flesh, and eyes of an unnatural yellow-green, irises long and cat-thin.

Imnada. Her certainty washed over her like a warning from her father's ghost. *Imnada,* his voice whispered up from the void. Older than the Fey. A demon race. A dead race. This one would be dead soon. She, with Alonzo's help, would make it so.

The smoky billows rose high before dispersing out across a roof of dim stars, dragging her spirit back to her bedchamber, her body torpid and slack, the sounds of her house unnaturally loud against the leaden silence of the smoky, spark-filled blackness.

She gripped the locket tighter, willing herself back into Alonzo's mind. His elation sped her own pulse as he bent over the man, caught like a herring in a fisherman's net, his breathing ragged, his face a sickly green as the silver sucked him dry. From the corner of her sight, Renata caught a glimpse of tangled golden hair and the ivory features of Bianca Parrino lying still upon a carpeted floor.

"Madame, are you awake?" her maid queried from beyond the door. "The gong has sounded to dress."

Letting go of the locket, Renata retreated into her body. She fought back the pressing desire to storm free of her bedchamber, call for a carriage, and fly to the actress's home. A fool's desire. Froissart expected her to be dressed and downstairs within the hour, ready to attend one more boring political dinner. Weakened from such a focused use of her powers, she had no strength left, even for the simple manipulation of her husband's feeble mind. She must appear. There was no escape.

Fury and desperation scalded her throat, and she gripped the bedclothes as if she would shred them in a shrieking rage. For the first time since she was a little girl, she allowed bitter tears to fall, her pain sharp as the blade Alonzo had used upon the Imnada.

Then, emotions mastered once more, she rose from bed, retreating to the privacy of her dressing room to do what she'd learned to do best and yet hated with all her heart: wait.

9

The sound of the door opening skittered along Bianca's shredded nerves. The creak of hinges threw her back four years to her darkest days. She went limp, pretending to be unconscious. A ruse that had always worked with Lawrence.

Slow, heavy footsteps sounded on the stairs, accompanied by the *thud-thud-thud* of something being dragged.

Unfortunately, Bianca knew exactly what that something was.

She'd tried turning off her mind to the sounds of violence coming from the floor above her. The scrape and crash of bodies. The painful grunts and curses. And finally the screams cut off almost as soon as they began, leaving an even more ominous silence in their place. She'd whispered to herself lines from plays, great long soliloquies, even stage directions. Anything to keep her mind from imagining, her thoughts from flying into a million broken pieces.

Now, as she feigned sleep, her chair rocked back

and forth, the man dumping and then securing his load in a chair back to back with hers. As her shoulders were yanked and the ropes at her wrists tightened, she bit her lip to stifle any whisper of a breath that might give her away.

A few minutes of this, a final tug on her bonds, and the footsteps retreated back up the stairs, followed by the slamming of the door.

Alone once more, she opened her eyes, stretching to look over her shoulder. Mac hung lifeless against his bonds, his face shielded by his blood and sweat-matted hair.

"Mac?" she whispered. "Can you hear me?"

The slightest movement of his fingers against hers. A shallow breath that became a strangled moan.

"It's going to be all right," she lied, her gaze drawn unwillingly to the narrow window set beneath the raftered ceiling. She wouldn't look at it. Wouldn't think about it. That would only bring on the panic, and she already hung by the thinnest of threads. "Say something so I know you can hear me."

She felt his body pulling against the ropes that lashed her wrists. His breath came quick and painful. And when he spoke, his voice was threaded with pain and hoarse from shouting. "The clans are safe, Father. I told him nothing."

"Let us out! Someone— anyone—help us! Please!"

Mac struggled up from a thick, soupy blackness to Bianca's frightened voice bouncing against his egg-fragile skull. Every inch of him hurt, but his left shoulder throbbed with an agony unlike he'd ever experienced, not even at the worst of the curse's onset. He vomited at the pain eating its way up through his flesh, stomach muscles convulsing, throat raw.

"Can anyone hear me?" Bianca called again. "Dear God, let us out!"

"Stop," he muttered. "Please stop yelling."

"Mac? You're awake. You're alive."

"Debatable." He cracked open his swollen eyes to a dank, mildew-smeared cellar. A few broken bits of furniture stood in a corner beside a set of rickety steps. At the opposite end, an enormous black fireplace gaped like a mouth, a few dusty, cobwebbed tools scattered on the cold hearth bricks. So the Feyblood had moved them from Bianca's house to a more secure location. Somewhere close to the river, from the smells blowing through the crumbling brickwork, the wind chilling his sweat-drenched body.

The silver net that had trapped him had been replaced. Now, wrapped round and round his neck, hung thin silver chains as if he'd rifled twenty women's jewelry cases. The freezing burn of the poisonous metal against his bare skin sent needles of fire chewing through his spasming muscles. Blood slicked his chest and arms, slid cold down his legs. Straining against the restraints holding him into a chair, he nearly passed out as his shoulder exploded, the pain numbing his arm, throwing splashes of light across his vision. He clawed back a scream at the cost of another round of retching that left him heaving for breath and weak as a kitten.

"I've tried. They don't budge," Bianca said, her voice trembling.

He looked up at the window. Was the light dimming? "How long have I been unconscious?"

"A few hours. I don't know." She struggled against the ropes. "There's no air in here, Mac. I can't breathe. We're trapped." With every sentence, her voice rose an octave. "Let us out!" she screamed before dropping to a half-sobbing whimper. "Please, I'll do as you ask, Lawrence. I swear."

There was obviously more to Bianca's terror than the current disaster, bad as it was, but he'd leave those questions for later—if there was a later.

"Deep breaths," Mac said, using the same easy tone he'd mastered while breaking colts for his father and later calming raw soldiers in the minutes before battle. "In through your nose and out through your mouth. Steady, even breaths."

He felt the tension in her body lessen slightly as she did as he instructed, but each moment he used to pull her back from collapse brought him one step closer. There was no telling how long he had until the Fey-blood returned. Until the sun set. Until the silver killed him.

"I'm sorry, Mac. I . . . I hate small spaces and locked rooms. When Lawrence . . ." She swallowed back whatever she'd been about to say. "Molly always tells me I'll catch a cold sleeping with the window open. My head knows it's foolish, but I can't help how I feel."

"I suppose we'll have to find a way out of here, then." Though how he proposed to do that, he had no idea. Every moment the silver leached further into his system. Every second the poison moved like acid through his veins.

Outside, the rain had turned to sleet. The tapping and rattling against the window beat against his pounding head, making it almost impossible to focus his scattered mind or harbor his waning strength.

"He wants Adam's journal, doesn't he?" Bianca asked, the brittle edge gone from her voice, though he sensed the tenuous control behind her quiet words. "That's what this is about."

His mind rolled back to the incessant pounding of the Fey-blood's questions, the torturously slow devastation he wrought with fists and boots and knife. Over and over until Mac's mind shut down, his body curled against the attacks. He'd given nothing away, but he'd emerged with answers. Answers that both reassured and terrified. "No, Bianca. It's me he wants."

"But—"

The secret of the Imnada had been discovered—that much had been demonstrated with dreadful certainty. But how far had it spread? How great was the danger? And could the threat be stopped?

"How much does Lord Deane know about the Imnada?" he asked.

"Sebastian has nothing to do with this. He wouldn't—"

"Murder an innocent man in cold blood? Why are you defending him? He's sold you to the dogs as well."

"I'm not defending him. I don't know anything about Fey-bloods or Other or any of the things you keep asking me. Sebastian caught me doodling the symbol I found in Adam's journal and asked me about it. Then he showed me the book and told me a story about a shifter warlord who betrayed King Arthur to his death. That's all."

"Did Deane and Adam ever meet?"

"No. He wanted to after he learned Adam had helped me pick out his birthday gift, but by then it was . . . by then Adam had—"

"Adam picked out a book for Lord Deane? What was it?"

There was a long pause when he thought Bianca might not answer. He sensed her desperation rising once more to the surface. It was obvious in the tension of the ropes, the shallowness of her breathing. "Think, Bianca. What book?"

"It was by Thistlewood or Thistlethwaite. I can't remember. Adam swore it would suit someone like Deane perfectly."

Someone like Deane. Adam must have recognized that the earl was Fey-blood. And in sending him the sorcerer Thistlewood's book he had tipped the earl off. Had Adam been that witless? Or had he had another motive for sending a message? One Mac couldn't begin to fathom.

He shot another glance at the window. Yes, the light definitely grew dimmer.

Jaw clamped against the blasts of pain ripping through his shattered shoulder, he worked at the ropes holding his wrists. If he could free a finger— hell, a fingertip—he might be able to loosen the knots enough to work his way out. But every excruciating movement pushed more of the silver's poison into his bloodstream. Already, his eyesight grew fuzzy. Darkness crept in around the edges as his muscles twitched with a tingly numbness. "Bianca, I can't. It's up to you. Try working loose."

"I'll hurt you."

"Do it anyway."

Immediately, the ropes tightened, cutting into his skin, sawing back and forth until he gritted his teeth against the burn, blood sliding hot down his palms.

Bianca's every breath came punctuated by a panicked sob, but she never paused, never tired as the minutes dragged on for what seemed an eternity. As the sun dipped ever lower in the sky.

Taking his own advice, Mac tried breathing deeply to stave off his own terror. By now, the humming burn along his bones was not completely due to the silver but to the coming sunset. A premonition of onrushing disaster jangled at the base of his brain. If Bianca was hanging by a thread now, what would seeing him shift do to her sanity? If she was like the rest of humanity, it would be a mixture of horror, loathing, and disgust. He would lose her forever. "Hurry."

She huffed as the ropes dug into his blood-slicked flesh. "I've . . . almost . . . almost got it."

A numbing, vicious tug on his hands sent a shooting, tearing pain up his arms and into his shoulder, but Bianca was free.

Scrambling out of her ropes, she knelt in front of him, her gaze locked on the wreckage that his body had become. "Dear God, Mac, what did he do to you?"

"Can you loosen the knots?"

She tugged at the cords binding his chest, struggled with those at his ankles. "They won't come. They're too tight."

"The silver, Bianca. Remove the necklaces," he gasped, a fiery burn licking up through his body.

By now his vision had become a blue sheet of flame, signaling the onset of the curse.

She leaned forward, lifting the anchoring weight of the chains from his neck, her scent and the warmth of her body like a drop of heaven amid the needling blast of agony. Freed of the silver, he lifted his head.

A choice lay before him: Did Bianca speak the truth? Was she ignorant of the Imnada and Lord Deane's perfidy? Or would he be setting free the woman who had betrayed Adam to his death?

Did he trust her or didn't he?

She fought with the ropes at his wrists, her fingers slipping on knots damp and slick with his blood. "Damn it, I can't get . . . just a little bit—"

His decision made, he nudged her away. "Go, Bianca. It's me they want."

She stepped back, the inches between them yawning wide as a canyon. "I can't abandon you."

"Go to the village of Bear Green. Find Jory Wallace. Tell him Mac sent you. Tell him to warn St. Leger and de Coursy. He'll understand." Nausea rolled his gut, a wash of cold sweat drenching his body.

"Mac, I—"

"By the Mother of All," he snarled. "Get the hell out!"

She touched his shoulder, the gentlest contact enough to make him moan, jaw locked, teeth clenched. "I'll do it, but against my will."

"Just go."

He heard the scrape of her chair being pulled across the stone floor. The screech of rusty hinges as she forced open the narrow window, followed by a blast of cold, damp wind against his face, the soft hush of snowfall. Bianca's grunts and rustles as she snaked her way out into the yard beyond.

"I'll find Jory Wallace. You can trust me."

He smiled through cracked lips. "I'm beginning to think I can."

She gave a hard bark of laughter. Then silence but

for the slosh and gurgle of drains, a steady drip from a leak in the roof, and a banging in his skull like musket fire. Or was that the jump and squeeze of his heart as the Fey-blood's curse pushed its way through him like an unstoppable rising tide?

Sagging against the ropes, he dropped his head onto his chest. Sensed the sun's final drop below the horizon like a grenade exploding in his chest, his mind ripped open in one horrific blast of dark Fey magic like a dagger to the brain.

He squeezed his eyes shut, tensed against his body's internal incineration, and waited. One . . . two . . . three . . . four . . .

Behind the black-bellied clouds, the earth turned on its axis. Day became night.

Man gave way to panther once more.

Outside, the temperature dropped with the onset of dusk. Snow swirled and billowed in a stiff wind, stinging Bianca's face, stealing her breath. Already the ground lay beneath a blanket of dirty white, and the normal street sounds bounced and echoed, oddly muffled by this blast of early winter weather.

She stumbled as a voice roared in her head. A shout of pain and rage and fear, but nothing like the terror driving her onward into the storm.

Head down, she scurried across the street, repeating Mac's directions like a mantra. Jory Wallace . . . Bear Green . . . Jory Wallace . . . Bear Green . . . It would take hours to travel to Surrey and back, and even if she managed to find her way there, how on earth would she convince a complete stranger to help her?

Second guesses and worst possible outcomes battered her as she moved through the narrow streets and filthy lanes, deaf to the shouts and crude laughter coming from dingy wineshops and greasy gaming hells. Brutal images filled her head, making her pulse rush and her mouth go dry.

She couldn't do it. Terrified as she was, she couldn't leave Mac alone. She had to rescue him somehow.

Spinning on her heel, she retraced her steps. Down a street marked by a few flickering lamps set in windows. A quick cut through an empty coal yard and across a muddy lane until the house loomed up before her once again, its dark windows as empty as staring eyes, its front steps covered in drifting snow. No prints marred the narrow passage to the yard behind. The Frenchman had yet to return. There was still time.

She knelt at the cellar window. "Mac," she hissed.

No answer.

She chewed her knuckles, peering into the darkness, swallowing back a renewal of her earlier panic. "Mac, it's Bianca."

Was that a movement below her? A sliding of black on black? Was she walking into a trap?

Only one way to find out.

Sliding her legs through the window's hip-crushing gap, she scraped and squeezed through, dangling for a moment by her hands, before dropping lightly to the floor and peering around her as her eyes adjusted to the dark. "Where are you?" she whispered.

Feeling her way across the room, she bumped against an empty chair. Squatted to find the abandoned ropes and discarded necklaces. By now she could make out the steps up to the ground floor, the cold hearth, the boxes in the corner.

"Mac? For the love of God, are you here?"

Movement from beneath the stairwell flickered at the edge of her vision.

Why the hell didn't you do what I asked?

She froze at the familiar voice. Deep. Luscious. A bit of that honey-smooth brogue.

But it didn't come from the corner of the room. Instead it rolled around inside her head, like a whisper or a thought, although it was nothing like either of them.

"Who's there? What have you done with Mac?" she gasped, smothering a tiny cry as one shadow disconnected itself from the surrounding gloom and an enormous paw stretched tentatively forward. She snatched up the chair, holding it out like a shield, fear splashing icy across her back, breath snatched from her lungs. "What are you?"

I think you know.

It couldn't be. Sebastian's tales of shapechangers and King Arthur and Fey and magic had been just that—tales. This was real life. This was reality. "The book . . . you can change into . . . but that can't be . . . it's impossible . . ."

Yet, here I stand talking to you.

His words from the very first afternoon they met. Her wildest suspicions blossomed into certainty: it was Mac.

Everything jumbled and spun in her head. She backed away, the chair's rough wood biting into her palms, the cellar wall cold against her spine. Concrete sensations keeping her brain from falling to the floor in a blubbering heap. "I don't know how or what you are, but—"

You're safe, Bianca. Put the chair down. I'll not harm you.

She dragged in a shaky breath. "Let me see you first."

Edging into a dim patch of light, a paw became the coiled strength of one muscled forearm that in turn became a pair of broad shoulders. All covered in black, rippling midnight fur. Last, his head emerged into view. Powerful and powerfully built, fangs as long as her index fingers extending white and savage, and always those familiar eyes shining pale yellow-green, pupils round and large and fixed on her with—she could swear—part chagrin, part arrogance.

Finally he stretched into full view on the stone floor. An enormous panther, long and lean and dangerous, his ribs lifting and falling in short, panting breaths, the twitching of his tail matching the beating of her heart.

Every inch of her body tremored with shock and fear, her knees barely holding her up. "Don't faint, Bianca," she muttered to herself. "You're dreaming. This isn't real. This isn't real. This isn't real."

She squeezed her eyes shut. Opened them again. Still there.

Pinched herself. Twice.

No luck. He was still there. All six and a half feet of lethal impossibility.

Why the hell did you come back?

His anger was like a slap on the face. She leaned upon the chair to steady herself, forcing herself to meet his feral gaze. "You didn't want me to see you like this, did you? That's why you sent me away."

I sent you away because I didn't want you hurt.

Strange as it seemed, once she grew used to the rumbling, growling quality of his voice blossoming up from inside her, she lost her fear. Less easy to overcome was the idea that the voice emanated from the animal lying supine at her feet.

"As soon as Adam left his journal with me, I became involved. You can't just think I'll turn my back on you."

That's exactly what I want you to do. Leave the way you came, and this time don't come back. Don't even look back.

"No." Convinced now that she'd fallen into some crazy netherworld, she swung past him to climb the stairs, each creaking step sending her heart into her throat as she strained to hear any sound that signaled the Frenchman's return. "I don't know what's going on. I don't know what you are. I don't even know if I'm going completely stark, staring mad. But I do know that we leave here together or not at all."

You barely fit through the window. There's no way I'll squeeze through. And the cellar door is too sturdy to break. I've tried.

With a shaking hand and a few dozen prayers, she turned the knob, throwing a relieved smile over her shoulder. "It's unlocked."

He must have trusted to the ropes to keep us secure.

"Can you walk? Or do you need my help?" Not that Bianca had the least idea how she'd shepherd a beast like this through the streets of London without being seen.

He limped behind her, his left front leg curled against his stomach, eyes glazed with sickness and pain. *I'll make it.*

Doubtful, but they had no choice. They couldn't remain here.

Hardly more hospitable than the cellar, the house's ground floor consisted of two empty rooms, front and back. So far, so good. The place seemed abandoned, but an oil lamp flickered low on a hearth beside a half-empty coal scuttle, various tools leaning beside the chimney where a smoldering fire burned. Their captor may have stepped out, but he intended to return soon.

"Leaving, shifter?" A figure loomed up in the doorway, his black coat hanging damp over his shoulders, the light from the lamp illuminating the snow speckling his dark hair, the leer on his face, and the ugly pistol he pointed at the panther's head.

Bianca threw herself back against the tiled hearth. Had the man seen her or had the heavy chimneypiece shielded her from his view?

Her fingers touched, then closed around the fireplace tongs resting beside her.

"You're stronger than the lieutenant," the Frenchman said with smug approval, "but that will only make your death sweeter."

A low, menacing growl met the man's taunt. Bianca tightened her grip on the tongs, fighting the urge to huddle on the floor with her hands over her head until the danger passed.

The man stepped farther into the room. "The chevalier should have killed you all when he had the chance. *She* will not make the same mistake."

The panther that was Mac crouched, ears pressed flat against its skull, tail lashing back and forth.

For one tense moment, no one moved. No one

breathed. And the only sound roaring in Bianca's ears was the crashing of her heart.

Then all exploded into chaos.

The great cat lunged, claws reaching for the man's throat. A flash of silver met the dusty air. A gun roared, belching smoke and sparks. The Frenchman flitted across her sight, his coat billowing behind him.

Now or never.

Tongs raised. Teeth clamped. Eyes focused on the spot where his neck met his skull. On the count of—

One.

Two.

Three!

Bianca stepped forward. Swung. Connected.

The Frenchman dropped to his knees, twisted, fell. And lay sickeningly still.

Dizziness tipped the room on its side, sickness clenching her innards with all-too-familiar horror. She dropped the weapon to the floor with a clang, doubled over, clutching at her stomach, and was violently, disgustingly ill.

She'd killed a man.

Again.

10

Bianca woke with a start, half expecting, half hoping to be in her bedchamber with Molly's off-key singing wafting from belowstairs. Instead, the dirty, abandoned storeroom where they'd hidden for the night proved to be as uncomfortably real as the naked man curled feverishly in the far corner. Dark hair clinging, sticky with sweat, to his forehead and his left arm cradled protectively against his chest, he murmured in a restless sleep. His words she didn't understand, but the tight-throated moans and white-lipped grimaces were more than comprehensible.

No longer hidden beneath a panther's camouflaging coat, a million shallow slashes marred Mac's torso, each one an ugly black ribbon against the background collage of purple and green bruising. His face had fared little better. A swollen eye, lips split and bloodied, a deep cut above his eyebrow. Yet nothing prepared her for the stretched and shining flesh scarring much of his upper back. A hideous burn, by the looks of it, long since healed over.

Not a crime to be laid at the Frenchman's feet. Someone else had tried very hard to kill Mac Flannery once upon a time. Had they ended as this last one? Struck down? Dead? Limbs a twisted rag-doll mess?

Bianca trembled as violent memories beat at the walls she'd put up all those years ago. She shoved the images aside as she'd done so many times before, instead concentrating on Mac: a human who could change into a panther. Or was it a panther who could become human? No wonder Mac was like no man she'd ever met.

He wasn't a man at all.

She locked that away with the rest of the things she wasn't going to think about. There would be enough time when they were safely away from here to unravel the enormous, colossal, unsolvable impossibility of Mac's existence. They were alive. Now they needed to remain that way. And here she'd been worried about a few nasty gossips and a sacking. She'd give her eyeteeth if that were the worst of her problems.

A cursory inspection of their refuge last night had uncovered little beyond a few empty boxes, a lot of occupied mouse nests, and a dusty leather haversack stuffed with clothing and an enormous wool greatcoat. This she now draped over Mac's naked body, then put a hand to his burning forehead.

He shuddered, coming alive like a drawn bow, every muscle coiled to attack before his unfocused gaze cleared in recognition. "Bianca?"

"I worried you'd not remember."

"Slim chance of that." He grimaced, pushing his matted hair out of his eyes. "The sun's up. You didn't see me . . . I mean, when I . . ."

She shook her head. "When I woke, you were as you are now."

This seemed to comfort him. He settled back against the wall, the coat sliding into his lap. Their eyes met, heat stealing over her cheeks even as the rest of her shivered in the early-morning cold. "You needed to stay warm. You're burning with fever," she explained.

He closed his eyes as if just speaking took more energy than he possessed. "Silver. It sickens us. Makes us easy to trap. Easy to kill."

That explained the net and the hundreds of necklaces looped around his neck.

"Are you all right?" he asked.

She touched the tender lump on her scalp, the hair around it stiff with dried blood. "I'll live, though what I wouldn't give for a hot bath and a headache powder," she said, trying for levity. It was that or fall to her knees gibbering mindlessly.

Mac must have sensed the churning of her thoughts and the wariness beneath her outward calm. "I never meant for you to find out, Bianca." He gave a gallows laugh. "Mother of All, that's the very last thing I wanted. A millennium of secrecy, and I've bungled it in less than a week.

"Here." He took the greatcoat and wrapped her back within its heavy folds. "Feverish or not, you need this more than I do."

"You'll freeze."

"Imnada don't feel the cold as humans do." He frowned in thought as he studied the room.

"Neither, apparently, do they feel embarrassment as we do," she muttered, inhaling the coat's combination of soap and sweat, brandy and smoke, as she studied Mac from beneath half-lidded eyes. No fat softened the whipcord strength in his exquisite chiseled frame. And even battered and bruised, he bore a warrior's precise movements and remorseless intensity. Enough to make her heart lurch painfully in her chest and heat to tingle beneath her skin. Enough to make her wonder what might have happened had the Frenchman not burst in on them.

Would that kiss have grown into something more? Would she have surrendered to the mind-erasing, body-scalding desire that had turned her inside out and upside down? Or would she have come to her benumbed senses and tossed him aside with her usual tongue-lashing?

She cast one more surreptitious glance at his long legs, hard-packed muscles, and square-jawed, steely-eyed face.

Who was she trying to fool? It wasn't a question of would she have surrendered, but how quickly.

He prowled the room, finally pausing by the far wall. Then, closing his eyes, he gritted his teeth and slammed his bad shoulder hard against the bricks. Again. And again.

"Mac!"

He dropped to his knees, face blanched beneath the bruising, a strangled moan escaping from between his lips. "Fucking bloody hell, that hurt."

"Are you insane?"

Sweat dripped off him, eyes cloudy with pain. "Had to . . . dislocated . . . better now . . ." He moved his fingers gingerly. "Feelings back." Grabbing the haversack, he rummaged through it, retrieving a linen shirt, a pair of breeches. "I need to find David. Warn him the Fey-bloods know. Time is running out."

"None of this makes sense. How could you exist and the world never know?"

"Mortals would"—he slowly eased his way into the shirt, hissing in pain at every movement of his shoulder— "would be amazed what shares this earth with them."

"Like these Fey-blood you keep talking about?"

He struggled to his feet, resting his back against the wall as he slid on his breeches with one hand. "The Other. Aye. They're the most common and, to the Imnada, the most dangerous."

"Because of King Arthur and the Imnada warlord's treachery?" She couldn't believe she was saying this.

"Is that what Deane told you? Treachery is a slippery customer, and there are always two sides to a tale, *mi am'ryath*." He glanced over at her, his gaze sorrow-filled. "I expected you to be long gone when I woke."

She offered him a tremulous half smile. "Where would I go? Home? To Deane House? They'd demand answers I couldn't possibly give."

He pushed off the wall to stand upright for the first time. Hovered for a moment before gravity took over, and he began to sway.

She grabbed him before he fell, her arms wrapping round his torso, her head coming just beneath his chin. Even ill as he was, he had the solidity of an oak, his furnace heat kindling fires everywhere they touched, his manhood pressed close between her thighs. "You can barely stand. Stay here where it's safe. I'll go find Jory Wallace."

Sliding his right arm around her waist, he drew her closer against him, the slightest hint of a dimple showing at the corner of his mouth. "Do you intend to dose me with enough laudanum to fell an ox? Again?" His smile glimmered like the weakest of suns, stabbing at her heart with a dull, unacceptable ache.

She stepped out of his reach, the October cold and definitely not Mac's embrace raising goose pimples up and down her body. "How did you know about the haversack?" she blurted. A stupid question, but it bought her time and space in which to calm her jagged nerves and the crackling heat engulfing her.

He accepted her maneuver with a tired shrug. "I've five such caches throughout the city, just in case."

"In case of what?"

He lifted his brows in a look of incredulity. "You have to ask?" He raised his right arm, palm up, as if in supplication. "My kind has lived beside you since the dawn of time. I'm Imnada, Bianca. Not a monster. Not a creature." He reached for her. "I'm a man."

She stared at their linked hands, his fingers blunt and capable and warm with promise. Lifted her eyes to his face, hysterical laughter bottled in her throat like cut glass.

"And an ally," he said, a glint of rueful humor in his haunted gaze. "Since events are now officially and irrefutably sticky."

After a garbled story of murderous footpads running amok near Cumberland Place, Mac and Bianca had been shown by David's housekeeper into a downstairs salon to await the master of the house. Mac had barely counted the number of wineglasses on the sideboard when David came bounding in, sporting his usual rakish seediness. Over the years, Mac had witnessed again and again St. Leger's personal blend of smooth-talking charm and scoundrel's magnetism that transformed perfectly normal women into giddy trollops.

He cast a surreptitious glance at Bianca and was curiously cheered by her lack of reaction. No blushing. No fluttering eyelashes or tossing of curls. If anything, she seemed to retreat into herself. Her expression hardened into implacability. Her actress's mask settled into place with the firmness of cement. Yet, he'd discovered her secret: she used that well-armored demeanor not to keep the world at bay but to hold her own fears tight within.

Had any man ever discerned her monumental struggle to bury all doubts and vulnerabilities beneath that famously cool exterior? Had any man ever tried? Or had they all taken her sleek, pleasure-loving façade at face value?

Adam perhaps. No wonder she mourned him. He'd been the only one to truly understand her—until now.

David had only a few minutes to work his charm before Bianca had been taken in hand by a maid to be fretted over upstairs. Once alone, David shed his gallantry, pacing the room like a prisoner.

"You brought her here? Didn't you hear my warning about Lord Deane? What the bloody hell were you thinking?"

"I was thinking that if it weren't for her, you and Gray would be attending my funeral."

"And she and the earl? How do you explain their connection?"

"I can't. Or at least, I can't explain where Deane fits in, but I trust she's telling the truth. Whatever Deane is up to, she's not involved."

David shook his head. "You've fallen under the famed ice queen's spell, haven't you? I can see why. The woman's a bloody stunner, and from the looks she kept throwing in your direction, it wouldn't take much to wiggle your way between those perfect thighs. Or mayhap you already . . . ?" He lifted his brows in question.

"She's not like that."

David merely offered a thin, knowing smile that made Mac want to hit him. Hard.

"Fine, if you don't want to talk about her, we'll talk about you. You look awful. Like death on a stick. How do you feel?" he asked, handing Mac a whiskey.

"Like I've been flattened by a whole convoy of runaway caissons." Mac accepted the drink but didn't taste. Instead he toyed with the glass, running a finger across the rim and swishing the amber liquid round and round as he talked: of the ambush at Bianca's house, the dirty cellar in Southwark, the hours he spent at the mercy of a man who'd unleashed a thousand years of fury with vicious precision on Mac's body.

David sat silently, only the sharpening angles of his face and the narrowing of his eyes revealing his growing rage. "You're sure he said 'she'? 'She' wanted you dead?"

"Whoever 'she' is, she was going to take great pleasure in killing me." Mac slumped in a chair, the room spinning enough to make walking straight downright dangerous. He remained weak, his guts cramping as his fever climbed, his shoulder aching down to the bone.

"You're certain we're dealing with Fey-bloods?"

"His powers scraped against my mental shields like a saw blade. I felt the mage energy's vibration all the way back to my fucking molars. They know, David."

Mac closed his eyes as the room spun, the walls sliding into a shimmer of hallucinations. Opened them again at the touch of a hand upon his forehead.

David stood over him, looking paternal. "Your fever's raging," he commented grimly. "How long did he have you trapped again?"

"Long enough." Memories clawed at him. Memories of pain when every breath was agony, the silver eating into his flesh like wires dipped in acid. And always the questions. Over and over, without end. With a what-the-hell last wish, he tossed the whiskey back, the heat scorching his throat to land like lead in his curdled stomach. "We need to send word to the Gather. To warn them."

"And how do you propose we do that?" David asked, crossing to draw back the curtain on a late autumn morning, the sun climbing through a haze of coal smoke.

"Your *krythos*. We can summon them with the far-seeing disk."

David dropped the curtain in place. "And have the Ossine's enforcers down on us like a pack of damned hounds? You know the penalty for contacting the clans. Exile becomes extinction. And despite the shithouse my life has become, I still like living it, thank you very much. If you're so determined to end on the point of an enforcer's sword, why don't you use your disk?"

Mac dug his hand into the borrowed coat pocket out of habit. He'd not noticed his *krythos*'s loss until this morning. And then it was far too late to go searching for it. His last link with home and family was no more. He shook his head. "Gone."

David shrugged, his dismissive indifference infuriating Mac.

"We have to do something," he chided. "We can't just sit back and let the worst happen without trying to stop it."

"Why not?" David argued. "Adam massacred an entire family of out-clans to keep our secret. Don't you find that disgusting and slightly hypocritical? That we destroy to keep from being destroyed? We're as guilty as the Fey-bloods."

Caught by surprise, Mac fell back on tradition. "Adam did what was required to keep us safe. The laws were put in place for a reason. The Gather acts only for our survival."

David sprang to his feet, the wolf revealed in his fierce gaze, bared teeth, fangs white as pearls, a quiver of rage surrounding him like an aura. "And will you enforce them, Mac? Will you do as Gather rules demand and take a knife to Bianca Parrino to claw your way back into their good graces? She helped you escape. Will you return her courage by slitting her throat?"

"No! But . . ." Mac collapsed into his chair, heart pounding, head blasting with a new fire. "It's not the same. She's different."

"Of course she is. But so were many who met their deaths because they discovered what we are." David resumed his seat, dropping his head in his hands as if he bore a great weight. "The Gather elders are fools and old men, frightened of their own shadows. So lost to stories of ancient treacheries, they can't see our race is dying now."

"What are you talking about?"

"The Imnada are failing. How many of us are left?

How many births replace those who have died? One to replace ten? And our powers? They're dwindling just as we are." David lifted his head, face ashen, eyes lost and staring. "This constant hiding in the shadows is dooming us to certain extinction."

Mac had never seen David like this. Never heard him utter such a blatant heresy. Not even during the first frenzied shock following the Other's curse. Even then he'd possessed a will of steel, holding longer than any of them to the hope their affliction could be overcome by their Imnada strength, their Imnada power. Perhaps that was what made his rage burn higher and hotter after that hope had been cruelly dashed. Shattered faith in his race and his own invincibility.

"You just said you didn't care what happened to the clans," Mac challenged.

David's dark eyes shone, and for a moment he looked as if he might continue to argue. Instead, he rose to pour himself another drink. Mac had lost count of how much he'd taken in just the few hours they'd been together, but surely it was more than enough. Hell, it wasn't even noon yet.

"I'll send word to de Coursy," David said. "And I'll get you to Wallace's before nightfall." He rang for a servant, passing Mac on his way out the door. "Even with all Adam's notes, do you really imagine you'll find a way to break the curse?" The desperate hope in the question twisted Mac's insides. "There must have been a reason Kinloch didn't tell us what he'd learned. Something you've overlooked."

"Only one way to find out," Mac replied. "But it's one more way than we had before."

David nodded, dropping a hand on Mac's shoulder. "Sorry to burden you with my moral quandaries, old man. Suppose it's an argument without an end. Stay here and rest while I have a chamber prepared and a bath sent up."

Mac nodded, slumping into his chair, letting the last frenetic hours spin away in a feverish haze. "David?" he asked, breaking the brittle silence.

St. Leger swung around, a brow raised in question.

"If you're right about the Imnada, what can we possibly do about it?" Mac asked. "We've been cast out. We're as good as dead."

David took a long time to answer, his gaze trained on some far-distant invisible point, a wild light in his dark eyes. "Perhaps that's our greatest strength, Mac. No one expects the dead to cause trouble."

In a mad scramble, Bianca retreated from the library door, hoping to make it seem she'd only just arrived at the bottom of the staircase as Mr. St. Leger emerged. In reality, her hand gripped the banister to keep her steady, her head swimming with snippets of the overheard conversation between Mac and this man.

Gathers, curses, the dying out of a race that until last night she'd assumed lived only within the pages of a picture book—why did every answer she gain only spin off a dozen more questions? She hated this constant state of confusion, this loss of control. It harked back to a time when these were all she felt and her life had been in someone else's hands. If she was ever to wrest herself free of the mess she'd fallen into, she would have to turn the situation to her advantage. She needed answers.

And she'd begin with Mr. David St. Leger.

His gaze brightened upon spotting her, and he came forward, hand extended. "Simply stunning, Mrs. Parrino. The color matches your eyes as if made with you in mind."

"Is that what you told the courtesan who wore it last?" she asked tartly, wishing she had her wreck of a morning gown back instead of this translucent confection of silk and lace and ribbons. It made her feel like the icing on an unusually erotic cake.

"Actually, I warned her she'd been nibbling between meals and was beginning to look a bit like a partridge, which is why the gown is here and the lady is not." He offered her his arm. "You must be famished. Breakfast is laid out in the dining room."

"I should see to Mac."

"Don't bother. He's sleeping, and if he feels half as bad as he looks, he needs all the rest he can get."

He seated her at the table before taking his own place, watching as she helped herself to eggs and ham, toast, and a restorative cup of tea. She hadn't realized how hungry she was until she began to eat, interrogation taking second place to her empty stomach. Seeming amused, St. Leger leaned back, now and then sipping from the cup of coffee in front of him. She refused to allow him to discomfit her and even offered him a narrow smile as she plowed through her second helping.

"Mac claimed you were different," he commented. "I'm beginning to believe he was right. Any woman—hell, any human—who isn't blubbering into their porridge or clawing the walls to escape is definitely one of a kind."

"Would either of those activities do me any good, Mr. St. Leger?" she asked over the rim of her cup.

"No, but they might make you feel a damn sight better." He leaned across the table to snatch a piece of bacon from a platter. "And please don't call me Mr. St. Leger. That was my father."

"What should I call you?"

"How about David? It's easy. Two little syllables."

She poured herself a second cup of tea. Or was it her third? Doctored it with plenty of sugar and milk. "I assume you're Imnada too?"

He smiled, giving a low whistle. "The papers didn't lie. Cool as a cucumber."

If St. Leger knew half of the whirlwind of thoughts racing through her skull, he'd sing a different song, but Bianca acknowledged his compliment with a gracious nod. Looking the part was half the battle. "So, are you?"

St. Leger straightened. "That depends."

"On?" she prompted as she studied him for signs of otherworldliness. Nothing jumped out at her unless one counted unearthly good looks as a clue. And yet, while Mac's saturnine features and forbidding expressions hinted at an ancient battle-ax-wielding paladin, David St. Leger possessed the golden, sun-kissed visage of your average Greek god: square jaw, piercing gray eyes, and a wide-shouldered, athletic build any tailor in London would drool to dress.

"On whether you plan on running to Lord Deane as soon as I let you out of my sight."

"Mac trusts me."

"Mac's not a cynic like I am. Despite mountains of evidence to the contrary, he still believes in outmoded ideas like loyalty, faith, devotion, and the love of a good woman. I've read the papers, Mrs. Parrino. I hear the talk at my club and the chatter in the park. And where there's smoke, there's usually fire."

"I had nothing to do with Adam's death, and I won't tell Deane or anyone about Mac or you. How could I without sounding like a bedlamite?"

"Wait a few hours and you'd have all the evidence you'd need," he mumbled.

"What's that supposed to mean?"

Has Mac shown you this little trick?

Her cup poised at her lips, she stiffened as the voice slid like glass across the surface of her mind. "My thoughts are my own, Mr. St. Leger. Not toys for your amusement."

"Impressive. Not a twitch," he said, his tone warm with approval before adding, "Your skeletons are safe in their cupboards, Mrs. Parrino. The Imnada can path mind to mind, but we're not psychics."

More's the pity, he added, his thought brushing against her consciousness with the same lewd invitation she'd experienced a hundred times in a hundred crowded ballrooms.

She gently placed her cup upon the table. "If you're looking for a replacement to wear this gown, I'm not interested."

"Spoken for already?"

Her gaze sharpened. "I speak for myself."

He scooped eggs onto his plate. Poured himself another coffee. "I can see why Mac's attracted to you. You're no shrinking wallflower. And you've made it this far, which means you're capable and quick thinking. All good assets. I've a feeling you'll need them before long."

"I'm certainly glad I've won your approval," she answered sarcastically.

"Unless"—he rubbed at his chin, eyeing her with new suspicion—"perhaps you were meant to get this far. You claim you speak for yourself, but Lord Deane's already shown a weakness for actresses. In fact, he married one. Perhaps he's pulling your strings and your arrival here is part of a larger plan."

She clenched her fork and knife in hands gone bone-white in anger. "Sebastian didn't send that brute after us. Whatever's going on, he's not involved."

David leaned in, a harsh light entering his eyes. "How can you be certain? The earl is Other and, as Mac may have told you, the Fey-bloods nearly exterminated us once. What's to stop them from finishing the job?"

"Seb's no murderer. He's a gentleman."

"Evil can easily cloak itself in wealth and breeding, Mrs. Parrino." St. Leger's gray gaze seemed to penetrate her brain. "While the heart of a hero can beat even beneath the skin of a beast."

"Mr. St. Leger said you wanted to see me."

Bianca stood in the doorway, dressed in a gown that looked as if it had been intended to entice rather than conceal. A sweeping low neckline of shimmering white seeded with pearls, the translucent skirts threaded with gold thread and more pearls. No one who saw her slender, gilded beauty would recognize the sweat- and dirt-stained woman who had risked her life to save him and fought like a lioness against a murderous Fey-blood. Like the mountain lakes around Concullum, Bianca held startling depths beneath her placid surface.

She lifted her chin, a small frown puckering her forehead. "Mac?"

He cleared his throat, shifting in bed, glad for the heavy shield of blankets. "We leave for Surrey in an hour."

Her frown deepened. "But we killed . . . I mean I . . . that is . . ."—she took a slow deep breath—"the Frenchman is dead."

"He is. But he wasn't working alone. There's a woman. I felt her malice and her resolve in my head like a stain. She watched as he . . . as he questioned me. I could almost feel her hand guiding his knife, sense her pleasure at my screams. Whoever she is, she's responsible for Adam's death, and if I'm right, she won't stop just because she failed to kill us. She'll send others, and they'll assume you know my whereabouts. They'll force you"—he closed his eyes against the bile clawing its way up his throat— "they'll force you to tell them," he whispered. "I won't let you suffer because of me, Bianca."

"I'd be safe with Sarah at Deane House," she answered just as softly.

"No," he snarled before taking a deep breath. "No. *You* may be certain of Deane's innocence, but I can't take that chance. Not until I completely understand the threat. Not with the lives of so many at stake."

"But how can I disappear to the wilds of Surrey and not expect anyone to notice? What will people say?"

He handed her a copy of the morning paper lying on the bed beside him. "David brought this up. I didn't want to show you, but perhaps it's for the best."

"'Butcher of Barleymow Court Found Butchered in Back Alley'?" she read.

"Above that."

"'Mrs. P—, late an actress of Covent Garden theatre, has left London in some haste. Is it to recover her health as some claim, or does she wish to escape the long arm of the law?'" Her jaw tightened, the paper trembling in her hands as she read.

"They've offered you the perfect excuse to quit the city."

"Yes, because they assume I'm guilty of Adam's murder. I have to say, this alliance idea isn't working out quite as I'd hoped."

"I agree. But we stay together and we stay safe."

"Do we?" she asked, her voice hoarse with emotion, a queer light blazing in her eyes. "Then why do I feel as if the real danger is only beginning?"

Bianca rested in a corner of the hired coach conveying them to Bear Green. The interior smelled of a mixture of camphor, soiled straw, and unwashed socks, the windows were coated with a dusty film, and the creaky springs groaned at every bend in the road. But the brazier held coals enough to keep her warm, the weather had cleared to a brilliant cloud-threaded blue sky, and she was alive.

Amazing how skirting death can turn once monumental concerns into petty problems.

She snuck a peek at her traveling companion from beneath lowered lashes. Mac slumped across from her, long legs stretched toward the brazier, face averted, dark hair falling forward over his brow so that only a narrow curve of jaw and cheekbone showed.

As she studied him, she tried to work up a little lingering terror—perhaps a touch of disgust. A hint of repugnance. Nothing. It was as if all her earlier shock had been overwhelmed by larger, more dangerous fears.

The heart of a hero. David St. Leger's words from this morning came back to her now as she watched Mac's fidgety attempts at finding a comfortable spot among the lumpy cushions with a typical sick man's grumbling. Mummified beneath a mountain of traveling rugs, he couldn't have looked further from heroic if he tried. At this point, between the mottled bruising, lacerations, and waxen greenish pallor, he resembled a corpse. Yet those work-scarred hands gripping and releasing the edge of his blanket, the tension leaping in his bruised jaw, and the keen-edged determination lingering in his bloodshot eyes all pointed to an unflinching courage, an unshakable resolve.

She couldn't help but wonder what it would feel like to be cared for by such a man. To feel safe and protected within the circle of his arms, knowing nothing could break the bond between them. To experience a love that burned as steadfastly as the devotion to duty in his warrior's gaze.

A lightning charge sparked over her skin, simmering up from her center in a quicksilver caress to flare between her legs.

What would it be like to go to bed with him? Would her heart thunder? Would her stomach clench with pleasure rather than dread? When had this dangerous attraction outstripped her guarded resentment? When had desire trumped astonishment and alarm?

Probably the very moment she'd lost the surprising

comfort of his solid presence. When she thought she'd never see him alive again. When his death had been a mere pistol shot away.

She refused to dig deeper into that troubling real-ization, afraid of what she might unearth. Already she felt like flotsam being swept along before a wave: Ad-am's murder, then Mac's entrance on the stage, turning her life upside down and inside out. She dare not wade further into such treacherous waters.

Mac shifted on his seat with a heavy sigh and mumbled, "Shite all. Why David sent us off in this rattletrap of a jarvey, I'll never know."

"Are you warm enough?" she asked. "Do you need another blanket? You can have mine."

He waved her off. "I'm fine."

"We can change seats if yours is too uncomfort-able."

He shook his head.

"I've some whiskey if—"

"Bianca, enough!" Mac exclaimed. "I marched from Portugal to Paris without expiring, I think I can manage twenty miles in a carriage even if it is about to rattle the teeth straight out of my head."

"It was Mr. St. Leger's idea. He said it would throw off anyone with a mind to follow us."

He grunted. "More likely his idea of a bad joke. Did I ever tell you about the time he sent me out after a Spanish guerrilla who'd made his headquarters in a convent? I was nearly emasculated by a gaggle of en-raged nuns." He gave a shuddering groan.

Bianca smothered a smile behind her hand.

"Of course, it's funny now," he complained.

"Can you . . . I mean, how . . ." Embarrassment

caused her to stutter as she sought a foothold on the questions swamping her brain. "Do you have a choice? Could you shift now if you wanted to?"

He looked up, and she flinched anew at his gaunt, sunken cheeks, the dark smudges beneath his dull eyes. "It takes strength and concentration. I couldn't manage either at the moment."

She turned to watch the passing landscape, though her mind recorded nothing of her surroundings, as she was too busy recalling Sebastian's tale of Arthur and the Imnada warlord Lucan. He'd paid for his crime, not only with his life but with the lives of all his kind. Adam *had* carried a dangerous secret. His life *had* been shrouded in mystery and fear. Just not in the way she'd imagined.

A chill slithered up her spine as she thought of the Frenchman's hatred, his twisted, venomous fury. Those moments before she struck would forever be inscribed in her memory. The way the light shone dirty gray, the thick dust hanging in the air, the spittle at the corners of his mouth as he hurled his threats, and the slick, cold feeling of her hands gripping the fire tongs. It was all locked in her head like the scene of a play.

Could Mac and St. Leger be right? Could Sebastian be a magical Fey-blood out to kill the remaining Imnada in a feud dating back a thousand years? Had she been an unwitting dupe in the earl's ongoing war? The idea didn't sit well. "Why do the Fey-bloods hate the Imnada? I mean, Arthur and the Round Table and Camelot, that's a story . . . a legend."

"As are we," he replied evenly.

"Do you mean King Arthur was real?"

He pulled the blanket higher up on his shoulders with a muttered oath.

"Mac?"

His pale gaze shone like rubbed pewter. "The Feybloods looked on us as monsters, Bianca. We didn't spring from the seed of Ynys Avalenn as they did. Our origins lay out among the stars, far beyond the Gateway, and thus their powers affected us differently or not at all. This made us a threat. Whether the Fealla Mhòr grew out of this long-standing insecurity or one crushing battlefield betrayal, who can say a hundred generations after? All I know is few Imnada survived the purges. And those that did kept themselves so hidden that none suspected they'd survived—until now."

Mac turned away to lean back against the lumpy seat cushions, his half-lidded gaze vague as if his thoughts drifted miles away.

They passed through a village, Bianca's attention drawn to a vicar hurrying down a churchyard path; a group of women chatting in front of a dressmaker's window; a young girl hanging laundry; sheep being herded by an old man and his dog. None of them with a clue that just beyond their awareness lay another world. One that seemed to hold both the stuff of daydreams and the creatures of nightmares.

She cut her eyes once more to Mac, stiffening when she found him watching her. His face had grown tight, darkness crowding his expression. Something else St. Leger had said occurred to her.

"Is it true the Imnada are dying out? Is that what you and St. Leger meant by a curse?"

"Listening at keyholes?" he asked, his gaze suddenly needle sharp.

"Searching for answers," she responded curtly. "Something in short supply at the moment."

"No, Bianca. The Imnada aren't cursed. Only four of us were imprisoned by a Fey-blood's dark spell."

The truth dropped heavy into the pit of her stomach, horror dawning with her sudden understanding. "St. Leger, de Coursy, Adam, and you." Her heart pounded with each name she counted off. "All of you served together in the army."

"Aye, Bianca. And all but for Adam suffer together now."

The coach turned onto a rutted farm lane, passing beneath a tangled canopy of autumn elms and oaks, the wide meadows to either side a thousand shades of dun. Then through a gate and into a farmyard, halting before a brick-and-beam house standing foursquare and solid. A cluster of barns and outbuildings stood farther on, the ringing of an anvil coming from the closest. Geese and chickens waddled between the legs of two horses tied to a fence.

A woman in a mobcap and apron came out onto the back steps of the house, eyes squinting in curiosity. Slowly, Mac unwrapped himself from his blankets, opened the door, and stepped gingerly down to meet her. "You must be Mrs. Wallace. I'm—"

Bianca had never seen anyone move so fast. One minute the woman's hands were empty, a hesitant welcome upon her features. The next she'd an ax hefted before her, its gleaming edge pressed to Mac's neck. "You're dead. That's what," she hissed.

11

"Good thing I was close to hand or Annie might have taken your head off." Wallace drew a line across his neck in vicious pantomime.

"Had I thought twice, I might have let her," Mac answered.

After the initial shock and fluster of their arrival, he and Bianca had been hustled into the house, where she had been offered a chair by the fire and a cup of sweet tea. Mac had been handed a towel to press against the bloody score on his neck. Unfortunately, it did little to stem his teeth-chattering fever or the throbbing ache infecting his joints. He clamped his jaw and fought to ignore it. Fainting was not an option.

Marianne Wallace set down two steaming mugs of coffee. "I'm sorry, Captain, that I took you for one of them. When it comes to my family, I'm not afraid of man or beast or those that fall anywhere in between, and I'll thank you to remember that."

The woman's firm tone made him feel about ten years old and four feet high. In real life, the bewitching siren he'd imagined sweeping Jory Wallace off his feet was tall and large-featured, with a wide mouth, a hawkish nose, and an expression in her eyes hinting at untold strength. She would have needed it to accept the husband she'd chosen—in both his forms.

Mac shot Wallace a questioning look as he took a fortifying gulp of coffee and nearly spat it out with a grimace. Whiskey didn't carry the potency of this thick, burnt-flavored, throat-scorching brew. It stung his cut lip before roaring into his stomach like lye. "'One of them'?" he wheezed and swallowed at the same time.

Jory sucked his coffee down, and only Mac's fleeting glimpse of a flask disappearing into a vest pocket explained why the sludge hadn't affected his host the same way. "Aye. We'll not be dragged into it, and so I told the fellow that came to recruit for the cause."

Mac tried and failed at a second sip. "I have the feeling I'm coming in near the middle of this story."

"Shoe's on the other foot now," Bianca chimed in, a little of the dangerous sparkle back in her eyes.

Jory chuckled before growing serious. "About a year ago, a chap showed up. A clansman from my old holding in Kilbanif."

"Imnada here? But . . ."

"I'm *emnil*. Outlawed and dead to them. I know. That's what I thought too."

"What did he want?"

"Said he and some others were frustrated with the Ossine-influenced Gather and their rulings. They'd started meeting in secret. Making plans. They hoped I'd join with them."

"To do what?" Mac's ill feeling returned, worse than before.

"Save the race from extinction. They believe the future of the Imnada depends on coming into the open. Making peace with the Fey-bloods. That we'll die out if we remain hidden away."

This constant hiding in the shadows is dooming us to extinction.

It was David's complaint echoed almost word for word. Mac sat up, a new tightness in his chest. One not associated with the silver poisoning. Could St. Leger be mixed up with these rebels? The man was reckless, desperate, and completely irresponsible. A perfect recipe for fomenting revolution. Mac barely heard Jory's next words over the rushing in his ears.

". . . packed him off the place quick. Then a couple months ago another fellow showed. This time from the Ossine."

The tightness crushed the breath from Mac's lungs. "An enforcer?"

"Aye. The Ossine know about this splinter group. Know and don't like it. I'd nothing to tell, but the punishment if I dare aid the conspirators was spelled out in grisly detail."

"Hence—"

"My wife playing executioner with a kitchen cleaver."

"Mac?" Bianca frowned. "This may make perfect sense to the rest of you, but I'm floundering with no script to follow."

A door slammed, bringing with it a brisk wind and the chatter of lively voices. "Pa said it was your job to mend that bit of wall where the bullock got through."

"Are your arms broken? I've the turnips still to see to. You do it."

"But Pa said—"

Two boys muscled their way into the kitchen. One Mac remembered from his first visit, but the older of the pair looked to be in his late teens by the swagger in his stance coupled with the belligerent glint in his eye.

"Henry, Jamie!" Jory barked, his mug banging against the table. "Don't come brawling in here like a couple of tinker's brats. We've visitors."

The two boys skidded to a halt and dragged their caps from their heads, manners chastened, eyes blazing with curiosity.

"You're late for luncheon. Where's Sam?" Mrs. Wallace plunked a plate of warm crusty bread upon the table. Another of crumbly white cheese and thick slices of ham. "And if you tell me you've locked him in the icehouse again, James Wallace, I'll set a switch to your backside. Don't think you're too old for a good hiding."

"He gets in the way, Mum," Jamie complained. "He's always underfoot except when you need a hand and then he disappears like a rabbit down a hole."

"That's no excuse for nigh freezing him to death."

"It's always my fault. Why don't you yell at Henry? He's the one who did it."

Mrs. Wallace spun to face her younger son. "Where's Sam now, Henry?" she asked ominously.

"He's helping Hetty and Aldith gather apples," Henry explained. "Really, Mum. Honest."

Mac shot a look over Jory's shoulder at Bianca, who watched the byplay with amusement.

"You came here before."

Mac returned his attention to Henry, who stood sidling back and forth with obvious curiosity.

"I'm surprised you recognize me."

"Were you set upon by highwaymen?" the boy asked. "Or did you fight a duel? Maybe you were in a battle?"

"Idiot, who would he be battling in Surrey?" Jamie jumped in with all the contempt of an older sibling for a younger.

"A bit of all of the above and a lot of none," Mac answered Henry.

"Make yourselves a sandwich," Mrs. Wallace advised. "Then, Jamie, go find Aldith and tell her I need her to help with the washing up. Henry, I want you to take Sam and Hetty and deliver this soup to the vicar. He's suffering dreadful from a cold, and this will do him good."

Both boys moaned, groaned, and complained, but one stern look from their mother had them slapping together a meal before heading for the door, their departure leaving a gaping hole in the cluttered, comfortable kitchen.

Jory took a last swallow of his coffee and rose from the table with a heaving sigh. "Now you see why I sent that rebel agent packing. I've a tie more binding than any clan allegiance, Flannery. These are my people now."

Bianca tarried by the well, tossing stones into the depths. Listened for the echoing sploshes as they struck far below. Strung too tightly to sleep despite her fatigue, she'd spent the afternoon exploring the farmyard. Nosing through barns and storage sheds, stroking the flat, sturdy heads of sheep shoving their way to feed, walking out into the orchard as far as the first stile to help gather the windfall apples.

The sounds, the smells, and even the sharp, earthy air lying on her tongue reminded her of her home an ocean away. Nothing here to hint at the incredible, magical secret hidden beneath the ordinary-seeming surface.

She heard the trills of children's laughter and looked up from her pile of pebbles. The boy Henry and his younger brother Sam swung on the kitchen garden gate while two little girls with identical snub noses, auburn curls, and matching aprons drew in the dirt with sticks.

Bianca watched them play, surprised at the tears pricking her eyes and the lump that caught in her throat. She'd long ago given up on the pretty fantasy of a life with a devoted husband, a cozy house where they would love and laugh and share their days, and children with their chubby hands, messy faces, and constant happy noise. Such a dream did not exist. She'd certainly never shared it with Lawrence. And after his death, when suitors had first come buzzing round her, she'd seen the falseness of their smiles and the deception behind their charming manners. They had wanted to win her, not because they loved her but because they saw her as an ornament to be worn upon their arms, a prize to be flaunted in front of their friends. And she, hardened and unmoved, had sent them on their way. Untouched. Untouchable.

The children's suddenly staring faces and hurried whispers alerted her to an intruder approaching. Wiping her eyes with the back of her hand, Bianca sat up straighter, smoothing her expression as if drawing a veil across her sorrow before turning to face Mac.

Bent-shouldered, he trod as if every step pained

him. The bruising on his face had become a grotesque palate of green, yellow, and purple, though the swelling had receded, the blood had been bathed away, and illness no longer clouded his gaze.

"May I join you, or is this well taken?" he asked with a gallant nod.

She shifted to offer him a seat, all too aware of his body so close beside her, the dampness of his newly washed hair, the masculine scent of his skin. "You look much improved."

"Marianne Wallace's medicinal tonic, three whiskeys, and four hours of uninterrupted sleep. Never felt better."

"Jory is the man in the picture. Adam's . . . his friend. The one I saw in London. Is that why we're here?"

"It is. And now you see why I knew you were mistaken about Adam. You could say it was their animal nature rather than their sexual nature that brought them together. Jory has agreed to let us stay on until I hear from David, but I had a hard time convincing him. I don't blame him for being unwilling. It's dangerous and he's a family to look after."

"And when you hear from David? What then?"

"If all goes as planned, I can petition the clans and enlist their help. If the Imnada are in danger, the threat belongs to us all."

"I thought you were in exile and unable to go home."

"That's where Jory comes in."

She should ask more questions. Force him to tell her his plans. She deserved that much after the chaos her life had become. But did she really want to know? Or would that only pull her in deeper? Entangle her in a world she had not known existed until a few short days ago? Perhaps this was her chance to distance herself from the danger surrounding Mac—the danger that was Mac.

She tossed another pebble down the shaft. "Do you realize how long it's been since I wasn't running from dawn to dark with fittings and rehearsals and performances and appearances? I'm not sure I know how to sit and do nothing anymore."

"It won't be for long. And if you grow too bored, I'll wager Marianne could find you plenty to do. There's never an end to the chores on a farm like this one."

"Are you well acquainted with farms like this one?"

"Aye. Though a fair bit larger, my father's place is much the same. I worked alongside him from the time I was old enough to toddle in his wake, knowing someday I would take over as clan chieftain and it would all be mine to protect and care for. Concullum was a trust and an honor."

"So what happened?"

"I grew up. What had seemed like the entire world to me shrank to the size of a prisoner's cell. I thought I knew better than my elders, thought I had all the answers."

She dropped her eyes to her hands threaded in her lap. "That sounds painfully familiar."

"My mother died. My father and I fought when we weren't ignoring one another completely. Life just . . . unraveled. And then I left for the army. And by the time I knew what I really wanted, it was too late. It no longer wanted me."

"That's what you meant when you said you couldn't go home."

"Ironic, isn't it?"

He stared off into the middle distance, his eyes trained on an invisible desire beyond the far horizon. The silence brittle as spun glass.

She cleared her throat, squaring her shoulders. Brushing a handful of pebbles into the well, where they fell with a skittering crash. "Not that I'm complaining, but how is hiding among the sheep going to convince people I'm not a murderess?" she asked brazenly. "Or win me back my job?"

He arched a brow as if understanding her attempt to shake him from his gloom. "I don't know. If nothing else, it will keep you alive long enough for the scribblers and gossips to sharpen their quills on some other poor blighter's reputation and Society's attention to turn to a new scandal." Although it was blackened and swollen, his eye still had the gleam of a scoundrel. "Is it my new rakish good looks that are driving you away?"

She offered him a cool appraisal. "You do look like something the cat threw up. No pun intended."

He puffed his chest out, tilting his head back to look down at her through hooded eyelids. "I thought it made me look gallant."

She laughed. "Not even close."

He placed his hand over hers; his touch was warm and strong and safe. "Trust me, Bianca. You'll see. It will come out all right."

She should have ignored the wild excitement flittering up her spine and the curling heat between her legs. She should remove her fingers from his grasp. She should have, but she couldn't. For a moment the children, the farm, the autumn birdsong, and this man before her combined to tug loose the iron vise of old grief. She caught a glimpse of what might have been had fate offered her a different path with a different man. Now fate turned once more, sending her places she had never dreamed she could go.

"Will it?" she asked, hoping Mac didn't hear the pleading in her voice.

"Of course. By the time you return to London when this is over, they'll be doubling your wages and begging you to return to the stage."

"And you? What happens to you when this is over?"

"I don't know. But I'll have a choice, and that's more than I've had in a long time." His penetrating stare glued her to her seat. Loss, uncertainty, suspicion, and loneliness hovered like ghosts within his gaze. Difficult to notice but easy to recognize. She saw the same within her own mirror every morning. "You'll have choices, too, Bianca. You're a beautiful woman. You could have any man you wanted. You don't need to be alone."

"Maybe I prefer being alone." She was drowning in the green of his stare, lost within the heat of his touch.

"And mayhap you were meant for laughter and sunshine and sweetness and joy."

"I have those things already."

He lifted her hand, kissing the underside of her wrist, his gaze slicing open her heart with the precision of a scalpel. "Do you?"

"You said you can't read minds," she said weakly. "You promised my thoughts were my own."

"And so they are, *mi am'ryath*."

Swallowing the lump in her throat, she never sensed his intentions until his lips pressed gently on her mouth, heat rushing through her like honey. She lifted her hands to his face, feeling the rough stubble of his beard, the tension in his jaw. Only by sheer force of will did she resist the desire, disentangling herself before she surrendered completely. There was nothing special about him. Nothing to make her risk her hard-fought freedom. Nothing to make her risk her wounded heart.

Pulling free, she lurched to her feet. Opened her mouth to explain, but nothing would come. There was no way for her to excuse her behavior or explain her reluctance. He said nothing, nor did he reach for her, but his hurt expression picked at her conscience.

Turning, she fled to the house.

Mac sought her trust. How could he know what an impossible thing he asked? She'd placed her faith in so few for so long. She'd locked her heart away in a box where no one could find it. No one could touch it. And no one could break it.

Ever.

"Adam did all of this?"

Mac circled the cramped room, his eyes raised to the hundreds of bunches of herbs and flowers hanging from the rafters before dropping to the stoppered jars on a long counter with rows upon row of drawers, their contents neatly labeled in Latin. Finally he perused the beakers and bowls, the pestles and mortars, the coils of copper tubing.

Adam's house had been ransacked, but this oasis of alchemy remained intact. It waited only for a hand to begin the process. Mac's hand.

"Aye," Jory answered. "It started simple enough

with a bit of storage and grew from there as he spent more time here. Made it easier for him to work without the worry of nightfall coming on suddenly."

"Why didn't you show me this place when I came before?"

"Wasn't certain it would do any good. Not until I'd had a look at Adam's journal."

"And?"

"Between his notes and my own recollections, I'm thinking there's a chance."

"You think?"

"Have you tried sorting through that mess? It's not as if I memorized the bloody process," Jory fired back. "Adam was the herbalist."

"I'm sorry." Mac rubbed the back of his neck thoughtfully. "I'd given up hope of ever breaking the Fey-blood's spell. Of returning home."

"Is that what you're looking for? A way back into the clans?"

Mac absently drew a finger over the dust-covered desk, only to realize as he lifted his hand that he'd written Bianca's name. Annoyed, he obliterated his folly with a single swipe of his palm. If only he could erase his feelings as easily. With her cold rebuff at the well, she'd made her position known. So why had some part of him hoped? Why had his imagination placed her by his side when common sense warned him off?

It was his own fault for daring to dream of a different ending. Wishing for more. A fool's wish, for there was nothing for him there as long as he lay under the curse. And when—not if—he broke the spell over him and reclaimed his rightful place among the Imnada, Bianca would be left behind. He would marry among the clans as tradition demanded. She would return to her life on the stage. He must remember that if he wasn't to become hopelessly ensnared in a trap of his own making.

"I had a place there," Mac answered. "A future."

"Aye, a future mapped out for you from birth by the Gather and the Ossine."

"I knew what I was when I belonged to the clans. I knew what was expected of me. In time I'd take over the leadership of our clan from my father. I'd marry the woman chosen for me. It was a life I understood."

"And yet, you ran away from that life and those obligations."

Brows lowered in warning, Mac turned to Jory with a hard look in his eyes.

The latter remained unfazed. "You left your holding and your clan. Ventured beyond the safety of the Palings. Took a commission in the army. To some Imnada, that's grounds enough to look on you with suspicion."

Mac had no countering argument. As he'd sought to explain to Bianca, he'd been young and headstrong when he seized the chance to leave home for life as a soldier. After all, the prized clan traits of loyalty, duty, and honor were equally valued by the military—the reason he'd chosen it for his career over his father's objections. Only time and distance had served to illuminate his true motivation: it had been an excuse to escape, from both the rugged emptiness of Mayo and the oppressive weight of his father's grief.

Mac dropped into a chair. "I'm tired of running. What's it gotten me? I remain as trapped as ever."

Jory smirked. "What, indeed?"

"If you're implying Bianca, don't be ridiculous. She's out-clan."

"And she looks at you with the eyes of a smitten woman."

"If by 'smitten' you mean fearful, suspicious, and disgusted, I'd agree."

"Give her a chance, man. You're not exactly what she was expecting, are you? You should have seen Annie when I first told her."

"How the hell did she accept it?" Mac asked.

Jory regarded him with bemusement and reproach. "Simple. She loved me."

Night closed thick and silent around the house. There were no lights but for a glimmer from the village seen fleetingly through the tossed branches of the coppice. No sounds but an owl calling from the churchyard, an answering nearby echo from the orchard. So different from the city where even the smallest hours before dawn held the clatter and hum of thousands and where a sea of torches, lamps, and candles created a permanent apricot haze even on the cloudiest nights.

Bianca lay upon her bed, staring at the ceiling. Her head throbbed. Her brain felt as if it had been fried like an egg. Even her hair hurt. Sleep had claimed her for a few hours, but Mac followed her even there. Restless dreams conjured ghosts, bent and strangely skewed, joints at odd angles, limbs furred or feathered, a rush of wings as a gathering darkness spread across her mind.

She tried closing her eyes to relax, but fears old and new continued to shiver along her bones. Memories she'd fought to suppress overwhelmed her shredded defenses. The feel of the tongs in her shaking hands. The shock in the man's eyes as he toppled. The way he fell, his limbs twisted in death. She'd lived with her guilt until it had become a permanent part of her. A scar polished over but never healed. A cancer on her heart.

Lawrence's death had been an accident. He'd come at her in a drunken rage, and she'd swung wildly, blindly, never for a moment believing one glancing blow would cause him to fall against an unforgiving brick hearth. A moment in time forever etched on her consciousness. No way to erase it. No way to outrun it. And now another death. Another secret she must bury.

Bianca.

The call cut through her fear like a sword, but she didn't move, afraid of what going to Mac would do to her already shaky resolve.

Why this crazy infatuation now, after so many years of remaining untouched and unaffected?

I know you can hear me.

Mac was brusque. He was arrogant. He was proud. But one slow quirk of that heart-stopping smile and her best intentions flew out the window. One moment of shared laughter or quiet conversation and she forgot why she was trying to avoid him.

I can't say I'm sorry for kissing you, because I'm not. But I am sorry I frightened you.

She could ignore him and have his voice bouncing around in her aching head all night, or she could indulge him and get some sleep. Rising from bed, she drew a wrapper around herself before stepping across the passage to his bedchamber. She would stand firm. She would be as frigid as her nickname. She would keep the space of a room between them.

"Mac?" she whispered, lifting her stub of a candle to light her way.

Over here.

Prepared this time, she barely flinched upon finding the panther lying on his side just beneath the open window. He lifted his head, his feral eyes gleaming with the reflected candlelight, though the expression in them was anything but savage. Instead, compassion burned brightly in his feline gaze.

Difficulty sleeping?

"How did you know?" she asked.

I can't sleep, either. She winced at the voice in her head. Not at the way it blossomed against her mind with the same clarity of the spoken word, but at the weakness threading the deep baritone. *I never meant to frighten you.*

"It wasn't fear that drove me away this afternoon. Or rather, it wasn't fear of you. It was fear of what you make me feel."

For a terrifying moment, the ice queen melted into a real person.

She grimaced. "Something like that."

The silence and the dark and the strange flickering shadows wrapped closely about her until she leaned against the bedpost, unable to leave as she'd intended. Her earlier fears and memories crowded around like restless spirits until the question spilled from her lips unbidden. "Do you ever feel the weight of your secret turning you into someone you're not? Or worse, crushing the life right out of you?"

*We have known no other way for uncounted genera-
tions. If it's a burden, it's one I no longer notice.*

"Did Jory feel the burden? Is that what led to his
marriage to Marianne? Just the simple joy in not hiding what he was or pretending?"

Mac didn't answer right away. Instead, the great
cat's eyes focused on her face with a piercing intensity,
his body still but for the gentle rise and fall of his ribs.
Are you speaking about Jory or about you?

Her throat tightened. Her eyes stung with unshed
tears.

What's wrong, Bianca? Let me help you.

She'd sought to put the horror from her mind, lock
it away as she'd always done before, but she was unable
to tonight. Instead, old and new mixed and merged
into a blur of sickening images. Memories pushed
loose from behind the walls she'd built until, without
thinking, she dropped to her knees, a hand upon his
shoulder, his fur thicker and softer than she had imagined.

Sobs tore at her stomach and hot, salty tears burned
her cheeks; she let them come, reveling in the loosening of the hard knot beneath her breast as she allowed
Mac to glimpse her dark past.

He curled himself around her, one enormous paw
upon her knee, his gentle strength a refuge. None
could touch her while he held her thus. None would
dare.

Do not weep, mi am'ryath. *You did what you must
to survive. We're alike in that regard.*

She'd prayed so often for Lawrence's death, for an
end to the torment of his step upon the stair, his hateful words, his heavy fist. But not by her hand. She'd

never meant for it to end with violence. She'd only wanted him to stop hurting her. To leave her alone.

Her hands unconsciously curled into Mac's fur, her tears falling upon his face as grief spiked painful and bitter against her heart. "Can you change back? Can you be . . . be Mac? I need . . . I need arms around me right now. I need to know this will turn out right."

Gods, Bianca. If I could do this for you, I would in half a heartbeat. But I cannot. This, you see, is my curse.

12

Bianca slept as she lived, curled into a tight, protective ball, hands tucked close to her chest, knees drawn up, a small frown line drawn between the perfect arch of her brows.

A wounded animal remembered its pain. So, too, did a wounded woman. Bianca had been hurt badly. Her marriage, a failure. Her husband, a bully who wielded his power with a brute's cruelty. He'd deserved any death that found him.

With his skin still tingling from his shift, Mac shut the bedroom window against a cold dawn rain, settling into a chair where he could continue to watch over her as he'd done through the night, first as she'd wept, then as she'd fallen into a restless sleep. The rain tapped against the glass, but the room was snug and warm, and Mac desired nothing more than to remain wrapped in this cocoon as long as he could.

Then, like a swimmer breaking the water's surface, Bianca gasped, her body stiffening, face white as marble, her half-dreaming, unfocused gaze locked on the window. "I can't breathe. Oh, God, I can't get out." A whimper trembled through her words. Echoes of her panic in the Fey-blood's cellar.

"Bianca," he soothed. "You're dreaming, *alanna*."

Beyond calming, she struggled free of the blankets, her breathing coming in staccato blasts like gunfire, eyes blind with horror. "Can't get out. Can't breathe." Half falling from the bed, she lurched for the window, scrabbling with the latch. Ragged sobs dragged free of her throat. "I'll be good. I didn't mean to do it. I won't argue. Please."

Her pleading turned his stomach. Between one breath and the next, he rose to join her at the window. Reaching around her, he eased her shaking hands from the latch. Slid the window up with a screech of swollen wood. Immediately, a sour wind billowed the curtains, squeezing his lungs with a blast of frosty wind.

Instead of shrinking from the cold, Bianca gulped great lungfuls of air, eyes closed, arms hugged to her chest. After a few moments she leaned her forehead against the glass.

"Bianca?" he said softly. "Speak to me."

"What do you want me to say?" Her shoulders hunched, tremors running the length of her back.

He didn't ask what had frightened her. He didn't have to.

Rainwater puddled on the floor at their feet. Her golden hair floated over his chest. But he didn't touch her. Or speak. Barely breathed. Tears shone silver on her cheeks. Dull, leaden misery lay heavy in her eyes. "I'm sorry."

His rage burned white-hot. What the hell had that son-of-a-bitch husband done to elicit such terror?

His imagination filled in every disgusting blank, fury torching Mac's throat. No wonder she had walled herself away from the world like a princess in a tower. Better a tower than a dungeon. "You've nothing to be sorry for," he said softly.

She glanced away, her arms hugging her chest. "You must think me mad."

"No, just horribly bruised, *mi am'ryath*."

Her head came up, her expression sharp and fearful and yet somehow full of hope. As tactile as a touch, her eyes roved over his shoulders, the long edge of his collarbone. Down over his ribs and the patchwork of ugly bruising crisscrossed by a map of raised pink scarring. Lower to his hips. His long legs. Back up to his member, which jumped with excitement beneath such intense scrutiny. He gritted his teeth. Willed himself to be calm despite the blood racing through his veins.

Her body remained poised to flee, but the horror of her memories had faded. Instead, there was grief and a sense of loss and the first glimmerings of something he refused to name. "What did that man do to you?" she asked, her voice breaking. "He . . . I never . . . oh, Mac . . ."

"Less than he would have liked, thanks to your courage."

"But your body . . . so many scars . . ." She traced his chest with one tentative finger. "Who could be so cruel?"

Uncertain whether she spoke of his recent wounds or her own ancient pain, Mac remained silent, though fire chewed through his belly at the sorrow haunting her delicate features. And where before he had wanted her trust, now it rankled like a burr. She shouldn't trust him, but he'd passed the point where he could turn his back on her. Hell, he'd left it miles behind him in his wild, predatory need to possess her.

Her gaping robe exposed the leaping pulse at her throat, the outline of her delicious curves, the shadow of her puckered nipples straining at the thin fabric of her nightgown. Mouth parched, his veins pulsing, he held his breath as she reached for him. Afraid of what her touch might mean. Afraid she'd retreat and he'd be left cold and bereft.

He need not have worried. Her palm came to rest over his drumming heart like a brand on his bare chest.

"You know me better than any living soul. I'm stripped to the bone with nowhere to hide," she whispered.

"No need to hide. We've traded secret for secret, *mi am'ryath*."

A slender line appeared between her knitted brows. "You called me that before. What does it mean?"

"It's a flower that grows near my home. It blooms in the dead of winter when there's a spell of warm sea breeze in off the ocean. When all else is cold and gray and lifeless, it's a bit of hope for better." He ventured to trace the delicate edge of one cheekbone, relieved when she smiled, her body slowly relaxing.

"Is it an Irish word?"

"Nay. Oi'm speakin' the language of me grannies when oi call on the ancient tongue." He sobered. "It's all but dead and gone. Just a few use it now. Those schooled in it and those too stubborn to give it up."

"Which are you?"

The agony of his exile. The death of the Imnada. His growing impossible desire for Bianca. All ricocheted like bullets round his scattered brain. "I'm both," he admitted.

"I asked you last night . . . but you couldn't . . . you weren't able . . ." She shuddered, her hand curling over his shoulder, her eyes as misty as a mountain stream. ". . . Mac?"

A word. A look. Both tore at his heart. Both offered him a glimpse of heaven. There was no future here for him. Not even if he was free of the curse. Free of the suffering that went along with being *emnil*. Free to love where he would. Not only was she a talented actress with all of London at her feet, but she was human. An out-clan.

And what was he?

He tipped her face to his.

A damned fool, that's what.

Terror burned through her. Terror and anticipation. So tangled Bianca couldn't separate them. She stood martyr-straight as Mac bent to brush his lips against hers. Arms clamped to her sides. Knees locked.

"Bianca?" he asked, worry furrowing his brow.

She could do this. Lawrence would not win. He would not imprison her for the rest of her life.

Mac released her, stepping an arm's length away. The space between them charged with desire and hunger and fear and sorrow. And loneliness. Always the loneliness. It was in the weight of her limbs. The grief in his eyes.

"Should I leave?" he asked in a deep, velvety voice.

No! she wanted to scream. *Don't go.*

But Lawrence was there. Like a jailer, he continued to bind her to him. His handsome, laughing face still bright with malice. His hateful words still beating against her heart.

Worthless whore.

Slut.

Adulteress.

Bitch.

She had been none of those things. But it had not mattered. Lawrence always believed the worst of her. He'd married her not out of love but to gain a possession. He'd worshipped her beauty. Her grace. Proud of other men's envy. Then warped by his own.

Fighting the urge to escape, she squared her shoulders, her body flushed with heat despite the October chill, her hair brushing softly against the small of her back. "I want you to know I don't normally entertain men. I know actresses have a certain reputation."

"As do soldiers. Mostly unfounded. The majority of soldiers I know are tough and leathery as old boots with gutter vocabularies and barnyard couth. Hardly the stuff of romantic daydreams."

"What of the officers?"

A smile tugged at the corner of his mouth. "Those *are* the officers." He clasped her hand, his thumb caressing her palm. The warmth and tenderness of his touch calmed her racing heart. "So why do you break your habit now, with me?"

She looked into his eyes, black with need. His jaw hard, a pulse leaping in the hollow of his throat. "Perhaps because you have never once groveled, flattered, preened, or swaggered to get into my bed."

"Inaction wins the day," he murmured, lowering his mouth to hers.

For a heartbeat, she froze. But this time she defied the ghost of her terror. And just like that, she broke through the hard stone walls of her prison, Mac's kiss sweeping her along into a sea of warmth, the frozen parts of her thawing within the circle of his arms.

Lawrence's sneering visage had been banished to the corners of her mind. He lurked still, but his power diminished, his hate washed away by Mac's desire.

"Bianca." His voice came ragged and broken close against her ear as he moved to nibble along her neck.

"Mmm?" she answered, her bones liquefying with every pass of his lips across her skin.

Was this what Sarah had wanted for her? Not the fortune or the title, but this bubbly champagne buzz coursing through her veins, an exhilaration equal to a thousand cheering audiences roaring in her ears?

"You're not listening to a thing I'm saying." Mac's voice sounded dreamy and far away. And she realized he'd been speaking all along as his lips made their way down her throat, his hands as busy as his mouth.

"Of course I am," she answered, the fluttering of her heart intensifying until she ached with an insatiable longing.

"Then what did I just ask?" He tipped her chin up with one finger, his eyes alight with amusement.

She blinked. Opened her mouth to answer. Closed it again. "I . . . uh . . ."

"That's what I thought. So, better to beg forgiveness than permission." As if she weighed no more than a child, he gathered her into his arms, carrying her over to set her on the bed, then stared down at her, tumbled and flushed amid a heap of quilts.

Once more her stomach clenched against a flash of memory. Lawrence above her. Lawrence, hard and ferocious. Taking what he wanted. Leaving her cold and alone and humiliated. Again she struggled back from the brink with muscle-trembling effort.

Mac paused, a knee resting on the edge of the bed. As if feeling her inner turmoil and the long arms of memory, he pushed her hair from her face with the gentlest of touches, though she felt the strength of his restraint like a shiver between them. "All it takes is a word. I'll take no woman unwilling or even one who harbors second thoughts."

"How about fourth and fifth ones?"

"You've only to speak and I'll leave. It'll be difficult as the storming of Badajoz, but I'll do it."

His words calmed her fears. She would not stop now. She had come too far.

"I want this, Mac. I want this with you," she answered, encircling his wrist with her fingers, holding him close when he would retreat. And with her other hand pulled him down to her. "I trust you."

She meant it as a compliment, but his face clouded for a moment. Just as quickly it cleared, and she couldn't be certain if she'd really seen the uneasiness in his expression. And then there was no time to think of anything. Sensation took over. She forgot everything in the slow exploration by his hands and—dear Lord in heaven—his mouth as he loosened the ribbons of her robe, slowly easing her free of her nightgown until she lay naked beside him.

"You're absolutely exquisite," he said, his accent

thick as treacle, his gaze drinking her in. Gooseflesh pebbled her skin, but within she burned as hot as an inferno, her inner thighs damp and throbbing.

Gray watery light moved across the floor and up the walls as he cradled her in the circle of his body, a thigh slung across her legs. His long and lingering kisses smoky smooth. A heady prologue to what would come next as he left her mouth to trail his deliciously slow way down her throat. Along her collarbone. South into the valley between her breasts, where he lapped lazy circles over one breast, then another until she whimpered, combing her fingers through his hair.

With every tender caress, desire became hunger, which in turn became raw, unstoppable need. He caressed the slope of her rib cage, the flat plane of her stomach, the rounded curve of her hip on their way to the source of this greedy hunger. Brushing against her. Preparing her. And then sliding easily within her.

Clamping her hands on his shoulders, she groaned her pleasure. Arching into him, wanting him closer. Her belly clenched, the torturous heat building with the enticingly slow movements of his fingers. If she could have sunk through his skin and into his blood, she would have gladly done it.

His own breathing quickened, his eyes darkening to the color of moss, irises enlarged to fathomless black pools. He drew himself farther on top of her, pinning her against the pillows, nudging her thighs apart.

"Say my name," he whispered in a broken voice, a wild, quivering need building low across her belly. "And say you want me."

Tears pooled in her eyes. Sarah had been so right. This was what she'd been missing and never knew. This runaway gallop of feelings as she stood poised upon a precipice. Stars whirling above her. Bliss a touch and a word away.

"Mac," she murmured. "I want you." Something spurred her to add, "But I won't beg."

He laughed. "The only one pleading is me, Bianca love."

"I want you, Cormac Cúchulainn."

Gathering her against him, his kisses came hot and demanding. His hands skimming her flesh, leaving shivery anticipation in their wake. Her center throbbed wet and ready for him. Lifting her hips to meet his questing fingers, she yearned to take him inside her. To feel him locked against her. His fingers retreated, and he entered her, slowly at first as she adjusted to his size and the explosion of sensations spiraling up from their joined bodies. Her inner muscles fluttered against him as he thrust, and she moaned, arching upward to answer his rhythm. The pleasure flashing like lightning through her veins as she raced toward a crescendo that seemed just out of reach.

But he refused to answer her building need. Instead, he drew the torturous hunger out in a long, exquisite dance. Every thrust spinning her closer. Every withdrawal pulling her back.

"I'll make you forget him if you let me," he purred, nuzzling her neck, the touch of his tongue against her ear shooting jolts of fire to her belly.

She locked her legs around him, feathering kisses over his granite-hard chest. Enjoying the strength of him. His lean, muscular beauty. His powerful soldier's build.

He answered by taking a nipple in his mouth. He swirled it with his tongue until stars shot into her eyes and she feared she might shatter into a million pieces.

Friction built between them like water surging against a dam. Heaven wheeled overhead. He groaned, head thrown back, face grim as he thrust once more, and she tumbled up and up into the stars. Rolling. Spinning. Diving. The tilt of planets. The crash of suns. He was there to catch her when she landed, body spent and relaxed, chest heaving, hands drifting like a breeze over her skin. She nestled against him, his fiery heat better than the thickest quilt.

As rain pattered softly on the window and Mac's heart beat steadily beneath her ear, she tried to feel regret for what she'd done, work up a good cleansing bout of shame to temper the deeper passions still blazing through her sated body. Perhaps even ponder the possible dire consequences of her headlong actions.

Yet, as Mac pulled her against him, his arm curving around her shoulder, his lips brushing the nape of her neck, she merely smiled into the darkness, eyes closed, for no ghosts invaded her thoughts. For the first time in years, she felt truly free.

Alonzo had come. Ignoring her husband's black scowl, Renata excused herself from the knot of men and women gathered around Monsieur Gaillart, newly arrived from Paris with all the latest gossip and intrigue from the French capital.

Despite her relief and her fury, she smiled serenely

as she passed through the crush of guests. Sympathized with Madame d'Humières about her gout. Commiserated with Madame Plouvier over her husband's new mistress. Reassured Monsieur Binchois that his bald spot did not show.

Crossing the foyer, she dropped her pose of gracious hostess. She was quite alone. There were none to see her flay Alonzo alive for keeping her waiting and, worse, for causing her worry.

Throwing open the doors to her morning room, she swept in like a bitter wind. "You'd better have a very good reason for pulling me away."

He remained seated in her presence. That was her first indication something was wrong. Then she smelled him, a caustic blend of urine, filth, and vomit clinging to his clothes. And finally he met her gaze, pain written in the slump of his shoulders and the gray pallor of his handsome features. "Gods deliver us, what happened to you?"

He pulled himself to his feet. "I wasn't certain you'd come."

"This had better be important. If you haven't noticed, my house is awash with guests, and Froissart does not like to be left alone to play host to this gaggle of French chickens. He's already suspicious of you and only my magical influence is keeping him subdued. But if my control ever unravels, he'll send you back to France—in pieces."

"Flannery escaped. I've sought him everywhere without success."

"You fool!" Alonzo's head snapped back at the force of her slap. Renata lifted her hand to strike again before catching hold of her anger. Curling her fingers into a hard fist before dropping her arm back to her side with a muttered oath followed once more by "Stupid, stupid fool."

Blood welled from the corner of Alonzo's mouth where her ring had cut him, but he made no move to wipe it away. Instead, he stood before her, no hint of his thoughts passing over his face, though even that brief physical contact between them had been enough to offer her a glimpse behind his impassive gaze. His shame flitted across her mind like a wraith.

She sank onto a chair, fingers drumming restlessly. Letting the fraught, chilly silence spin out between them as she regained her composure. "Didn't the silver work?" she asked finally. "The ancient sources are very specific about the metal's effect on the loathsome creatures. It *had* to work."

"The silver did just as you said it would. He was at my mercy."

"Then what went wrong?"

Alonzo bowed his head, a flush of angry heat crawling over his face. "The Parrino bitch. She struck me from behind. By the time I came to, they'd long fled. I've searched throughout London for them but picked up no trace."

A tight-lipped smile escaped her iron control. "Like most men, Alonzo, you underestimate a woman's strength and her cunning."

His gaze cut to the fire before settling once back upon her face. "All's not lost."

"Tell me you at least learned the names of the others who murdered my father."

He winced but did not back down. "Flannery wouldn't betray his friends, though I did everything but slice him from crotch to gullet. He's strong, I'll give him that," he said with grudging approval.

She dug her nails into her palms in frustration, rage burning in her chest. "So you risked coming here simply to tell me you've no news and no prisoner?"

"No. I came to bring you this." A notched glass disk lay in the palm of Alonzo's hand.

13

Mac knelt by the fence, a nail between his lips as he fumbled for the hammer. Sweat stuck his hair to his head, and his back and shoulders ached, but between yesterday's recuperation and the pleasurable activities of this morning, he felt less like a walking corpse and more like a man on a mission. Though right now, his mission was to make repairs to the cattle shed while Jory spread a final layer of chalk and peat over the ground before the cows were brought in for the winter.

He recalled similar farming duties completed side by side with his father, the air holding a crisp chill, a skein of geese flying low over an autumn sky to glide into the lake, the encircling mountains rising blue and misty from the holding's green valley floor.

As if on cue, a woman's voice lifted in song in a traditional ballad, one he'd heard his mother sing often. But today the voice belonged to Bianca: he knew even before she emerged from the kitchen doorway, hair bundled in a kerchief, her satins and silks replaced with a simple dimity gown covered by a snowy white apron. Their eyes met and she smiled, her cheeks stained with a sunrise blush.

His chest knotted, his hand tightened around the handle of the hammer, and for one poignant, perfect moment, peace and happiness were his.

Mac had long since disappeared with Jory, and Marianne had departed for the village with the girls. Grateful for time alone to muse on all that had passed this morning, Bianca sat on an upturned milk pail beside the byre, a bull calf watching her from behind his mother's flanks, the cow's breath steaming the chilly air. Frost nipped at Bianca's snuffly nose and her toes had gone numb, but she merely pulled her shawl closer around her shoulders, plucking a stem of grass to flick between the fence boards to tempt the bullock.

"His name's Jasper."

She looked over to find the youngest Wallace son watching her with the calf's same pose of reluctant bravery. She took his age for six or seven. Slight in stature, he bore the same red hair and high cheekbones as his father, but his muddy-brown eyes and wide mouth were all Marianne.

"Jasper's a fine name," Bianca said. "Did you give it to him?"

He sidled toward her, one toe dragging in the dirt, then the next, his fingers fiddling with a piece of twine. "Mum did. She names all the animals. But she says next spring I can have a spaniel pup and name him myself. I can't decide between Idrin and Anoraeth."

"They're both very good names."

"Idrin's important and Da says he's the father of us

all, but I like Anoraeth better." One more step. One more twirl of his twine. "His stories are more exciting. There's one where he steals a magic ring from the Fey that lets him travel through time, and there's another that has him visiting the land of the dead."

"He sounds very brave."

"Father said Anoraeth was second in courage only to Lucan, Arthur's war leader, who died with the king at the final battle."

At the mention of the familiar name, Bianca's stomach clenched, her hand curling around the edge of her shawl. "Your father knows a lot of grand stories."

"He says telling the old tales makes them come alive. But he won't always tell them, even when we ask. Some nights he stops in the middle and goes out to the barn. Mum says we're not to disturb him then. Aldith does anyway, but I never do." He puffed out his chest with pride.

"Perhaps your father grows tired after telling so many stories."

"No, miss. He gets sad."

By now the boy stood beside her at the fence, his earlier shyness forgotten.

She gave an encouraging smile. "I don't think we've been properly introduced. I'm Mrs. Parrino."

"I know. I was hiding from Henry 'neath the cupboard in the kitchen when Mum and Dad were telling Jamie about you."

"Scamp."

"I didn't mean to listen, but I was afraid to come out. Henry said he wanted to toss me in the sheep's trough for going through his things. I needed a bit of chalk and Henry has so much and mine's all gone."

"So what did you overhear?"

"Not much, ma'am. Honest. Only that you and the captain are here from London and the captain and my da knew one another from the before times."

"Before times?"

"Aye, before Da was driven out by his family for marrying Mum. They made him leave and never come back. That's why we aren't given a clan mark and why Da and Jamie fight all the time."

"A mark?"

"Sammy! Where are you?"

Speak of the devil. Jamie Wallace came striding toward them, his gaze sharpening when he spotted his brother in the company of Bianca. As he approached, he straightened from his adolescent slouch and combed a hand through his wind-mussed hair. "Good day, Mrs. Parrino," he said with a dignified nod. "I hope Sammy's not being a pest."

"What's wrong with your voice, Jamie? It sounds all deep and funny-like."

Jamie shot Sammy a killer glare.

"Your brother was amusing me with tales about Anoraeth and Lucan and your parent's Romeo-and-Juliet courtship."

His face turned red, his eyes cold as ice. "Just silly children's stories, ma'am."

"No they're not, Jamie. You take that back. Da says—"

Jamie wheeled on his brother with a look that made Sam close his mouth with an audible click. "Get yourself back to the house, Sam. There's work to be done."

Sam gave Bianca one last impish grin before turning on his heel and running across the yard.

"Don't let Sammy bother you. He's just a baby," Jamie advised.

"I suppose you're too old to believe in stories."

"Hmph," he grumbled, once more all adolescent anger. "Tell my father that. He never thinks I'm old enough—for anything. But one day I'll make them listen . . ." He suddenly seemed to realize who he had spoken to, for he smacked the fence post, startling the bullock back behind his mother. "Like I said, ma'am. Those are just baby stories. Nothing for you to worry over." He glanced at the thickening clouds. "It'll rain soon. Best get inside."

He walked away, his back stiff, his head up, and Bianca smiled, seeing in this stone-faced, upright first son no hint of comfortable, contented Jory. Instead, the defiant pose and hard-edged gaze put her in mind of Mac.

She placed a hand over her stomach, her smile erased as quickly as it had bloomed.

A boy with Mac's dark features and solemn gaze. A girl with his green and gold eyes and flashing smile. The thought burst and died like the spark from a flint and steel.

Never during her marriage had she quickened with child. A fortunate lack, as it turned out. One she thought long since laid to rest. But this morning had taught her just how much of what she'd always thought had been wrong while she was hostage to painful memories of Lawrence.

As Jamie predicted, a chill rain spattered the ground and pattered against her shoulders. She lifted her shawl over her head, banishing her wild thoughts with the ease of long practice. Mac was a dream with no substance, a chimera built on imagination and fantasy.

And she'd learned long ago the folly of dreaming.

*　　　*　　　*

"It's amazing, isn't it?"

Thinking herself alone, Bianca swung around, catching back a gasp. Mac stood in the stillroom doorway, brushing rain from his hair, shaking the weather from his oilskin coat.

"When did you return?"

"Just now. Jory had some calls to make in the village, so I decided to collect and organize what we need from Adam's stores."

"This is why you came to Surrey. To do what Adam did. To break the curse."

"It is."

"Do you think you'll be able to?"

"I have to. I have no future otherwise."

Inhaling the confusion of sweet, musty scents, Bianca regarded the hundreds upon hundreds of specimens dangling from the rafters. It kept her from having to meet Mac's eyes and see the determination in his face. It also kept him from seeing the foolish tears burning on her eyelashes.

"It must have taken Adam months to gather all this," she said with a forced cheerfulness, reaching up to pull down a bunch of simple lavender, the dry sprigs crackling in her hands. Their perfume lingered, soft and grandmotherly. "But if anyone had the patience to find these plants, Adam did. I can still picture the last afternoon we spent together. He stopped by to borrow a book and stayed to help in my garden. Afterward we sat in the parlor and chatted about Dr. Smith's view on Linnaeus's order *Decandria Monogynia*."

"Now, that's friendship," Mac answered. "Or torture,

depending on your perspective. Adam once asked my opinion on Basil Somebody's account of some bishop's garden. We were under fire at the time, so my answer was short, to the point, and not repeatable."

She laughed. "Poor Adam. He *was* quite keen. His interest in botany was far more clinical than mine. I loved the beauty. He loved the science. My father was of the same mind. He could prose on about Dillenius and Sherard for hours. Guests to dinner came prepared with paper and pencil."

Arms folded over his broad chest, Mac leaned against a shelf, regarding her with an intimacy she found both alarming and compelling.

A proper lady would have been embarrassed. A decent woman would have felt ashamed or awkward. After all, she'd welcomed him into her bed. She'd risked scandal and the loss of her reputation. She'd stripped body and soul, gone against every vow she'd made, and thrown every bit of practical good sense out the window for a rippling abdomen and a pair of muscular shoulders.

But instead of seemly discomfort, anticipation cruised her skin and heat gathered in the pit of her stomach as she imagined his body beneath the heavy coat, the long, lean length of him, his sun-bronzed skin. A strange ache knotted her chest when she remembered the way he'd gentled her through the worst of her fears, his soft laughter, their whispered conversation.

"Your father and Adam sound like two of a kind," Mac said.

"They were. Perhaps it's why Adam and I grew so close. He reminded me a lot of my father and of my life before England." She bit her lip as she began to smile. "My aunt Eustacia once said my father would rather make love to a shrubbery than a real woman. My father responded by saying if his choice were between the boxwood and my aunt Eustacia, she was absolutely right."

"A botanist and a comic. You're fortunate. After my mother's death, my father became a different man. Emotionless. Distant. So wrapped in his own grief, he couldn't see his children were as miserable as he was. It was like Siobhan and I had lost both parents."

"Is that your sister?"

"Aye. She was a wee sprout when I left. No more than eleven. I shouldn't have abandoned her. If I'd been a good brother, I'd have stayed. Taken care of her."

"You did what you had to."

"Did I? Or was I selfish and thoughtless?"

"Is that why you want to return? For your sister?"

"I return because to be without clan or kin is to be completely alone. To have an enormous part of me missing. A gaping emptiness that nothing can fill. I'd do anything to be whole again."

"My father died a few months after my marriage. I know that feeling of isolation and the desire to belong."

He straightened and strode across the room, coming to a halt before her, head tilted to the side as if she were a specimen he wanted to study. Mac's gaze seemed to pierce her very thoughts. How had this man grown so familiar to her —and so dear? How had she lost her head so completely?

"The past is unchanging and the future is uncertain, Bianca," he murmured, tipping her chin upward when she sought to evade his stare, "so we need to hold tight to the few precious moments we have and hope for the best."

"*Poor Richard's Almanack*?" she teased.

He gave a short bark of laughter. "One of Mac Flannery's trite maxims. Hardly philosophical, but it's the best I can do."

Warmth rushed to her cheeks, a new strength rising from the wreckage of her old defenses. Is this what Sarah and Deane held between them? This easy camaraderie? This sharing with someone who cared? Had she ever had this with Lawrence—even in the beginning, when she'd been full of hope and innocence? She couldn't remember. Too many years and too much misery lay in between.

Fear and excitement and desire and dread boiled up in her until she felt as if she might explode. She had spent so many years building walls to keep everyone out that to step through the breach and risk everything on a crazy whim threw her into a panic, her heart drumming under her ribs, her palms damp, her mouth dry.

"What are we doing, Mac?" she asked, suddenly afraid. Of what she was feeling. Of this closeness that threatened every barricade she had used to protect herself from hurt. "This can't be. Can it?"

He cupped her chin, caressed the line of her cheek. "You should be used to impossible by now."

"Most should be among Adam's collection. Those missing, we'll have to search for in London," Jory explained.

Mac sat opposite, their heads bent over the book,

Mac with pen and paper to hand as Jory studied Adam's notes. Since Jory's return home, they'd spent the past two hours poring over pages of complicated instructions mixed with endless lists and haphazard directives. Perfect work to take his mind off Bianca and the growing tangle he'd made of their relationship.

Hold tight and hope for the best? You should be used to impossible? He sounded like a bloody book of bad proverbs. Eighteen months of enforced solitude had made him rusty; he just hadn't realized he'd become a tavern bounder with the most wretched poetic banter in history.

"Are you certain about this plant? Haymaids?" Mac asked, dragging himself back to his current problem to face the scrawl of Adam's handwriting. "I've never heard of it."

"It's alehoof, sometimes called ground ivy. See there? In the margin he's noted it alongside its Latin name." Jory withdrew a flask from his pocket, topping up the coffee Marianne had placed at his elbow. He offered it to Mac, who—understanding now how Jory downed the stuff without gagging—accepted with a nod of thanks.

"Cooks as if she'd been raised in heaven's kitchen, but her coffee is worse than the devil's spit. Like drinking burnt glue," Jory said with a sigh.

Mac took an experimental sip of his own. Burnt glue laced with whiskey wasn't much better, but he tactfully remained silent.

Fog swirled close around the house, but it carried none of the dank London stench nor did it lay thick with sulfur and smoke at the back of Mac's throat. Instead it held the damp, loamy mustiness of forests thick with oak and ash and rowan. He felt his senses stir, his instincts heighten. Tonight he would be free to venture beyond the refuge of a locked door. He would use the cover of the fog to stretch his limbs and shed the confines of his human shape for a few precious hours. Who knew when such an opportunity might come again?

Mac pulled free Adam's *krythos* from its pocket. Ran his fingers over the familiar notched edges and the smooth, glassy surface. Adam must have felt the same inexplicable need to hold on to the far-seeing disk despite its deafening silence. That discovery underscored his friend's death as standing beside his grave never had. Adam was gone. The break in their friendship would never be healed. There would be no more trading of brotherly insults or good-natured ribbing. No more whiskey-laden conversations.

"Is that a *ph* or a *qu*?" Jory turned the book one way then another. "Adam's bloody handwriting. Could the man crowd more letters to a page?"

"We're lucky he didn't cross his writing to save on paper." Mac stretched, listening to the scratching of Jory's quill and the snap of the afternoon fire. Damn, but he grew maudlin. He should be dancing for joy. He had Adam's journal. He had a potential remedy for the Fey-blood's curse. He had a beautiful woman in his bed.

He also had Fey-bloods on his trail, a body that resembled a side of pounded beef, and—oh, yes—a beautiful woman in his bed.

Bianca deserved better. She deserved someone who could love her as she ought to be loved. Someone free to offer her a life and a heart not divided into daylight and darkness, man and beast.

He rolled his neck, his shoulders, his arms. Shifted in his seat. He needed to concentrate. Focus. Pull his mind out of his breeches.

Jory shoved the book across to Mac. "What do you think: *ph* or *qu*?"

Mac scanned the page. "Maybe *bl*?"

Jory snatched the book back with a grumbling, "Damn it to hell. I've had enough of this tedium. My head's about to split in half."

"Here, now. Both of you take a break before your eyes cross." Marianne knocked the door wide with a shove of her hip, her hands filled with an enormous tray. Behind her came Bianca carrying another platter, napkins draped over her forearm.

Perfect.

He'd not thought about the blasted woman for ten complete seconds and here she was in the flesh. Flesh he now knew intimately. Flesh sweet as summer fruit and warm with life. Flesh he wanted to free of those confining clothes and devour one delicious inch at a time.

Jory leaned back with a sigh. "How do you do it, Flannery?"

"Pardon?" Mac started up in his seat. "Do what?"

"This." Jory waved a hand over the spread of paperwork. "How do you keep from going barmy sitting at a desk all day, staring at a mess of numbers?"

Mac rubbed his forehead in hopes of alleviating a growing headache. "Not much choice. The farms at Concullum are lost to me."

Instead of leaving the tea and food, Marianne joined them at the table, her sharp eyes falling upon Adam's journal with a frown. "Any luck on finding what you seek?"

"It could be months before we've riddled it out. And that's being optimistic." Mac rose to work off his frustration, offering Bianca his seat, restraining himself from touching her as she smiled at him in response. He made himself look away before he kissed her stupid. "It would take a damned brigade of scholars to make sense of Adam's notes."

As Marianne fixed plates, she and Jory exchanged a look that was all too easy to interpret; their desire to help warred with their concern over the danger Mac represented. He couldn't blame them. He'd react the same way if he had children of his own to protect. But without Jory's help, he didn't have a glacier's chance in hell to unravel Adam's journal. Even with his assistance, it was a mind-bending puzzle.

Marianne pasted on her best hostess smile, but the fear in her eyes gave her away. "Ah, well. It will come, but for now have a bite. You need some feeding up. You're thin as a fence rail and pale as a prisoner." She poured out a beer from the pitcher. "And no wonder, working in that horrid city. You need some fresh air and proper looking after."

"Leave off pestering the man," Jory scolded goodnaturedly. "Don't you have enough children of your own to worry over?"

Marianne shot her husband an imperious look. "I'm thinking Flannery would be a sight more biddable than any of my own flesh and blood. Do you know what Jamie has done now? He's—"

"*Erythronium americanum.*"

The three of them swung their attention toward Bianca, who'd bent over to read Adam's journal.

"What's that?" Jory asked.

"*Erythronium americanum*. That's the plant here."
She pointed at the page Jory had been deciphering.

He leaned in close. "*Er*. Of course."

"Do you know what it is?" Mac asked, coming back
to stand behind Bianca's chair.

She looked at him over her shoulder, eyes shining
with knowledge. "Adder's-tongue. It has a pale yellow
flower and mottled leaves. Blooms in April and May."

"Now, where on earth did you learn all that?" Jory
asked.

She grinned. "My father studied botany and our
housekeeper used to distill the juice from the leaves
and dose me with it for all sorts of complaints. Swore
it cured everything but death."

Marianne paused in the midst of lighting candles
against the lengthening afternoon shadows, her eyes
fixed on Bianca. "Are you men thinking what I'm
thinking?"

Jory flicked a cautious glance toward Mac, then
pushed pen and paper across to Bianca. "She's not a
brigade, but she might be all we need."

14

"He's gone, Jory."

Bianca looked up from studying her notes to see Marianne's pinched face, her hands fumbling with her apron.

"I've not seen him since luncheon. I've combed the farm and the house. No sign of him."

Jory's pen stilled, his features guarded but not afraid. "Did you ask the children?"

Marianne sniffed her exasperation. "Tight as poacher's traps, the lot of 'em, but I caught Sammy leaving the window ajar and Henry shoving a jacket and shirt beneath his bedcovers. He's out there, I know it."

Jory's eyes cut to the window, where dusk settled over the fields. They'd been locked inside for hours studying Adam's journal, Bianca lost in cramped, blotted pages of genera and species. Even so, she knew the moment Mac departed, and why. The window framed the darkness like a painting.

"It'll be fine," Jory said. "He knows not to pass beyond the last field and to keep free of Squire Fruddy's park."

Were they speaking of Mac? Bianca's stomach tightened.

"But what if he doesn't, Jory?" Marianne's strained voice interrupted. "Jamie's getting bolder by the minute. Last month it was for an hour or two. Now it's been most of the day. You've got to go after him. Find him and bring him home. What if"—she glanced toward Bianca with a frown—"what if someone comes upon him? One of those Fey-blood following from London? Or worse, an Ossine assassin. Jamie's still just a boy. He doesn't understand the dangers."

"He's older than I was when I first ventured out alone."

"That may be, but you did it among your own kind. You had the security of kin and clan around you. Jamie's had none of those advantages."

"I've given him what guidance I could," Jory said quietly, rising to take Marianne under the arm, guiding her firmly back toward the door.

She didn't go quietly, her voice high-pitched, threaded with anxiety. "It's not enough. He thinks it's a game. A lark."

The two stood at the door in low conversation. "You're working yourself into a state, Annie. Jamie's a clever, capable lad."

"So you won't go. You'll just let your son run wild."

He angled her farther into the passage, so that only the tip of her bobbing cap and a few shaking ringlets were visible to Bianca over the bulk of his shoulder. "Flannery's abroad," he said in a quiet voice. "He'll look after the boy."

"Flannery's not his father," Marianne huffed. "Fine if you won't go; I'll get Henry. He and I will look."

"No." Jory grabbed her by the wrist as she turned to go. "Annie, please. Let the boy be. Dragging him back will only make him worse."

She wrenched away, departing in an agitated swish of ruffled skirts.

Bianca grabbed up the closest book, diving into it as Jory returned to stir up the fire with a crackle of sparking embers. "You'll have to forgive my wife," he said. "Since that Ossine's arrival, she's been a bag of raw nerves. She's sure the clans are looking to make trouble for us."

She looked up from the page, eyes wide with innocent confusion. "I'm sorry. Did you say something?"

His lips curled into the same glitter-eyed smile she remembered from Adam's house. "I've read of your acting abilities, but never imagined I'd get a front-row viewing without traveling up to London Town."

Her features remained placidly unconcerned, slightly bewildered.

"Your book, Mrs. Parrino." Jory pointed. "It's easier read right side up."

Her own smile glimmered with the flash of a dimple as she closed her ridiculous prop with a thump of dusty pages. "I should be the one to apologize. I'd no right to listen in on a private conversation."

Jory stabbed at the embers, though the fire already danced merrily. "*Hmph*. With Marianne, an argument's not a private conversation. It's a knock-down, drag-you-over-the-coals fight. She's fearless where her bairns are concerned."

"So Jamie's gone missing?"

He stared into the flames, his gaze grown serious. "Aye, the lad's eighteen going on thirty. Thinks he knows it all."

"I remember being young and confident. Seems a lifetime ago now."

He snuck her a look over his shoulder. "I'll wager your father wanted to lock you in your room and throw away the key until you were too old for such mischief."

"He used to threaten me with the convent as a joke. Then I met my husband and the jokes stopped."

"Your father didn't approve?"

Bianca shrugged. "Like your wife, he thought I was too young and naïve. That I would end being hurt."

"But you married anyway."

"Oh, yes. Like Jamie, I knew everything. An old man's warnings counted as nothing to me. Lawrence was what I wanted, and my father had never been able to deny me anything." She shifted the notes that were spread on the table, though her attention wasn't on them. Instead, she recalled a very similar conversation with Mac. They had both paid dearly for the folly of their youths. "It must be hard seeing your children grow and know they'll soon be off on their own."

"You want to keep them wrapped in swaddling forever, but if they're to learn to stand on their own, you must nudge them from the nest and let them try their wings, even when it scares your hair white."

She looked to the night beyond the window. "And if they come to harm? Or make a mistake? How do you know if they're ready to fly free? Or if the risk is too great?"

Jory's gaze returned to the flames, the light hollowing the toughened angles and lines, making his eyes glow dull. "Life is risk. Play it too safe and it's no longer living, just surviving."

That was exactly what she'd been doing: playing it safe while life passed her by. But dare she take Jory's advice and risk more?

Dare she place her hand back in the fire?

The animals hustled and shoved each other in an attempt to shelter within the safety of the sheds and byres and away from the predator in their midst. Only the farm's bull ox stood his ground, slamming against the fence boards, small, dark eyes lit with fury. A lamp burned in the kitchen window, but no one came to the door or plucked back a curtain. They knew who walked tonight.

He skirted the barn at the edge of the orchard, picking through the gloom with little problem, his eyes catching and holding the thin, pallid light of the goddess moon as he leapt to the top of the stone wall, lifting his head to the wind, inhaling the scents of woodsmoke, cut hay, wet earth, and animal dung.

No clutter of buildings or crush of humanity. No maze of cobbled streets beneath his paws or lamplight to avoid. No fear of discovery.

As he gave himself up fully to his aspect, he shed the despair that ate at him with the destructiveness of silver, ignored the Fey-blood threat stalking him like a shadow, and reveled in the uncomplicated joy of simply being alive.

Dropping lightly to the ground beyond, he followed the wall until he came to the edge of the coppice, the trees rising up like sentinels before him. He swung his head to the east, where lights from the village danced like fireflies. A dog barked. Laughter sounded. The human world. A world forever barred to him as long as the curse held sway. A world where Bianca lay waiting, perfumed silken flesh amid tumbled sheets.

She had looked upon him as both man and beast and had not shrunk in horror. Amusement curled his lips. Well, perhaps a bit of horror at first. But over and over she had shown herself to own the courage of the clans as well as a gentle vulnerability that touched a chord deep within him: shared secrets and shared danger. It made him dare to dream when he knew he shouldn't. Not if he wanted to return to the clans. To Concullum. To his life as Imnada.

Defiantly turning his back on the tangle of conflicting desires, he plunged into the wood, the dark welcoming him like a brother.

Bianca opened the kitchen door and squinted into the dark. Behind her, a clock chimed the small hour of two in the morn. Ahead, a pinprick of light and the comforting smell of pipe smoke drew her from the house to join the man standing alone by the well, his gaze upon the belt of trees beyond the meadow.

"I'm sure Jamie will be home soon," she said, as much to reassure herself as to comfort a worried father.

"A boy on the cusp of manhood can find plenty of trouble if he's of a mind to." In the glow from his pipe, Jory's gaze flickered demon red, his craggy features hollowed and skull-like.

Gooseflesh raised the hairs on Bianca's arms. Her stomach clenched with a sudden unreasonable fright as wild fancies conjured the Frenchman's granite visage from the fog that hung heavily in the air.

"Mac's out there, too, isn't he?" she asked, rubbing warmth into her arms, drawing her heavy woolen cloak closer about her hunched shoulders.

"Aye," Jory answered around his pipe stem.

"Do you ever . . . I mean, it must be hard not to indulge when you get the chance."

"It's dangerous. Being unmarked and *emnil* makes it doubly so."

"But Mac risks it."

"He does. Once in a while, it's worth any risk to assume your aspect for pleasure rather than in shame. To become one with all the creatures the goddess touches in her travels across the heavens."

"Adam came here for the same reason, didn't he? To walk out under the night sky without fear of being discovered. To forget the curse and his exile for a little while."

"Aye. He loved the city, said the bustle kept him from thinking overmuch or too deeply on things he couldn't change, but it was a two-edged blade. Crowds can distract for a time, but they can also make a soul feel lonelier than a ghost."

The pain of Adam's death returned a hundredfold. Especially now that she realized how little she truly knew about him, how many secrets he'd held back. Surely, if she'd been a true friend she would have recognized his loneliness. But then, had Adam ever seen it reflected in her own eyes? Or had they both dissembled for so long that no stray emotions escaped their rock-hard exteriors? She certainly would never have admitted that she had not been completely and perfectly content in her whirlwind life onstage and in Society.

Not even to herself.

Not back then.

Only in the short space of days since Mac had swooped into her drawing room like an avenging angel had the quiet hours preyed on her mind with their might-have-beens and their worthless regrets. And only since leaving the bustle of her familiar London haunts had the infinite spinning heavens made her feel like the tiniest grain of sand upon a beach, vulnerable to the first in-rushing wave, easily lost to the vastness of the sea without someone's comforting hand to steady her.

She scanned the far-off line of trees once more, looking for that someone even as she chided herself for a sentimental fool who deserved any grief that grew out of such a ridiculous hope.

"A good friend, Adam was," Wallace said quietly, holding his pipe between his teeth. "To live apart from your own is a hard thing for any man, Mrs. Parrino. I'd not go back and change what happened, the Gather and their blasted rulings be damned. But time and again it's pleasant to speak of home with one who shares your memories and understands your loss."

"Did Adam ever mention me?"

Another brilliant flare as Jory inhaled. "Aye, he did."

A lump formed in her throat. "Did he count me as a true friend?"

Jory's mouth curved in a queer smile. "He did. He said the papers called you the ice queen, but that one day you'd meet someone to crack that frozen rime, and when you did, he wanted to be there to see it."

It was her turn to scan the fog-shrouded distance like a sailor's widow, tears standing upon her lashes as she sought an impossible glimpse of Mac amid the black-on-black shadows. "I don't know how he did it, but I think he has. I'm terrified and ecstatic, and oh, how I wish Adam could be here to tell me 'I told you so.'"

Threading between rowan and holly, elm and oak, Mac's heightened Imnada senses took in the panicked scramble of a rabbit as it fled before his predator's scent, the hush of an owl's wings in the trees above, and the scratch of a field mouse down among the rocks.

Breaking into a small clearing where a spring escaped a rocky outcropping, Mac knelt to drink, ears flicking back and forth, attuned to the slightest quiver in the wind, the softest footstep. He and Bianca might have shed their pursuers, but he had no doubt they were tracking them with every Fey-blood trick they could summon.

The wind shifted to the south. Immediately, Mac froze, water dripping from his muzzle, eyes slashing the dark to where a shape huddled low amid the brush.

Mac's brain prickled. His heart sped up. His chest tightened.

Imnada. One of his own kind.

Jory? Is that you?

The shape moved a fraction of an inch, but enough for Mac to catch a glimpse of the mottled reddish gray fur and black-tipped ears. A lynx. Mac's heart stopped, his breath clogging his lungs. It couldn't be, could it?

Adam! Mac's pathing sliced the air between them.

The animal rose from the cover of the brush, darting into the trees.

Wait! Adam, come back!

Mac blasted his thoughts with a cannon's force as he leapt after, his ground-eating strides carrying him through the wood, his senses attuned to the veriest sign of the lynx's passing. The snap of a broken twig. A vine moving without the aid of a breeze. The crunch and scrabble of claws upon bark.

The animal moved with the speed of one familiar with the wood, but Mac had years of tracking skills on his side. They broke from the tree line at the same moment, the lynx twenty yards to Mac's right. It veered toward the hedge guarding the Wallace orchards, barely visible against the dappled shadows.

Mac cut the corner, bringing himself within a body length, and with one great leap slammed the smaller animal to the ground, where it lay hard on its side, ribs heaving.

Even knowing it was impossible, disappointment raged. Not Adam at all, or even his ghost. The animal was too small, the ruff about its neck a dirty white, its coloring more gold-brown, whereas Adam's fur had been almost silver-gray.

Was this an Ossine enforcer sent to watch the farm? Was Jory more involved with the rebel Imnada group than he let on?

What's your business here? Who sent you?

No answer, though Mac felt the animal's fury and fear in the drumming of its heart and the pounding of its blood hot and fast beneath its skin.

Recovered fully from his first foolish hope, Mac studied the shapechanger. No more than three stone, it retained the spotted winter coat and slight build of a youngling. He opened his mind, probing deeper, hoping to discover some inner clue to this stranger's identity.

The answer shocked him. No clan mark. No holding signum imprinted upon its mind.

An *emnil* like himself. Like Jory.

Who are you?

Again no answer, though Mac felt a push back against his mind like fingers brushing lightly over his skin. A half-forgotten comment from Jory jogged a memory: Adam and Jory hailed from the same holding—Kilbanif, in the high northern mountains of Scotland, where the winds raged down from the arctic and few dared leave the deer trails to cross into the small glen where the Imnada sheltered.

The same holding.

The same clan.

The same aspect.

In the instant Mac's hold eased, the lynx scrambled to its feet and bounded away like a ghost in the night, its direction confirming what its stubborn silence had not, for it headed straight for the barn buildings and the safety of the Wallace farm.

Mac regarded the youngling with the first stirrings of a wild thought, one that was surely impossible. *Jamie Wallace? Is that you?*

15

He came to her as the sun speared the sky with the first shafts of morning light. For one terrifying moment, she knew only the weight upon the bed, the smoky, masculine scent of bare skin, a hand caressing her hip. Then a cool wind shredded her darker dreams to ragged streamers, and she recognized the callused hand and the bronzed skin's spicy smells of wood and field, and finally welcomed the gentle weight as he pressed her into the warm curve of his side.

She blinked up into his almond-shaped eyes, surprised both at the joy she found in his arrival and the ease with which she'd overcome her initial discovery of it. She sported with a legend. Bedded a myth. Possessed her very own frog prince.

If only he could be saved by a mere kiss from his fair damsel's lips.

She spooned into his furnace heat, his bare chest pressed against her back, his erect manhood nestled into her backside. "You're home," she whispered.

He pushed aside the heavy fall of her hair to nibble

the sensitive spot behind her ear, his hand draping over her hip to lie beneath her breast. "Do you know how good that sounds?"

His lips burned a path down her neck to her spine, his hands caressing and kneading her breasts until her nipples stood puckered and jolts of electricity sizzled along her nerves. Rolling her over, he lowered his mouth to suck at her bottom lip before he kissed her, his tongue swirling and retreating in a teasing give-and-take that had her answering his kisses with her own.

She closed her eyes, swimming away on the bliss of Mac's caresses, a smile lifting the corners of her mouth. It was only as a hand skimmed the inside of her thigh to nudge her legs apart that memories slashed like daggers into her consciousness. Her breath clogged her chest, cold splashing across her bare flesh, and arms that had been comforting were now confining.

Mac's voice seemed to come to her from down a long tunnel. "Open your eyes, Bianca. Look at me."

With reluctance, she did as she was told, seeing not Lawrence's ruddy face and drink-dilated pupils but Mac's familiar chiseled features, the slant of his dark brows, the aquiline nose with the bump on the bridge, the strong chin bearing a day's stubble of beard. Yet the first wriggling notes of panic remained in the turning of her stomach and the instinctual need to escape the prison of his arms.

As if sensing this, Mac rolled away, though his eyes remained fixed on hers, the calming expression in the clear green-gold depths easing her humiliation.

"I don't know what to do," she whispered, her voice raspy and choked with shame. "He lives inside me like a virus. His words. His anger."

"Look at me, Bianca," Mac said evenly. "Look at me, and we'll go from there."

She nodded. Pushing her hair back off her face, she lifted herself on an elbow, telling herself she was studying him as an artist might consider a composition. As if she would sketch him, she observed the way muscles connected to bone, how light and shadow emphasized the stark austerity of his war-hardened body. As her awkwardness dissipated, she focused on the individual scars and lingering bruises covering his torso.

As she grew bolder, she let her fingers follow the path of her gaze. He lay with his arms behind his head, a smile playing on his lips as she traced the ridge of his collarbone down over his chest, which rose and fell in quick breaths. For an instant their eyes locked and she faltered, uncertain of this new and titillating freedom.

"You're safe with me, Bianca," Mac said, his voice a deep rumbling beneath her palm. "You control what happens here now."

She nodded, accepting his reassurance, and returned to her cautious yet thorough appraisal of his body. Her hands moved to his rippled abdomen, then finally his manhood, erect amid the bush of curling hair at his groin.

He closed his eyes as she explored the velvet softness of his skin, the hardness of his member. But as she let her fingers glide from root to tip, a gasp escaped his clamped lips.

A steady building pressure throbbed against her own center as she learned his body with her hands and mouth, the shape, the scent, the movement of his muscles, and the expressions chasing each other across his face. With each stroke, his breathing grew more ragged, his pulse leaping wildly at the base of his throat. Exhilaration raced like champagne within her blood as this strange new power thrilled and excited her. Bending above him, her hair fell like a golden curtain around her as she took him in her mouth.

Mac gasped, his hips jerking off the bed. The wet, throbbing heat between her legs increased until she felt both light as down and stone heavy with arousal.

Slinging a leg across his hips, Bianca leaned forward to capture Mac's face in her hands. The rough stubble of his jaw rasped against her skin as she kissed him, a desperate craving scorching her blood. His tongue thrust deep as if he were making love to her mouth.

With a groan, she lowered herself onto him, her muscles stretching to take him completely. Another plunge, and she felt her urgency growing and spreading. No imprisoning arms held her captive, no chilling dread sat like a rock in the pit of her stomach. Just trembling spasms of building anticipation as the two of them caught and held a rhythm, the crush of their bodies causing her desire to coil tightly, release only a thrust away.

Mac's hands grabbed and held her to him as he answered her thrust for thrust, his pace steadily pushing her closer to the point of no return.

With a moaning, she felt every nerve in her body explode, amazement bursting in her mind like fireworks. Even as aftershocks vibrated through her, each one ripping her into a thousand pieces, she felt Mac climax, his body coming off the bed as he spilled his seed, sticky and hot, inside her, finally reaching to drag her down against him, the sweat of his skin salty on her lips, the taste of his mouth as intoxicating as brandy.

She lay sated and relaxed upon him, feeling the steady rhythm of his heart beneath her ear, his arms encircling her loosely. He dropped a kiss on her forehead, another on the top of her head.

"Is it always like that?" she asked, eyes closed, body still humming with frissons of delicious pleasure.

"No, *mi am'ryath*," was Mac's drowsy answer. "This is something special."

Despite a leg going numb and an itch on his left shoulder blade, Mac never moved as Bianca dozed in his arms, her hair spilling softly over his chest. Instead he reveled in the way she fit perfectly against him like a puzzle piece, in the girlish silken curls framing her ears, at the way she bit her lip as she slept, tense and on her guard even in her dreams.

He ran a hand idly up and down her ribs, his body slack with satisfaction and yet already stirring as she shifted provocatively against him.

"Oh, no," she said when his hands crept north along her inner thigh. "If we don't rise from bed now, we never shall."

"I thought you were asleep."

"No. Just thinking."

"About what?"

She shrugged, her gaze elusive, her expression giving nothing away she did not wish him to see. "I'm thinking about food. Let's go downstairs. I'll help Marianne cook breakfast while you help Jory with the feeding of the animals."

He nuzzled her neck as if he might imprint her scent upon his mind. "How completely domestic. Like an old married couple."

A chance remark, but it had an instant chilling effect, as if someone had slid a knife blade between them. Then she smiled, and while the moment passed, the memory lingered, underscoring how fractured the ground they walked upon was every minute spent together. They wouldn't speak of it, but they both felt reality closing in despite their attempts to hold it at bay.

She rolled to edge of the bed, standing to stretch her arms above her head, giving him a perfect view of her ripe, hourglass curves before she grabbed up a wrapper.

As she moved about the room, Mac lay back to watch, surrendering to the fantasy of a life in which hard decisions were unnecessary and Bianca never left his side.

The vision came as clear to him as the sunlight spilling over the chamber floor, turning her hair white-gold, her skin pink. A farm like this one where weeks turned into seasons and then into years in perfect tranquillity: a warm, lighted kitchen to come home to, bodies twined together within a feather-soft bed at night, children banging up and down the passages in a joyful noise.

His gaze fell to the taut, creamy satin of her stomach.

Would they be dark like him or inherit the golden curls of their mother? Green-eyed or blue? Right-handed or left? He caught back a breath as this morning's daydreams jogged loose last night's revelation.

Would they be Imnada or human?

For that question, he already had an answer, although it turned all he thought he knew on its head. But then, what belief of his hadn't been shaken to the core over the last weeks? If someone approached him claiming to be the goddess moon personified, he would not bat an eye.

"Mac?" Bianca turned from bundling her hair up in a twist of pins and combs. "Is something wrong?"

"Jamie's Imnada."

Her brow furrowed and her eyes narrowed before clearing in dawning comprehension. "That makes sense."

"It does?"

"Last night I thought Jory and Marianne were concerned he'd gone to drink with his chums or to set a few traps on the squire's lands, but if he was . . . out there . . . no wonder they worried."

Mac pushed himself up against the headboard, rubbing a hand over his chin as he thought. "But how? Jamie Wallace is a half-breed. Part human. Unmarked. According to the teachings, he shouldn't be able to shift. Hell, he shouldn't even exist."

Bianca threw him a swift glance, her eyes dancing with amusement. "Just what every adolescent wishes to hear. Will you tell him he's a freak or shall I?"

Mac's mouth hardened into a straight line, his brain afire with this new twist. "I'll say naught to Jamie, but I've got some questions for his father."

Reluctantly, he rose from the warmth of their shared bed to bend over the washbasin, splashing water on his face. Yet, it wasn't the sudden cold that sent a shiver up his spine but the brush of fingers across his upper back.

"Does it ever pain you?" Bianca asked softly.

He looked over his shoulder, only able to see the very edge of the scar, the flesh stretched and ugly. "Seldom now, though for weeks after I thought I might die. Months more that I wished to."

"Was it the war? Waterloo? I heard the fighting was fierce there and the casualties tremendous."

"Its origins lay on the battlefield, but no. The Ossine removed my clan mark as part of my exile."

"They burned it off you?"

"It is the law." Mac closed his eyes and saw the cold-eyed emotionless stares of the enforcers as they approached where he stood shackled within the Gather's circle. He recalled his futile struggles against the silver chains pinning him down and the stink of his flesh, the pain like being thrust into a furnace as the visible symbol of his belonging was charred away. Only the stripping away of his signum, the mental bonds connecting him to the clans, had been more traumatic. "Burning is the only way to obliterate the mark completely. The fortunate ones die from their wounds within days."

A small, hard gasp escaped her lips, her fingers dropping away. "That's barbaric. Inhuman."

He turned to cup her face, using his thumb to trace the rounded curve of her cheek. "But we're not human, *mi am'ryath*. Not completely."

Her eyes flickered and she would have drawn away, but Mac caught her wrist. "We don't just wear the skins of animals, Bianca. We possess their spirits, their very souls." He felt her breath against his chest, smelled the citrus spice of her skin, knew when her tension eased into something different. Something he began to cherish despite himself. "We will destroy any threat to our survival without a qualm. But we will also fight to the death to protect those we love."

Jory's eyes, dark and angry as storm clouds, met Mac's. "They've lied to us for countless ages, Flannery. We aren't forced to marry within the clans or risk extinction. My children inherited my gifts along with my blood. And yet, they'll never bear a clan mark nor be entered into the Ossine's scrolls. They'll forever be considered rogue. A target for any zealous enforcer."

Rubbing a hand over the back of his neck, Mac paced off the perimeter of the stillroom. "Why would the Gather do that? Why, when our numbers are dwindling, would they cut off our chance to grow strong again?"

"Who can say? All I know is my son becomes more bitter and reckless with every passing year. I've been able to control him so far, but the day is coming when he'll force a confrontation with the Imnada. I know it. Marianne knows it. It's our greatest fear."

"That's why you sent the rebel clansman from your holding away. That's why Marianne nearly took my head off with her cleaver."

Jory gave a tired shrug. "Perhaps I did wrong by encouraging the children. Recounting the legends and schooling them in the laws and teachings. Perhaps it was my way of holding on to what I'd lost. Of making sure I didn't forget."

"You couldn't know where it would lead."

"No, but it's raised the younglings with a false hope. Jamie resents this exile. He views the Gather elders and the Ossine as his enemies. The rebels seek to take advantage of that and recruit him to their side, but I refuse to allow my son to be caught up in a war that isn't his."

Mac slid into a chair. "Yet, if he carries your blood and your powers, he should be recognized. Given the mark and brought into the clan. It *is* his war."

"A war that can't be won."

"Jory, listen—"

"No. You listen, Mac. I've told you about the younglings' powers. That's where I end it. You can stay until St. Leger contacts you, and I'll help with Adam's journal, but don't push my hospitality or my patience."

"If that's your wish."

"It's my order, and you're a soldier," Jory answered. "You should know how to take orders."

"I'm very good at taking orders." Mac smiled. "But I'm even better at waging war."

He'd known he shouldn't be there even as he'd cast off his clothes and fallen into bed beside her. His brain whirred with the reasons the two of them were a very bad idea. And yet, after a day spent studying Adam's journal, he'd needed the comfort of her body and the reassurance of her quiet words.

He'd found both.

Now, she lay enticingly in his arms, her scent in every ragged breath he took. He glanced at the clock, though it was unnecessary. He knew what time it was. His body burned with it.

He brushed aside her hair to lay a kiss behind her ear, drawing in a last lungful of the sweet citrus smell of her skin before he rolled out of bed.

"Mac?" she said, still half-asleep as her hand smoothed over the depression in the bed where he'd just been.

"I have to go."

She stretched, every sensual curve and dimpled hollow a source of torturous arousal. Thank the Mother of All for the chill of the bedchamber. At least he wouldn't completely embarrass himself.

"Stay. Your secret is mine," she said. "You've nothing to hide anymore."

"Don't I?" He pulled on his breeches and dragged a shirt over his head, feeling the sun drop in the sky with every beat of his heart. "To shift in freedom is a gift and a joy. To be forced to assume my aspect is best done in solitude. I don't want you to see me like that, Bianca."

"Mac—"

"Not now. Not ever." The sun edged behind the trees, the light gray and flat, the temperature dropping. He pulled on his boots. "This is my life, Bianca. This is how it must be."

"I hate what the curse has done to you."

He leaned over to offer her one last kiss. "So do I."

The household settled for the night, Bianca lay in bed awake and listening, every sense tuned to the world beyond the walls of her bedchamber.

Would it always be like this if she stayed with Mac? Every night lived alone in neck-tightening suspense. Every day a constant counting of hours until the curse took hold once more. A life severed in two, with both halves blighted by dark magic.

There would be nothing for the two of them as long as the curse held sway. He had not said as much, but it was there in the sorrow caught within his eyes, in the gentle distance he maintained between them despite their passion.

If only he would agree to let her travel to London for assistance from her contacts there. Among the botanists, herbalists, and apothecaries, surely one of them would be able to help. Mac worried about her safety, but what other option did they have?

Dratted, irritating, stubborn man. After all that had happened, did he still believe her incapable of taking care of herself?

She rolled over, punching her pillow into shape, and froze, heart in her throat.

Had she just heard a gunshot?

She strained to listen over the drumming of her heart.

There it was again, distant but unmistakable. Was it Squire Fruddy's gamekeeper after poachers? Or did they hunt larger, more otherworldly game?

She sprang out of bed, wrapping a dressing gown around her against the chill. Peeled back the curtain to stare out into the night, casting prayers to any deity who would listen.

Please, don't let it be Mac. Please let him be safe. Please let him come home.

Nothing moved, not even a breeze to stir the distant line of trees. She opened the casement a crack. A blast of cold air hit her face, chilling the sweat that lay clammy over her back. She waited, each minute ticked off in deep, steady breaths. She paced the perimeter of her rug. Counted to one hundred. Then did it again.

Finally, she latched the window and let the curtain drop. Another few minutes and she lay back down in bed to stare at the ceiling.

But the fear didn't leave her.

As long as the curse remained, it never would.

Could she live with that?

Would Mac give her the choice?

16

The sun gilded the tops of the trees and threw long finger-like shadows out over the meadow as Mac and Bianca walked the autumn woods, enjoying the last moments alone before night and the curse parted them. Already his skin prickled, darkness crowding his vision as his tendons knotted and muscles burned. Pausing to catch his stolen breath, he squeezed his eyes shut and clamped his jaw tightly. "Bloody hell."

A hand rested lightly upon his arm. "Should we return to the house?"

He opened his eyes. Apprehension dimmed Bianca's summer clear gaze, her face pale but composed.

With a determined shake of his head, he straightened, taking her in his arms. "There's time yet. And I would spend what I have holding you."

She lifted a hand to push his hair from his brow, pressed a kiss upon his lips. "Don't you mean arguing with me?"

"There's no argument. You're not going."

She pulled out of his embrace, a subtle movement

that didn't feel like the cold shoulder but had definite
icy tones about it. Perhaps forbidding her was the
wrong way to end the discussion, but they'd been over
the same furrow so many times in the past weeks, and
he'd run out of tactful ways of saying that over his dead
body would she travel alone to London in search of
the last plant listed in Adam's notes.

Aquameniustis.

He never thought he could hate a word, but just
saying each irritating syllable made him grit his teeth
to keep the oaths from flying. Jory hadn't recognized
the name. Nor had Bianca. Neither had the local
apothecaries they'd asked, the farmers they'd con-
ferred with. Not even an old gypsy they'd met on the
side of the road outside the farm gates who swore her
herbal lore came straight from the queen of the faeries
herself. An idle boast, as it turned out.

None had heard of the blasted plant.

But there it remained, clear as day in Adam's journal. Or at least, as clear as any of the writing in Adam's
journal was. The pages devoted to his last and greatest
research project were also the messiest, as if he'd written them in haste or as inspiration struck, his mind
speeding along, his hand desperate to keep up.

The ink was smudged in places, blotted in others,
the words running together so that individual letters
were barely discernible, and only after hours of patient
work did they manage to decipher the bits they had
succeeded in recovering.

"So you're simply giving up?" Bianca asked, bending to grab up a stick, which she swung against the tall
meadow grass as if decapitating marauders.

"Of course not."

She gave a particularly nasty swipe of her stick, snapping its tip against a tree. "Mac, we've done as much as we can without outside assistance. We need to consult experts, scholars whose botanical knowledge isn't ten years out of date and whose research techniques aren't rusty as an old rake."

"Agreed."

"Then you agree that traveling to London makes sense. The Horticultural Society is there. Kew Gardens. The Royal Society. Someone's bound to recognize Adam's mystery plant."

"Agreed again."

"Then I'll leave in the morning. The mail coach comes through on its way from Brighton every day."

"*We'll* leave in the morning," he amended.

She spun around, her stick coming perilously close to his head. "You can't go."

"No, what I can't do is allow you to jaunt off to London by yourself. It's not safe."

She seemed to consider this for a moment. "Easily solved: I have friends I can stay with."

"If by friends you mean Lord Deane, the answer is no again. Even if he's not involved in Adam's murder, what could you possibly tell him that won't raise more questions than it answers?"

"I'm an actress. Dissembling is my bread and butter. I'll think of a plausible explanation." She laid her hand on her hip, eyes sparking. "You know it makes sense. You just don't want to admit it. It's the perfect solution. No one could get to me behind the walls of Deane House."

"But you won't *be* behind the walls of Deane House," he pointed out rationally. "You'll be traipsing about London, looking for a damned plant and landing in who knows what kinds of danger. No, Bianca. We go to London together or we find another way."

"Fine." She chucked her stick away. "Suit yourself, but you know I always get my way in the end."

He grabbed her hand, refusing to relinquish it. Instead, he pulled her close, tipping her chin to his. "So you keep informing me."

He lowered his mouth to hers, letting the fullness of her lips, the tease of her tongue, and the heat of her body ease his frustration even as new urges throbbed painfully. He nuzzled the column of her throat as he cupped her breasts, rubbing a thumb over her taut nipples. She moaned, leaning into his touch, sparking a wild arousal along his limbs to rival the curse's fire.

Despite what the papers said, Bianca Parrino was no ice queen. Instead, she resembled a diamond. A stone of a million facets. Ever changing. Always alight with a brilliance undimmed by circumstance. It's what he admired about her. What he began to adore.

"I never knew . . . it was never . . ." she murmured between soft gasps.

"Don't think about him, Bianca. Don't allow his ghost to hold you captive." He sucked in a sharp breath as her hand burrowed under his jacket to untuck his shirt.

His heart thundered, his breathing came quick and shuddering with every slow caress of her fingertips. He would take Bianca here. He would defy the curse and make love to her upon a soft blanket of bracken beneath a scarlet and orange sky, the scents of earth and wind mingling with the spicy notes of her perfume. But even as he loosened her gown to taste her flesh—even as her fingers glided over his skin, leaving a ripple of yearning in its wake, his member pulsing with raw need—another sensation sang like steel over the surface of his mind or like a woman's nails across his back. A curving, curling, tentative touch, but one he recognized.

His *krythos* was lost no longer.

He reached out to understand the intruder seeking entry to his thoughts, using all his skills to follow the mental connection back to its origins and the mysterious woman at its heart. The *krythos* sang to him, drawing him further and deeper into the current until on the very edge of his mind hovered an image, a glimpse of his enemy. He sought to imprint her upon his memory when the bond between them shattered, an explosion ripping through his skull like shrapnel, dropping him to his knees, pulling him into a fetal ball, his throat raspy with his own screams.

Blood dripped from the cut on her cheek to fall upon the virginal white of her gown, a broken glass edge all that was left of the Imnada's far-seeing disk.

Renata closed her fist around the jagged shard, the pain acting like a drug on her flooded senses, the void's spiraling smoke and cinders still dancing across her vision. "He was there, Alonzo. I felt his power. His mind. It roared in my head like a raging beast."

Alonzo's eyes gleamed. "Did you discover where he hides?"

"No, but he lives and he lusts. I felt his desire as my own. So sharp, it dampens my loins and fires my need."

Hunger narrowed Alonzo's dark gaze. A fierce, brutal

desire amplified by the surrounding mirrors and her own stolen yearning. And this time she did not deny him.

It was only as Alonzo plowed her like a spring field that she sensed someone watching their joining. A brush of voyeuristic prurience tempered with confusion and then rage. She turned her head on the pillow in time to spot Émile standing dumbly within the doorway, eyes bulging, face three shades of scarlet.

A tiny hitch in her plans, but one she had long prepared for. Playing to her audience, she lifted her hips to take Alonzo more deeply as he thrust himself inside her. Parted her lips in a cruel serpent's smile. "Welcome home, husband. Or should I say farewell?"

With a shift of his arms and a twist of his pelvis that had Renata pinned safely beneath him, Alonzo released a powerful blast of mage energy.

Émile Froissart, with his greasy bourgeois body and his peasant's manners, never knew what hit him.

Mac lay upon the grass, staring up at Bianca, her eyes shining with unshed tears, her hand gripping his sleeve as he tried to sit up.

"My *krythos*," he croaked, his throat scraped raw. "The Fey-blood has it in her possession. For a heartbeat, I sensed the touch of her mind upon my own."

The temperature dropped as the sun sank lower toward the horizon. His body cramped, his nerves aflame with the curse's blue fire. Every breath came laced with glass. Every movement pushed the needling, searing agony closer to his heart.

"Let me help you," Bianca urged. "If you lean on me, we can get you back to the house. Jory can—"

"Leave," he answered. "Leave now and don't turn around. Not for any reason."

"I can't. What if she returns? What if something happens?" She grabbed him under the arm in an effort to hoist him up. "It's a short walk. We can make it."

He clamped his jaw against a scream, his weight too much for her as he slithered back to the ground. "Please, Bianca. If you . . . if you care for me, just go."

"I'm not going anywhere."

"Bianca, I . . ."

Too late.

Swallowed by the curve of the earth, the sun's golden edge disappeared, the curse boiling up through him like lava, nerves flayed raw. With a roar of fury and despair, he stripped off his clothes even as the flames consumed him in a blue-white inferno. He toppled back to the turf as lightning arced through him, corrupting his body, spearing his brain.

True to her word, she did not leave. Blind to all but the river of flame, still he sensed her presence like a rock upon which he might anchor himself. An oasis of calm where all else was a fiery whirlwind.

"'By night I sought him whom my soul loveth: I sought him, but I found him not,'" she quoted as night overtook them both.

As oblivion claimed him, he answered her, his lips curled back over extended fangs, a rumble deep in his pounding chest. *My mistress with a monster is in love.*

Aquameniustis. The last plant on the list. Underlined twice. But nothing else. No other clue to its identity. Was this its common name? A variant? Did it bloom in the spring or fall? Was it found in England? Abroad? Bianca had never heard of it, and none of the references in her encyclopedias and compendiums yielded any clues.

Papers strewn around her, notes written and crossed through and written again, she toiled long into the night. Using context and her own botanical knowledge, she worked around the worst of the handwriting and ink splotches, but even that wasn't enough in some instances. Still, she labored on. A cup of tea and a bowl of stew had been her supper. A worried look and a whispered discussion had been her cue to slip free of the house and come here to Adam's stillroom.

She found most of the ingredients listed amid the abandoned jars and discarded boxes, the shelves of dried plants and the bundled aromatic herbals hanging from the ceiling. These she placed in a special compartmented container, each separated and marked.

The methodical, exacting work was just what she needed to pull her mind out of the worn rut of her endless spinning thoughts, the frightening images of Mac's transformation.

Engulfed in a coil of blue fire, his body lost within a vortex that wove and spun and turned upon itself. A creature emerging like a butterfly from a caterpillar's cocoon. A panther, sleek and lean and dangerous in its beauty. A panther that bore the body and soul of the man she loved.

Her stomach shriveled into a hard little knot, and she fought back the urge to bang her head against the desk. What had happened to the haughty, remote, self-reliant Bianca? The one who held herself above, aloof, and apart? The one who had trained herself *not* to care? The one who did not go around telling men she loved them?

She bent over until her forehead rested on the desk. She didn't know. Cared less. Like a moth drawn to the flame, she wanted Mac, and to hell with being burned.

She rubbed her hands over her face, willing her exhaustion and her embarrassment away. Rolled her shoulders and shifted on her seat to bring some feeling back to her numb posterior before refocusing her gaze on the dancing squiggles in front of her itching eyes. She would concentrate on her immediate problems: the notes and the draught Mac would use to break the curse. The rest would fall as it would with or without her fretting.

Unfortunately, her immediate problem brought her right back to the dratted *Aquameniustis* and Mac's stubborn refusal to let her pursue answers in London without him tagging along like a honking great bull's-eye for the Fey-bloods to aim at. Tonight only underscored the tightening circle, the growing danger. There had been no word from St. Leger, and while Mac said nothing about the man's continued silence, she knew he worried. Had the Fey-bloods discovered and eliminated him? Had he been caught by an Ossine enforcer?

The soldier in Mac chafed at the slow, deliberate unfolding of Adam's notes, the methodical precision, the careful trial and error. She felt it in the mounting tension running like a fast current just beneath his skin, in the nights she entered his room to find him gone, hunting beneath the crescent moon. In the mornings when he took her with a fierce hunger, his wild passion pulling her along until she matched his unchecked need with her own.

Much longer, and she knew he would do something foolish, if only because he saw no other way. Wasn't a cornered animal the most likely to lash out?

But where he found the slow process of the scientist irritating, she enjoyed it. Her mind sharpened and cleared with every clue she followed and every hypothesis she put to the test. This she could do. This she could offer him—his life in return for hers. A life free of the haunting pains left by her marriage, wounds finally cleansed of so many years of hopeless bitterness.

The acrid smell of pipe smoke made her raise her head from her notebooks to see Jory, weary and careworn, at the threshold of the stillroom.

"He's slipped out again?" she asked.

"Aye. Marianne is up and pacing, and I'll not get a wink if I don't go looking for him."

"Mac will keep Jamie safe."

"Is that what you think? Mac brings the danger. He doesn't solve it."

She stiffened in her chair, chin lifted in anger. "That's not fair. Mac's counting on you. How can you turn your back on him when he needs you most?"

"Simple," Jory answered. "I've a wife and children to worry over. They come before anyone else. I've allowed you to stay, I've assisted as I could, but things grow complicated. Damn it, you've Fey bloods after you. What if they track you here?"

"What if they do? Or what if that Ossine fellow who threatened you returns? Who'll stand with you against them? Jamie? The younger children? It's as your wife said: you've no clan or kin to help you now."

"And you think Flannery will be able to stand up to them? Alone?"

"Not alone. There are others. St. Leger. De Coursy. All four of you are Imnada and all four of you share a similar exile." Warming to her argument, she felt the blood tingle through her body as she spoke, the words flowing like wine, her tone imposing but not arrogant, as if she stood upon the stage before a rapt audience. "They would stand with you. They would be clan and kin and family to you if you let them."

Jory's shoulders hunched, his bright eyes dimmed. "You're quite an orator, Mrs. Parrino."

"It's my profession, Mr. Wallace."

He shook his head, his voice a growl of frustration. "For eighteen years I've managed to live without interference or trouble. I've married, raised children, worked this farm. None questioned who I was or where I came from. Now, in less than a year, all of it hangs in the balance."

"No," she answered sharply, "for eighteen years, you hid away, pretending to be something you weren't. I know all about hiding the truth behind a mask. And, like you, I needed Adam to remind me who I was. And Mac to force me to remember. I'll not go back to those dark and lonely days. Will you?"

17

―――

"Are you certain you want to do this?" Marianne asked, offering Bianca a cup of coffee, which she gracefully declined. "Surely, the captain will have a few choice words when he discovers you've gone."

"I'd wager more than a few, but that's beside the point."

A dim morning sun barely speared the parlor windows; the farmyard beyond wrapped in fingers of trailing mist. It had still been dark when Bianca dragged herself out of the warm nest of her quilts to wash and dress. Tiptoeing down the stairs into the kitchen, she'd been met by Marianne in wrapper and slippers, hair still in rags, face bearing the sagging smudges of someone who'd been pulled from her bed too early.

Bianca sympathized.

She'd been up all night formulating her plan to leave Bear Green for London. Only when she woke with a page of notes on the tannins associated with *Anthemis nobilis* stuck to her ink-smeared cheek had she decided she'd better retire for a few hours' sleep. Waking before dawn, she reviewed her decision inch by inch, looking for a way that did not include going behind Mac's back, but always came to the same conclusion.

"He may be furious, but he'll thank me for it in the end," Bianca explained.

Marianne cast her the doubtful look of a woman long familiar with the male mind. "I don't know about that. Men get ill-tempered when women claim they act for their menfolk's good. They take it as an insult to their masculine privilege."

Marianne's words of caution took root for a moment, giving Bianca pause. "Be that as it may, to London I go. Stall Mac as long as you can. Tell him I've gone into the village with the girls or I'm walking with Sammy over the hill toward Culler's Down. Anything, so long as he doesn't ask questions."

Marianne folded her arms over her chest. "And when you don't come back? What then?"

"By the time he realizes what's happened, it'll be too late in the day for him to travel."

Marianne sniffed. "Either that or he'll go haring off after you, come shift or no, and risk being set upon by hounds or a poacher. Or shot at by some lunatic who thinks he's seeing monsters."

The idea slid cold and shivery up Bianca's spine, but she shook it off, clasping her valise with a pronounced snap. "If I worry about every little thing that could go wrong, I'll never leave."

"You must care very much for the man to do this for him."

"That's a discreet way of explaining it."

"Well, I don't care how he brangles when he finds out: I know Flannery will be happy when that draught is complete. To be declared *emnil* is a living death for an Imnada of the clans. They walk and they breathe but they're never quite the same afterward. It's as if a part of them has been cut away. Even after almost twenty years, Jory has days when he shuts himself away to brood on things best left in the past."

"I understand that sort of pain. To be cut off from the best parts of yourself. To be completely alone in the world and unable to rely on anyone and trust no one."

"But now with you and the captain having an understanding, that's all changed. He'll build a life outside of the clans as Jory has."

But would he? Or would his desire to return home trump his desire for her? And even if he chose to remain in London, what sort of future would there be if the Fey-bloods declared a new war on the Imnada—a Fey-blood like Sebastian?

Was she mad to risk the earl's help? Was he the killer St. Leger assumed he was? And would Mac believe she'd betrayed him by turning to Seb for help?

Was she causing more problems than she was solving?

Bianca fought off these pointless thoughts before they ran away with her. She'd have hours on the road to dwell on the potential for catastrophe. No sense in giving up before she even made the attempt.

A carter's wagon waited in the farmyard, a gruff-looking chap handling the ribbons. With a leering stare and a smile showing more gaps than teeth, he offered his hand, hauling Bianca up beside him on the bench.

"I'll be back as soon as I can."

Marianne offered her hand a reassuring squeeze. "I hope so, child. I surely hope so."

Mac woke late, stretching to relieve a lingering ache in his shoulder, new stiffness in his back and legs. His temples still pounded from the destruction of his *krythos,* his brain was muzzy, and he felt a painful throbbing against his skull.

For the first time, he'd sensed his real enemy. Not the Frenchman but the woman who controlled him. She'd been elusive, a subtle but potent twining of instinctual magic and honed skill. Obviously a powerful Fey-blood, for none but one gifted in the mage arts would have been able to tap into the *krythos's* energy long enough to make a connection. Had she known what such a mental link offered him? For although she had invaded his mind, he been given a glimpse of her as well.

He'd smelled her heavy musky-sweet perfume, seen her gold-flecked brown eyes and black hair, and sensed the hatred that lay like a blight upon her soul.

Ignoring the tipping and heaving of his bedchamber floor, he rose to splash cold water on his face, rake a hand through his disheveled hair, and drag on his clothes. A glance out his dormer revealed a sun hanging well above the barn roofs. He'd not just slept in: he'd slept half the day away.

Downstairs, the kitchen smelled of yeast and lemons and nutmeg and fig. Marianne's hands were white as she sifted and measured flour and shoveled great loaves into the oven. At the table, copper-haired Aldith rolled dough while the small, auburn-haired Hetty shaped scraps into tiny animals.

Mac's eyes traveled over them, looking for some sign of their latent abilities. Too young yet for complete manifestation, but still, a casual touch of his mind on theirs revealed the girls' future power. It danced and sparkled on the surface of their thoughts like stars scattered over an endless sky.

"You've missed breakfast and lunch, but there's jam and biscuits if you're hungry," Marianne offered, wiping her forehead with the back of her hand.

Mac grabbed a biscuit from a tray, smearing a glob of strawberry jam on one flaky half. Heaven. "Is Bianca in the stillroom?"

Something passed over Marianne's face, and she jerked her head toward the door. "Best speak with Jory."

He nodded, a queer, uncomfortable feeling invading his stomach as he choked down the rest of the biscuit. "I'll do that."

In the yard, all hands had been gathered. Sammy and Henry rushed back and forth between sheds and byre while Jory worked with Jamie, man and boy bearing the same wide stance and capable, quick movements. Both scowling black as thunderheads.

As Mac crossed the farmyard, he studied the eldest of the Wallace younglings. His questions grew with his frustration. How could the Ossine not realize that the goddess's powers passed with their blood? And if they did know, why had they kept it secret? Did the Gather elders possess this knowledge? Was the Duke of Morieux a party to the deception? Had Gray de Coursy's grandfather lied to them all? Had age-old prejudices won out over a possible new future for the failing clans?

Jory looked up, eyes narrowing as Mac approached. He leaned his rake against the fence and jerked his head toward his son with enough meaning the boy nodded before grabbing up his tools. As Jamie passed Mac, the youth's gaze slid over him with a mixture of admiration and antagonism.

Mac's discomfort grew.

"Where's Bianca?" he asked.

Jory raked a hand through his hair, the shaggy red mane already dark with sweat, his forehead glistening. "Gone."

Mac's stomach fell into his boots. "Tell me everything."

Jory peered meaningfully over Mac's shoulder, the interested gazes of the children drilling into his back.

"Inside. Now," Mac snarled.

Within the cold gloom of the stillroom, his gaze took in the neat stacks of paper, the box filled and labeled with samples from the bunches and drawers, the journal closed and bookmarked with that same ragged piece of ancient coat lining. Then his vision narrowed to the single piece of stationary held down by a chunk of quartz.

He picked up the stone and scanned the first few lines on the sheet of paper, barely noting the fact that she'd left all in readiness for him.

"She departed just after sun up," Jory explained. "A carter was hauling a load into the village. From there she was going to catch the mail for London." He pulled a watch from his vest. "Be there in an hour or two if the roads are fast."

"And you let her leave? You never once tried to stop her?"

"She's a woman grown, Flannery. And a woman who knows her own mind." Jory regarded him with a steady eye and a grim set to his jaw.

"A woman who'll get herself killed if she's not careful."

"She said she had friends she could stay with while she hunted down that last plant. Said she'd be safe there."

Friends.

He closed his eyes on a string of hair-curling profanity.

The goddess help them all. She'd run to Lord Deane.

"Take me with you."

Mac didn't even bother looking up from shoving the last of his belongings into his haversack. Not difficult. He'd nothing beyond a change of clothes, Adam's journal, Bianca's letter. "No."

"That's unfair. Just because you're angry at my da is no reason to take it out on me."

Mac straightened to face the young man who stood within the doorway, alive with excitement and determination, his mouth a white-lipped line in his tanned face.

"I'm not taking my anger out on you," Mac answered reasonably. "The last thing I'll do to repay your father's hospitality is to steal away his son."

"You're not stealing if I go willingly," Jamie argued. "I want to leave. I have to get away from this farm. It's the only way I'll find out the truth."

"What truth?"

"The truth about who I am. Where I come from."

"You're James Wallace of Line Farm, Surrey."

"That's not what I meant, and you know it better than anyone. I've heard you and Da talking. You want to return to the clans as much as I want to see them for myself. You can take me with you when you go back. They'll listen to you."

Mac gave a scornful bark of laughter. "If you've been eavesdropping, then you also heard I'm *emnil,* an outcast like your father. They'd kill us both on sight. Stay here and you grow to a ripe old age. Attempt to breach the Palings and contact the clans, and you'll be dead in a week."

His jaw squared, Jamie shot a hot, dangerous glare at Mac. "I'm eighteen. I don't need you or my father to give permission. I can do it on my own."

"You don't need our permission, but you sure as hell need our help. The holdings are well hidden behind the shielding mists of the Palings. If you lose yourself there with no guide, you'll be wandering for months. And even if by some miracle you found your way through the clan's defenses, they'd have your guts for garters before you took one step onto holding lands."

Jamie slouched in the window embrasure, arms folded belligerently over his chest. "If you won't take me, there are others I can contact. They'll listen."

They. Those rebel Imnada Jory had mentioned. A faction being hunted by Ossine enforcers. A group who would welcome Jamie Wallace and then use him for their own ends. Mac might not agree with Jory's decision to deny Jamie any hope of a reconciliation with the clans, but he understood the love that drove Jory's choice.

"That may sound like the answer, but it can only lead to trouble," Mac answered. "Do you want the enforcers to return for your father? Or your brothers and sisters? They won't spare them if they believe a threat to the clans exist."

"And that threat is me?"

"If you force the issue, yes." Mac took a steadying breath. He had no time to argue with the boy, but he also couldn't leave the situation as it was. "Be patient. If the rebels are strengthening, as your father thinks, you may get your wish. But if you push, it could all explode in your face."

Jamie stood spear-straight, gaze crackling. Lips pulled back to reveal pearl-white fangs. "I knew you'd be like Da. 'Be patient.' 'Be cautious.' I'm tired of waiting. I'm Imnada whether the clans acknowledge me or not."

Storming out of the room, he slammed the door behind him, his tread loud on the stairs before another door slammed, followed by Marianne's plaintive call to her son—a sorrowful end to their conversation.

Mac knew he'd handled their talk all wrong. He should have listened, tried to explain Jory's concerns. Would Jamie have understood? It was hard to say. The boy was a hothead, impatient and angry at the world. Unwilling to heed the advice of those older and wiser. Those who understood the dangers and hoped to keep him from falling prey to them.

And he was the spitting image of Mac at eighteen. Hell, maybe even now at twenty-eight.

Hoisting his haversack onto his shoulder, he followed Jamie's headlong flight at a more sedate pace. Marianne stood at the kitchen window, a hand holding back the curtain, her back rigid as a bayonet, hands shaking.

"Give him a few hours alone and he'll calm down," Mac suggested.

She turned, regarding him with resignation, eyes bright with unshed tears. "I knew it would come to this in the end. If he seeks them out, they'll kill him."

Again Mac was struck by the similarities between Jamie and himself. The oppressive feelings of being trapped. The certainty that anywhere must be better than home. And the burning desire to stand on one's own out in the wider world. "Should I go talk to him? Maybe I can—"

"You've done enough." Jory had come in through the front and was slapping his gloves against his thigh. "The boy will be all right as soon as you've gone and things get back to normal."

"Jory, perhaps it would do some good," Marianne said hopefully, a hand on his shoulder.

He shook her off with a frown. "I said you're free to go, Flannery. If you don't get a move on, it'll be dark soon."

With nothing left to say, Mac nodded his assent.

"I've a horse already saddled," Jory said as they walked together out into the yard, where a dark bay stood at the rail. He took the horse's reins, emotions chasing each other across his haggard face, too rapid for Mac to catch any hint of his thoughts. Then he straightened, his golden-brown gaze defiant. "If you can't find Bianca and need a refuge, come back here. We'll see you safe."

Stunned, Mac shook his head. "I don't understand."

"You're one of the clans," Jory answered, his words slow and deliberate, as if he'd given them much thought. "As am I, whether we're acknowledged or not. You're welcome here. If the time comes when we must fight, we'll fight together."

Mac swung up into the saddle, gathering the reins. "If you don't hear from me by tomorrow night, send word to St. Leger."

Jory's eyes flashed with understanding. "Perhaps you've thrown the Fey-blood from the scent. Perhaps the threat is past."

"I've a feeling this particular adversary won't give up until I'm dead and buried."

Jory stepped back as Mac turned the horse around. He took one last look at the cheerful house and cluttered farmyard, then he was through the gate and cantering down the lane. Only at the wood did he catch sight of Jamie stepping from the trees, gaze fastened on Mac, hand raised as if he might call him back.

Turning his mind from the trouble he had left to the trouble awaiting him, Mac spurred his horse on, and Line Farm was lost to view.

18

Despite the killing pace he'd set, Mac arrived in London too late to do anything but stable the horse and find safe haven in his apartments, the rooms somehow dingier, chillier, and lonelier than he remembered. He spent the hours of darkness pacing the floor, fearful that Bianca was at Lord Deane's. Terrified that she wasn't. Thus, it was an unfashionably early hour that saw him approaching the palatial monstrosity that was the Earl of Deane's town residence.

The London palace's majestic façade of arches and pillars rose up over St. James's Place like a declaration of supremacy. The iron gates, the rows upon rows of windows, and the stretch of manicured gardens leading to the tall front doors had been constructed to intimidate and overawe in an ostentatious display of power. The earls of Deane had served on king's inner councils, commanded great armies, and ruled over parliamentary ministries stretching back into the distant past. They'd had the intelligence and strength to gain influence and the cleverness and ruthlessness to keep it. They'd also managed to do it without a hint of scandal marring their sterling reputations or a damaging blot upon their characters.

Until the current Lord Deane—Sebastian Commin—had risked authority, connections, and patronage to marry a Billingsgate fishmonger's daughter who'd risen to fame on the London stage.

It had been the talk of the summer and fall, Society in an uproar over the impetuous and indecent wedding between two such disparate personalities. The men had chuckled and nudged each other over Lord Deane's lust-fed folly, while the women had been furious such an eligible prize had been plucked from under their noses by a woman hardly better than a whore.

The result of this outrage and ostracism ended in an advantage to Mac. No line of carriages blocked the gate. No stream of calling-card-toting visitors or patronage-seeking toadies trolled the terrace steps or wandered among the boxwoods. And Mac was alone in the three-acre anteroom as he awaited the return of the liveried footman.

He paced the room's perimeter one more time. Twenty-eight . . . twenty-nine . . . thirty steps to the west wall. Turn. One . . . two . . . three . . .

"His Lordship will see you now." The footman's insolent gaze raked Mac with passive contempt.

"I didn't ask to see the earl," he replied, matching the servant's frigid tones. "I need to speak with Mrs. Parrino."

The man's expression hardened. "This way, Captain."

Arguing would only get him thrown out on the street. Best to face Deane once and for all and determine the damage for himself. Tucking his hat under his arm, Mac followed the footman through a series of awe-inspiring public rooms into a smaller yet no less impressive suite of sitting rooms, and then to a corridor ending at a pair of double doors. A quiet rap and a murmured voice from within, and Mac was shown inside.

"Captain Flannery, my lord," the servant announced to a man bent over the desk, his dark hair only slightly silvered with gray, his granite face set in concentration.

"Thank you, William," the earl answered without looking up from his writing. "That will be all."

No sound but the scratching of pen on paper, the tick of a clock in the corner, and the snap of a fire within the enormous marbled hearth, but Mac's head buzzed, his skin crawling with a prickling electrical charge that set his teeth on edge. David was right: the Earl of Deane was Fey-blood, his power tangible.

"I've come to see Bianca Parrino," Mac announced.

Deane held up a hand as he continued writing.

Mac ground his jaw, fists clenched. "Is she here or not?"

"One moment and all will be answered, I assure you," Deane responded.

Empty of patience, Mac shoved forward, slamming his hands on the desk, startling the earl from his correspondence. "My moments are precious and I've few to spend awaiting your pleasure, so either tell me she's here or send me on my way to look elsewhere."

Rather than answering Mac's temper with his own, Lord Deane sat back in his chair, his fiery golden gaze nearly blinding. "So you're Captain Flannery. I've heard a lot about you."

Mac curled his fingers around the edges of the

desk, the temptation to heave it up and over the arrogant earl almost overwhelming. "Where is she?" he demanded.

"Bianca's safe, Captain. You have my word."

"That's not what I asked."

"No, but—"

Mac leaned forward to within inches of the earl's face, exhaustion, dread, and frustration pushing him as close to the brink as he'd ever been. "Get her. Now."

Rather than showing fear, Lord Deane quirked his mouth into a smile as he rang the bell behind him. "You've just lost me a hundred guineas, you know. My wife's a hopeless romantic. She wagered there was a man behind Mrs. Parrino's arrival." A different footman arrived. "Edward, find Mrs. Parrino and bring her here. She has a visitor." The man bowed and departed, and Deane turned his attention to Mac once more. "While we wait, you and I have important matters to discuss." He motioned toward a chair. "Don't you think?"

Mac straightened but refused the seat, conscious of the sword hanging at his side and the pistol he carried in his coat pocket. Would it come to that? Would he have the strength and the resolve to kill this man in cold blood? There would be no way he could escape the house unremarked. He would be caught, tried, and executed. The Imnada's secret safe, but at the cost of his life.

"No need to resort to violence," Deane said as if he sensed Mac's dilemma. "I'm no threat to you," he paused, "or to the Imnada."

A sing of steel, and the point of Mac's sword rested at the base of Deane's throat, piercing the folds of the earl's cravat. The slightest push and the man would choke on Mac's blade, his talking days over. "Do you want to die, Fey-blood?" he snarled.

Deane's eyes never wavered, his body tense but unmoving.

"At ease, Captain," came a barked command from the door.

Mac swung around, guts knotted, mouth dry, brain awhirl with confusion. "Gray!"

"I arrived in London the day before yesterday," Gray explained. "I never saw David. We must have passed each other on the road."

"What the hell are you doing here? With him?" Mac demanded. "Damn it, Gray. What's going on?"

Mac had sunk into a chair only after Lord Deane had eased himself beyond the reach of his sword and Gray had extracted the weapon from his white-knuckled grip.

"I came at the request of Lord Deane," Gray answered. "My visit overlapping yours is merely a happy coincidence."

"Happy for me, at any rate," quipped Deane, rubbing his neck.

"But why? He . . . he's . . ."

Gray propped himself on the edge of the desk, one booted leg swinging. "Yes, he is. He's also one of a handful of men and women who know of the Imnada's existence and are devoted to opening a new dialogue between Fey-blood and shapechanger." As Gray continued to explain, Mac's suspicions of ambush intensified. He'd been so convinced of David's involvement in the rebel plot that he'd never given a thought to de Coursy's complicity.

"Do you know what you've done?" he demanded when Gray had finished. "You've betrayed the clans. You've condemned the Imnada to death."

Gray's steel-blue eyes narrowed. "No, I've offered us hope for the first time in a thousand years. It's our only chance. We can't just wall ourselves away behind the Palings and pretend the outside world won't invade sooner or later, because it will. Our safeguards weaken. The powers that went into their weaving fail as we do. It's only a matter of when. Better to choose our own ground than wait for the enemy to choose it for us."

"Then you agree they're the enemy."

"Some. Perhaps most. But not all. And definitely not Sebastian."

Deane acknowledged the compliment with a gracious nod, though he remained safely on the other side of the desk, beyond Mac's reach.

"How long have you been in league with them?" Mac asked.

"I was approached upon my return from France and shortly after Grandfa—after the Gather acted on our malady."

Mac snorted his disgust. Malady? David was right. Gray couldn't even speak the word "curse," as if saying it out loud increased its power.

"There were mitigating circumstances that brought all of us together in common cause," Gray said. "Circumstances, I'm happy to say, that are no longer a concern, thanks to one of our number. But it showed us how much we've lost by hiding behind the Palings' wards and how much we have to gain if we join forces. The purges happened more than a thousand years ago, Mac. The reasons are barely remembered except as legend."

"*He* remembers them." Mac pointed to Deane. "He related them in detail to Bianca. Arthur betrayed and struck down by his treacherous Imnada war leader. The Fey-bloods rising up in rage to avenge their fallen king. A moving faery tale."

"Which is just what they believe us to be," Gray answered. "The Other think we're extinct—killed off during the Fealla Mhòr. Our return now will be a new beginning, a new chance to live in peace."

"Or a new opportunity for them to renew their hatred." Mac's brain was as rattled and unsteady as a jug-bit drunkard's, words pelting him from all sides, only half of it making sense. But he clung to the few clear thoughts in his head. Focused on those. "Was Adam part of this conspiracy?"

"He'd made his presence known to Sebastian, but there had been no actual contact."

So Mac had been right. The gift of a book had been the signal for a meeting. A meeting that never took place. "Because Adam was murdered by a Fey-blood. Did you know this at the funeral? Was that why you tried to fend off my questions? Because you knew Adam had been killed by one of your associates?"

Gray's lips pressed together, his eyes dangerous. "You don't know that for a fact."

"Yes. I do. That's what David was on his way to tell you. I was attacked and almost killed by one as well. Only Bianca Parrino kept me from ending up in a box alongside Adam in St. James's cemetery." His gaze snapped to Lord Deane. "Ring any bells, my lord?"

Gray and Deane exchanged impenetrable looks, though Mac sensed the unease his tale had sparked. They hadn't known, and it worried them.

"The Fey-blood killed Adam. Now she's after me," Mac continued. "Still trust your so-called friends?"

"I acted for the good of our race, Mac. You have to believe that."

"Did you?" Mac snarled. "Or did you do it to get back at your grandfather for abandoning you?"

Gray's hand tightened around the knob of his cane, his eyes drilling into Mac's skull with a lethal glare.

"And if dear old Granddaddy wouldn't come to your rescue before, don't expect him to do it when the Ossine's enforcers catch you. The Duke of Morieux will probably be the one to swing the axe." Mac turned back to Deane. "I've been patient, but no longer. Where's Bianca?"

"All that righteous anger and now you're desperate for an out-clan, Mac?" Gray asked, returning Mac's thrust with a quick strike of his own.

"Back off," Mac snarled. "While you've been playing traitor, I've been trying to break the fucking curse so we can all go home. Without Bianca's help, it will take me weeks to riddle out the last of Adam's notes—time I don't have if this Fey blood shows up again. Time none of us has."

"Is that all you want with her?" Gray asked, one regal brow arched in infuriating superiority.

"That's all. Period. End of story."

Deane looked up, eyes widening, a pained expression chasing its way across his features. "Come in, Bianca. Thank you for joining us. We were just . . . uh . . . speaking about you."

*   *   *

There it was in black and white. Well, maybe not black and white but definitely stated emphatically for all to hear. Mac needed her—not as a woman but as a gardener. Talk about humbling. She'd been desired by dukes and courted by princes, and here a lowly army captain dismissed her as nothing more than a convenient tool like a trowel or a sharp pair of secateurs. Useful because she could tell a *Fraxinus* from a *Taxus*.

And, like the silliest of schoolgirls, she'd fallen for his pretty words and been lured by sweet promises.

Again.

One would think she'd have learned by now. One would think her heart would know better.

One would think she'd be immune to the pain.

One would be very, very wrong.

Yet, none of that touched her face or marred her pose of carefree ambivalence as she alighted upon the edge of a sofa, settling her skirts around her. To look at her, none would ever know her heart lay scattered around her in pieces. Thank heavens Sebastian and Major de Coursy had slipped unobtrusively away. This was one time when she did not relish an audience.

"What I told Gray. What you heard. I didn't mean it." Mac's excuses bounced off her like spent arrows.

A living death. A part of their soul cut away.

Marianne's words haunted Bianca. When desires cooled, how long before resentment overcame respect and desire turned to bitterness? How long before Mac saw her as the source of his pain, the root of all his problems? How long before the insults became blows? "You don't need to explain."

"I may not need to, but I damn well want to." Mac started pacing the room as she clutched the sofa arm with a sinking heart, wishing the floor would swallow her whole. "You and I, Bianca. We were never supposed to happen."

"An impossibility like young Jamie Wallace?" she asked flippantly, the muscles in her face faltering under feigned composure, her shoulders inching closer to her neck.

"Something like that," he answered with a cynical twist of his lips. "The Imnada have lived apart for so long, it's difficult to imagine another way. To trust where trust is synonymous with betrayal."

"Jory did it."

"He did, and was outlawed for his pains."

Was this his way of saying good-bye? The fantasy of the snug farm, the warm bed beneath the eaves, the laughter and voices of children floating through the house—she had conjured them and for a few brief happy hours had imagined them within her grasp. But, like props and sets, they had been an illusion. The curtain had closed, the fantasy no more than paste and paint.

Mac rubbed a hand over the back of his neck, his gaze sharp, his face rigid with strain. "For the past eighteen months, I've lived with one dream—to find a way home. It's hard to simply let go. But—"

"Then don't, Mac." Fear caught at her heart. She didn't want to hear any more stammered explanations. She didn't want to know she was a useful appendage. "Go home to Concullum. See your sister. Repair relations with your father. Take up the life you lost. I'll do the same. It will be as if we never laid eyes on one another."

"It's that easy for you dismiss the last weeks?" His stare seemed to scythe right through her. "To pretend nothing happened between us?"

"I didn't say it would be easy. Those days in the country were fabulous, and I'll never forget them—or you. But we have to face some cold facts."

"This is madness. You're actually going to sit there and pretend this was some sort of foolish lark? Damn it, I know you better than that, Bianca."

On went the armor. "Do you? You forget who you're speaking to. I can play any part I choose."

His anger by now was palpable: she recognized the signs—a flash in his eyes, a tensing of the muscles in his jaw. "You might be able to fool the gullible prancing sods who flutter around you with their poems and their presents, but you aren't fooling me," he shot back. "That was no act, though I'd lay any odds you're performing now."

"You have your clan, Mac, as I have London. This is where I belong." Layer upon hardened layer, stone wrapped in steel wrapped in a gemstone brilliance. She smiled around the lump clogging her throat, cutting off her breath. "I didn't realize how much I would miss the bustle and pace of the city until I was trapped in Surrey with naught but the cows for company. Besides, I prefer being on my own with none to tie me down to the drudgery of domestication."

She thought she saw him wince, but it was an expression so quickly replaced by harsh purpose, she couldn't be sure.

In his agitation, he picked up and put down a porcelain urn from a sideboard, a Wedgwood jug, a brass candelabra. "You can just chuck it all away without a second thought?"

"Who said it was decided in haste? I've had time to think it over. It's the best thing to do. The *only* thing to do. You know it as well as I."

She braced herself for effusive arguments, denials, perhaps even a declaration of some sort. It wouldn't be the first time she had cut off a man's presumptions with one swift blow. Just the first time she'd done it while her own heart felt like lead in her chest and her head throbbed with the effort. But no declarations followed. Instead, Mac put down the pewter bowl he'd been holding and answered with a simple "If that's how you wish it to be."

"It's the way it must be." She gripped the arm of the sofa, wishing it were his throat. She had not wanted a scene, but she might have expected a little protest. A dollop of dismay to make her feel less horrible. The man groveled. She held herself aloof. That's how it was supposed to happen—how these situations had always spun out in the past. Anything different seemed odd and awkward, like ill-fitting clothes. "Besides, I learned the hard way that wishes count for little in this world."

He did not reply, his silence damning, the way he could not look her in the eyes all the evidence she needed to know she'd chosen right when she chose to cut things off cleanly. Best the cauterizing slice than the slow, seeping wound.

His gaze was dark and unreadable, his face as empty as her own. "I'm happy we cleared matters between us."

Was that what they'd done?

Then why did Bianca's thoughts tumble in her head and she retained the distinct urge to slam the nearest heavy object over his thick head?

She smiled though her cheeks ached and her eyes burned. "Clear as crystal."

She'd dismissed him. Offered him her hand to kiss as regally as if he were a petitioner before the court. With monumental effort, he'd answered her indifference with his own, though in truth he'd wanted to shake her until her teeth rattled. Knock her over the head. Drag her kicking and screaming from Deane House and . . . and what? Take her to his meager rooms and ravish her? Send her back to Line Farm, where he could keep her safe? Tie her in a chair and force her to listen to his pleas until she believed him?

The answer would be all of the above. Unfortunately, none of those options, tempting as they were, would inspire her trust or gain her forgiveness. She'd been viciously abused by a man who'd twisted her love for him into a weapon. Who'd used his strength to batter her into submission while wielding his words with surgical precision. Mac would not be accused of doing the same. Not even if it meant walking away and not looking back. He'd told her once that all she had to do was say the word and he'd relent.

He'd hold to that promise no matter the consequences.

Unheeding of his pace as he retraced his steps to the entry hall, he rounded a corner smack into a woman coming the other way. Steadying her with an arm beneath her elbow, he looked down upon a diminutive beauty with gold-flecked gray eyes, a mouth made for smiling, and Fey-blood magic singing in her veins. It lifted the hair at his neck and vibrated like a struck tuning fork along his bones.

"We should install footmen with whistles to handle the traffic," she joked as she returned his speculative gaze with one of her own. "Though recently the crowds have been rather thin, so perhaps not."

"I'm sorry, my lady. I wasn't paying attention."

"Your thoughts must have been taken up with Bianca. She does have that effect on people, Captain Flannery."

"You know me?"

Her smile widened to one of impish mischief. "I do now. But where are you going? You've only just arrived. After battling your way past our phalanx of footmen, I expected you to stay for as long as the siege lasted. Lay in supplies. Bring on your sappers."

"I've done enough damage for one day, my lady. My only option now is a graceful and orderly retreat."

"My, the warlike metaphors are flying this morning, aren't they?" She laughed. "Well, if you won't soldier on, perhaps you can leave it to me to scout the terrain."

He grimaced.

"Too much?" She shrugged. "Perhaps you're right. Don't worry, Captain. I'll talk to her. She's a tough nut. Always has been, but I'll see what I can do on your behalf."

"You're kind, my lady, but it's probably for the best." He bowed and continued on down the corridor, his feet as heavy as his heart.

"The best for whom, Captain Flannery?" Lady Deane called after. "Bianca or yourself?"

19

⸙━━━⸙

"Sweeting, is that you lurking about out in the corridor?" Sarah called as Bianca passed the door to one of Deane House's six spacious public salons. "Come in and have something to eat, my dear. I've cake and those little yellow biscuits you love so much, and there's tea warm in the pot."

Drat! Just what she hadn't wanted after a long afternoon spent meeting with Dr. Hove at Kew Gardens. The renowned botanist and plant hunter had been very sympathetic but not at all helpful, and Bianca wanted only to change out of her grubby clothes and settle into a hot bath. Besides, tea and cake with Sarah was like stepping into the confessional: she'd wheedle and pry until Bianca gave in just to stop the onslaught of questions. And at this point she didn't know what answers she could give that wouldn't make her sound a few pages short of a full script.

"The cake is plum—your favorite," Sarah cajoled.

Snagged fair and square, Bianca surrendered to the temptation of plum cake and tea, entering the

salon like Daniel into the lion's den. Hardly designed
for companionable tête-à-têtes, the cavernous space
echoed, the gilded, elegant furniture was unwelcom-
ing, and even the allegorical figures cavorting on the
painted ceiling seemed to wink down upon all visitors with smug superiority.

She shivered as she took a seat, though a fire
blazed in the hearths standing at either end of the
room. Perhaps it was the dog-with-a-bone stare
Sarah turned on her, an expression that always boded
ill. It meant Bianca was in for a lecture or an interrogation—or both.

"I thought you said builders working on the chim-
neys kept you from going home to Holles Street upon
your return to the city."

"I might have stretched the truth a tiny bit."

Sarah eyed her as she poured the tea. "So it would
seem. So now that your handsome captain has chased
you down to declare his undying devotion, what are
you waiting for?"

"Your sources have failed you, Sarah. That's not
why he came. We had some unfinished business, now
concluded. That's all."

Sarah plunked her teacup down with a noisy
rattle of the saucer, a motherly scold forming in the
creases of her brow and the stubborn lines around
her mouth. "'Unfinished business, now concluded'—
you make it sound as if he were balancing your ac-
counts. Men don't come rushing to a woman's side
before breakfast without a very good—and non-
businesslike—reason." She folded her arms over her
chest and stared sternly down her nose. "You chased
him away, didn't you?"

"I didn't chase anyone," Bianca said, nibbling on a biscuit.

"You did. That's exactly what happened. Let me guess. You channeled that 'Gloriana meets Attila the Hun' personality you've perfected and, like any sane man, he ran for the hills."

"I don't do that."

"You do. You've been playing that fearsome empress of the world role for as long as I've known you, and why not? It works. The men you don't terrorize outright end up worshipping at your feet like a passel of overawed eunuchs."

"Now you're being ridiculous." Bianca rose with a sudden urge to exchange her tea for something stronger. A double dose of sherry might do it. Ignoring the disapproving stares from countless generations of Sebastian's forbears, she poured a glass from a sideboard decanter, downing it like a sailor with his daily grog ration.

Sarah observed her over the top of her china cup. "So . . . will you tell me what happened between you and the captain or must I guess?"

The sherry hadn't helped. Perhaps some cake. Three or four slices ought to do it. "Why should I bother? You seem to have my personal life well in hand."

Sarah dismissed her waspishness with a wave of her ringed hand. "All I know is that you've been stomping about, looking dark as a thundercloud, since you arrived and now you're swilling sherry like a maiden aunt. If those aren't the signs of man trouble, I'll eat my best bonnet."

Man trouble? That would allow that Mac was a man. But he was so much more than that, and while Bianca had shoved that one simple fact aside, in the end the truth was undeniable and insurmountable. While he remained trapped within the curse's power, he would never allow himself to love her. And if he broke free of the dark spell, he would leave her and return to his clan.

Easier and less painful to leave him first.

At least, it was supposed to be.

"Bianca, dear heart," Sarah interrupted, "you're murdering that poor slice of cake. Come and sit down before you maim any more of the food."

"What?" Serving knife clutched in her fist like a dagger, Bianca looked up from her mangled dessert. "Oh, right. Sorry."

"Remind me not to annoy you" was Sarah's skeptical response.

Bianca sat back in her seat, fortifying herself with another quick dose of sherry and the mutilated remains of her cake.

Sarah turned her attention to her tea, though she shot concerned glances at Bianca between sips. "You can't just crawl back in your shell, my dear. Not if you want a chance at getting the happy-ever-after. Take it from me: sometimes you have to fight tooth and claw for it."

"Who says I want to fight for it? Or that it's worth fighting for?"

"I do. You think marriage to Sebastian hasn't got me terrified? Or that I wouldn't shed this gilded monstrosity"—she waved her hand to indicate the salon— "in a heartbeat if I could? You don't think Seb hasn't endured a crippling loss of reputation and prominence for marrying a lowly actress? Alone, the two of us were safe. We risked nothing."

"So why did you marry? You had your career and social standing. He had his."

"Because we loved one another, you twit. Because we were better together than we were apart. And sometimes that's all it takes."

"And sometimes not even love is enough." Bianca shoved the unfinished cake aside, her throat tight, her mouth dry. "I appreciate the advice, and I know you mean well, but it's just not . . . even if Mac and I wanted to . . . and our lives allowed us . . ." She gave a rueful chuckle as she twisted her napkin round and round. "Let's just say it's not possible, for reasons too complicated to go into. You and Sebastian are simply the exception that proves the rule." She rose, placing her plate on a side table. "Thank you for the refreshments and the conversation, but I think I'll return to my rooms."

"Bianca, dear heart, listen to me—"

"No," Bianca retorted, refusing to be drawn further into conversation. Her head throbbed and the cake she'd eaten sat like a brick in her stomach. "You don't and you can't understand. Not this time."

Sarah's normally cheerful gaze turned solemn, her gray eyes sparkling with strange glints of gold. She tilted her head, sizing Bianca up with guilty chagrin. "Sit down, Bianca. You're not alone, and I understand far more than you could possibly know."

"Both of you? As in 'you'"—Bianca's goggle-eyed stare moved from Sebastian to Sarah while her mind raced headlong in a thousand directions—"'*and* her'? As in 'the two of you'? Together?"

"You make it sound as if we've confessed to stealing the crown jewels or kidnapping the prince regent," Sarah blurted, only slightly shame-faced. "It's not nearly that exciting, I can assure you."

"No? Discovering your best friend is a magic-wielding sorceress? I'd say it rates pretty high as a topic of interest with me."

"Here. This might help." Sebastian pushed a drink under her nose.

Accepting the glass, Bianca looked up to meet his somber gaze. "And that story you told me, the book you let me borrow, and all the questions—you weren't trying to finagle information out of me. You already knew the Imnada existed. You knew because you were in league with them." She tipped the glass to her lips, welcoming the brandy's warmth, still trying to grasp the whirling thoughts as they passed through her consciousness. "At least I wasn't wrong. You weren't involved in Adam's death. You aren't the cold-blooded murderer they claimed."

"I'm glad to know you came to my defense. I only wish you'd approached me sooner. I might have been able to help."

"Mac didn't trust you."

"He still doesn't, and with good reason if indeed Other are targeting Imnada. But I still don't see how it can be one of us. Only a handful are aware of their existence. A handful of men and women I would vouch for with my life."

"Could one of them have changed his mind and decided the only good shifter is a dead shifter?" Bianca asked.

"I thought of that," Sebastian replied, "but our

group is small, and none among us fits Captain Flannery's description of your murderous Frenchman."

Recalling with perfect clarity those moments before she struck the man down, she said, "The man mentioned a chevalier. The chevalier should have killed Mac, but she would finish the job."

Sebastian's expression sharpened. "Are you certain? The fellow mentioned a chevalier specifically?"

"Very certain. Every moment from that horrible night has been seared into my brain. I couldn't forget it if I tried."

"What did you do with the book I gave you?" he asked.

"I suppose it's still at my house. That is, if my house is still there."

"Never mind. Wait here," Sebastian said, leaving the salon.

His departure seemed to suck the warmth from the room. Bianca and Sarah regarded each other with a new, wary awkwardness.

"More cake?" Sarah offered shyly.

Bianca shot her a how-could-you look of exasperation.

"None of that," Sarah scolded. "You'll give yourself wrinkles."

Bianca arched a brow in question.

"I did think about telling you, sweeting, really I did, but you're so damnably rational and utterly sensible. I wasn't certain how you'd react. You might have been accepting or you might have had me clapped in irons and packed off to an asylum."

Conceding the truth of Sarah's worry, Bianca took another long swallow of her brandy while continuing to cast her curious sidelong glances.

"And you can stop staring at me as if I might turn you into a toad any moment. I can't whip up magic like Cook bakes a casserole. I don't pop in and out of existence, and I can't zap, poof, or otherwise zing. Quite disappointing, really, if you think about it, but our gifts don't work like that."

"So what can you do?"

Sebastian burst back into the salon, carrying an enormous tome beneath his arm. "Here it is. I knew I had a copy of the *Peruzzi Treatises* somewhere. It's not his best work, but it gives you the idea." He offered the volume to Bianca.

"What am I looking for?"

"The author."

She read the spine, opened it to the title page. "Gilles d'Espe. The same man who wrote that book on the Imnada."

"The very same. He began as a professor at the Conservatoire de Sauvageon in Paris, but he became obsessed with the idea that the Imnada somehow survived the ancient wars. That they were out there and still a threat. He collected every scrap of information ever written about them. Financed and led expeditions in hopes of discovering their hidden holdings, but of course he found nothing but a bout of lung fever and a swift loss of his family's fortune. The Other discounted his scholarship as the insanity of a once-brilliant mind broken by drink and the death of his wife, but it didn't stop him. If anything, it sharpened his desire and he grew increasingly drawn to the darker magics in an effort to prove his lunatic theories."

Bianca flipped through the rambling chapters. "Not so lunatic after all, but what has he to do with Mac?"

"He was the *chevalier* Gilles d'Espe, and he and his household were brutally killed during the final days of the war."

It didn't take a genius to connect point A to point B and come up with the sickening circumstances of d'Espe's death. "Mac, Adam, and the others," Bianca said. "They killed him, didn't they?"

"D'Espe must have discovered the truth somehow. They would never have allowed him to live after that."

"I learned the truth and I'm alive."

"You were lucky. You had two things working in your favor. One: you aren't Other."

"And two?"

"Captain Flannery loves you!" Sarah exclaimed.

Both Sebastian and Bianca shot her irritated looks, which she answered with a smug smile.

"So d'Espe placed the curse on the four of them?"

"Gray would never explain and I didn't press him, but the pieces all fit. Fey-born powers don't affect the Imnada in the normal way. Spells go awry. Mage energy bends and warps in odd and unexpected ways. He may have been trying to subdue them. Instead, he just made them very angry."

As all Mac's slips and enigmatic comments came into focus, her queasy feeling spread throughout her body. The curse on the four of them had been a result of warped Fey magic. A last-ditch defense from a man who'd bitten off more trouble than he could chew when he confronted the Imnada soldiers. He'd paid for his inquisitiveness with his life. In a way, so, too, had Mac and the others. Which was less painful: the quick obliteration or the slow, grinding destruction by infinite degrees?

Sebastian's gaze darkened, a troubled look passing over his stony features.

"There's more, isn't there?" Bianca asked.

"The chevalier's daughter is here, in London. She's the wife of a wealthy munitions merchant attached to the French embassy. Or should I say 'the widow': he died of a heart seizure a few days ago. They plan on shipping his body back to France for burial, but . . ."

"But what?"

"Madame Froissart has chosen to remain in London."

Bianca rose in a rush of heavy skirts, hands tightening to fists. "I need to warn Mac. He needs to know. To be on his guard."

"I thought you and Flannery had concluded your business, darling. All obligations at an end," Sarah said.

"So I should just let him be killed and do nothing to warn him? Don't be preposterous," Bianca snapped, nerves winding tight, heart racing.

"The turtle finally emerges," Sarah muttered.

"Perhaps a message sent to the Horse Guards," Sebastian suggested. "And I'll send word to de Coursy."

His offers faded into the angry buzz of Bianca's thoughts. Where could Mac be? How could she find him? She straightened, the answer like the sudden blaze of a newly lit candle. Concentrating her thoughts as if she were physically reaching for him, she pictured the scarlet of his uniform and the gold of his braid, the sheen of his dark hair and the intensity in his gaze. *Mac. Mac, where are you? Please, if you're out there, answer me.*

Nothing.

Mac, Madame Froissart is the chevalier's daughter. She's the one. She murdered Adam and now she's after you.

No answer. No way to know if he'd heard her. But for the barest of moments, the hairs along her arms lifted and she felt a prickling sensation between her shoulder blades. Someone listened.

Madame Froissart, Mac. She's the one.

With a cry, Renata broke contact, retreating back into her body, leaving behind the ember-streaked void and the voices that called to her from the infinite pillars of rippling, lung-choking smoke. Doubling over into a chair, she clutched her skull, pain ripping through her brain, spotting her vision, turning her stomach. "Bianca Parrino is here. In London."

"You touched her mind?" Alonzo asked, mouth folded into a grim line, eyes alight with recent passion.

"For a moment only. Wherever she is, it's warded against magic. The protections too strong. They prevented me from fully bonding with her."

"Then we've failed."

Her body felt clammy with cold sweat as she pushed her hair off her face, placing the remaining two golden strands of hair back into a tiny ormolu box. "No. This is a perfect solution, and it was clever of you to think of retrieving them from the Parrino town house. Very clever." Opening her jewelry case, she placed the ormolu box within. "Once we have her, we have Flannery."

She stretched, letting the silken robe she'd donned upon rising from bed slither from her naked body. She studied herself in the mirrors, caressing the round pertness of her breasts, pinching the taut, dusky nipples still bruised from Alonzo's lovemaking before running her hands down the slope of her rib cage to the flare of her hips, brushing the hair between her legs, her quim wet and throbbing. Alonzo's hungry gaze followed her every movement, his tongue running over his lips, his cock hard once more.

"London's enormous. It could take forever to find her," he said, his voice raspy.

She met his eyes within the mirror, rising from her seat with a smile of invitation on her kiss-swollen lips. "Do you think so? She cannot stay warded away from my powers forever. And when I find her, I will control her. You wait, Alonzo. I shall have Flannery on his knees before me within week. And before I kill him, he shall watch as I take away all that is most dear to him. He shall watch and understand my pain."

20

⸭━━⸰⸭

At the familiar polished vowels and public school consonants coming from the corridor, Mac lifted his head from the report on his desk. If he was lucky, the always-churlish sergeant on duty would send the unwanted visitor on his way. Mac was in no mood for guests. Instead there was a short burst of "Yes, sirs" and "No, sirs" before Gray de Coursy appeared in the doorway, a valet's dream from the top of his stylishly cut head of golden hair to the tips of his champagne-polished boots. The bloody sod looked as if he'd just stepped from the pages of a gentleman's magazine.

Mac fought down the overwhelming urge to beat the shit out of him.

"Working hard?" Gray asked, scanning Mac's overflowing desk as he closed the door behind him.

"If you must know, I'm trying to complete a report due to General Burrell. My unexpected trip out of town has me trying to catch up."

Gray's gaze settled on the blank piece of paper beneath Mac's hand with a slight lifting of his eyebrows.

"All right," Mac growled, "so I'll settle for starting the bloody report."

Mac had been here since this morning and he'd yet to write one word. Work was not the solace it had once been. His reports had lost their luster, his ledgers no longer enticed with their brain-numbing columns and rows, and his office walls closed in like the jaws of a trap.

And now the cherry on top of his horrible day was settling himself on the only other chair in the room and regarding Mac as if he were a particular tasty bit of prey.

"Did you come to offer me more of your justifications?" Mac asked. "Or are you hoping to convince me not to turn you and your associates into the Ossine once I'm reinstated into the clans?"

"What makes you believe you will be?"

"This." Mac pulled the journal from a drawer and slammed it down on the desk between them. "Adam broke the curse before he died. I plan on following his notes and doing the same. I'm this close." He pressed his finger and thumb together.

"And you assume once you're no longer tainted by the Fey-blood's dark magic, you'll be welcomed home with open arms. The pronouncement of *emnil* reversed."

"That's the plan."

Gray leaned forward in his chair, resting a ringed hand upon the top of his cane. "You'd really return to Concullum and pretend the last two years never occurred? Have you forgotten the agony as they stripped the clan mark from your body and the signum from your soul? Can you forgive them their deafness as you pleaded for your life and they did nothing while you lay bleeding and broken?"

"Is that what this is about, Gray? Revenge? You'd destroy the clans to get back at your grandfather?"

For a moment Gray's eyes gleamed with some hidden emotion, but the expression was gone so quickly, Mac couldn't be certain he had seen it, and when Gray spoke, there was nothing in his voice to betray he might be less than in perfect control. "What of Bianca Parrino? Is it so easy to leave her behind?" he asked.

Mac gritted his teeth against Gray's dispassionate reserve, the man's placid gaze boring into him like the point of a dagger until Mac's fury erupted. "You want to know how easy it is? It's like I've taken a bullet to the gut, every damned second an agony. Does that make you happy? Is that what you wanted to hear?" He brought his fist down hard on the desk, the pain jolting up through his arm driving away the despair, but only for a moment before it roared back.

"No, it's not what I wanted to hear." Once more, Gray rubbed the eagle's head decorating the head of his cane. "Does she know this?"

"After yesterday, she thinks me the biggest son of a bastard to ever walk the earth, and I can't blame her. I missed my chance."

"Did you *want* the chance?"

"What's that supposed to mean?"

Gray shrugged as he flicked a nonexistent speck from his breeches. "It's none of my business—"

"You're right. It's not."

"—but it seems to me if you cared for the woman as much as you claim, you'd tell her so."

"It's complicated."

Gray continued to eye him with the same bland expression that made Mac want to grind his teeth to nubs. "Can we talk about something else? Mayhap the betrayal of the clans by the heir to the leader of us all? The threat of an attack by the Ossine? Or how about the treachery of your Fey-blood conspirators?"

Gray remained unfazed. "I'm aware of the difficulties."

"That's the understatement of the century."

"Did you ever think our accursedness was meant to be, Mac? That perhaps the mother goddess set these events in motion to compel us out of the well-worn paths of our forefathers? To make us chart a different future from the one we'd always imagined?"

"Destiny?" Mac snarled. "That's your argument?"

"We need fighters like you. Men who've stood in the ranks. Who don't run when the firing starts. Who can inspire loyalty among our friends and fear in our enemies." Gone was the even tempered stoicism, replaced by a zealot's enthusiasm.

"Enemies? You're speaking about your own kind. Does that make the Fey-bloods your friends? No, this is your war. Mine ended on the field at Quatre Bras. I'm through fighting. Just ask the army. I'm a battlesick liability these days, good for nothing more than shuffling papers."

Gray crossed one booted foot over the other, the gleam of his diamond ring winking as he turned it this way and that. "I'd hoped to sway you without mentioning this, but Bianca told me about Jory Wallace." He paused, his normally supercilious blue gaze even smugger than usual. "About his younglings."

Mac's fingers tightened on his pen.

"What will happen to them? Unmarked by any clan, they're vulnerable to the first enforcer who stumbles upon them."

"They're just children. Leave them out of it."

"Children the Imnada need if we are to endure beyond a few failing generations," Gray said without flinching. The once-timid fledgling had found his wings and become a merciless hunter.

Mac threw himself to his feet, pacing the office, hands clasped behind his back. "The clans will never accept the marking of half-breeds. Just as they'll never accept a clan member taking a mate outside the bloodlines."

"Not as things stand now, no. The Ossine are too strong, their sway too great over the Gather. But if we were to make inroads into their power, then there is a chance."

"How does throwing your lot in with the Feybloods accomplish that?"

"They understand what it is to be different, to stand apart from the humans while being of their world. They are our natural allies, Mac. You know that as well as I do."

"And the Fealla Mhòr means nothing? The purges? The treatment of the Imnada as demons to scare their children? That counts for nothing?"

"We have to start somewhere to rebuild the trust between us. I choose to do it now, before it's too late."

"And the Fey-blood who's tracking us down?"

"Here's your answer." Gray reached into his coat pocket, pulling out a slim wafered letter that he handed over.

Immediately a familiar orange-cinnamon scent

wrapped round Mac and his fingers tightened on the swoop of feminine writing with an unwelcome thrill.

Bianca.

Had Lady Deane done what she'd said and talked Bianca round? Mac's heart gave a humiliating jump as he broke the wafer and unfolded the thin sheets, Bianca's perfume filling his head. Instead, a few dashed lines was all that met his eyes. His hand crushed the paper, his mind racing ahead. "Renata Froissart?"

"You were wrong, Mac," Gray said quietly. "This Fey-blood isn't after the Imnada. She's after the four of us. Vengeance for the killings at Charleroi."

"Adam left none alive."

"So we thought, but obviously someone knew we'd been there and what we were. The question now becomes: How do we stop her?"

Mac smiled, ideas clicking into place, plans forming. "You let me worry about that. I'm tired of playing her game. It's time she learned the most dangerous animal is the one with nothing left to lose."

Bianca laid the book aside, rubbing her temples. Not even the two cups of coffee she'd had after dinner could keep her weary shoulders from slumping or stave off the dismal nauseated feeling in the pit of her stomach. An entire day with no word from Mac. Nothing to let her know whether he'd received her note. Nothing to let her know whether he still lived.

She straightened her shoulders. No. She would not think that way. Mac was safe. Silence did not necessarily mean something sinister. And he'd made it clear their alliance was at an end.

Pulling free the last volume in her pile, she opened it to the index and ran her finger down the column, knowing almost before she began what she'd not find.

Aphyllon.

Apios.

Apocynum.

But no mention of *Aquameniustis* anywhere.

She slammed the book closed. Scanned the shelves on every wall without leaving her seat, knowing she'd exhausted her last resource. Lord Deane's extensive collection held infinite wonders, but it was definitely thin on botanical resources.

It shouldn't be so blasted difficult. It hadn't been once.

In years past, the knowledge had been there. As she worked and studied alongside her father, she'd been adept at identification, had the sharp thinking and analytical skills to understand the botanical mysteries her father brought her. But now? Now she was fooling herself by thinking she could again be that clever girl she'd once been, the one with her life ahead of her and the world at her feet. She'd traveled too far and experienced too much to return to those bygone elysian days when her biggest worry had been making sure her father changed out of his wet socks and taken his powdered rhubarb for digestion.

In the end, necessity and survival had won the day. She'd become an actress.

A pretty face with a sharp wit and a chilling demeanor. Loved by thousands yet understood by no one. She was the role she'd created, the stereotype of the leading lady, and there was nothing left of the real Bianca but a few botanical meetings and a ridiculous excuse for a garden.

"You're up late." Sebastian stood just inside the library door, dressed as if he'd just come home, though a look at the clock showed the hour to be almost four in the morning. "Or perhaps you've risen early."

"You had it right the first time." Bianca shoved a plate of wilted sandwiches across the table toward him. "Hungry?"

He accepted with a tired smile, dropping his gloves on the table, falling into a chair. "Famished."

"An enjoyable evening?"

"If you count meeting with three ministers, four government secretaries, a half dozen functionaries, and the prime minster enjoyable."

She grimaced. "Not even close."

"At least I only had to bite my tongue a half dozen times tonight. Sarah must be growing on them."

Now that he'd come closer, Bianca saw the gray cast to his skin, the dark smudges below his eyes, and the tired lines biting into the sides of his mouth. Did he still think his unpopular marriage worth the complications it had brought him? "Sarah has a way," she said. "You wait and see. She's got more charm in one finger than most women have in their entire bodies. They'll be eating out of her hand by this time next year."

"For her sake, I hope so." He glanced at the stack of books. "A little light bedtime reading?"

"Research, but it's hopeless. I've been away from the field too long."

"Why bother, then?"

"What?"

"I mean, it's not your problem, is it? It's Flannery's. Let him work through the night searching for the answer. You've done more than enough."

She winced at the harshness of his statement, though she couldn't fault his argument. After all, it was the same one that had been rolling around in her head all evening.

Why?

Why hunt through endless volumes?

Why keep up the search for an impossible plant for an impossible man that she loved with an impossible love?

She wanted to tell him that the search for the missing plant had become a search for her own lost identity. That a busy mind was a mind unable to dwell on what-ifs and useless regrets. That the clatter and chaos of the city kept her awake after the peaceful nights of Line Farm.

She wanted to, but she couldn't.

Because Mac was the real reason she worked. He may have hurt her, but he'd also forced her to remember who she'd been before Lawrence had twisted her into someone else: a stranger who kept the world at bay for fear of being hurt again. And in doing this he'd offered her indescribable wonders and a fantastic world both more beautiful and more frightening than she'd ever imagined.

Of course, there was no way to convey her reasoning in any way that would make sense to someone who'd never felt the slow grinding away of his spirit like grain through a millrace.

A hand covered her own, and she looked up to meet Sebastian's eyes. "He hurt you, Bianca, and were I not an emissary for peace between our races, I'd rip his poxy head off and shove it up his—"

"Seb!"

"He doesn't deserve you. That's all I'm saying."

She tossed off a tired smile. "If someone told you, in order to marry Sarah, you would have to give up all this"—she gestured around her—"your wealth, your family, your connections, everything about you that made you special, could you do it? If it came down to giving up a piece of your very soul to possess her, could you?"

He sat back, his gold-brown eyes thoughtful, his craggy features set in stern lines despite his exhaustion. "I don't know about the wealth and the power," he answered with a wry curl to his mouth, "but the soul bit? Now, that much I've done."

"Were Mac to choose me, he would lose everything all over again. He would never see his family. Never be able to go home. I can't ask him to do that, Seb. I *won't* ask him to do that."

"What if you didn't have to ask?"

She stared at the words on the page in front of her but saw none of them. Instead, memories she'd fought to push aside rose up like ghosts: waking with Mac's warm body spooned against hers, his strong arms holding her close, the scent of his skin, the shadows in his eyes, the scarred and puckered flesh of his back where his clan mark had been burned away, the softness of his dark hair . . .

The clock chimed the half hour.

She lifted her head from the page. "It's late. Sarah will wonder where you are."

He rose with a yawn, dusting sandwich crumbs from his breeches. "I know when I've been dismissed, but let me say this: Don't let pride keep you from telling Flannery how you feel. He's not a stock character in a play and you haven't read the ending. He might surprise you."

"I've weathered surprises enough from him, don't you think?"

He shrugged. "Just some stale advice from an old married man, but one who knows we males are extremely dense when it comes to intangibles like love. Sometimes it takes a good clubbing over the head before we see what's right in front of our noses."

"Is that what Sarah did?"

A smile hovered over his mouth and lit his bright eyes. "I've the scars to prove it." Then he sobered. "One more thing before I slink off to bed. If Madame Froissart is the woman seeking vengeance on Flannery and the others, be careful. She's not a woman to be trifled with, and I would never forgive myself if you were hurt and I could have prevented it."

"I didn't come to London to hide. I came to help Mac."

"Which brings us back to my original question: Why bother?"

"Because I can't just give up. What if Mac never finds the answer? What if he never breaks the curse? To be so close and fail would destroy him."

"Unless Froissart gets to him first."

"That's not even close to funny."

"No, Bianca, but it wasn't meant to be."

The thin crescent shell of Berenth—the waning quarter moon—rose above the house across the street. Tonight's shift had come at a price. His joints ached and a feverish stiffness infected his bones as the concentration needed to harness the moon's power drained away as fast as he could focus it. Normally, the Imnada avoided shifting during the dangerous period between Berenth and Morderoth, the night of no moon. It took too much energy and left them too vulnerable. But normal had held little sway over Mac's life for years, and none at all in the last eighteen months.

Normal Imnada rarely ventured beyond the warded mists of the Palings, preferring to remain close to their safeguarded holdings and among their own kind.

Normal Imnada did not go against their clan leaders and fathers to join the army. And they did not, could not—were forbidden to—take a mate outside of the bloodlines.

Gray claimed he sought to change this. He sought to pull down the wards and protections that had safeguarded the Imnada for generations and thrust the sheltered clans back into a hostile world. He struggled to give the Imnada a future.

But would he?

Or would he and his followers be slaughtered by the Ossine's enforcers or betrayed by the Fey-bloods?

They needed fighters if they hoped to gain anything more than a painful death. Men who'd seen battle and knew war.

Men like Mac.

His gut twisted, his heart beating painfully under his ribs at the choice he faced: join with Gray or betray him.

To join the fight would mean a permanent exile. No hope of returning to the clans. No way to reclaim that life. But did he even want to anymore? That life seemed as tattered and broken as a fallen battle standard. Shot through with new ideas and new imaginings and a face as pale and perfect as the goddess herself.

Round and round, his mind whirled like a Catherine wheel. A constant buzz like the whine of a million bees vibrated through his skull, muddling his already confused thoughts. He shook his head, seeking to stop the endless dizzying spin of possible outcomes, but it only made his temples throb and his stomach lurch uncomfortably as if he'd drunk too much.

Why was he here? What had brought him to this street on this night? He couldn't remember. Couldn't focus. He closed his eyes, laying his head upon his paws, seeking a calm amid the storm as he struggled to concentrate.

One . . . two . . . three . . .

He counted the beats of his heart while Berenth's sideways grin seemed to laugh at his attempt to pull himself together.

Three . . . four . . . five . . .

Froissart. The name swam up out of his fogged brain. Renata Froissart. Daughter of the murdered chevalier. She was the reason for his patient waiting. She was the enemy that sought to destroy him.

Snatches of memory burst against Mac's mind—the yellow edge of the woman's blood-soaked skirts, the globe on its mahogany stand, the sun streaming through the top of the far trees . . .

So much misery spun off from that one bloody day outside Charleroi. So much death and sorrow and violence.

He scanned the windows of the Froissart town house. A light shone in a second-floor window. Shad-

ows moved back and forth behind a heavy curtain.
He'd seen no sign of Madame Froissart, but she was
there. He sensed her presence like the bitter tang
of blood lying on his tongue and in his throat. Fey-
blood magic hanging thick in the air like smoke over
a battlefield.

He would end this. He must. And soon. For there
wasn't much time left before Morderoth, a night,
when not even the evil magic of the curse could over-
power the will of the goddess. A night when shifting became impossible and the Imnada were at their
most vulnerable. During the purges, the Fey-bloods
had struck when the darkness of Morderoth stretched
over the land.

Renata was the daughter of the chevalier.

She would know this.

She would use this.

Mac would be ready.

21

"I'm looking for *Aquameniustis*. A-Q-U-A-M-E-N . . . Have you heard of it?"

The nurseryman scrubbed a hand through his thinning hair before slapping his hat back on his head. "Naw, none of that, but we've got some fine hedgehogs." He motioned toward a wicker cage where three of the bristly balls of fur appeared to be sleeping. "Good for beetles, they is. A right good price."

"I don't want hedgehogs," Mac explained slowly. "I want bloody *Aquameniustis,* whatever the hell it is."

The man shook his head. "Try the fellow at the end. He might have what you're looking for."

Since Mac had already spoken to the fellow at the end, as well as with ten other vendors, he merely nodded and turned away to pass among the market's bustling crowds thronging the courses between wooden stalls heaped with fall vegetables, tottering crates, and barrels stacked man-high. Bands of frustration tightened his shoulders.

He had traveled the length and width of London,

or so it seemed. From the elegant offices of Reverend Hodges and the botanical society to the vine-cluttered shop of Dr. Newcomb of Seething Lane until he was sick to death of uncomfortable hackneys, greasy chop-house food, and musty offices and anterooms. Adam's plant was a fiction, an invention, a fraud. Poor science, said one. Poor penmanship said another.

If only Bianca were there to help him.

Is that all you want with her? If you cared for the woman as much as you claim, you'd tell her so.

Gray's comments continued to rankle like burrs beneath Mac's skin, the tension in his shoulders sinking like a stone into his chest. Why hadn't he declared when he had the chance? Was it gallant sacrifice, as he'd told himself while feeding draft after draft of the same unfinished letter to the flames; or was he the coward that Lady Deane and Gray claimed he was, unable to take that final and irrevocable step?

By now the morning sun had climbed through a filmy layer of smoke and cloud. Sweat had dampened Mac's coat so that it stuck to his back, and his throat was chalky with thirst. He'd seen a tavern just beyond the market's edge in Bedford Street. Some rashers and eggs were just the fortification he needed to continue his search.

He took a deep calming breath, only to catch a whiff of an all-too-familiar scent.

Bianca? Here? Or had he simply conjured her from his thoughts and a bad case of wishful thinking.

He scanned the shifting sea of faces.

A swirl of blue gown. A gleam of golden hair. Was that her just ahead, dodging that overturned cart of turnips?

He shouldered his way through the crowd, but by the time he'd bulled his way to the cart, she'd disappeared.

He paused between a vendor hawking carrots and parsnips and a greengrocer extolling the freshness of his young cucumbers and crisp new peas. Passed a keen gaze over the stalls ahead, nostrils flared for the elusive scent of her. Turned to the right. Jogged up half a row before the silvery bell of her voice floated on a musty breeze.

Two stalls away, consulting with a gentleman in apron and gaiters holding a tall, thin flower studded with delicate white blooms. ". . . for less than a hundred guineas. You'll not find another like it in the city."

"I'm sure you're right. Well, thank you for showing it to me. It's lovely, but I'm afraid I'll have to decline."

"P'raps another time, miss." The man placed the flower back amid the potted blooms and shrubs around him. "Now, as I was saying: old Mr. Ringrose—he's your best bet for what you're asking for. If he don't have it, no one does."

"How much?" Mac asked over Bianca's shoulder.

Bianca whipped around, flashing him a wide-eyed stare.

"The orchid? One hundred guineas, Captain," the nurseryman answered.

"She'll take it."

Bianca stiffened. "I will not. It's far too expensive."

"Do you want it?"

Her gaze flicked longingly toward the plant.

"We'll take it," Mac repeated.

"No, we won't."

"It's my money. If I want—"

"Thank you, Mr. Sullivan," she said to the hovering

nurseryman, handing him a shilling. "This is for your trouble."

Pocketing the coin, the man tipped his cap with a wink as Bianca turned to regard Mac with a cool, appraising gaze. Only the tight hold on her reticule and the slight trembling of her fingers gave her away. "What are you doing here?"

"I'm here in search of that last bloody plant, but what the hell are you doing?" he growled. "What if Madame Froissart should turn up, or some more of her hired toughs?"

"So you did get my note. When I didn't hear from you, I couldn't be sure the major had found you."

"He found me."

"Were your hands broken? Did you have no ink or paper that you couldn't dash off a sentence letting me know?" He wouldn't say her comment dripped with sarcasm, but there was a definite waspishness to her tone.

"I should have, but—"

She held up a hand. "You're right. It's no longer my concern."

"That's not what I was going to say."

"No? What *were* you going to say? That you hoped buying me an expensive gift would make up for the fact I worried myself sick over you for the last few days? I warned you once, Mac Flannery, I can't be purchased with pretty baubles. Just because you and I—"

"You and I what, Bianca?"

She flushed but met his gaze without wavering. "It doesn't matter. Good day, Captain."

"Hold on." He grabbed her arm. "There was no ulterior motive in my offer." She continued to spear him with a doubtful stare. Heat prickled the back of his neck, and he dipped his head, suddenly self-conscious. "All right, perhaps a slight touch of ulterior motive. But you wanted the flower. I wanted . . . oh, hell, I wanted to see you smile."

She folded her arms over her chest. "That's absurd."

"Is it?"

Just then, an enormous out-of-breath young man with shoulders wide as a ship of the line and a face like a platter bulled his way through the crowd. "You can't be running off like that, mum. His lordship will have the skin from my back if I let anything happen to you."

"There's the answer to your question about my safety," Bianca said. "As you can see, an entire regiment would find it difficult to outmaneuver Donas here."

Risking a curt set-down or even a fist to the jaw, Mac tucked her arm under his. Now that he had her alone on neutral ground, he refused to let her escape without a struggle. "You're dismissed, Donas. I'll see Mrs. Parrino back to Deane House, where she will stay this time."

A dangerous line appeared between her lowered brows, her jaw tightly set, but she didn't argue or pull away. Instead, she nodded toward the footman, who looked as if he might do enough arguing and scene making for the two of them. "Tell Lord Deane I'll be home by tea."

Donas glowered at Mac. "I suppose, if you say it's all right, mum, but—"

"Please." She laid a gentle hand upon his arm, giving him a smile that would have called birds from the trees and the sun from the sky.

The footman caved, his broad face turning bright

red. "Very well, mum. I'll let His Lordship know." He turned to Mac with a stare that could strip paint. "But you better not let anything happen to her, ya hear?" He offered him one last threatening look and cracked his knuckles before disappearing into the crowds.

"It's amazing how you do that," Mac said, firmly tucking her against him lest she change her mind and go pelting after the besotted Donas. "One smile and he's ready to charge the cannon's mouth for you."

"Don't tease. He's a sweet boy and takes his duty very seriously. You of all people should respect a slave to duty."

Despite her queenly rebuke, Mac felt desire flood him as well as affection and an unexpected optimism. The woman he'd discovered at the Wallace farm was still there, just buried beneath a hard, frosty layer of winter. But, like the delicate petals of the *am'ryath*, it would take just the slightest warmth for her to bloom again.

He opened his mouth to say the words he'd penned over and over. The arguments he'd concocted as he stood outside Deane House.

A barrow bumped his knees. "Here, now, fella! Out the way, then."

Coming to his senses, Mac moved aside, swallowing the explanations and excuses. He couldn't speak. Not yet. Not until Renata Froissart had been dealt with and the curse had been lifted. He could offer nothing until then. But after . . . after, he would not let her go until she believed him. Until she trusted him again.

"I never meant to hurt you." Hardly inspiring. He'd said it at least a hundred times to her since they'd met. No wonder she continued to eye him with obvious doubt and a dangerous glitter in her eyes.

"So you buy me a flower and think all is forgiven?"

A crowd of laughing men pressed through between them, their faces red with cold, fists tight about their sacks. For a moment he and Bianca found themselves separated as the group passed, and only Mac's grab for her hand kept her from being swept along in their wake.

He shoved her into the alley between two stalls where the noise was muffled somewhat by the canvas draped across the crates of cabbages and turnips.

"You're right, Bianca. From now on, I promise never to buy you anything. Ever. You could be starving and I wouldn't deign to purchase you the smallest crust of bread. On my honor."

"Now you're being ridiculous."

"See, I didn't spend a penny and I succeeded anyway. You're smiling."

"I most certainly am not."

"You are. It's there. The tiniest hint of the smallest little smile, but it's there." Unthinking, he touched the corner of her mouth; her skin was cool, her lips warm.

A barrel-chested vegetable seller tucked his head out to growl at them. "Here, now, are you buying or gabbing? I've customers what can't see the merchandise with ye blocking the way."

"This isn't the place for conversation," Bianca said.

"You're right." Mac took her hand as they passed through the aisles toward the market's edge.

"Have you found what you were looking for?" she asked.

He flicked his gaze over the porcelain curve of her cheek, one gilded curl peeping from beneath her stylish bonnet. A smile tugged at the edges of his mouth. "I begin to think I have," he answered quietly.

"Really? I've come up empty-handed, though three nurserymen, including Mr. Sullivan back there, all said to call on a Mr. Ringrose. They say for anything out of the ordinary, he'd be the one to see."

Surprise surged through him. "You're still searching?"

Pink rose in her cheeks, her chin hardening defiantly. "It's a puzzle, pure and simple, and I've always loved a good challenge. It's nothing to do with you, so don't get any ideas."

Oh, he had ideas, all right. All of them indecent. Hope rushed in to replace his earlier exhaustion, and he had to clamp down hard on the smile fighting to break free. He jerked his head back the way they had come. "So, how do we find this Ringrose?"

"'We'?"

"I promised young Donas. Remember?"

"He has a shop near London Bridge."

As they fought their way through the crowds, small details took on heightened significance. Her long, tapered fingers resting lightly on his arm, the way her gown slid provocatively over her hips as she walked, the smell of her hair as she bent her head toward his. Unable to stop himself, he noted this new awareness of her with a mixture of joy and sorrow.

Bianca had become more than a means to an end. She *was* the end.

A woman he could love.

A life he might live.

Passing a young girl sitting cross-legged on the curb, he dropped a few pennies into her apron, accepting in return a bunch of faded blooms, which he held out for Bianca. "I know I promised no gifts . . ."

She shook her head. "Between the gleaming gold braid and the roguish Irish charm, the women of London must not stand a chance."

"Too bad it's only one woman I'm interested in winning over."

She held the flowers to her nose, her expression softening. "You're a ridiculous, irritating, infuriating man, Captain Mac Flannery."

He pushed a curl off her cheek. Drank in the growing faith he sensed behind the beauty of her gaze. "You got it half right."

Mr. Ringrose's apothecary shop leaned drunkenly in the shadow of London Bridge, in an alley running behind the giant pipes and pumps of the nearby waterworks. Its windows were clouded with filth, its weathered signboard hanging from one rusted chain. The stench of feces, dead fish, and mud stung Bianca's eyes and choked the breath from her throat even through the handkerchief she pressed to her mouth.

"Are you certain this is the right address?" Mac asked, looking a bit pea-green himself.

Through her watering eyes, Bianca checked the paper one final time. "This is it." She jumped back as a rat the size of a lapdog scuttled out from under the rotted foundation to disappear down a nearby drain. "You'd think someone as well-known as this Ringrose fellow would be able to afford a decent workplace."

Mac threw her an encouraging smile. "Mayhap the rare-plant business isn't what it used to be."

She hiked up her resolve with a lift of her shoulders. "Well, we won't find out by standing here."

Mac turned the door handle, ushering her inside.

A bell tinkled over the doorway as they entered, an answering chime echoing from somewhere in the back, but Bianca's attention was all for the Aladdin's cave of treasures that lay before them.

Narrow aisles ran between shelves heavy with old and weathered books mixed in with jars big and small containing specimens preserved in brine: here a small toad, there what looked like a hairless rat, the third Bianca couldn't even begin to guess and, by the looks of it, was better off not knowing. Another aisle held shrunken heads—of men and women—some with hair, some without. A trio of mysterious bottles labeled XXX and with a skull and crossbones stood like soldiers in a row beside a stuffed parrot and a glass dish of eggs the size of apples. Just beyond was a wall that contained nothing but drawers from top to bottom. She pulled open a few to find small bundles wrapped in cloth, colored stones, a fish skeleton.

From the ceiling hung thousands of bunches of dried plants, so many tucked against each other that the ceiling joists had disappeared from view. In addition, running the perimeter of the shop were wide counters containing live plants growing in glorious profusion. She recognized sweet marjoram and garden rocket. A small pot of rush leeks peeked from behind the wide leaves of an endive. One wall held a profusion of featherfew blooming as if it were July. Another contained great blowsy peonies, which typically only burst into flower in April.

Vaguely, she registered Mac's hand giving hers a reassuring squeeze, his muttered oath mixing with her own, the clamor and chaos of the bustling wharves cut off as the door swung shut with the clang of a prison cell.

Dizziness overcame her, a strange tilt and spin as if the earth had suddenly shifted for a moment beneath her feet, the light growing flat and gray, her stomach rising into her throat. She closed her eyes, inhaling through her nose and out her mouth, feeling Mac's tension in the grip of her hand, the heat in his voice.

"This place reeks of magic, Bianca. We need to leave. Now."

Her eyes snapped open, the world steadying as she gripped his arm tighter. "We can't. Not if we want to find the last plant on Adam's list."

Mac shot her a strange, worried look. "Bianca? Is something wrong? You seem unwell."

"Who's there?" From behind the curtain, a voice as crackly and old as dry paper piped up. "Who is it, Badb? Can you see them?"

"I'm here seeking Bartholomew Ringrose," Mac called.

Something black and swift as an arrow dove on them from the ceiling, brushing so close by Bianca that she felt the whisper of its talons pass her cheek. A crow half again a normal size alighted upon a chair back, studying them with eyes shiny black as marbles.

"Well, Badb? Do we know them?" the voice asked, still from the anonymity of the back rooms. "Are they who they say they are?"

A croak from the crow, a twitch of its glossy head.

"See for myself?" the voice whined. "Well, I shall, won't I? I hope they don't expect to be fed. I've only lunch enough for two."

A hand pushed aside a faded, once-luxurious

velvet curtain separating the store from the rooms behind, and out stepped a skeletal man with a long white beard, flowing silver hair, and bushy eyebrows like whisk brooms. Dressed in a shabby suit of threadbare clothes, he had a napkin stuffed into his shirt and a striped and tasseled cap perched upon his head. The combination of all this should have given him a clownish air, but there was nothing humorous in the expression blazing from his glittering silver eyes.

"What's so important you feel the need to interrupt someone's luncheon? I warn you, I haven't enough for any guests. Besides, it's chops and gravy, Badb's favorite, and she doesn't like to share."

The crow fluttered from her perch upon the chair to land upon the man's shoulder. With twin pairs of gimlet eyes, they sized Mac and Bianca up with raking stares that could curdle milk. A headache blazed up behind her eyes.

"We're looking for a plant. We were told you might have it," Mac said.

"A plant? You're bothering me for a plant? What do I look like, the corner flower girl? Buy the woman a bunch of violets and be done with it. Come bothering me for a plant," he muttered. "Badb, can you believe it? As if I've the time for such nonsense. And us just settling in to our luncheon."

The crow squawked, skittering a few steps up and back on Ringrose's shoulder.

"I'd wish you good day, but I'd be lying. Now, push off and let me get back to my chop." He turned away, obviously already dismissing them from his mind.

"I can see why the plant business isn't booming," Mac muttered.

Ignoring the mounting discomfort at her temples, Bianca shushed him with a wave of her hand. "We're looking for *Aquameniustis,* Mr. Ringrose. Have you heard of it? You're our last hope."

The man peered at her closely for the first time, his stare giving her a pins-and-needles feeling as it traveled from the tip of her head to the tips of her boots. The thudding behind her eyes doubled in intensity, spreading from her temples to overtake her whole brain. It throbbed with every beat of her heart.

The crow bobbed its black head and flapped its wings. "What's that?"

"*Aqua—*"

"Hush, woman. I heard you the first time. Just getting my bearings."

Bianca sucked in a breath, her hand tightening on Mac's. Here it was. The answer they sought. Even now, the plant they needed could be hanging inches away or tucked among the vines and greenery growing rampant around the room.

"*Aqua . . .*" he mumbled to himself, combing a hand through his beard, eyes lost in thought. ". . . *iustis.* Sounds familiar. On the tip of my tongue."

Bianca crushed her reticule as she awaited his answer.

Ringrose stopped, hands still tangled in his beard, eyes narrowed. "Never heard of it. Sounds made-up to me. Now, be off with you and let me get back to my luncheon."

He started to dive back behind the curtain, but Bianca snatched his sleeve. By now her eyes watered, her vision narrowing. The pain seized her brain in a vise-like grip, pushing down into her spine, and she wanted to be sick. "If you remember or come across it, please send for me—Mrs. Parrino." She handed him her card. "It's very important."

His glittering gold stare moved from the card to her face and back again. "Parrino, is it? The one who murdered the chap in St. James's Park?"

He twitched free of her, diving behind the curtain, leaving Bianca shaky-kneed and splashed with perspiration, hopes cracking in her chest.

"It's over, Bianca. Come along."

She hung back, expecting the old man to return, tell her it was all a mistake, and present her with the specimen. Like a child anticipating a treat, she dragged her feet, throwing expectant glances over her shoulder—right up until the door closed behind them, and they were left standing out upon the street, a buzzing in her head, and a pain in her heart.

"I'm not giving up," she vowed.

"Maybe David's right. Maybe I'm chasing phantoms," Mac said, a harshness to his features she'd not seen before.

The chill in the air acted like a slap to the face, the worst of her sickness seeming to fade in the brisk river wind. "The answer is out there. Adam wouldn't have listed it if it didn't exist. We just have to find the right person to ask."

Mac looked on her, eyes blazing in his stark and pale face, cupping her cheek in one shaking hand. "I have found exactly the right person, Bianca."

"Thank you for coming with me. Sebastian's been too busy and Sarah isn't exactly up on her swordplay. And since the truth has come out, they both have barely let me out of their sight."

"They rise in my estimation every minute. It's unsafe for you until Madame Froissart is contained."

"You mean killed, don't you?"

"She's dangerous, Bianca. Any Fey-blood powerful enough to manipulate my *krythos* is a force to be reckoned with. I'll not have you hurt."

"A bit late for that," she said with a rueful twist of her lips.

She moved up the stairs and into her bedchamber, the hearth black and cold, curtains drawn against a dim afternoon, Mac's tread slow behind her. "Gray explained what happened . . . why Renata Froissart seeks you."

Mac's face tightened until the bones stood stark and sharp under his skin, eyes like dark pools, fists clenched. "Did he?"

"He told me everything, including Adam's role. You didn't kill anyone, Mac. It wasn't you who murdered the chevalier and his family. It was Adam. He killed all of them."

But I would have if I had been there in his place," Mac answered. "I would have wielded the sword just as effectively. I would have done my duty and eliminated the threat."

Her heart galloped in her chest. "And now?"

He gazed at her with an expression she'd never seen before. It frightened her and thrilled her at the same time. "I could no more harm you than I could cut off my own arm."

Gripping the back of a chair, she turned away, unable to face the intensity in his pale eyes. Her headache had receded, leaving in its place a hollow emptiness, his words seeming to echo against the fragile shell of her skull.

"Why did you want to come back?" he asked. "Couldn't Deane have sent someone round for your things?"

"He could have, but I needed to see the place, if only to convince myself that the last few weeks haven't been some grand hallucination. That I won't suddenly open my eyes in my own bed and discover you and the Imnada and Fey-bloods and . . . and the two of us together wasn't just a crazy dream."

"Are you convinced?"

"I suppose I have to be, but it's almost disappointing. I think I expected a unicorn to meet me in the hall or faeries to be dancing on my dining room table. It's just musty and damp and no magic in sight."

"As I recall, unicorns only show themselves to virgins, and the Fey are a dour, arrogant lot. You'd never catch them doing anything as frivolous as dancing."

"Have you ever met one?" she asked, trying to keep the tone light despite the tension humming in the air. She knew that if she turned, he'd be watching her, his eyes focused like a beast upon its prey, body coiled like a spring. Crossing to the cabinet beside her bed, she slid open the top drawer, drawing out her pistol.

"No, though I've heard of Imnada who have and some who've never returned from the meeting or come away shades of their former selves." He spied the weapon in her hand, taking a startled step back. "Bloody hell, Bianca."

"Relax. This is what I came to collect." He continued to eye her as if she'd run mad. "You asked me once how I managed to fend off all those unwanted suitors. Now you know. I keep it by my bed, just in case. Always have done since Lawrence . . . well, since his death."

"You're a constant surprise, Bianca Parrino."

"I told you once before, I do what I must." A shiver jumped down her spine as she placed the gun in her reticule.

Sarah called love a risk. Jory spoke of living versus surviving. Even Sebastian in his way had thrown a gauntlet at her feet. Clasping her hands together in front of her, Bianca breathed slowly through the fluttery excitement bubbling through her. "It all looks a little flamboyant and tawdry after Line Farm. Pink-and-gold wallpaper? It's like a bordello in here."

"You can't compare this place to the Wallace house. May as well compare apples to pumpkins or yourself to Marianne. There's no similarity."

She rubbed the dust of weeks between her fingers, glancing back at him over her shoulder. "Isn't there? I'd say we have quite a lot in common."

His gaze flickered and was still. "I stand corrected. You and she are much alike. You both made the mistake of falling in love with a shapechanger."

Dust forgotten, she dropped her hands to her sides. "Was it, Mac? Truly? I sent you away, but now I have to know. Was what we had between us a mistake? Was it nothing to you but a way to keep me close and persuade me to help you with Adam's journal?"

Risk it all. Throw the dice. Ask the question. That's what she'd done. Now it was up to Mac to offer the response. The silence stretched thin as wire between them, until she wished she'd held her tongue. Here, then, was her answer, much as it grieved her to admit it.

Unable to withstand the damning quiet, Bianca flung herself away, but a hand grabbed her arm, holding her captive. He spun her around until she stood pressed against him, the buttons of his uniform poking into her skin, his grip cutting off the circulation to her fingers, his dark gaze burning a hole through to her brain.

She didn't care. It was enough that he held her. That he would not let her escape. It was hope where she'd had none.

Slowly, Mac reached up to push a stray curl behind her ear, his gaze alive with a scorching hunger until she felt she must melt beneath his devouring stare. "Nay, Bianca," he said, his voice hoarse, his breathing ragged. "No mistake and no trick. Not then. Not now."

He lowered his mouth to hers in a kiss, gentle despite the urgency radiating off him like heat off sand. Even in his ruthless need, he held back, the strength it took visible in the rock-hard tension of his muscles, the racing of his heart beneath her palm. She shivered with love for this man who could offer her such a precious gift.

Threading her fingers into his hair, she pulled him closer, as if he might come to his senses if she allowed him time to think, or as if *she* might, given the opportunity. After all, they'd settled nothing between them. Not really. The curse still clouded every moment. Renata Froissart still hunted them. Mac's decision to return to the clans had not changed. And as far as she knew, she remained unwelcome at the theater.

But who the hell cared?

Not her. Not while his tongue dove deep into her mouth, his erection pressed temptingly between her legs, and every nerve in her body jumped with wicked impatience.

She wanted Mac's hands upon her body, his lips

plundering her mouth. She needed him moving inside her, slow and deep until the sweeping, thundering rush of ecstasy shattered her. She wanted to feel all these things. Time for weeping later.

As if they raced against fate, pulse-pounding urgency drove them onward. Hands fumbled with buttons and ribbons as they unwrapped each other, breath coming in quick gasps, her hair tumbling loose down her shivering spine. No whispered endearments. No playful banter. Just a powerful urge to lose themselves in the pleasure of the moment in case a moment was all they had.

He backed her against the bed, the two of them falling onto it, skin meeting skin. His body curving over hers as she caressed the scarred muscles of his back, his mouth making its delicious way down over her neck to her breasts. His tongue teased her nipples erect, his teeth grazing them until she arched into his tantalizing fingers.

Questions were driven away as they took comfort in the sinful need to escape. Fear and heartbreak pushed aside as he thrust hard into her, her hips lifting to welcome him. The tempo rapid as he pounded into her, flesh sweat-slicked and salty on her tongue, legs locked around his waist in a savage need to escape fate and a future apart.

Pressure claimed her as every muscle twisted tighter and tighter, friction drawing her satisfaction closer with every thrust. She opened her eyes, wanting to see his face, wanting to memorize every line and angle, the curve of his brow and the shadow on his jaw. His gaze met hers as if he strove to do the same, his eyes like twin embers, raging with lust and fire and sinful greed. His face tightened, his jaw jumping, and with a cry he found his release. She tilted her hips to take him deeper, feeling her own desire peak, bliss spasming through her in a dazzling haze of sweet, arcing explosions. Tears stung her cheeks.

As he rolled her over onto his chest, his hands skimmed the line of her back, his touch once more gentle, his eyes no longer alive with a dangerous light but warm with mischief. "Pink and gold are my new favorite colors, *mi am'ryath.*"

Mac's deep voice vibrated along her bones, his incredible heat keeping her warm despite the chill of the room. And yet, she was deaf and blind to it all. The answer bursting into her head like the spark of a kindled lamp in a dark room.

Am'ryath.

The language of the Imnada.

Of course!

The second golden strand of hair shriveled and curled into dust upon her open palm, the endless sea of billowing smoke and exploding cinder fading into the crackle of her sitting room fire.

Close. Too close. The Imnada had almost recognized her intrusion. She'd felt him seeking her out, the questing touch of his mind invading the void where she lurked like a wraith. Only the ancient graybeard's interruption had saved her from discovery. For that, perhaps she would spare him his life. She could afford to be generous now that her quarry had been cornered.

She leaned back in her chair, enjoying the silence of

her widow's solitude. Alonzo would be here soon, his demands on her body no less fervid, though far more enjoyable, than poor dead Émile's. But until then, she could bask in the full appreciation of her coming success, for with the knowledge gathered this afternoon she would reel Bianca Parrino in like a fish.

Bait the trap.

Catch an even greater prize.

Her quiet laughter shattered the stillness like a bomb blast, and tilting her hand, the line of gray ash drifted onto the floor, where a maid would sweep it away.

22

"How could we be so blind? It was staring us in the face all along and we never saw it. *I* never saw it."

Bianca had donned a dressing gown as she rummaged among her books, but she could be wrapped in a coat of chain mail and still Mac would smell the spice and sex coming off her skin like the headiest of perfumes, taste her luscious core on his tongue. His cock hardened anew at thoughts of pearly flesh and tight, wet heat, and he fought back the urge to sling her across his shoulders and carry her back up to her bedchamber, where he'd peel off the silken slip of fabric with his teeth and stake his claim once and for all.

So much for keeping silent until he dealt with Renata Froissart.

Fangs extended, he felt the feral ruthlessness of his aspect like lava in his veins.

Bianca Parrino would bear his mark. She would carry his scent.

He would rip the throat out of anyone who dared harm her.

She belonged to him—now and forever.

Victory dancing in her eyes, she looked up from her book. "We can't find *Aquameniustis* because there is no such plant. It doesn't exist."

From cock-hardening arousal to being doubled over as if he'd had the breath kicked out of him. "Are you saying Adam didn't break the curse? There's no way to stop the Fey-blood's magic?"

"No. I'm not saying that at all." Caught up in her discovery, she seemed completely unaware of the horrible despair closing over his head until he couldn't breathe. "I'm saying between Adam's poor handwriting and my own ignorance, I transcribed the notes incorrectly." She slammed the book closed, snapping him free of his panic like a fist to the jaw. "Where's the journal now?"

A throbbing pain lanced his temples; he wanted to be sick. "In my office at the Horse Guards."

"Good. It doesn't matter yet, but we might have to be certain when it comes down to it." Her head remained buried in the book she held; she barely even glanced up to toss him a quick, reassuring smile.

Where was the bewitching siren who'd lured him onto his knees, her whimpers as she came around him sparking his answering release? He grabbed her, dragging her into a chair. "Bianca, please. Speak slowly and calmly. Is there or is there not a way for me to break the Fey-blood's spell?"

She nodded. "I think so, yes." A slim crease appeared on her forehead. "No, I don't think. I know. I'm absolutely sure of it."

Exhaustion rushed in to replace his earlier panic. "Explain."

She pushed her hair back over her shoulder and

clasped her hands in her lap, her face aglow with a new strength. Not the showy dazzle of the actress or even the opalescent shine of the passionate lover, but a deep, calming light that turned her blue eyes to stars. "Adam wrote down the name of the plant, but in his haste and excitement he wrote it not in English or even Latin. He wrote it in the language of the Imnada. That's how the plant was originally known to him, so that's how he wrote it down. Like the *am'ryath*."

"Then we learn what plant he meant and—"

"And we have the answer. Yes. The rest falls into place like links in a chain. The draught. The end of the curse. The lifting of your exile. You can go home, Mac. It will be over." She swallowed, her hands tightening on the book she held, the light in her gaze dimming as if someone had shuttered a flame. "It will finally be over."

He leaned in, cupping her face between his hands. "And if I've decided I don't want it to be over just yet?"

"You don't mean that." Bianca gulped back a quick breath. "Not really. All you've wanted, all you've fought for, has been to break the curse and rejoin the clans. What if you give that up for me and then come to regret it?"

Here, then, was his choice. The vow he'd not been able to say because to do so would set him upon an irrevocable course—a course taking him away from his safeguarded clan holding. Away from the open moors and misted vales of home.

"It won't happen, Bianca."

"You can't be sure."

"I'm more certain of what I feel for you than of anything since I turned my back on my father's suffocating grief and left Concullum to join the army."

"How can you give up your dream?"

He leaned in to kiss her, feeling the rightness of his choice sing in every cell in his body as their lips met. "By taking on a new one, *alanna*."

"Well? You know the language. What do you think?" Bianca pushed Adam's journal across to Mac.

Upon their arrival at Deane House, Bianca had hustled Mac through the halls to the library, praying she'd not run into Sarah. The woman had a knack for sniffing out scandal, and it wouldn't take more than a tilt of her nose to smell the delicious contentment curling off Bianca like smoke.

No, she would face the questions when they came, accept every I-told-you-so her friend uttered, but not yet.

She wanted time alone with Mac. Time to discover the habit he had of running a hand through his hair when he read and to recognize the single-minded intensity he maintained even at rest. She needed to commit to memory the male scent of him and the way his lashes swept down over his high cheekbones like shadows. And finally, she sought to remember the tingling, bubbling happiness that tugged at her lips and sent butterflies fluttering through her stomach whenever their eyes met in a moment of shared desire.

All these moments she would lock away in her heart so that if the worst happened, she would not forget. Ever.

"It could be"—he turned the journal sideways, squinted at the slash and loop of every letter—"it looks like 'Og'mnithris.'"

She observed his long fingers, the sprinkling of hairs upon the back of his hand, the silver white scars on his wrist from the Frenchman's ropes, and an ache pressed against her chest and under her ribs with the power of this new emotion. "Never heard of it."

"Nay, it's as you said. It's a word in the language of the Imnada. A language hardly spoken anymore."

"But Adam spoke it."

"Aye, he did."

"So, what does it mean? What's Og'mnithris?"

Mac rubbed his chin, his cat-slanted green eyes locked on the word, his gaze distant. "It's a small shrub. Grows in river basins and near streambeds, anywhere swift water moves. In English, it would be . . . it would be called death-bringer."

"What kind of a name is that for a healing herb?"

He touched the aromatic sprig of rosemary that lay pressed between the pages of the book. "It isn't used by healers, Bianca. The Ossine burn the leaves and inhale the smoke. They say it carries them beyond their bodies and through the Gateway, where they're reunited with the ancestors."

"So it's a narcotic or an opiate. A substance that makes one see illusions."

"No, Bianca. There's nothing of illusion about it. To inhale the smoke is to indeed tear free of the body and walk into death. But it's temporary. The body remains alive to welcome the wandering soul back. To actually ingest death-bringer would be fatal. The rift would be irrevocable. The body would die, the soul left as naught more than a shade with no anchoring form to return to."

A chill swept over her as if a window had been

thrown open, the air suddenly dank and cold like the must of a newly opened crypt. She shook off the sensation with effort, though the prickles of gooseflesh running up and down her spine remained. "Then you must have read it wrong. It can't be the plant you know."

His face grew solemn, his gaze distant as if he saw something invisible to her. "No, this is the final key, the solution we've been searching for. I feel it as if Adam whispers it in my ear."

She cast a swift glance around, half prepared to catch a glimpse of an apparition. "But Adam didn't die. He broke the curse. I saw him at night. He was himself, not a ghost or a . . . or a hallucination."

He focused on her again with a shrug of his shoulders. "I can't explain how he did it. Only what I know. Death-bringer is powerful magic and, in the hands of anyone but the Ossine, poison."

"Then it's as you said: there is no answer. No way to break the curse."

"No, Bianca. You've found it. Don't you see? Without your help, I never would have known what to look for. I never would have come as far as I have. It's just as you said, Adam broke the curse. He used the death-bringer. And so must I if I'm to finally be rid of the Fey-blood's magics."

"What if something goes wrong?" She pinched her lips together in a rush of exhaled breath. "What if the poison kills you?"

Another shrug, as if death were as trivial as a missed meal. "Then I die, Bianca. But I die knowing I made the attempt."

"I don't want to lose you. Not now. Not when I've only just found you."

"You'll not lose me." He tipped her face to his, his mouth curled into a heartbreaking smile, though sorrow touched the corners of his eyes. "Trust me."

She blinked away tears. "How did I know you were going to say that?"

Descending the front steps, Mac met Lord Deane coming from the mews, his face drawn, his gaze grim. "Come to grovel an apology at her feet?"

Mac collared him, nerves raw, emotions running like a river in spate. "Look, Fey-blood. I've no choice but to tolerate you, but don't push it."

Deane's eyes flicked to the hand on his lapel, gold flashing in his somber eyes. "Gray warned me you were the perfect soldier. Question nothing. Toe the line. Do as you're ordered. No matter the cost to you or others. Does he paint an accurate picture?"

"If this is your idea of a recruitment speech, you'll have to polish your delivery. Bianca's inside with your wife. I want you to keep her there. Do whatever you have to do, but don't let her out of your sight."

"You believe Renata Froissart remains a threat to her?"

"I've felt the woman's madness, her lust for vengeance. She grows impatient and reckless. She would use any weapon against me that came to hand. Including Bianca."

"Is she a weapon? Or is she a tool?"

Animal fury choked closed Mac's throat, the panther riding just beneath his skin. "I'd take care if I were you, my lord, lest a slip of the tongue cuts your throat."

Instead of responding with rage or even mild

alarm, Deane relaxed, amusement twitching the edges of his mouth. "Not an answer, but it will do." He threw a swift, shuttered glance to the house. "There's something you must know. I've sent a letter to de Coursy, but he rode for the north this morning."

"Go on."

"Stories are circulating. Stories of demon shifters walking among us once again. Stories of monsters bearing the forms of men, dealing blood and death and evil rivaling anything hell might bring forth."

"You believe Madame Froissart is the source?"

"I do. Trouble is brewing. The rumors are gaining strength like tinder before a flame. If she's not stopped, she could throw all that our group has accomplished thus far into jeopardy."

"She could awaken a new Fealla Mhòr."

Weariness hovered in Deane's eyes. "The Other are only a few months away from a conspiracy that brought us to the brink of war with the human world. Suspicions still run high and fear remains rife among my people. All it would take is the right spark for the bloodshed and deaths to begin all over again."

"Then I'll just have to make sure that spark is snuffed, won't I?"

With a nod, Mac descended the last steps to the drive, Deane's voice checking his stride. "Bianca cares for you, Flannery. Don't make her regret it."

Mac squeezed his eyes shut and said a silent prayer to the goddess, his heart like lead in his chest as he walked away. One order he could not promise would be carried out.

*   *   *

A watchman called the hour of three, but the lights within the Froissart house still burned bright, the party of dark-clad men who'd entered shortly before midnight still inside. What did they do in there? What plans did they hatch? A footman had left an hour ago and had not returned. The young man had come within a breath of Mac's hideaway, his gaze passing without seeing over the enormous dark form crouched in the gloom of the alley.

Since then, there had been no other movement from the house, and Mac was left to stand guard in a cold, misty rain that silvered his fur, hung in droplets from his whiskers, and made a long night downright uncomfortable.

At four, a carriage drew up to the curb, rousing Mac from a half-lidded doze to narrow his gaze on the man emerging from the town house to stand in the guttering light from the doorway, his fur-collared coat turned up around his neck, a hat standing tall upon his dark hair. He turned to speak to someone beyond Mac's vision before entering the carriage. A few words in the clipped abruptness of Lyonnais French, but enough for Mac's heart to race as he growled low in his throat, ears clamped against his skull, tail lashing. He knew that voice. Had heard the oozing oily viciousness of it as his flesh had been peeled off him in strips and pain had lived in every soft-spoken ruthless syllable.

The Frenchman lived.

The hunt was on.

23

⟡

Dawn barely pinked the sky when Bianca left her rooms for the library and the stack of books still to be studied. One problem solved. A greater and potentially lethal problem created. There had to be something she'd missed. Some clue among Adam's writings overlooked in the excitement of yesterday's success. But what?

The house was quiet, with only a few servants up and about, starting fires, cleaning and dusting the unending maze of rooms, setting the table for breakfast.

Worrying at her dilemma like a dog with a bone, Bianca ignored them all as she wandered through the Blue Salon, the Round Room, the gallery. Only occasionally did a whisper penetrate her concentration.

". . . one what done it with that dead chap in the park . . ."

". . . don't look like a fancy woman . . ."

". . . don't believe it . . . hurt a fly, she could . . ."

She barely acknowledged the snatched comments, other than to note that the papers had not yet lost interest in the lurid circumstances surrounding Adam's death. They still sought to spin tales from vicious gossip and sly innuendo. Somehow that didn't bother her as it might have done a month ago or even a week ago. A bulwark stood solid now between herself and the slings and arrows of outrageous fortune. Mac was an anchor holding her safely in place. A net when she fell. Wings to help her fly.

She sailed through the hushed remarks unscathed until a cleared throat and a touch upon her sleeve drew her back from her thoughts to find Donas standing at her shoulder.

"Pardon me, mum, but a letter's come for you." He handed her a wrinkled folded page, the inexpensive paper thin and stained.

Her stomach clenched as she fumbled with the simple blob of sealing wax, trying to still the slight trembling in her hands as she read the scrawled words written there. "Is His Lordship awake?" she asked.

"He's not here, mum. A message come last night and he left straightaway for his estates in Berkshire. None know when he'll return."

Bianca barely heard him, her mind already skipping ahead as she worked out the next minutes, the next hours. Flinging the page down, she hastened for the stairs and the pistol she'd retrieved from Holles Street. "Call us a carriage, Donas. We've a meeting to make."

"You let her leave? Alone?" Mac stood in the drawing room of Deane House experiencing a depressingly familiar stomach-rolling feeling. Did he need to nail

Bianca's feet to the floor to ensure she stayed put? Were his worst nightmares coming true?

Lady Deane's hands clenched into fists in her lap, her gold-shot gaze hardening. "Not alone. She took Donas with her."

The shambling muscle-bound mountain from the marketplace. Mac's heart rate ratcheted down from terrified to merely scared witless. Then he read the hasty explanation Bianca had penned before she left, and his fear exploded back into white-hot panic. The man could be the fucking Matterhorn and he'd stand no chance against the Frenchman's battle magic or his blade. Nor would Bianca.

"Shit all! When did they leave?"

By now Lady Deane had risen from her seat, her imperious gaze growing more frightened by the moment. "An hour ago."

Plenty of time to travel into the City. Plenty of time to fall into a cesspit of trouble.

"Shit," Mac snarled again as his hand fell to the hilt of his dagger, the taste of blood in his mouth where he'd bitten down hard to keep from shouting his rage. One . . . two . . . three . . . He counted the jagged spasms of fear lancing his innards.

"What's going on, Captain?" Lady Deane asked.

Mac paused in his rabid pacing. "I followed one of Renata Froissart's men last night. Where do you think the bastard went?"

"By the murder in your gaze and the way you're gripping that knife of yours as if you mean to lop off my head, I'd say to Mr. Ringrose's apothecary."

"You got it right in one. Whether the man's in league with Froissart or merely a dupe to her schemes,

I don't fucking care. Bianca is walking into a trap. Renata Froissart sent that message, I'm sure of it. She lured Bianca there, knowing I'd follow."

"Bianca went there for you, Captain. She felt there was no other way."

"Is that supposed to make me feel better? This curse has cost me my family, my clan, my friends, and nearly my sanity. I'll not let it claim Bianca too." He pulled himself together. Running headlong would gain him nothing but a faster death. He needed to think things through before he ran willy-nilly into the Fey-blood's den. "Get word to your husband if you can, my lady. He'll know what to do."

"And you?"

"I'll visit Ringrose. If Bianca's not there, he'll know where she's being held."

"What if he doesn't want to say?"

"Then he dies, my lady."

She gripped the back of a sofa, the deep green of her gown only emphasizing the chalky pallor of her skin. "If Bianca is the bait for this trap, won't you be giving them what they want if you simply walk right in?"

"They'll learn to be careful what they wish for." His smile revealed extended fangs, his body alive with the power and precision of the panther. Lady Deane's recoil only adding to his already keen-edged nerves. She was right to be afraid of him. Right to fear the Imnada. They suffered no enemy to live and defended their own to the last breath in their bodies.

Bianca was his.

He would kill for her.

If need be, he would die for her.

* * *

Mac's reconnaissance of the area around Ringrose's shop offered him little to go on. The windows remained as crusted over with city grime as ever; the sign creaked in the fitful breeze off the river; a scrawny, half-fed dog slunk out of the yard with a dead rat in its mouth. Nothing else stirred and no voices sounded from within. Drawing his knife, he tried the door, the latch turning easily, the overloud tinkle of the bell jangling down his spine and into the pit of his stomach.

The interior seemed even filthier and more cluttered than it had yesterday. Ignoring the buzz of Feyblood magic skittering along his bones like nails on a slate, he traveled up and down the aisles, boot heels crunching on broken glass, liquid puddling on the floor around gobs of unidentifiable flesh. A plant lay shredded in pieces among the remnants of its shattered pot as if someone had flung it against a wall, the sweet fragrance of its torn and broken petals mingling with the acrid stench of embalming fluid and rot that clung to his nostrils and the back of his throat.

Shadows crawled like inky wraiths over the walls as if unseen watchers followed his every move, and a draft stirred the faded curtain sealing off the shop's back rooms. A draft that carried with it the faintest hint of orange and spice—and blood and fear.

He'd barely put a hand upon the curtain when a shadow dropped from the ceiling in a rush of black. Instinct took over. Mac dropped to his knees, back bowed to the floor as Ringrose's crow swooped past, talons poised to claw his eyes out, beak sharp as a razor.

The bird squawked, wheeling around for another dive, but Mac was faster. He grabbed up a piece of the broken clay pot, firing the missile as the crow plunged. The shard struck the bird's outstretched left wing, causing it to tumble in a ruffled ball of feathers and feet end over end to the floor, where it skidded beneath a cabinet and lay unmoving.

"Badb!" Ringrose charged through the curtain to scoop up the bird the way a mother would cradle a child. "Look what you've gone and done. She'd not hurt a soul and you've killed her. Speak to me, Badb. Speak to Papa."

Reaffirming the grip on his knife, Mac regained his feet, noting the tear in his jacket where the bird's claws had raked the cloth on a path to his jugular. "Where's Mrs. Parrino?"

The old man continued stroking the dead bird, murmuring under his breath, his bent shoulders and skinny fingers shaking as he struggled with his emotions.

"How much did Renata Froissart pay you to write that note?" Mac growled. "Where is she? What has she done with Bianca?"

Ringrose lifted his head, tears streaming from red-rimmed eyes, his face twisted in anguish. "I don't know what you're talking about. I've not seen Mrs. Parrino since yesterday when the two of you rudely interrupted my luncheon."

"And the man who came here last night? A tall fellow. Dark hair. French."

Again Ringrose shook his head. "You're mistaken. No one came last night. You must have this shop confused with another. Now go away." His gaze narrowed. "Go away. Leave before it's too late."

Small chance of that. There weren't two such magic-heavy rabbit warrens in all of London. He knew what he'd seen and he'd seen the Frenchman entering this shop. He felt Ringrose's deception in the sour stench of sweat and fear rolling off him. He knew more than he was telling.

Mac grabbed him by the shirt, only the veriest thread keeping him from wringing the scrawny man's neck as he'd broken his bird's. "Tell me what you know, old man."

"Mac? You got the note I left with Sarah. You came." Her voice. Her scent.

Releasing Ringrose, Mac spun round to see Bianca standing at the curtain, her golden hair tumbling loose from its pins, a smudge high on a cheekbone that looked all too much like a bruise, but other than that she appeared to be unharmed. His immediate terror abated, though he remained on his guard.

He crossed the room toward her outstretched arms, wanting to touch her, hold her, assure himself this wasn't some cunning hallucination. "Are you hurt? What's the old man done to you? Where's Froissart?"

He'd made it only halfway when a second figure emerged from behind the curtain, dragging Bianca back against his brawny chest, his other hand holding a pistol to her temple.

"Are you in such a rush to meet death, shifter?" the Frenchman asked. "For that is what Renata has planned for you. A slow and very gruesome death."

Fey-blood magic pulsed the air like a dissonant chord. It jolted along Mac's nerve endings like a constant strike at his funny bone. How much of it was attributable to the Frenchman, Ringrose, or the hidden presence of Froissart was impossible to determine from the cacophony blurring his vision and making his head throb. "You tried and failed once. What makes you think this time you'll be any more successful?"

The Frenchman's lips curled in a cruel rictus of a smile, his eyes empty as death, the grip on his pistol unwavering. "Her."

Bianca lifted her chin as the barrel of the pistol dug into her neck.

Mac's hands curled to fists, his body aflame. Every ounce of fear and sorrow and guilt accompanied the ribbon of his pathing. *I'll not let him harm you, Bianca.*

Bianca's gaze clouded, and she answered with a barely perceptible shake of her head.

"Throw down your weapons, shifter. Now."

Mac tossed his dagger to the floor with a clang, pushing it forward with the toe of his boot. Then he pulled his brace of pistols from under his coat, laying each one down, shoving them one by one toward the Frenchman's feet.

"And the blade you've hidden away in your boot."

Mac hesitated until the Frenchman pressed his gun into Bianca's neck once more. Kneeling, he drew a second slim blade from his boot, adding it to the pile. "Let her go. She's not part of this."

"Isn't she? Defiling herself with a shifter lover? Taking a demon into her bed? If you ask me, she deserves whatever happens to her."

"What do you want?" Mac asked. "Tell me and I'll do it if you'll just let her go."

The man's smile widened, a ruthless light glowing in his dark eyes. "For starters, I want to see you on your knees."

"As you wish." Mac's eyes burned, his heart thrashed against his ribs. Sweat washed cold across his back as he bent slowly. First to one knee. Then the other.

Something oozed through the leather of his breeks, and a jagged pot edge drew blood as it ground into his knee.

"Mac, don't," Bianca murmured.

But Mac had already bowed his head, arms loose at his sides, surrender evident in every rigid muscle. He trained his eyes on the floor, on the broken greenery, the pieces of shattered drawers, the dark feathers turning and drifting over the boards. Behind him, he continued to hear Ringrose's aggrieved murmurs as he crooned to his dead familiar. And something else: the whisper of fabric across a carpet, the brief sound of a quick, indrawn breath.

"You thought you could win against us, shifter? You thought you could kill and not face justice?" the Frenchman jeered. "You'll beg for the kiss of my blade before I'm through with you. You and then the rest of your filthy kind."

Rage swept Mac like a fever, but he remained where he was, subservient, submissive. Whatever it took to buy him a few seconds. Until . . .

Drop, Bianca. Now! Mac's pathing ripped the air between them.

With a cry of pain, Bianca threw herself to the side, catching the Frenchman off guard as she fell.

Mac's third and final blade—whipped free from his back, where it had rested against his spine—flew toward the Frenchman's heart. Only the man's sudden grappling with Bianca's deadweight kept him from being speared like a pig on a stick. Instead, the blade bit into his breast just below his collarbone. The force of it threw him backward, blood erupting in a ribbon of scarlet.

Bianca rolled clear of the fight as Mac snatched up a second knife from the pile. The Frenchman lay on his back, arched against the pain, his left hand grasping to remove the dagger from his shoulder. Mac stood over him, adjusting his grip for a final downward thrust. Their eyes locked in a terrible drawn-out contest of wills.

"You fail—again," Mac snarled.

"Kill him, Renata," the man gasped, his eyes gazing beyond Mac. "Do it now."

The reek of Fey-blood magics intensified until Mac's eyes watered, the grip on his dagger growing slick, a buzz along his nerves until every hair stood on end. He knelt until the point of his blade touched the man's chest. "Where's Froissart?"

Bianca's whispered words touched Mac's ear and mind simultaneously: "She's here."

A shadow speared the floor, the oppressive smell of scent hanging like a cloud in the air. The Frenchman's eyes darted about, then froze and glazed over, his breath coming in quick, rasping pants.

"We finally meet face-to-face, Captain Flannery, though I've seen you many times through Alonzo's eyes and even reached into your mind as easily as sifting through a jar."

Mac straightened. At last he looked upon the woman behind Adam's murder. A woman whose journey, begun in vengeance on four, threatened to drag the entire races of Imnada and Other into a new conflagration if she wasn't stopped. He recognized her deep-brown eyes, her blue-black hair, her intensity of expression. But now the skin stretched tightly over the bones of her face, and her hands curled like talons at her sides. Power rolled off her in waves until Mac grew nauseated, the floor seeming to roll in the sudden dizziness that overtook him. He tightened his hold on his knife lest it slide from his trembling fingers. If only Bianca weren't in the way, he could gain a clear shot. A quick kill.

"It's over," he said, even as he sought to path instructions to Bianca, but something blocked him. He could gain no connection with her mind.

Renata's eyes gleamed. "In this we are in agreement, shifter. It is over and you have lost. Just as your friend Kinloch surrendered to me in the final minutes of his life, so, too, will you know the shame of begging before the end. As will Gray de Coursy and David St. Leger."

Mac flinched.

"Yes, I have discovered them. It took time and seeking both on this plane and in the void, but I have found them and soon they will know the same degradation and shame. They will see their end coming, with no way to prevent it."

"He didn't do it. He didn't kill your father." Bianca's gaze remained riveted on Mac's face, her hands lost in the folds of her skirts.

Renata's eyes burned black and soulless, her fingers gripping Bianca's bare arm. "You fight for him. How sweet, but how simple to turn that defense into an attack."

Fey-blood magic crackled the air around Froissart like a twining ribbon of fire before leaping to entangle Bianca within its powerful embrace.

"Do it! Now!" Froissart screamed.

The muscles in Bianca's neck went rigid with strain, her pupils dilated, and a dark presence crouched at the edges of her gaze. "She's . . . there's something . . . I can't control . . . Oh, God, I'm sorry, Mac."

She raised her right hand.

Mac caught the glint of steel, the stench of black powder. He only had time to shout, "Bianca, no!"

A deafening roar shook him to his knees, a searing pain lanced his head, and Mac fell tumbling into an endless void, the darkness rushing up from below to swallow him.

24

Deep breaths in and out. Slow, calm, easy breaths to relieve the panic blistering her mind. She had air to breathe. The walls were not closing in. No one ever died from a locked door.

She stalked the area of her makeshift cell, trying to rub warmth back into her freezing-cold arms, relief and disgust warring for dominance in her sloshy, scattered head.

She had not murdered the Frenchman. She could erase that debit from her life's account, more's the pity. She shuddered, recalling his powerful arms wrapped round her body, the gloating in his voice as he sought to humiliate Mac before he murdered him.

But he had not been the one to strike the killing blow. They had made Bianca do it. They had used her as a weapon against the man she loved.

She stumbled, her knees buckling from under her as she sagged against the wall. She pressed the heels of her hands to her eyes as if she might erase the image of Mac's body sprawled at her feet, blood pooling beneath his head. As if she could claw out the slithering hatred that had infected her mind, taking her over, compelling her against her will.

In the moments she'd been under Renata Froissart's influence, she'd felt the woman's warped perversion. Her hatred and the desire to be avenged had eaten into her soul until there was only a black and empty hole where her heart had been. A hole she'd filled with dark and powerful magic.

Bianca could only console herself with the bitter knowledge that the shot had not been fatal. Mac lived still, though for how long was anyone's guess.

Long enough for the Frenchman and Renata to annihilate him in a death of inches until there was naught left but a husk for the ragpickers, another victim left to rot in London's streets.

Long enough for him to dwell on Bianca's apparent betrayal and hate her for it.

She banged a fist against the wall. No. She would find a way out. She would put right the mess she'd created. She would find Mac before it was too late. Another try at the door. Still locked, and no amount of fiddling, pulling, pushing, or kicking did anything but frazzle her already shaky nerves. Another study of the empty room as if some answer might magically write itself upon the walls. Not that escaping from the room would accomplish anything except get her into more trouble. She and Mac had been brought to the Froissart house this time, the center of the spider's web.

She sank upon the floor, drawing her knees up tightly to her chest, wrapping her arms around them. Loosed her mind as if unfettering a caged bird. *Mac, where are you? It's Bianca.*

A faint shimmering touch brushed against the edge of her awareness, but she closed her eyes, concentrating on reaching out, seeing the thought in her head and then letting it go. *It was Renata. She can control people. Somehow she can reach into my head—into anyone's head—and make me do what she wants.*

The shimmer grew stronger until it became a prickling, listening tension that twitched her shoulder blades. *You have to believe me. You have to . . . you have to trust me.*

No answer to her plea, but the shimmer flared brightly, a warmth wrapping round her as if arms embraced her. Then, as if a shadow blotted out the sun, the warmth fled beneath a cold, sour wind, and Bianca was left alone once more.

Mac swam in and out of delirium, every movement sending shock waves of pain from his skull into his stomach until his throat ached from retching. Like ghosts, voices came and went. Some angry, hitting his fractured mind like bullets, and others stealing softly and poisonously into his consciousness like thieves. But all with one goal: to discover the secrets of the Imnada. To learn what they could of the five clans before they destroyed him.

He clamped his jaw against the agony and said nothing, though each session ended with another slash of the Frenchman's knife across his flesh and another blow to his broken body. Mac merely curled tighter into himself and endured.

Once the voice changed from the unceasing interrogation, and he lifted his head to Bianca's shadowy presence, which acted like ice water on his burning body. He reached for her, trying to answer, to reassure her, but before he could focus on her words, she'd vanished. Swallowed by a whirling pool of darkness, to be replaced by a girl whose shiny black eyes and narrow face seemed oddly familiar. Then she, too, was gone and he woke alone, the chamber empty, no candle or fire to ease the impenetrable gloom.

His first thought upon opening his eyes was that the horrible clawing ache along his bones and the slow one-by-one crush of organs was a result of the silver-threaded cords binding him hand and foot.

A notion revised as soon as he looked to the window and the slender gap between the heavy curtains showing the dimming afternoon light.

No, this brand of perpetual incineration was much worse.

The Fey-blood's curse fought to consume him as it did every night, but the goddess moon's absence from the sky prevented the forced shift. Mac was trapped in his human form while two great magics battled for his soul.

Sunset. Morderoth.

The longest night began now.

The sound of a key turning in the lock brought Bianca's head up. Shadows hung thick and close around her, and the air held a dank, musty chill along with a strange metallic taste that seemed to coat her tongue like fuzz. She had no idea how long she'd been here, and despite repeated attempts she had never felt Mac's touch upon her mind or his voice sounding in her head.

The latch clicked and she threw herself to her feet to take up a position on the wall beside the door. She braced herself for the attack, fists clenched. Tension wiring her back. She'd get one chance only. She'd better make it count.

The door opened with a sudden jerk before easing slowly wider, a gnarled hand upon the frame. As the intruder stepped through, Bianca brought her fist up in a quick cut to the jaw, dropping her jailer to the floor like a puppet whose strings had been cut.

"See there. I knew I should have gone in first," a voice sulked. "Now he'll likely wake with a knot on his head and a foul temper to match, and who will he blame? Me, of course."

Before Bianca could react or recover, a girl entered the room to kneel beside the body of Mr. Ringrose. Almost boyishly thin, with a crop of short, black curls and eyes as shiny as beads, she wore nothing but a trailing cloak of black feathers, while her skin where it peeked through her garment glowed with an almost deathly pallor.

"Badb? But you're a . . . were a . . . crow."

Catching sight of Bianca's shocked stare, the girl smiled, eyes dancing, mouth curved impishly at the corners. "Aye, among an infinite number of things, but we've no time to discuss it now. The sun has set. He'll be at his weakest this night." Before straightening, she took a dagger from a sheath on Ringrose's belt.

Was this a trap? Another of Madame Froissart's manipulations? A dream?

"No dream and certainly no conjuring of hers." The girl's brows drew into a pouty frown as she handed the dagger to Bianca.

"But I saw you attack Mac," Bianca stammered even as her fingers curled around the blade's handle with a grateful squeeze. "I saw him strike you down."

The girl's feather cloak ruffled as if annoyed. "Make a decision. I've not much time. Come with me or stay here and await your fate."

Bianca hesitated, glancing again at Ringrose's unconscious form. "We can't just leave him behind."

The girl grinned, though no warmth reached the jet sparkle in her black eyes as she bent to touch Ringrose on his forehead. "There. He will return to the shop. Wake and be as irascible as ever. Satisfied?"

As Bianca watched, the body on the floor took on a translucent rainbow glow, pinks flowing into reds, which in turn flowed into purples and blues. With every changing shade, Ringrose—or what had been Ringrose—faded until there was nothing but specks of dazzling color bursting against the darkness. Then even the bursts died away, leaving only the gloom of a moonless night and no body at all.

"Come on." Grabbing Bianca's hand, Badb pulled her from the room into a narrow, whitewashed corridor, locked doors to either side. The corridor led to a kitchen. Spotless, organized, and empty of life. No glowing stove or bustling of servants. It echoed with the sound of their footsteps on the tiles, the rasp of their breathing.

The girl took the lead, Bianca following as they crept up the stairs to the main house, pausing at the green baize door. "He's being held in her bedchamber upstairs."

"How do you know?"

Badb threw her a look of disgust. "Because I do,

that's all. But it's late and he hasn't much time." Bianca started forward, but the girl grabbed her sleeve. "They will seek to use you against him as they did before. Do not allow Renata Froissart entry into your mind."

"How can I keep her out? I'm not one of you. I don't have any powers. I can't change into a bird or a lion. I don't have a wand I can wave. I'm improvising here."

"You're doing fine." The girl reached up to tap Bianca's forehead with a tip of her finger.

Light flared, washing the inky stairwell a brilliant silver before it faded, leaving a faint halo burning at the backs of Bianca's eyelids.

"My wards will protect you," the girl explained, "but they will not last long. You will have to move quickly."

"Can't you just do what you did to Mr. Ringrose and carry us all out of here?"

"I'm afraid not." Her curls bobbed as she shook her head. "Bartholomew is a Realing. Disrupt the magic holding him together, and he will return to his source back at the shop."

Bianca wished even a word of her explanation made sense.

The girl seemed to understand, for she threw Bianca another, almost sisterly grin. "It's not important. Just know that Bartholomew is safe, I can't carry anyone anywhere, and you need to hurry."

"Aren't you coming with me? Strength in numbers and all that?"

"I can't. I'm not allowed. Get you out: those were my instructions. I've done more than I should already."

"Who gave you those instructions? Who sent you? Was it Lord Deane? Gray de Coursy?"

But even as she spoke, the feathers of the girl's cloak seemed to curve and ruffle up around her face, the trailing end whipping around her body until all of it was a moving, shifting curtain of black growing smaller until it was no larger than a crow. But instead of taking flight, the bird itself took on the same prismatic glow as Ringrose, body fragmenting as it moved from violet to indigo to blue and continuing down through the color spectrum in a sparkling cloud of multihued light.

"Wait," Bianca rasped. "You can't leave me."

But the brilliance of the flashes had already dimmed, fading until they resembled dust motes caught by the sun before disappearing completely.

Bianca touched her forehead, feeling once more the faint buzz of whatever safeguards had been offered to her. And with a deep breath and a swift prayer to any and all gods out there, she stepped through the green baize door.

A touch on his shoulder jerked Mac awake to struggle uselessly against his bonds, the silver cutting into his wrists and ankles until he moaned in agony. He cracked his eyes open against a candle held close to his face, every muscle tensed, waiting for the blow of a fist or the searing pain of the knife.

"Dear God in heaven, what have they done to you?"

Mac let out a suspended breath, his relief mixed with terror. "Bianca, love. Is it you? I was dreaming of a girl in a cloak all of feathers."

She kissed him, her tears spilling onto his face, her sobs uncontrollable. "I'm so sorry, Mac. Renata was in my head. I couldn't . . . couldn't . . ."

He tried to smile around the pain engulfing his body, the constant fire burning under his skin. "'Tis all right, *alanna*. I know her powers. She would use you to destroy me, body and soul. Which is why you need to run before they find you here."

"You're coming with me." A sharp tug, and he had to bite back a scream. His wrists were free. Another, and his ankles were no longer bound. "They're busy downstairs. If we hurry, we can escape before they ever know we're missing."

She draped his arm around her shoulder, hoisting him against her. The flames within him leapt and snarled, his knees almost buckling.

"Can you walk?" she asked, struggling to keep him upright.

"I can," he said, forcing one foot in front of the other in a somewhat straight line, every shuffling step tearing at muscles cramped with fever and reopening the jagged cuts imparted by the Frenchman's blade.

"The sun's down, Mac, and you haven't changed. Does that mean—"

Already Mac felt Bianca weakening, his weight bearing down on her. They'd never make it to freedom. Not like this. She hitched him farther onto her shoulder, her breath coming in quick pants.

"The curse remains. It's Morderoth, the night the goddess moon hides her face. Shifting's impossible, so I suffer in the torture of between."

She reached for the doorhandle with her free hand, her other arm wrapped around his midsection. He could feel his broken ribs grating under her hand, blood trickling over his torn flesh and drenching her gown.

The corridor beyond lay in darkness but for a single candle upon a table at the top of the landing. Mac focused on the flickering light to keep the anguish from overwhelming him.

"Just a bit farther," Bianca hissed under her breath as he flagged halfway down the corridor.

He nodded now that speech took too much effort. Counted silently in his head Ten steps to the stairs. Another twenty to the first floor. Then another landing. Another set of stairs. An entrance hall. A street. Too far to travel and too many opportunities to be caught.

By now he heard Renata and the Frenchman locked in heated conversation, perhaps an argument. As their voices rose up the stairs, Mac and Bianca caught a word here and there.

". . . Amhas-draoi should know . . . Scathach's army . . . steps to eliminate . . ."

". . . will make him talk . . . others pay . . ."

". . . kill or be killed . . . them or us . . ."

Mac's sentiments almost exactly. Fey-blood and shapechanger. All Gray's efforts would be for naught. There was too much hatred and too many years of suspicion to be overcome by a few idealists. War would come. To the death this time, for when the shielding power of the Palings was breached, no Imnada holding would be safe from Fey-blood attack.

By now the pain had overtaken him until it filled every cell in his body, but with it came an unnatural calm and a purpose that sent him, not toward the second set of stairs and escape, but toward the closed door.

Gray was right. The four of them had been offered a chance to break free of the hidebound traditions chaining them. Mac had been given love with a woman whose courage, loyalty, wit, and beauty constantly amazed him. He'd found a truth kept hidden from his kind for centuries—a truth that could spell their ultimate survival. But only if those who would begin a new Fealla Mhòr were stopped.

"What are you doing?" Bianca said as he dragged himself free of her supporting arm to stand wobbly but upright.

"Following my destiny, Bianca."

She fought to hold him, to slow him. They were so close. The unguarded front door lay a mere twenty paces away. But whereas before he'd clung to her, hunched and battered, now he stood on his own. His blade-like gaze scythed the darkness of the corridor, his body as bristling with energy as a summer storm. She sensed a difference in him, a wildness, a power as raw as the surging of the ocean, as if he'd shed his humanity. This, then, was the otherworldly Imnada. This was the fantasy creature come to life.

"You'll be killed," she pleaded, though she knew before she spoke that her words would be turned aside by the aura of invincibility he wore like impregnable chain mail. "You'll be killed and I'll . . . I'll be left alone. I can't go back, Mac. I've felt too much. You've made me feel too much." She hated the whine underpinning her words, but the truth was indisputable.

He brushed his lips over her brow, the girl's magic mingling with the power of his kiss. "Then I'll just have to win, won't I?"

Sliding the knife free of her grip, he flashed her a last killer smile before moving toward the murmur of conversation, then turned to face her at the very last moment. "Go, Bianca. This is not your fight. It never was."

Before she could argue, he placed a hand on the door, adjusted the grip on his knife, squared his bloodied shoulder, and slammed like an army unleashed into the room

Bianca had always imagined battle to be a glorious affair of snapping banners and rattling drums. Brightly plumed officers upon prancing horses and heroic last stands amid the roar of cannon. A clash of chaotic, noisy thousands over scarred and sacred ground.

This struggle was dirty and bloody and fierce— and oddly silent. No shouted commands or inspirational battle cries, just a street scrum over broken furniture and a bloodstained rug. The air crackled with the same summer heaviness of a coming storm, and a taste of metal coated the back of her mouth.

Renata lay beside an overturned chair, a torn ribbon, jewel-bright gold against the ebony cascade of her hair. Her skirts sodden with blood but for a few inches of untouched hem that retained the delicate pale stitching of woodland flowers.

Locked together, Mac and the Frenchman exchanged cruel and wicked blows, Mac already a mess of bruises, blood streaking his face and arms, slicking his bare back. Which blood was the Frenchman's and which flowed from wounds already sustained by Mac in the torture of long hours? Bianca couldn't tell.

Unlike the fight at Adam's house, there was no brutal joy or wild excitement. Mac fought with grim-faced purpose. Each ring of knife on knife made her stomach tremble. Each grunt and snarl and swiftly drawn breath threw her heart into her throat as she waited for the feint that would end it. The parry that would be turned to an attack. The point where Mac's broken body could no longer endure.

She scrambled in search of a weapon. A book? A paperweight? A broken china figurine? But they fought too close to allow for any interference. Any intrusion could be the second the Frenchman needed to press his advantage. Already Mac slipped, his knee giving out, his arm falling to his side, ripped open by a blade's jagged edge.

Transfixed, Bianca watched, hands gripping the doorframe. Eyes focused on the man she loved bleeding out before her.

Pinned back, Alonzo reached into the hearth, dragging out a flaming log, striking Mac across his scarred back in a shower of embers and sparks that spun and fell to the carpet or flew upward onto the drapes.

Mac reared back in a cry of rage, eyes wide, the irises vertical slits in a face that bore nothing of the human in its ruthless savagery or chilling brutality.

"Alonzo!" The scream tore the air like the lash of a whip.

Bianca's head whipped around to stare at the risen shape of the woman, hair trailing wildly over her shoulders, a hand clutching a single glittering strand like thread or the silk from a spider.

End it!

The order slid into Bianca's mind like a creeping

tide, a whisper filling the cracks left by her doubt and her fear. End it now and she would no longer need to fear Mac and the predator that hovered at the back of his gaze, the monster that could rend her limb from limb if he chose or spill her blood with the ease of instinct.

Smoke curled and thickened as sparks ignited and flames crept unguarded over the floor. Then Renata was at her side, pressing a pistol into her hand. This time Bianca would not miss. She would center the bullet in Mac's chest. She would kill him, and he would look into her eyes and know she had won.

No, Bianca shook her head, but the power of the voice would not be dislodged. It clung like the smoke that clawed at her lungs and stung her eyes.

A stumbling, off-balance lurch, and Mac's knife flashed in a quick thrust, punching deep into Alonzo's gut.

The man dropped to his knees on the blazing rug, his face drained of color, his hands grasping the handle of the blade lodged in his stomach as if uncertain how it had gotten there.

End it now!

The command tumbled and turned her like a stone upon a beach until Bianca saw no choice but to agree. To end the fight and destroy the creature that would destroy her if he had the chance.

The pistol's grip was warm against her palm, the heat of it comforting against the cold infecting her body, numbing her until she felt nothing, knew only the voice. Saw only the point she must aim for in order to shatter Mac's heart as he stood above his beaten enemy.

She closed her eyes, hoping blindness would delay the moment she must choose, and that's when she sensed it. A warmth beyond the heat of the pistol and the unrelenting pressure of Renata's hand over her own. This was a winking, darting sliver of heat that uncurled from a spot in the middle of her forehead, stretching downward, wrapping her in a strange, dancing silver light.

Kill him. For Father. For Alonzo.

Like the blade impaling Alonzo, the force holding Bianca sank deep into her brain until she was left once more bereft of any but Renata's cold, hollow echo beating against her mind like a hammer strike against an anvil.

Kill him now.

The wards crumbled. The protections disintegrated. Bianca must obey or be rent apart by the strength in the voice.

She lifted the gun. Cocked the hammer.

End it!

Mac's gaze met hers, his eyes a blaze of knowing. His body awash in blood and gore, humming with unspent violence. He lifted his hand as if in gratitude or farewell.

Tears streaming down her face, Bianca turned and fired, the scream as the bullet struck tearing her apart.

She had done as she was told.

She had ended it.

25

A burning white light seared the backs of her eyelids, pulling Bianca from the tumult of the endless nightmare in which Mac's broken body was carried away by a giant crow, disappearing behind a wall of silver blue flame.

She opened her eyes on a choking gasp of pained breath to find herself in her Deane House bedchamber, tucked up under blankets and quilts, Sarah's anxious face hovering above her.

"Donas," she ordered. "Go tell His Lordship she's awake."

The young footman was alive? The last Bianca had seen him, he'd gone down like a felled tree beneath a well-swung cudgel. "What's happened?" she croaked, her voice rusty, her throat sore. "How did I get here?"

"What do you remember?"

Bianca tried to concentrate, but memories slid away just as they swam to the surface. A pistol's deafening report followed by the gagging stench of black powder. The slithering, clinging presence in her head cut off as Renata went down in a spray of blood and bone. And flames licking up walls, over fabric, devouring all in its path as the town house burned. "I killed her. I killed her to save Mac."

A line creased Sarah's brow, her mouth thinning. "Rest now, darling."

Bianca struggled to sit up, but the blankets held her captive, the weight of them pinning her down. "Where is he? He should be here. Tell me where Mac is."

"Careful. You've been unconscious for a week. We thought we'd lost you."

Why was Sarah evading her questions? Why couldn't she remember anything beyond Renata's death? Why unless . . .

The giant crow. The wall of flame. It hadn't been a dream. She'd killed Renata, but it hadn't been enough. It hadn't been in time. Mac was dead anyway. She'd lost him.

She closed her eyes, the grief and ache in her chest almost unbearable.

A draft of cool air hit her face as someone entered the room. She opened her eyes, hoping for a miracle; but it was Sebastian, whose solemn visage only cemented the pain in her heart.

"She's asking for Flannery," Sarah murmured, rising to greet her husband. A touch. A shared look. All things Bianca would never know. Would never experience. This was why she'd armored herself. To keep from feeling this small and alone and frightened again.

"What have you told her?" Sebastian asked.

"Nothing yet. Perhaps it would be best coming from you."

He took the seat beside Bianca's bed that Sarah

had vacated, his features drawn into austere lines, his golden eyes dimmed.

"Mac wouldn't leave when he had the chance. He wanted to end the threat to the Imnada. He called it his destiny," Bianca said, blinking to hold back her tears.

"I wish I could say he'd succeeded, but despite Renata Froissart's death, events have moved beyond any hope of containment. I fear the secret of the Imnada is a secret no longer. What happens now is anyone's guess."

"So Mac died for nothing."

"Died? I think"—he shot Sarah an accusatory look—"there's been some confusion. Flannery's not dead, Bianca."

She sat up among her pillows despite the sudden whirling of the room and spinning of her stomach. "What? Where is he?"

"We don't know. Flannery delivered you to us that night. We tried to convince him to stay, at least until we could have him seen by a surgeon, but he resisted. By then I believe instinct had taken over. He wasn't solely Captain Flannery. Not even solely human. And a house of Fey-bloods, even those who meant him no harm, overloaded his every animal sense of survival. He fled. Disappeared completely, and we had no word for five days."

"Five days when we despaired of you as well," Sarah interrupted.

"We sought news of him but heard nothing until a letter arrived this morning. Flannery is alive, though where he is or what he does is not written."

"He didn't even wait until you woke or even looked

at you once you were taken from his arms. I'm sorry, sweeting," Sarah said, her indignation toward Mac evident in her voice.

"Don't be. He's still alive. That's all that matters."

"But he abandoned you. He left you without a farewell. No word. No nothing. All as if you were naught more than passing acquaintances." Sarah's anger for Bianca's sake touched her deeply. She'd always taken for granted Sarah's breezy charm and dramatic flair. Only lately had she found that the new Countess of Deane possessed hidden strengths and unflagging loyalty. "I thought for certain he loved you. I'm not usually wrong about such things."

"He's doing what he must."

The gesture amid the flames of the town house. The words they'd spoken. Bianca might wish it had ended differently, but she understood Mac's leaving. *Trust me,* he'd said. That was what she would do. Trust that he would return. Trust that he would succeed.

Trust that he loved her.

With his hand on the knife at his waist, Mac gazed upon the floor of rose-and-gold marble, the milk-white walls stretching stories above him into an enormous vaulted ceiling painted in dazzling frescoes he could only catch glimpses of in the flickering torchlight. Ahead of him four corridors stretched away into infinity, all of it mirroring his dream, down to the golden light spilling from some unseen source and the sound of burbling water as if a fountain were close by.

The magic of the place carried the raw, elemental power of the true Fey. It beat against his skull like a sword striking a shield, sank through his healing flesh into his blood like frozen needles through his veins.

He swung around, but where the apothecary shop's peeling door had been, a row of tall, arched windows now stood. Draped in scarlet velvet tasseled with silver cords, they looked out upon fields of flowers, a haze of mountains on the far horizon.

No way but forward. No idea why he'd been summoned here.

"Hello!" he called out, his voice bouncing back to him in a ripple of echoes from each of the branching corridors.

Ticklish misgivings slid coldly across his shoulders, lifting the hairs at the back of his neck. Why would creatures as elusive and indifferent as the Fey bother with him? He'd have to tread very carefully if he didn't want to end up a pawn in their schemes.

"Ringrose! Are you there?"

"Who is it?" a familiar voice creaked from down the left-hand corridor. "We don't want any. Go away."

"It's Cormac Cúchulainn. An Imnada of the five clans!" Mac shouted in answer.

A faint circle of light bobbed closer as someone approached. "The five clans . . . the five clans . . . almost fifteen hundred years they fall silent with nary a peep, and in the space of six months I can't turn around without falling over them."

The flickering light revealed itself to be a lamp Ringrose carried high above his head, but it was the girl by his side who drew all Mac's attention. The girl from his fevered dreams. The same short, dark curls. The same trailing cloak of crow feathers over skin as pale as bone.

"He's the look of the clans about him, eh, Badb?"

Ringrose said. "Don't know what it is, but I can tell an Imnada from a league away. Two, if I'm wearing my spectacles. So you survived, did you? Happy to hear it, though you can tell that woman of yours she needs to keep her hands to herself. Ungrateful filly." Ringrose rubbed his jaw.

"I know why you're here." The girl stepped forward, her smile welcoming as she reached on tiptoe to put a finger to Mac's forehead. "You're here for the death-bringer. You want to know how to harness its power without losing yourself to death and Annwn's dark paths forever."

Mac rubbed at the spot, prickling heat bursting behind his eyes. "Who are you? What is this place?"

The cloak's glossy feathers ruffled with a light whisper as the girl shrugged. "Does it matter? The important thing is that we have what you seek: the answer to your questions." The girl grinned and grabbed his hand. "Come this way and all will be explained."

Mac dragged his hand free. "Why should I believe you or accept your help? When have the Fey ever offered assistance without wanting something in return?"

No longer smiling, the girl's lower lip jutted out in a childlike pout.

"I told you he wouldn't be a pushover like the last one," Ringrose snipped. "He's savvy. Had to be to survive this long."

"We helped free your woman from Madame Froissart. We offered our protections to her. Now we seek to hand you your greatest desire. And you still question us?"

"I don't question your generosity or your courage. Only your motives."

"I told you," Ringrose asserted. "Too clever by half."

"Oh, hush, Bartholomew." The girl waved him off like a pesky insect. "See here, son of the Imnada. We held up our end of the bargain. We told him how to unravel the dark spells binding him. We assisted in gathering what he needed. We even offered up the secret to surviving the death-bringer's influence. Now he wanders the paths of the dead. Unable to do as he promised. Unable to repay us for our kindnesses."

"What did Adam promise you, exactly?" Mac asked.

"A simple thing. A small thing. Hardly worth mention—"

"He offered us our freedom, that's what he did," Ringrose interrupted. "Should have known better than to trust a shapechanger. Like trusting a bear to watch a honey tree."

"This is a prison for you?"

Ringrose smoothed a hand over his long beard, his gaze flashing to the arched windows with an expression akin to physical pain. "One without bars or chains but no less painful. We can look upon our lost home, see the heavens spin, the fields beckon, but we are unable to enter without suffering instant death. A sentence most diabolical."

"What was your crime?"

"We assisted . . . that is, we did not . . . he is not . . ." Ringrose sighed. "We're powerless to speak of it. Suffice to say, we have served long and suffered greatly. Will you help us, son of the Imnada?"

"And for this you'll give me the death-bringer. You'll show me what I need to do."

"Yes, yes, anything."

"Agreed," Mac said before he could think better of it.

Badb smiled and took his hand while Ringrose's step came almost sprightly. "It is simple, shapechanger. So simple. The answer to both our dilemma and yours is in the blood."

He stood at the table, months of tireless effort distilled down to no more liquid than would fill a teacup. The surface shone flat and oily, the consistency resembled a melting jelly, and the smell was enough to singe his nostrils and bring tears to his eyes.

Three full turnings of the moon it had taken him. An eternity. Every newspaper torturing him with glimpses of her life. Every letter he began only to feed to the flames, an act as painful as the curse's nightly awakening. He'd told himself again and again that he did it for her. Should the draught fail, better for her to move on than find herself chained to a man tainted and twisted, whose spirit remained an eternal prisoner of dark magic. But in his heart he knew he did it as much for his own pride. Curse or no, she would stay with him, but pity was no substitute for love, and sympathy was a slow killer of desire. He would see both in her eyes, and that he could not bear.

But now it was done. One last component and Adam's draught would be complete.

He could face her free of the curse. Free to love her as she deserved to be loved.

With a finger, he traced the three recent scars slicing across his other palm, the tingle of magic fizzing beneath his healing skin. Before he could second guess Ringrose's final instructions, Mac took up his silver-bladed knife and reopened the newly healed wounds, blood welling up like a scarlet thread. Tipping his palm up, he let the blood drip one-two-three into the cup, where it lay like a stain before sinking and becoming lost amid the dark, gelatinous concoction.

Done.

Bought with pain, heartbreak, loss—and now blood.

Closing his fist around the stinging wound, Mac eyed the mixture with eagerness and repugnance. He lifted the cup to his lips, held his nose, and swallowed all of it without coming up for air.

Placing the cup back upon the table, he walked to the door, where the western sun faded over the churchyard to be lost amid the distant hills.

Closed his eyes.

Waited. For life or death, he knew not.

Shading her face from the lowering sun, Bianca stepped down from the gig. Accepted her bag from the blushing, pimply young man who'd offered her a seat in his conveyance at the coaching inn and spent the next hour talking nonstop to her about his prize herd of Hampshire sheep. Needless to say, it had been a long hour of travel.

But with his departure, the silence took over. An unnatural quiet that held an almost stifling expectancy, as if the very breeze had been chained. Bianca almost wished for the never-ending chatter of her gallant to break the strange calm.

No golden-leaved wood or autumn birdsong this time. Winter gripped the rattling branches of the oaks standing sentinel around the house and the snow-dusted fields to the west. A small group of cows moved in the straw-covered byre, their warm eyes trained on Bianca as they chewed their chaff. Smoke curled from a chimney into the twilight sky.

"Jory? Marianne?" Hoisting the strap of her leather satchel upon her shoulder, she headed for the house. "It's Bianca. I've come back."

A tickle between her shoulder blades raised goose-flesh up and down her arms. She paused, a hand upon the kitchen door, her other crushing the satchel's strap in a clammy fist.

"They've all gone to Dorking for the day."

That voice. That deep, rolling, honey-smooth Irish baritone that shot yearning all the way to her toes.

She turned, swallowing the anxious flutters of fear and excitement bursting up through her chest. Half hoping. Half dreading. Had she been right to come at Marianne's urging, or would this be the final relinquishing of dreams she'd nursed through the endless months of searching for Mac without success?

He stood within the shadow of the stillroom door-way. Despite the cold, against which she was bundled in cloak and muffler, he wore naught but a pair of leather breeches, his shirt clasped in his hand. The golden afternoon light picked out every fading scar. Too many to count. His Imnada blood had been the cause of his maiming, but it had also been the only thing that kept him alive after suffering from wounds too terrible for any normal human to survive.

She lifted her eyes to the stark angles of his face, the grim set to his jaw, the prideful light glowing in his green feline eyes. "'If the mountain will not come to

Muhammad, then Muhammad must go to the mountain,'" she quoted.

"How did you know where to find me?"

"I didn't until Marianne wrote to tell me you'd turned up here a few weeks ago. But for the last three months, I've hunted everywhere, Mac. I asked at the Horse Guards. I spoke to David St. Leger. I traveled to Yorkshire to Gray de Coursy's estate. None knew where you'd gone. Lord Deane and I turned London upside down and found nothing. It's as if you fell off the face of the earth."

"I sold my commission. It was for the best. They were happy to be rid of me."

"And David? Gray? Even Jory? They'd not heard anything from you, either."

"The work made it impossible."

"I'm aware of your work, Mac. I'm also aware of the reasons you felt compelled to hide yourself away, but three months without a word? I began to think . . ." She paused to steady her breathing. "Mr. Harris asked me back to take the role of Desdemona in *Othello*. Adam's murder has finally been eclipsed by a scandal involving a man from East Grinstead with three wives. My notoriety has faded to a few sideways looks and more invitations to dine than I can accept."

"Congratulations," he said. "It's what you wanted."

"Once, but no longer." She hated the quaver in her voice, but Mac's impenetrable gaze pinned her down like a bug under glass. "Or at least, it's not all I want anymore."

"You shouldn't have come, Bianca."

His words hit her like a punch to the stomach, driving the wind from her body, the hope from her heart.

She gripped her bag like a lifeline, the leather smooth where years of hands had worried it. "Is this why you didn't write? Because you've changed your mind?"

He drew a shuddering breath, the orange disk of the sun picking out hollows beneath his cheekbones, making deep wells of his eyes. His fingers curled to fists, his body taut as a wire. "I feel the same as I ever did," he said through a clenched jaw, his breathing shallow and quick. "Nothing has changed."

"Then what?" She glanced at the light seeping between the trees upon the far-off hills, the skies above growing feathery and purple, and the truth dawned on her: "You did it. You finished the draught."

His chest heaved, a sheen of sweat glistening on his skin, dampening his brow. "I've done what I can. It's up to the goddess now whether my plea is answered."

She looked from the sun back to him. "But you said the death-bringer . . . you said it was poisonous. You said you didn't know why it didn't kill Adam."

He offered her a wan half smile and a shrug. "I still don't know, but it's too late to worry now."

The bag fell from her shoulder into the dust, her heart banging like a bird against the cage of her ribs, her steps becoming almost a run as she crossed the space between them. "That's why you didn't want me to come, why you kept silent for so long: in case it fails. In case you . . . in case you die. Are you mad?"

He braced himself against her advance, though his gaze flickered and he was the first to turn away. "There was nothing for us if I didn't make the attempt."

She took him by the arms, wanting to shake him until his teeth rattled. "There is nothing for me if you die trying, you great lummox."

The sun dipped below the farthest hill, backlighting the heavens, streaming upward into the blue and silver clouds. A flock of crows took flight in a chorus of rushing wings to rise like a black cloud into the sky. A cow's bell rang low and sad from the nearby byre.

Bianca stared deep into his eyes. Refusing to look away. Refusing to cry. He cupped her face in his hands, lowered his mouth to hers. The heat and the power of his kiss bursting like fireworks against her jagged, paralyzing fear.

She was faintly conscious of the sun diminishing to a fingernail glimmer of gold before it oozed at last beneath the horizon.

The wind picked up, pressing her skirts to her legs, tugging at her bonnet. Branches scraped and a shutter banged. An owl called from the churchyard. But still she stood within Mac's embrace, his arms like steel around her, his heart beating steadily beneath her palm. The minutes drifted past like the streamers of cloud above. Minutes when no spiraling cataclysm of fire engulfed him. No clawing agonies warped his body against his will.

He remained as he chose. His form unaltered.

Lifting his head, he smiled down at her, his skin golden, his eyes like molten silver. "I still breathe and I still stand. The curse is broken, *mi am'ryath*. It's finally over."

She combed her fingers through the crisp hair at his neck, loving the way her body molded into his, the strength in his stance and the desire in his gaze carrying her away on a shimmer of desire. "Something new has just begun."

*   *   *

They lay in each other's arms, their cooling bodies still damp, the cresting pleasure of their joining still buzzing within him like the growl of the ocean or the sough of the wind through the high mountain passes.

Moonlight spun the world in silver, great pools of it streaming into the bedchamber. Bianca's head lay in the crook of Mac's arm, her white-gold hair spread over the pillow and ribboning his chest, her body as shimmering and pale as the goddess above.

He dropped a kiss upon her temple. "She watches us."

Bianca propped herself up on an elbow, her skin washed in the luminous silver light, reigniting heat barely banked. "The same goddess lights the holding at Concullum, Mac. It shines upon your family and your clan." In her deep-blue eyes, a lingering question. "It lights your path home."

"*Un fieuyn commdedig. Calmmys aeshav,*" he whispered. "So beautiful and so passionate." He leaned up to kiss her deeply and irrevocably, his scent tangled in her hair, alive on her skin. "I love you, Bianca. For now and forever. And I am already home."

Glossary of the Imnada

Berenth. The night of the last quarter moon. This begins the period when the Imnada's powers to shift at will begin to ebb and it becomes both more difficult and more dangerous.

Bloodline scrolls. The written history and genealogies created and maintained by the Ossine. These records are used to select mates for the Imnada from the five clans.

Clan mark. The crescent symbol tattooed on the upper backs of the male members of the Imnada, signifying their full acceptance into the clan upon their majority. Both males and females are also marked mentally with a signum identifying their clan affiliation and holding.

Emnil. An exile who has been formally sentenced by the Gather and had his clan mark and signum removed and his name erased from the Ossine's bloodline scrolls. An *emnil* is considered dead to the clan and his life forfeit if he attempts any contact with a clan member or a return to clan lands.

Enforcer. The warrior arm of the Ossine whose job it is to track down and eliminate any potential threat to the Imnada.

Fealla Mhòr. The Great Betrayal: the betrayal and murder of the last king of Other, Arthur, by the Imnada warlord Lucan. This event triggered a vengeful purge of the Imnada by the Fey-bloods, who had always mistrusted and feared the shapechangers.

Fey-bloods. (slang) Also known as the Other. Men and women who possess the blood and magical powers of the Fey.

Gateway. The door between earth and the galaxy where the Imnada first originated.

Gather. The ruling council of the Imnada, consisting of seven members: the chieftains from each of the five clans, the head of the Ossine, and the Duke of Morieux, who is hereditary leader over the five clans.

Idrin the Traveller. Among the first Imnada to come through the Gateway and settle on Earth. He is considered the father of their race and from his seed the five clans sprang.

Imnada. A race of shapechangers and telepaths divided into five clans overseen by the ruling Gather.

They wield no magical powers though they are sensitive to its presence and can identify those who possess magic. At first they existed peacefully with the magical race of Other but when the Imnada betrayed King Arthur to his death, they were hunted down in the wars and uprisings that followed. In the ensuing centuries, those who survived grew reclusive and fiercely suspicious of all outsiders to the point that most believe the Imnada no longer exist.

Krythos. Also known as a far-seeing disk. A notched glass disk about 2.5 inches in diameter. It is used to augment and amplify the Imnada's natural telepathic abilities over long distances.

Lucan. Leader of the clans during King Arthur's reign. He conspired with Morgana, the king's half sister, to place her son Mordred upon the throne. His betrayal led to Arthur's murder. He was captured by the Fey for his treachery and imprisoned within the Bear's Stone for all eternity.

Morderoth. The night of the new moon when the shift is impossible for the Imnada.

Mother Goddess. The moon from which the Imnada derive their magical powers.

Ossine. Shamans and spiritual advisers to the clans, they tend to be the strongest and most powerful of the Imnada. They maintain the bloodline scrolls used for selecting each Imnada mating pair. They protect the Imnada from out-clan interference with their armed militia of enforcers, and from their ranks is chosen the keeper of Jai Idrish, the Imnada's most sacred relic and the key to the Gateway.

Other. See **Fey-blood**.

Out-clan. Slang for someone who is not a member of the five clans.

Palings. Magical mists conjured and maintained by the Ossine of each clan. They are used as a natural force field, disguising and shunting people away from the hidden holdings. In recent years, these warded fields have weakened as the clans' powers have weakened.

Pathing. Speaking mind to mind. Imnada can use this telepathy to speak to one another over short distances or when they are in their animal aspect. For longer distances, they use the amplifying power of the *krythos* to connect with each other mentally.

Priestesses of High Danu. An order of Other women devoted to a contemplative life in service and devotion to the gods.

Realing. A magical servant bound to a specific person or place.

Rogue. An unmarked shapechanger without clan or hold affiliation.

Signum. The mental imprint set on every shapechangers mind at birth by the Ossine. It identifies clan affiliation and rank. Those cast out of the clans have their signum stripped, denoting their outlaw status.

Silmith. The night of the full moon when the shift comes easiest and the powers of the Imnada are at their height.

Warriors of Scathach (Amhas-draoi). An Other brotherhood of warrior mages who serve as guardians between the Fey and human worlds.

Ynys Avalenn. Also known as the Summer Kingdom, this is the realm of the Fey.

Youngling. A child of the Imnada who has not yet reached maturity or been marked.

Keep reading for an excerpt from

SHADOW'S CURSE

Book Two in the Imnada Brotherhood Series

by Alexa Egan

Available from Pocket Books in October 2013

1

LONDON, MAY 1817

The man stood over his victim, his knife flashing in the dim light of Silmith's round yellow moon. The scent of blood and urine hung on the stale breeze. The clink of a money pouch echoed in the quiet of the alley. David hung back in the shadows, awaiting his moment. The thief would have to pass by him to reach the street and escape within the warren of dockside wharves and warehouses. When he did, David would be ready. It was a scenario he'd perfected over the course of the past year.

Not once had he allowed his prey to escape his own brand of justice. Not once had he been caught or even seen except as a ghostly shape, an enormous rippling shadow with glowing yellow eyes. Some called him a demon or a monster: the newspapers who prospered from his exploits and those who worked the darkness for their own gains. But those who'd been saved by his intervention labeled him a guardian angel, a mysterious hero.

He was neither. Merely bored.

And angry.

Very, very angry.

If any member of the five clans of Imnada were to discover he spent the time between sundown and sunrise saving the lives of humans, they'd think him mad. Not that he cared what they thought anymore. He was *emnil*, dead to his clan. An outcast and an outlaw.

And while he was no longer doomed to pass his nights in his clan aspect of the wolf, these small, vicious hours had become a solace, the cluttered, squalid stews, his personal hunting ground. The Fey-blood's recent discovery of the Imnada's survival only added to the knife-edge thrill he craved like an addict. Something he knew all too much about these days.

The clouds passed over the full moon, the breeze kicking up in starts to ruffle the fur along his back, the bristly ridge at his neck. He lifted his face to it, felt it curl over his muzzle, bringing with it the salty tar-laden stench of the Limehouse docks. Just then the victim moaned, stirring as he regained consciousness, a hand groping feebly for the knot at the back of his head. Shoving the pouch in his coat pocket, the assailant lifted his knife with deadly intent. Theft soon to become murder.

Thought fell to instinct, and, with fangs bared in a vicious snarl, David sprang.

Callista rubbed a cloth over the last silver bell before placing it back in its case alongside the other three. Closing the lid, she secured the lock with a roll of her thumb over the circular tumblers. But instead of putting the mahogany box back upon the high shelf beside her bed, she remained at her desk with the box in front of her. Her finger followed the familiar loops and swirls decorating the lid. Her mother's box. Her grandmother's. Her great-grandmother's.

Necromancers, all.

The power to walk the paths of the dead had been

gifted the women of her house, stretching back beyond anyone's memory. At least that's what Mother had claimed. Callista couldn't know for certain. She'd never met any of the women of her house beyond Mother to ask them.

Now she couldn't even ask Mother.

Callista slid open the top desk drawer, removing a bundle of old yellowed letters wrapped in a frayed ribbon. The wax was dried and crumbling, the writing smudged and faded. Mother had kept them all. Every single missive she'd sent to her family that had been returned unopened. The proud and prominent Armstrong family of Killedge had never forgotten nor forgiven the shame of their daughter's elopement. Callista pulled free the top letter, reading the words though she knew them by heart. A newsy cheerful letter, despite the anguish and the dread that had prompted this last desperate attempt to reconcile. Mother had died a month later.

The letter had been returned a week after the funeral.

The door behind her opened, a breeze stirring the hair at the back of her neck, raising gooseflesh over her arms. As Callista quickly slid the packet of correspondence back into the desk drawer, she felt Branston's thunderous stare bore into her, his fury like a shimmer of red behind her eyelids.

"I almost wish Mr. Corey hadn't found you in time for your appointment," he said. "Better to postpone the summoning than have poor Mrs. Dixon's hopes dashed so cruelly."

"Your concern for the grieving mother is touching," Callista answered wearily. "I'd not have taken you for a sentimentalist."

"What I am is a businessman, and you, my dear, are the business. A fact you keep forgetting."

As she rose to confront her brother, his small,

washed-out blue eyes narrowed, his nostrils flared as if he smelled something rank. "That's where you're wrong. I know it all too well. You haven't let me forget for one moment in the past seven years."

His hands flexed and curled into fists, his well-fed body wired with tension. "Is that what your sulks are about? Your feelings are hurt? You don't feel appreciated? Is that why you decided to dash a grieving mother's hopes by telling her you were unable to speak to little Jonny?"

"It's not right to take these people's money without offering them something in return."

Shoving his hands in his pockets, her half brother shrugged away from her. "We offer solace. Reassurance. Hope. Worth it at double the price," he said, in the same tone he used to hawk her skills during their years traveling town to town and fair to fair. "We're their only link to their loved ones beyond the grave. To the infinite knowledge of the future the spirits can offer us."

"Yes, if I'm able to find the spirit they seek and the client's questions are answered. But I never found that woman's son. I walked as far as I dared into death. I tried every path I knew. I couldn't lie to her."

"Perhaps you need to delve farther? Walk paths you've yet to explore?"

"I'm not trained for the deeper reaches. Mother died before she could teach me those lessons, and without the proper instruction it's too dangerous to attempt."

"I don't bloody care." He spun round, jaw clenched. Brotherly concern, a pose obviously too difficult to maintain. Not that he'd ever tried very hard. Perhaps if they'd been closer in age or she'd been born a boy or he'd not been an ill-tempered, spiteful good-for-nothing sod. "Do what you need to do to satisfy the customer, Callista. If you won't risk it, then lie. If you'd done that tonight, the old cow would have left here pleased as punch, thinking little Jonny was with dear old dad doing ring-the-rosy in heaven. She'd have been happy to be comforted in her time of grief. I'd have been happy to relieve her of her money."

"We've only begun to recover after the fiasco in Manchester. Do you want to be arrested this time? Or worse? Mother always said—"

"What I want, Callista"—he slammed his hand upon the table—"is for you to do as you're told. I don't give a damn about your bloody bells or your Fey-born gift or your sainted mother. She's dead, and if it weren't for me, the only gift keeping you from the gutter would be the one between your legs. So, you'll tell these sniveling, drippy, hand-wringing women with their sob stories whatever they want to hear, because if you don't"—he shoved his face close enough for her to smell the whiskey on his breath—"I'll make you very, very sorry."

She refused to cower before him, though she knew it only made him angrier. Instead she locked her knees, forced her shoulders square, and met him glare for glare. "You're no longer my guardian, and I won't be forced to act as your circus sideshow any longer."

His gaze grew icy, a wicked smile dancing over his mouth. "The next time you leave, I've told Mr. Corey he can return you in any condition he sees fit. He's more than willing, and, knowing him, any struggle on your part will only increase his ardor. You suppose that high-flown aunt of yours you're always running on about will acknowledge you once you're ruined and stuffed with a man's bastard child?"

Cold splashed across her back, nearly buckling her knees. She gripped the edge of the table. "You wouldn't dare."

"Wouldn't I? Victor Corey wants you for his wife, the gods only know why, and I've accepted his proposal. It matters little to him whether he beds you before or after the ceremony."

Callista wanted to be sick. "I'll not marry Corey. He may dress like a dandy and ape the manners of a gentleman, but he's nothing more than a common street thug."

Branston grabbed her, his fingers digging into her upper arms until tears burned in her eyes. "If Corey wants you, he'll have you if I have to drag you bound to the altar. Do I make myself clear?" he spat.

"Completely."

He released her to pat her cheek, an unpleasant smile stretching his wide mouth. "You make it so much harder than it needs to be, Callista. Haven't I always ever seen to your best interests? Haven't I always been there to take care of you, unlike those high-and-mighty relatives of your mother's? Corey's an important and wealthy man with important friends. You should be happy he wants you."

She crossed her arms over her chest, eyeing him like the disease he was. "Your persuasive abilities continue to amaze me. It's no wonder none of your schemes have ever paid off."

Annoyance flickered in his gaze. "Get some rest. We've two appointments tomorrow, and I want you at your best. I'm going out. Mrs. Thursby will be here should you need anything."

Hardly a comfort. The old bawd acting as Branston's housekeeper was another of Mr. Corey's associates. Since setting up shop in London six months ago, their household had slowly been taken over by the gang leader and his underlings. But why? What really lay behind his continued and growing interest in them?

"Where are you going?" she asked.

Branston chucked her chin as if she were ten years old. "Worried for me? Don't be, dear sister. I'll always be here to look after you. Always."

She crossed to the hearth, though no warmth touched her frozen, shivering skin. Always was what she most feared.

No matter how many times he did it, David St. Leger always hated this part.

With held breath and steady hand, he eased the silver-bladed knife across his opposite palm, blood welling behind the thin cut. Holding it above the glass he'd prepared beforehand, he waited as three drops large fell into the viscous slime-green liquid, then snatched up a napkin to wrap around his wound. Already the initial sting became a steady throb moving up his arm into his head until spots bounced in front of his eyes and his stomach squirmed ominously.

He'd almost left it too late.

Swirling the liquid round as if he were appreciating a fine brandy, he raised the glass to his lips, closed his eyes, and downed the vile, greasy brew in one shuddering swallow.

He wasn't sure which was worse—the cure or the curse.

Placing the glass on a nearby table, he sank into an armchair, leaning his head back against the cushions until the dizziness passed and the potion took hold. The clock struck the hour. A log in the grate fell apart in a shower of sparks. Rain pattered against the window.

And then there were the sounds that didn't belong. A far-off click of a latch. The brush of a boot against carpet. A rattle of a knob. Not a servant. He'd sent the last one to bed on his arrival home an hour ago.

Taking up the knife once more, David waited—and listened. He'd take no chances. Not with the Ossine's brutal enforcers stalking the countryside in search of rebel Imnada. Not when wielding silver might be the difference between life and extermination.

Sooner or later they were bound to suspect exiled clan members of collusion if not outright allegiance to the traitors. And when they did, David would be ready. They'd not lay their hands on him again.

He'd die first. And take a few down with him before he went.

The sounds came closer. David hung back, the knife ready, every muscle tensed for the attack. The door opened and a shadow fell across the floor. Unhesitating, he lunged, his arm sweeping out to catch the intruder. A shout erupted. Glass shattered. A knife flashed. The intruder's neck ended trapped in the crook of David's elbow, his back arched against the silver pressed to his kidneys.

"Are you barking mad, St. Leger?" the man growled from between clenched teeth.

David closed his eyes on a string of profanity. Dropped his arm and his blade.

Captain Mac Flannery.

"Is this how you greet all your guests or am I special?" Mac snarled, his cat-slanted green eyes narrowed in fury.

"You'll always be special to me," David quipped with a smile despite his shaking knees and the renewed rush of dizziness spinning his head. He tossed the knife with a clatter onto a nearby table. "But if you lurk around doorways in the middle of the night, you can't complain about the less than friendly welcome."

"I knocked, but I expect your housekeeper's retired for the night."

David cast a glance at the mantel clock. "It's two in the morning. Of course she's retired." He poured himself a drink. On an afterthought, he poured one for Mac, who was rubbing at his waistcoat. "What the hell are you doing here at this godforsaken time of night anyway? Shouldn't you be home making mad, passionate love to your new bride?"

"I wish. I came to let you know there's an enforcer skulking around London."

"Let him skulk. I've done nothing wrong, unlike some people who are up to their necks in traitorous revolution." David settled into a chair. It felt good after the busy night he'd had. He tossed back the whiskey, feeling the burn all the way to his toes. "Much as I appreciate the warning, couldn't it have waited until morning?"

"You've always been more of a night owl. I see things haven't changed."

"Darkness suits me," David said with a sly curve of his lips. "Does Gray know about this meddlesome Ossine?"

"Gray's gone north to Radcliffe. I haven't heard from him in weeks. I'm starting to worry."

"And so you should. If the enforcers ever discover his involvement with the rebel Imnada and their Fey-blood conspirators, he'll end in pieces and us right alongside him."

Mac rubbed his temples as if his head pained him. "I know, but Gray doesn't listen. Personally, I think this whole rebellion is his way of getting back at his grandfather."

"Do you blame him? The old man could have saved him. He could have saved all of us. Personally, I think a nice blade between dear Grandpapa's ribs would be much easier, but to each his own."

A tense silence sprang up, though neither strove to break it. The three friends had reached a tacit agreement. They never spoke of the last chaotic days of war when a dying Fey-blood had set his vicious spell upon the three of them. Nor did they talk of the cure they had discovered that had fast become a deadly addiction. They could not stop. They could not continue. Either choice brought sickness and, finally, death. In their struggle to free themselves of the enchantment, they had ended trapped and tainted by the magic of the Fey—again.

Mac found solace from his pain in love, Gray in revenge.

David found it at the bottom of a whiskey bottle.

"So, now that your message has been delivered, care to stay for a drink—or three?" He started to rise.

"There's another . . . small matter."

David sighed, dropping back into his chair. "There always is."

A shuffling step sounded from just outside the door followed by a click of a heel on the parquet. David snatched up his silver blade and was halfway to the door before Mac grabbed him. "Wait."

David swung around, eyes wild. "What the hell—"

"Caleb!" Mac called. "Show yourself. It's all right."

A thin man with a long, pockmarked face and dingy brown hair stepped into the study. His eyes darted around the room as if gauging safety.

"St. Leger won't harm you. Will you, David?"

"That depends on who the devil he is." He turned once more to the sideboard. Mother of All, but he needed another drink.

"This is Caleb Kineally," Mac began. "He's—"

"Imnada." David finished Mac's sentence at the first mental brush of shapechanger magic against his mind. "I take it he's one of Gray's rebels."

Mac ran a hand over his haggard face, and for the first time David noticed the waxen pallor of his friend's features, the smudges hollowing his eyes. "Aye. He needs to lie low while that enforcer's on the loose."

"Is there a reason you're telling me all this?"

"I want you to look after him."

"Me?"

"While Gray's gone, you're the only one I trust to keep him safe. Bianca's been through enough already. I can't ask her to place herself in danger again. Not with a baby on the way."

David's resolve wavered at mention of Mac's out-clan bride, but he shoved his better nature aside. Mac had asked for the trouble when he'd bought into Gray's mutinous rhetoric. It wasn't David's problem nor his cause.

"It's just until things quiet down," Mac pleaded.

"No. It's too dangerous. You and Gray can delude yourselves into thinking you'll make our lives better by defying the Ossine. I know the truth. You'll end up dead. But you won't take me with you."

"We're dead either way though, aren't we?" Mac answered. The simple truth of those words hit David like a kick to the stomach.

So much for tacit agreements.

"Please, David."

He'd never heard Mac beg. Not in Charleroi with battle looming and the Fey-blood's spell singeing their veins like acid. Not when he'd been brought in chains before the stern-faced Gather to have the sentence of *emnil* pronounced. And not even when his back had been a charred wreck and death seemed a mercy. Mac did not beg. He suffered. He endured. It's part of what David had always admired about his friend.

"You once told me the dead were the only ones who might make a difference," Mac said. "You once believed in the cause as much as any of us."

"Did I? Must have been drunk at the time." David tossed back his whiskey. Was this his third or his fourth? He'd lost count.

Mac eyed him over the glass with a last-throw-of-the-dice look on his face. "What if I told you the name of the Ossine on Kineally's trail is a man by the name of Beskin?"

David's back twitched with remembered pain, the whiskey turning sour in his gut. Eudo Beskin remained in his head as a brutal nightmare from which there was no waking. If keeping Kineally safe thwarted the dead-hearted bastard, he would do it gladly. "Very well. He can stay. But that doesn't make me one of you."

Mac smiled his success as he placed his glass upon a sideboard. "Scoff all you like, St. Leger." He tossed a newspaper on the sofa open to the headline MONSTER OF THE MEWS PREVENTS MALICIOUS MURDER. "But you're one of us whether you admit it or not."

The man sat at his usual corner table, his plate emptied of dinner, a brandy before him. Those in the crowded chophouse who noticed him at all dismissed him without a second glance. Just as he'd planned it when he set the spell in motion that repelled eyes and minds, allowing him to disappear while remaining in plain sight. A useful gift. In his early days on the street, it had kept him alive in the chaos of London's slums when food had been his primary goal. But as his skills grew so did his ambitions. After all, why be given such a talent if it wasn't to be used?

". . . big as a bear with teeth like a lion's and claws like the barber's razor. Seen it myself . . ."

". . . this before or after you'd spent your week's pay on blue ruin . . ."

". . . found old Moseby last week, gutted like a mackerel in an alley near the steel yard . . ."

". . . wager his old woman did him in rather than some slavering monster . . ."

The nearby conversation grated on his already strained temper. He'd not come to hear gossip from two red-nosed drunken knaves with less in their heads than they had in their pockets. He checked his watch, sipped sparingly at his drink. Half his success came as a result of keeping a clear head among a rabble of half-soused alley scum.

The door opened and Branston Hawthorne scrambled in as if he had a constable on his tail. Out of breath, he darted his suspicious eyes round the room before sidling over to slide into the seat opposite. "So sorry," he wheezed. "A group of us were meeting to discuss these rumors about the Imnada. Hope you weren't waiting long."

"*What* are Imnada?" Victor Corey sipped unconcernedly at his brandy. It wouldn't do to show too much interest. Keep them guessing. Keep them off their stride. Never show your hand. That had always been his way.

"Don't you know about the shapechangers?" Hawthorne asked, disbelief creeping into his voice.

"Damn your eyes! Would I ask the question if I knew?"

Corey hated that he must rely on fools like Branston Hawthorne to instruct him in a magical world that should have been his birthright. He hated that the knowledge this bootlicking poltroon took for granted, Victor Corey, king of the stews, scrabbled to grasp. But grasp it he had. It had taken years to fully understand his power, both its limits and its possibilities. The results had gained him wealth and influence, if not admiration. No matter. The world may not respect him, but it feared him. An emotion that served him twice as well.

It flickered now in Hawthorne's gaze. Corey relaxed back in his seat, swigging his brandy as if it were the gin he craved. "Who or what are Imnada? They must be important if they kept you from our meeting."

Hawthorne licked his lips, rubbed the side of his nose with one pudgy finger. "Yes . . . I mean no . . . I mean of course. I'm happy to explain. The Imnada are shapechangers. Used to be plentiful as the coins in your pocket until they betrayed Arthur at the last battle. Their war chief cut the king down where he stood"— he snapped his fingers—"just like that. But the Other showed them. For their treachery they—"

Corey scowled. "*King* Arthur? Is that the Arthur we're talking about?"

"Aye, last great king of our kind, old Arthur was. Said to be more Fey than human. But it didn't stop the Imnada from doing him in. He bled same as anyone with a sword stuck through his gut. Afterward, the shifters were hunted down, the whole monstrous lot of them. Killed in droves like vermin until none were left . . . or so we thought, the sneaky buggers. It's said they've returned bold as brass and twice as dangerous."

Corey leaned back in his chair. "They change shape? Into what exactly?"

Hawthorne sighed as one might when confronted with a small child's incessant questions, his long exhale choked off at a single cold stare from his host. "They shift from man to ruthless wild beast. As soon as kill you as look at you. The Other are organizing. We'll not be taken unawares by a bunch of dirty shifters."

"Pitchforks and torches?" Corey said smoothly. "I'd love to see a mob like that parading down Bond Street amid the hoity-toities. Give them a good scare." He held Hawthorne's gaze long enough for the man to shift uneasily in his seat, before glancing away with a lift of a shoulder and a wave to the barman. "Enough about your bogeymen in the night. I invited you here to find out what you plan on doing about your sister's defiance. I don't appreciate being made a fool of, and I'm sure you don't want me to change my mind about our arrangement."

He regarded Hawthorne's unease with satisfaction. "No, of course not, Mr. Corey. You've been more than generous with your offer and I'm indebted to you for your patience in the matter."

"You're indebted to me for far more than that, Hawthorne. And I expect payment in full. The girl or the coin. Which will it be?" Though, he already knew the answer. He'd made sure Hawthorne was up to his neck in debt with no hope of repayment. Not that it had been difficult. The man had the business acumen of a babe in the cradle.

Hawthorne straightened in his chair, his chubby face breaking into a smile. "You'll have Callista, Mr. Corey. No worry on that score. I've given her a good talking-to. There won't be any more of her foolishness." He took a long greedy swallow of his wine, dabbing at his mouth with a napkin, unaware of the red drops flecking his neckcloth. "She can be a handful at times, but a stern husband should settle her down right quick."

Corey smiled. Oh, he'd settle Miss Callista Hawthorne down all right. Once tamed, she'd make good bedsport. The woman was ripe for a man's attentions. All she needed was the right man to show her the way.

But while he would enjoy introducing her to the pleasures of the flesh, it was Callista's gift of necromancy he truly desired. She was his key into death. And when one possesses the key, one controls the door; both who goes in and, more importantly, what comes out.

Annwn was full of dark spirits bound to the deepest paths of the underworld. Dark spirits who only needed a guide to lead them up to and through the door between realms. Once that door was breached, Branston Hawthorne with his round little body and unctuous pandering would be the first to die. And from there, who knew . . .

With an army of the underworld at Corey's command, his grip on London would tighten like a noose. They called him a gang lord.

Soon, they'd call him mayor.

Perhaps in time they'd hail him as king—or better. Arthur might have been the last great king of the Other. Victor Corey could be the next.

Some thought him mad to take a dowerless nobody as his wife, but he knew better. Callista Hawthorne would bring him the world as her marriage portion.